**Reading Extravaganza**

ead the book then pass on to family or friends
ill in table below so we can see how many people have read it

- Share photos on social media #cityreads #wallsendreads
- Return to Wallsend Library

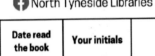

North Tyneside Libraries @NorthtyneLibs

| Date read the book | Your initials |
|---|---|
| | |

Cahill Davis Publishing

Cahill Davis Publishing

First published in Great Britain in 2022 by Cahill Davis Publishing Limited.

First published in paperback in Great Britain in 2022 by Cahill Davis Publishing Limited.

Printed and bound in Great Britain by Clays Ltd, Elcograf S.p.A



ISBN 978-1-8381820-9-0 (eBook)

ISBN 978-1-8381820-8-3 (Paperback)

Cahill Davis Publishing Limited

www.cahilldavispublishing.co.uk

To my Grandma, who I was lucky enough to be loved by for 38 years. I carry your heart in mine.

# 1

# *Goals*

## Derek

Derek had been a podgy child, then a chubby teenager and now what he liked to refer to as a "robust" adult. Derek saw himself as a role model for larger people, and whilst acknowledging people come in all shapes and sizes, he felt we should all embrace a little extra squidge now and then.

He had, in fact, not always had this attitude. His wife, Brenda, would call him a pig. Even "bloody fat swine" at times of heightened debate. *What a vile woman she is*, he thought. Derek had tried losing weight, more for Brenda than himself. He'd tried a protein only diet (his whole being had reeked of excrement), a liquid diet (the shakes had made his heart race), a points diet (he'd saved his points up every day and then ate a multipack of crisps) and Slim to Success (he'd replaced half a cheesecake with more pasta than that which would fuel Usain Bolt for a month). No fad diet was ever sustainable or enjoyable in the slightest for Derek.

After a barrage of taunting and belittling him, Brenda would be an ambassador for his latest diet, giving Derek a false sense of support. Then, a few weeks in, when he was struggling or the weight was coming off, she would sabotage with his favourite meals. He would come home to creamy carbonara, cheesy fish pie, homemade minced beef pie smothered in gravy, or rich lasagne and garlic bread. Then, the diet would end, destroyed by a controlling Brenda, petrified he may gain a little more confidence as the pounds dissolved. The bottom line was Derek liked his meals, his treats and snacks. The pleasure of food was one of his life luxuries, and he didn't feel the need to restrict that. He had enough misery dished up from Brenda most of the time.

Granted, he could eat one more potato than most pigs, but so be it. Life is short, and he'd had friends who had dropped dead a decade ago. Slim friends, at that.

Life was for living, so he embraced his love handles. Derek said no to any more conscious dieting the night he ditched his eleven-stone unloving handle, Brenda. Then, he calmly sat down and wrote his future goals.

Derek had five goals on his list, two of which were the most important to him:

1) Be true to himself.

2) Meet people who will accept him as he is.

Thirteen simple words, but they felt like a big challenge for this big man. He would break the goals into bite-sized pieces. He pondered over what he believed would make him feel genuine, authentic, truly himself. He knew his immediate thoughts on being true to himself, but would that cause turmoil for his second goal? There was a lot to contemplate. He looked over at Des, his ever-loyal Labrador, who returned the glance with everlasting love. At least Derek knew good old Des would always accept him.

Derek went to bed that night, his head full of questions, scenarios, solutions and actions. Brenda had left that evening for what he knew would be the final time, the explosive showdown leaving him with a mixture of emotions. It had been a long time coming, no doubt, but there was something bittersweet in this final argument and ultimate resigned acceptance between them that the marriage was over. He surprised himself, thoughts ruminating more about a future of feeling free to do what he wanted rather than grieving for the end of decades of marriage. In his exhaustion, he felt some positivity.

At work the next day, it wasn't hard to see that Derek wasn't being himself.

"What's up, bud?" asked his closest colleague, Jeff.

"Ah, nothing really, just a bit tired," he lied. His life had taken a significant direction change of late, his split from Brenda being something he had considered for years. Executing it was a very different thing.

Derek was still processing the situation from the night before—the erupting reaction of him expressing his needs more assertively over the last month or so. Their marriage hadn't been working for a long time. Both of them knew that. Brenda had turned nasty and critical. Derek would refer to her secretly as "the witch" or "poisonous bitch" on occasions of intensified emotion. He could never do anything right, and affection was fleeting. Brenda was no longer his comfy pair of slippers. Prior to this, she'd never accepted him for who he was. Derek could never be his true self in front of Brenda. It felt suffocating and increasingly toxic over time. Enough was enough; Derek had muted himself for far too long.

Historically, Derek would secretly indulge in an hour or so of pleasure and contentment when she was out with her sister or at her coffee morning. The day she had come home early and caught him had led to an evening of arguing, upset and confession. It wasn't all new to her; no massive revelation. Derek had tried many times before to make her understand and see his point of view. Tried, and failed. All the conversations over the years, Brenda's negativity and the disgust on her face, as if he had announced he had just drowned a basket of kittens. The times he'd clarified that it would change absolutely nothing between them, she'd turned on her victim mode. Derek would reassure her, but she wouldn't budge. Like a concrete pillar, she'd hold her ground, refusing to compromise.

"I won't have people thinking I married a pervert, Derek." "You can't do this to me." "Just be a man, for Christ's sake." She could be excruciatingly vile at times. But in the early days, Derek had been reluctant, even a little frightened, and there had still been some love for Brenda.

They were childhood sweethearts. Derek had been in the same year at school as her big brother, Clarence, and they'd lived a few streets apart. Brenda was beautiful, with her long, silky blonde hair and blue eyes that sparkled like diamonds. He was tall and plump but "with a warm face", as his mother always said. Derek's mother was his world, and he thanked her for his respect of women, even Brenda.

He had tried. God, had he tried. All his married life, until the last six months of it, Brenda had come first. Holidays, cars, furniture, everything. She'd always get her own way. The décor in their house, the food each day, when and where they would go out. Was he a doormat? Bri, his closest childhood friend, and Jeff had made the odd comment. His late friend Arthur, on the other hand, used to just speak his mind directly. Derek chuckled, recalling some of the comments Arthur had made.

"She's a mad cow, Derek, get her culled." "Stop letting the old hag dictate who you are." "To me, you are a perfect character." What he would give to see Arthur now.

Derek saw himself as being passive; anything for an easy life. But he definitely had a backbone. Hadn't the break-up proven that? Twenty-seven years of marriage. It was all he knew, and it hadn't all been bad. But resentment had crept in. It's a funny thing, resentment. An insidious poison going through the cells of the body, building, gaining strength, bubbling away. It would never have been Derek wanting to be himself that broke the marriage. No, it was always going to be resentment, harboured from Brenda's vicious ways, her control, the need to present a perfect marriage to the world. For God's sake, no one was even interested in their lives. That summed Brenda up—the bloody front and keeping up with the Joneses. But no one gave a hoot. They were too bloody interested in what they were having for tea. It was only Brenda who cared, and possibly some of her cronies, who had nothing better to moan about.

The relentless lines and sneers that poured from her had intensified over that last month. The name-calling and put-downs. At first, Derek had tried to resist, but he'd become increasingly depressed and suppressed. Suffocated by pretence and false smiles. Enough was enough, and it really was enough. Then, last night happened.

Today was the start of his new life. He would tell people in time. Tell them the whole story. He wasn't ashamed. It just needed to be a reality in his head before others knew. It had been such a secret for so long. They would struggle to understand—folk are judgemental parasites at times. He had to get it right; digest it in his own mind before he explained to others. Did he owe people explanations? No, quite frankly. But he did want people to understand, and that took planning and patience. In the meantime, what went on behind closed doors was his business. He rubbed his hands together and smiled. There was relief, delight and, dare he say, happiness running through his veins where resentment had so recently flowed.

Derek spent his week at work like he usually did, with no great deviation to his routine. He did, however, have time for a lot of thinking and reflection. After years of ranting and moaning from Brenda, he truly relished that time. Cartington's had been Derek's place of work for over fifteen years. Laid-back, easy, and the team were a nice bunch. Cartington's was a transport and trip firm, providing minibuses, limos, coaches and organised trips for the public of Newcastle upon Tyne, North East England, to enjoy. Derek was a good all-rounder and had taken on extra responsibilities over the years. It suited Derek to do his job around nice folk and then leave it at work. No stress, no worries and always plenty of cakes and homemade pies going around the office.

Each evening that week, Derek arrived home, popped his wellies on and took Des for a walk. Des would come bounding towards him, tongue hanging out, almost grinning, delighted to see his dad. Des knew the walking route well after eight years and led the way as Derek trundled along, deep in thought. Much of his previous dog walking mindfulness had been dreaming of a future where he didn't feel constrained. Or he had used the time as an opportunity to cool down from another verbal attack or incessant lecture from Brenda. Thinking about it, he loathed her. But now she was gone. The walks would become symbolic of Derek's future; the "new me". An opportunity to breathe in the fresh—well, slightly polluted—air and dream about what could actually become a reality.

Derek didn't aim big: health, happiness and comfort in his own skin were his M.O. Acceptance, of course, was important, but that came after his own agenda: to be his true self. With Des by his side, who loved him unconditionally, and fire in his belly, he knew he could do it. So, where to start?

# 2

# TV Dinners

## Derek

It was the end of the working week and Derek's first Friday night without Brenda. Although he continued to be elated about his emancipation, it did have somewhat of an impact on his routines. He was a creature of habit for the most part, and some of the habits Brenda had instilled, he actually enjoyed. Like the Friday night banquet they would indulge in. Brenda would cook the feast. Given she had retired, she was in all day on a Friday and would prepare their supper. She might have been a spiteful cow at times but she was a good cook.

Derek had eaten sandwiches, microwave meals, sausages and eggs all week. Luckily, Tasmin had brought a few homemade pies into work, so he'd had his fill of slices of those, with leftovers to take home. She'd beamed with pride at his feedback, shovelling more onto his plate at lunchtime. Derek didn't mind; he'd genuinely enjoyed the steak and kidney. He rubbed his stomach. Maybe it had deflated a little over the week?

For the first time, Derek felt a pang of loneliness. A distinct missing sensation for the vindictive anchor he'd had in his life all those years. Friday night feasts were always a time of relaxation, watching TV, limited talking and eating copious amounts. Brenda had never seemed to call him a greedy pig on Friday nights as he'd troughed down her offerings. There was never a starter but always a hearty main: roast dinner with all the trimmings, pasta bake and homemade garlic bread, fish pie and veg, steak and roasted Mediterranean veg, hunter's chicken, potatoes and steamed asparagus. His mouth started to water. Pudding would always be stodgy, warming and satisfying: his favourite sticky toffee pudding with succulent dates and lashings of thick yellow custard, homemade rice pudding with nutmeg, tangy ginger sponge and custard, sweet moreish apple pie with Cornish creamy ice cream.

Derek was ravenous. He got out of his chair, Des staring as he made his way into the kitchen. The cupboards were bare apart from a few staples: bicarbonate of soda, three stock cubes, a tin of baked beans, spaghetti, flour, tomato and basil soup and Weetabix.

"Takeaway it is," he mumbled. He could write a list and go to the local supermarket, Foodways, tomorrow. Margherita pizza and chips ordered, he made a cuppa and flicked through the TV channels. Naff all on for a few hours. He and Brenda would usually watch a film until Jonathan Ross or Graham Norton came on. As his tummy rumbled, he continued to search for something to watch. All these channels, yet nothing on. He chuckled at the irony.

"Bugger it." He put the remote down whilst an advert for the latest in beauty products played away. He would start his shopping list as he impatiently waited for his takeaway.

Derek pondered the best way to write the list. Perhaps meals and ingredients needed, or just a load of different foods in the hope a week's worth of meals could be made. He had never had this responsibility before and suddenly felt inadequate. His mind started wandering back to the takeaway.

"Concentrate, you useless old arse."

Right, start with breakfast. Cereal, bread for toast, butter and jams. His favourite was apricot. Ooh, and maybe some lemon curd. Milk, lots of milk for cereal and cuppas. Tea bags, coffee and maybe some hot chocolate.

"Great start, eh, Des?"

Des looked up, a possible rolling of the eyes.

"Dog food," Derek said, suddenly reminded. "Can't forget you, old boy."

Now for meals. Perhaps a vague list; he could always ask for help in the shop if he needed it. Derek looked up from his notepad to see *Dine in With Me* starting on TV. Something he hadn't really watched before, as Brenda loathed reality TV. They were in Bristol. Four hungry people taking turns to cook a thoughtful, adventurous meal for one another in an attempt to win one thousand pounds at the end of the week.

"No bloody decency these days, Des," Derek announced at the thought of people letting strangers root around their homes on TV.

The doorbell went, and Des went berserk.

"Shut up, Des, you daft bugger," he said as he shuffled to the door to get his takeaway.

The smell of melted cheese and vinegar caressed his nasal passages as he brought the food back to the living room with him. "Mmmmm," he whispered, sitting down to eat out of the box. Des's eyes lit up. Tilting his head, he stared at Derek's knee, ogling the food.

As Derek sat munching away, he continued to watch the programme. It showed a middle-aged man, Tony, in his kitchen. He was messing around with pans and ingredients, slurping a glass of wine. Tony's menu, to the delight of his guests, was carrot and coriander soup with homemade sourdough bread for starters.

"Sounds nice," said Derek, nodding.

Tony explained his main was rack of lamb, roasted sweet potato and parsnips with tenderstem broccoli and jus.

"You mean a posh Sunday roast, you pompous twerp."

Dessert, Tony proudly announced, was Eton mess. Derek was mesmerised as Tony got to cooking. The programme kept skipping to snippets of his guests and their expectations: a woman getting her nails done in a salon, saying she was looking forward to a hearty meal; a young lad questioning the ingredients of Eton mess; an older lady adamant she still had the winning menu.

"Wouldn't mind tasting Tony's menu, Des; sounds bloody lovely." The advert break came on, and Derek used it as an opportunity to make a cuppa and put his takeaway rubbish in the bin.

"Go on then, Son." He motioned Des over as he scraped the batter scraps into the dog's bowl. "No big, bad mammy to tell you off for eating nice things now, is there?" he continued, smirking.

With the kettle boiled and a few half pieces of biscuits salvaged from the bottom of the biscuit tin, Derek rushed back in to see how Tony's masterpieces had turned out. The soup was just being served to his patient guests, who oohed and stated that it "looks delicious" as a white bowl with golden goodness inside was placed in front of each of them. They tucked in and devoured their slices of sourdough bread. Derek thought it looked tasty.

Next up was the main course. During this, the four contestants discussed politics and their dreams and aspirations. A bit of tension in the air, exactly how the producers of the show would want it. *Tony's main course looks the business*, Derek thought as he dunked his broken biscuits. A big portion of meat, plenty of veg and gravy. Derek's stomach rumbled. Maybe it was indigestion—he couldn't be hungry after his takeaway, could he?

The guests ate their mains, critiquing the jus and meat tenderness. After the main course, two of the guests went rummaging through Tony's bedroom wardrobe.

"Bloody nosy sods. Why are they doing that?"

The snooping guests pulled out a karate outfit and had a chuckle, claiming Tony to be a "dark horse".

Pudding was next. Derek felt himself getting a little excited to see the guests' reactions. He was more of a hot pudding man himself, but anything sweet after dinner was always welcome in Derek's eyes.

"Eight out of ten for presentation, my old mate Tony," he said, chuckling.

The guests seemed to enjoy it, although a few minutes later, the older woman was criticising it in the taxi on the way home. *Two-faced bugger*, thought Derek. All guests scored the food. Tony was two points behind Mags, the older woman, who'd apparently cooked the night before. Cindy and Adam were cooking on the other two nights. The episodes were back-to-back tonight. Great, he was getting into this *Dine in With Me* lark. He let Des out the back to do his business during the break, then settled back down, excited at what the contestants were going to cook next. After all, it could even help with his shopping list.

# 3

# The Weekly Shop

## Derek

Derek had slept soundly. He awoke feeling refreshed, physically and mentally lighter and, for the first time in a long time, optimistic. Of course, he would naturally have hard days, weeks even, he knew that. This would eventually become the odd difficult hour, minute or second—it was part of the grieving process. Even though he knew his split with Brenda was for the best, it was still the end of an era.

Des stirred, perked his head up and looked longingly at Derek. Sometimes, he really wished Des could talk. Oh, the conversations they would have.

"Righto, Son, let's get up. We've got a busy day ahead."

The two of them journeyed downstairs, Des in front as always, looking back at his master with jubilant eyes, knowing breakfast was imminent. A quick toilet stop in the garden for Des and then he dashed back in, hovering around his food bowl. Breakfast was served, and Derek once again went to the fridge to assess his options. Knowing his fridge wouldn't have miraculously filled itself overnight, he still opened it, chuckling to himself before rummaging around the freezer for something, anything, edible. Ah, treasure: a few slices of fruit loaf. They would do, even if there was no butter. He was sure there was some marmalade in the cupboard.

Sitting down to his breakfast, Derek considered the day ahead. He would start with his food shopping. He revisited his list from the night before as he savoured his fruit loaf. Despite no butter, it was tasty and sweet in his mouth. Adding a few more items to the list, he sighed with contentment. The house felt quiet, but in that moment, it was peaceful waves washing over him.

He had arranged to meet Bri at the local pub, The Spitting Feathers, later in the day. It would be good to catch up and talk through the whole Brenda situation with him. Over the years, Bri had witnessed first-hand what a vicious bitch Brenda could be. Jibes at Derek's weight, his apparent inadequacy, belittling and mocking him. Bri wanted the best for Derek, and once Derek was ready to disclose more of the truth, he felt Bri would stand by him.

"Right, old son, walkies for you." Des barked a grateful thank you, and Derek quickly pulled on some jogging trousers and a T-shirt. Another thing Brenda used to have a go at him about.

She had mocked him on many occasions: "Derek, you look like a bag of shit in those jogging bottoms." "Being fat doesn't give you an automatic right to live in grey, elasticated sports trousers that, ironically, you would never exercise in because you never get off your backside."

True, Derek did wear them a lot, but since Brenda had never let him wear what he wanted to in the house, why should he have made an effort? Adding to this, his weight had crept up with his unhappiness. Granted, he had become a little tubbier these last few years, as comfort eating became the only way to tolerate his miserable home existence, but being bigger was fine with him, and name-calling certainly wasn't. Thinking about the taunts made him seethe. Derek would never criticise anyone's weight or anything else about someone. Bloody hell, diversity makes the world go round. Suddenly overwhelmed with emotions, he decided he needed some fresh air.

"Morning, Dekka. Morning, Des," Susan from next door called out as she got into her Fiesta.

"Morning, Susan. Have a nice day," he replied politely as always, wondering why after eleven years of living next door to Susan, she insisted on calling him Dekka. He had never introduced himself as Dekka, and Christmas cards had always been signed Derek. Where had Dekka come from? It made him sound like a DJ from the nineties. She would be calling him Del Boy next. Maybe it was something she did with everyone—bizarre nicknames to try and sound in touch with the cool kids. Perhaps Susan was simply trying to cling to her youth as she crept into middle aged. Whatever it was, Derek found it irritating.

As Derek walked Des to the park on the next estate, he wondered about nicknames, where they came from and how people imposed them on others who may not want them. *Nothing as strange as folk*. He wondered if he should start calling Susan Suzie, Sue, Suzie-Sue or something as silly as S. Her surname was Williamson, so maybe he should start calling her S Willy. He could only imagine her reaction to that.

Twenty minutes later, Derek and Des were back home. As Des retired to his dog bed in the lounge, Derek walked upstairs to his bedroom, humming as he went. Was that a little spring in his step? He was sure it was.

Derek turned the radio on. It was nice to be able to control the noise in the house. Brenda had some mental obsession with the hoover. She was forever plugging that bloody thing in. *I bet she used to plug it in and swear about me as she hoovered the non-existent dirt*, Derek thought, chuckling to himself. Mad cow. She would probably be hoovering her sister Linda's house within an inch of its soft furnishings, driving her mad as well. Actually, come to think of it, Linda was a pain in the arse, just like her younger sister.

Brenda hadn't been in touch all week. She had said she didn't want to hear from him and wouldn't be making contact until she felt ready. Derek knew she would be absolutely livid that he hadn't tried to contact her. He also knew she had been to the house mid-week whilst he was at work, as more of her clothes and rubbish were gone. Bloody marvellous; he wanted rid of all the ridiculous lotions and potions she wore to try and reverse the years of being a misery and smoking like a chimney most of the late eighties and early nineties. *Nothing could cover up her stone heart.*

He didn't mind her leaving a little make-up though—Chanel Rouge Coco brought back some nice memories. She had bought it in duty-free nine or so years ago when they'd gone to Tenerife.

Derek got ready quickly. He had plans for the whole weekend and was looking forward to his first as a single man. Jeans and a jumper would do for Foodways. He would be looking for a whole new wardrobe over time though; a reinvention.

"Right, Son, I won't be too long." He glanced at Des, who looked back with love in his eyes. "Alright, alright, I will bring you back a treat." Des made a little sound that Derek recognised as contentment. Derek swore that dog had a human's soul. Picking up his car keys, he left the house, praying he would avoid Susan.

It only took fifteen minutes for Derek to get to Foodways. Getting out of his Astra, he grabbed his bags for life, pulled the nearest trolley and sauntered into the supermarket. Brenda would do all the shopping for most of the year. Derek often only went at Christmas, liking to peruse all the festive gorge: rich cheeses, succulent meats, salty snacks and puddings galore. He was peckish just thinking about it. *Supermarkets sell everything these days*, he thought. *No need to go anywhere else really. There's a cashpoint, a bureau de change, a dry cleaner, a cobbler, a pharmacist. It's a clothes shop and you can buy all your weekly food. Magical.*

With his list eagerly out, Derek set about getting a full week's worth of supplies. As well as the list, he would see what he fancied, getting ideas and asking staff if needed. It was a whole new life skill, and so what if he was over sixty years old? He came from a generation of women who looked after men. He'd never expected Brenda to look after him, but he'd just so happened to be the breadwinner of the two. His newfound singledom would allow him to enjoy learning about cooking and cleaning, getting some household independence.

Derek smiled to himself, feeling adventurous. Scanning over the fruit and vegetables, he was amazed at the range of produce. He was unsure what half of it was.

"Okra. What the bloody hell is okra?" he said aloud, forgetting where he was.

A woman turned to him, giggling. "Very nice in a curry, I say." She smiled, walking away as Derek blushed.

He walked mindfully up and down the aisle, looking over the rainbow of colours and feeling slightly overwhelmed by his unfamiliarity with at least half the produce. He tentatively stepped closer to the vegetables, frightened they may snap at him like a caged animal.

"Hmm, sweet potato. That's ok, I know you, sweet potato, old pal." He smiled, picking up one of them and turning it over in his hands. Sweet potato wedges—he had enjoyed them on a few occasions. "Why not," he said as he placed two in his trolley.

"What's next? Courgette. Looks like a cucumber or a marrow to me."

"It's from the same family. Cousins, I believe," chirped in one of the shop floor staff. "Nice roasted in a ratatouille or with pasta."

"Thanks. I love a bit of pasta," replied Derek.

A courgette went into the trolley, followed by broccoli, a pack of baking potatoes, an onion and some carrots.

A few loose chillies. Derek liked a kick to his food and was looking forward to creating some masterpieces. Fruit next. Derek was an apple and banana kind of man. He liked strawberries in the summer but avoided pineapples—they stung his tongue. He then came across mangoes. He liked the flavour of mango in a juice drink, but he'd tasted an actual mango many years ago and felt the taste compared to that of furniture polish. *Don't you just hate it when a flavour of something tastes nothing like the real thing?* he thought. *How fraudulent. Ah, bugger it, let's try it again.*

The next aisle was full of toiletries and cosmetics, with an opticians and pharmacy. He sprayed and sniffed, fancying a new scent for the new him. There were a few that tickled his fancy. A David Beckham spray and a spray that smelt like summer, coconut and sandalwood. He put them both into the trolley. "Because I deserve it."

Up and down the aisle he went, enjoying every second. Brenda used to moan about doing the shopping, claiming it was a tedious chore. She was lying. It seemed like good fun to him; an adventure of food, colours, tastes and new characters. Most others seemed in a good mood too. People were picking their favourite items and trying new things. Lists in hands, children in trolley seats, eating chocolate. People talking on their mobiles, asking for ingredients and sharing what they were getting for that night. Derek was loving the Foodways vibes, enjoying the people-watching as much as the food exploration.

Crisps, biscuits and cereal were the next few aisles. He grabbed some of his favourite crisps, some custard creams and chocolate. He needed them for sustenance at work as well as for treats. Porridge, check. Cornflakes, check. The fresh meat and freezer aisles seemed to never end. His trolley was getting noticeably full, but he didn't want to stop. He had nothing in the house to eat. He could make this shop last him a good while and just top up over the coming weeks. He justified it in his head. The meat choices from different parts of the world were vast. Brenda called anything from another country she didn't like or couldn't be bothered to try or cook "foreign muck". Funny how she liked some "foreign muck", such as pasta and the odd mild Indian dish, but she wouldn't dream of trying certain foods and, therefore, Derek hadn't tried them either. He scoured the choices, determined to find something he hadn't tasted before. He settled on a Mexican dish, the ingredients already there in the pack. If he liked it, he could perhaps make it from scratch at some point. Up and down, up and down he continued. Gathering some frozen chips, a few ready meals, pizzas and some frozen veg. Although he was inspired to cook, Rome wasn't built in a day. Plus, he still had work.

"One step at a time," he said.

Eventually, he came to the end of the aisles. Bloody hell, he had been in here over two hours. He found a friendly faced cashier and started loading his mountain of goods.

"Morning, love. Actually, afternoon," he said.

"Hi there, do you want a hand with your packing?" she replied.

"Yes, please, love. It will take me another two hours, otherwise." He chortled.

Derek chatted with Louise, the checkout operator, as she scanned his food. She commented on a few of his items that she had tried. Derek wanted to know more—what she'd had them with, what the taste was like, how many servings it made—but he was conscious of the queue developing behind him. He was fascinated by the whole supermarket encounter and felt he had been missing out all these years. After placing the last item in one of his bags and paying, he thanked Louise, wished her a nice day and set off towards the exit.

On the way out, there was a huge noticeboard publicising local things on the wall. Glancing quickly as he moved past, he observed a music teacher advertising his services, a poster for the local church fete and a photo of a missing cat.

Derek packed his bags into the boot, pleased with his achievement. He drove back home, daydreaming about the meals he could produce in the week ahead. He decided to set himself a goal of making two new meals a week to develop his culinary skills and expand his palate. It would give him something to do; a new hobby. Deep down, Derek knew it wasn't long before he'd start to feel lonely. He wasn't used to being on his own. Even the pain in the arse that Brenda had become was still company. He sighed. Could he really go it alone? Could he really be his true self? And would his true self be accepted?

# 4

# *Experimenting*

## Derek

After what felt like another hour putting all his shopping away, Derek boiled the kettle, grabbed the biscuit tin and retired to the lounge. Des sharply followed, keeping the biscuit tin in his line of vision.

"Only Rich Teas for you, Son," Derek said, fishing one out the tin for an already salivating Des. Derek settled back into the sofa. He took out his shopping list, now crossed out, and realised how much extra he had bought. Brenda had some old recipe books somewhere in the kitchen. He would hunt them out later.

For now, he decided to turn his laptop on and have a look online for the first of his recipe challenges. He had bought enough food to open a bloody restaurant; he could definitely find a recipe to start his new hobby. As he loaded the laptop up, a thought came across his mind. A thought he had buried so many times, fighting against it like the sun fighting to shine through a cold winter day. For periods of time, the urge had quelled. Brenda had made sure of that. He knew she would have a devious way of checking his internet history. Derek could manage a laptop, just. He was certainly no IT whizz kid and used only simple programs at work. Brenda had done a beginners IT course about eighteen months ago. She even knew how to blog. He often thought she'd done the course to check up on him. Call it paranoia. It had worked, and he had stayed away from doing any research after she'd told him to man up and stop being a pervert.

He could feel himself getting annoyed. A pervert? Who the hell did she think she was? You can't bloody call people perverts. A pervert is someone who preys on people in a sexual way. A depraved and sick individual. Someone who exploits others for sexual gratification. How could that nasty cow put him in the same bracket, for God's sake? He knew how: because she was an ignorant bitch, frightened of what the bloody neighbours might think. Worried about her silly friends, the women at the WI, those at Knit and Natter, the over fifties keep fit group. Worried about saving face, worried about judgement. So, instead, she'd branded her husband a secret pervert, and the "pervert" had had to swallow his urges, bury his thoughts, suppress his secret and comply with whatever Brenda wanted.

Derek jumped up, seething, giving Des a fright. "Sorry, Son, didn't mean to startle you." Foaming with anger, he paced the lounge, desperate to ring her. He had so much to say. In that moment, he hated her. All the love, all those years of marriage and nice memories dissolved, leaving resentment.

He grabbed his mobile, shaking with emotion as he scrolled for her number. Prodding the keypad with ferocious anger, he dialled her number. Straight to voicemail. "You've got to be taking the absolute piss," he said. Adrenaline was pumping through his veins. He had to say what was on his mind. He could ring Linda. That was who she'd said she would be staying with when she'd stormed out earlier in the week. He searched for Linda in his phonebook and pressed the call button, biting his lip while he waited for her to answer.

"Linda, it's Derek, is Brenda there?" he blurted before she had the chance to speak.

"Ah, hello to you too, Derek. Yes, I'm fine, thanks," Linda spat out sarcastically. "She's not here, Derek. She went to Tenerife with Joan two days ago and said she's away a fortnight. Try her bloody mobile, I'm not her keeper. Goodbye."

Derek kept the phone to his ear after Linda clicked off. He had to take a few seconds to absorb what she'd said.

"Bloody Tenerife. *Bloody Tenerife*. Who does she think she is, Shirley friggin' Valentine?" he shouted. His temperature was soaring. Des scurried into the kitchen.

Fingers shaking, he dialled Bri. Bri answered after only two rings.

"Bri, mate, what time are we meeting? You aren't going to believe what that cow Brenda has done."

"Mate, calm down, you sound hysterical. I'm out with our Bonnie at the moment and her mam. I can be at The Spitting Feathers in an hour or so. Will it keep till then?"

"Yeah, of course, sorry. That's great. I may have calmed down by then. See you soon. Enjoy your time with the kid."

Derek put his phone down. He needed a beer, feeling on the edge between screaming with frustration and crying. Des looked at him sheepishly as he entered the kitchen.

"Sorry, Son, I didn't mean to frighten you," he soothed as Des rolled over, giving Derek his belly to stroke.

Derek opened the fridge, looking at all the food as he hunted for a beer. *There they are.* He pulled one out and cracked it open, thinking he better line his stomach, as he intended on spending the rest of the day in The Spitting Feathers.

Toaster out, Derek popped four slices of bread in. Two slices of toast never seemed enough. *The recipes can start tomorrow*, he thought. Smothering his toast with butter, Derek watched it melt, turning into liquid on his hot, moreish bread. He then spread over a thick layer of lemon curd. The toast almost glistened. Shoving it in his mouth, he absorbed the sweet taste. With the other three slices consumed in the same way, Derek felt that satisfactory sugar rush.

A quick shower and change of clothes. He had got all hot and bothered from his attempted phone call to Brenda and speaking to that smug cow Linda. A shower would soothe his mind and body. Stripping off and getting into the cubicle, Derek automatically started to contemplate. The shower had been his sanctuary over the years, that and walking Des. It was his time to think and some time away from Brenda's negative voice; an escape. He would often sing in the shower, normally his favourite Style Council song or a bit of Leonard Cohen if he was feeling especially melancholic. Sometimes, the latest catchy chart song. Derek thought he had an alright voice. True, he would never sell out stadiums but he could hold a note or two. Brenda used to tell him to pack it in. Another chance to be a spoil sport, put him down and, as Derek always thought, show her envy, since she sounded like a constipated turkey shitting out a brick when she sang. He quietly laughed, then went straight back to being angry.

He let his mind wander as he washed himself with the strawberry shower gel. Why did shower gels aimed at women always smell so much nicer than those aimed at men? He could practically drink this shower gel. He sang for the last few minutes of his shower, washing his hair and letting the water run down his back, gently massaging him.

Now, what to wear. He opened the wardrobe and looked across his clothes. Colour coded, bland and boring. Clothes he had worn for years, the same style, colour and fabrics. Clothes that Brenda had insisted on buying every Christmas and birthday, despite him pleading with her not to and asking for anything but. Another way to control him. He moved the trousers to one side, revealing the green holdall he used to use for squash in the late nineties. He pulled it out and opened it, feeling like a child at Christmas. His heart beat faster with excitement and anticipation even though he knew what was inside. He opened the bag ferociously and clumsily. He pushed his hand inside and felt warmth flow through him. And then he snapped back to reality. Not today. No, not today.

Right, blue jeans and his maroon polo shirt. He wanted to get to The Spitting Feathers as soon as possible, meaning he'd get there before Bri and most likely have a pint alone. Not that he minded; you were never really alone in The Spitting Feathers, with the familiar, friendly locals. Derek would find someone to talk to or just enjoy people-watching.

He went downstairs and looked in the hallway mirror, turning sideways. "Think me belly's gone down a little here, Des," he called out as he smoothed over his stomach. Shoes on, wallet and mobile in pocket, and off he went.

The Spitting Feathers was only a seven-minute walk from Derek's house. It was a walk Derek could do with his eyes closed. He had got to know the nearby residents as he'd passed them over the years, often saying a quick "hello" and "how are you?" He wondered if people would judge him differently in the future, if it got to that stage. If they would still be as pleasant and friendly. Sadness crept over him. *Bloody stop it. Stop being an idiot and worrying about what people think*.

He thought back to something his good friend Arthur used to say. "We are only this big," he'd state, putting his thumb and forefinger a couple of inches apart. He'd meant that in reality, we are insignificant, and people don't really care what others are doing. Of course, we care about our loved ones, but most people's interest in others is limited. Derek always found conversations with him so insightful and wise.

"Really, Derek, do you give a flying fuck what the woman three streets away is up to?" he would say, or "Derek, my love, no one is interested in you; they are too busy thinking about what to have for tea."

Derek laughed, a warm, love-filled laugh. He missed Arthur. Three years ago, Arthur had passed away from stomach cancer. Years of alcohol misuse and self-neglect had ravaged his body. Sadly, he'd only had four wonderful years of sobriety and clarity before being diagnosed and beginning his battle. A battle he'd boldly fought but ultimately lost.

Derek had opened up to Arthur, and Arthur had accepted him the way he was, thoughts, feelings, desires and all. He missed that closeness. Bri was a great friend, and he had Jeff and a few others from work. But no one was like Arthur. He'd just got people and understood that they had to be who they wanted to be.

"Are you going in, old son, or staying out here all day?"

"Sorry." Derek shook his head, leaving his thoughts. He smiled at Jack awkwardly—a local at The Spitting Feathers—realising he was already outside the pub and not knowing how long he'd been stood there, lost in his own mind.

"Yeah, mate, gasping for a pint. How's you? How's Angie?" Derek asked.

"Sound, all sound. And your Brenda?"

"We split up. For the best really. Long time coming."

"Ah, right. Ah, well, onwards and upwards, eh."

*Men never know what to say*, Derek thought as he nodded, following Jack into the pub. Bri arrived half an hour later as Derek was sinking his second pint.

"Hi, mate," Bri said, giving Derek a shoulder hug.

"At last. Nice to see you."

The next hour was filled with Derek updating Bri about the last week. Every detail, apart from the catalyst, of his explosion with Brenda. Insight into the final straw, the build-up and the aftermath. Derek mentioned the phone call, Linda, Brenda being in Tenerife and his newly found culinary independence. Bri's face said it all.

"But why now, Derek? I mean, you never seemed that unhappy."

"I've had enough. I'm over sixty, and I let her chip away at me for too long. She wouldn't let me be myself. I was a version of who she wanted me to be. She's a spiteful bitch, Bri, she really is. She made me feel like a loser for a long time. I was basically living a lie."

"Living a lie? Bloody hell, that sounds a bit dramatic, mate," Bri said, chuckling.

"I don't know how to explain it, I just know I feel lighter and as though I have something to look forward to for the first time in forever." Derek paused, taking a breath. "There are things I will miss—companionship, someone making me a cuppa—but I don't think I'll miss anything about her personality; it turned so toxic. The only good memories are old memories, and they've been pushed out by the last few years of her trying to change me." Derek sighed and looked down at his hands. "I'm not explaining it the best. My head is still a bit of a whirlwind. It's been a lot this week, mate. But I do appreciate you listening."

Bri squeezed Derek's shoulder reassuringly. "Anytime, Derek, you know that."

The two friends drank some more, talked about fantasy football, Bri's wife Eileen, his grandchildren and work. Two old friends with lots in common. The hours passed with ease. Derek felt good.

"Right, mate, time for me to go," Bri said, looking at the clock on the wall. Derek's eyes flitted to it too, seeing it was gone 10 p.m. "Eileen will be expecting me."

"Yeah, I best get back for Des. Listen, Bri, will you come around for tea one night next week? Thursday?"

"Sure, mate. Sounds nice."

The friends hugged and said their goodnights before heading off in different directions.

# 5

# *Pie Thursday*

## Derek

Derek's week so far had been pretty uneventful. He continued to adjust to life as a single man. Learning new skills in the house, enjoying the peace and quiet—albeit a little lonely at times—cooking new foods and researching. Every night when he got in from Cartington's, he made a new masterpiece in the kitchen. His appetite had well and truly returned, and he was thoroughly enjoying experimenting with new flavours and foods. Last night, he had made BBQ chicken, sweet potato fries and roasted veg, his plate a mass of colours and textures. It had easily been a nine out of ten, he'd thought as he'd tucked in.

Tonight, Bri was coming for tea. Derek was nervous; it was going to be a meal neither of them would forget. Earlier in the week, Derek had managed to get Tasmin from work's pie recipe off her and was going to attempt to make it for Bri. *Would you have ever thought it*, he chuckled to himself, *Derek Morgan making a pie*!

Research had formed a large part of his free time that week. He had been on websites and forums, reading stories of people similar to him. It had helped, on the whole, albeit daunting and overwhelming at times. Some of these forums could be quite abusive, full of what people called "trolls". But it had been helpful in assisting

Derek to make more sense of everything and his future plans. Bri would be his guinea pig. Well, second guinea pig, as Brenda had been the first, and that certainly hadn't gone well.

Derek started ruminating on the evening, predicting, worrying. What if Bri was disgusted or disowned him? He could lose his lifelong friend. Surely Bri wasn't that shallow. Derek could really do without losing a close friend at this point in his life. But he couldn't go on like this. His marriage was over, and something had to come out of it that made Derek happy. He didn't actually need anyone's blessing, he just wanted it and couldn't cope with any more loss.

"You'll always accept and love me, won't you, Son?" Derek said, looking down at Des. Des's marble, adoring eyes looked back with unconditional love. Humans could learn a few things from animals.

Derek started preparing the pie recipe. He had under two hours before Bri would arrive. *Plenty of time to prepare the pie and veg, have a shower and get changed*, he thought, although he knew he would need at least three times longer than usual to get ready.

Tasmin's pie was legendary at work. Derek knew he wouldn't make it the same on the first or hundredth attempt, but he was up for the challenge and was thriving in his new hobby. Radio on in the background, he took pride in his preparation, and forty-five minutes later, the pie was in the oven and the veg peeled and cut for boiling.

*Maybe just one drink to steady the nerves before getting ready*. Just one gin would take the edge off. He couldn't have too much—it was a school night—but one would most definitely help the nerves. He poured his drink with trembling hands.

*Get a bloody grip*, Derek thought, moving upstairs. Opening the wardrobe, he reached to the back, grabbing the green holdall. His heart was pounding. Unzipping the bag, he felt the warmth of comfort from the content, tainted by a fear soaring through his veins. It was real. This was it. The beginning of possibly the end. This one decision could change everything: his state of mind, his next move, his future, his lifelong friendship. It could alter everything.

Would it come as a shock to Bri? Would he say he's always had an inkling? Would he be pleased for Derek? Or would he be disgusted like Brenda was? Jesus, was it all worth it? Necking the gin, Derek looked at the bag. Yes. Yes, it was worth it. Of course it was. Enough was enough. He felt suppressed, muted, or as Arthur used to say, "My sparkle has been dulled".

It took Derek almost a full hour to get ready. By the end of the hour, with ten minutes spare until Bri arrived, he had drank three gins and felt tiddly. Luckily, the pie was looking delicious and the veg was roasting nicely. The smell of home cooking and goodness filled the kitchen. Derek inhaled with comforting satisfaction. The food would be good, even if it was to be the last supper.

Derek loitered in the hallway, waiting to hear the doorbell go and the usual second doorbell in the form of Des barking. He felt as if he were waiting for a job interview: sweaty palms, dry throat. *Why does time drag when we don't want it to and fly by like a Red Arrow when we wish it would last longer?*

Then, the noise came; the doorbell rang. It sounded like an emergency evacuation siren to Derek, and for a second, he contemplated escaping out the back door. He froze. *So, this is what flight, fight, freeze and flop is, then*, he thought. *I can't do it. Pretend I'm not in. Hide*. He felt the tears building up, ready to burst their dam.

Derek was still frozen to the spot at the end of the hallway. This was Bri, his closest friend, the best man at his wedding, his goddaughter's father. *If he won't accept me, no one will*. It was the ultimate test for Derek. It was literally now or never.

"Coming," he shouted.

Ten steps away from the door. Ten steps and the future would be decided. Ten, nine, eight, seven, six, five, four, three, two, one. Hand on door handle. Door open. Bri standing on one side of the front door, Derek on the other.

"What the bloody hell, Derek?" Bri's chin almost hit the doorstep.

"Hi, Bri, come on in, and please, do call me Debbie."

# 6

# *Dinner with Debbie*

## Derek

"What the hell, Derek?"

"You've already said that, Bri. Please come inside."

Bri remained on the doorstep, eyes massive, mouth open, looking as though he were about to collapse.

*Shit*, thought Derek.

"Please come in, Bri," Derek said, starting to panic. "Let me explain."

After what felt like an eternity, Bri followed Derek inside, mouth still open. The fact he'd actually come inside was a good start. Bri took his coat off and hung it in the usual place, over the banister, like he had done for years. A comfortable routine. But his mouth was still open as he continued to stare at Derek.

"Close your bloody mouth, mate, will you? A fly will land soon." Derek nervously chuckled.

They walked into the lounge in silence. Bri kept opening his mouth to say something, then closing it again. It was the longest few minutes of Derek's life.

"Is this a joke, mate?" Bri asked nervously.

"No, Bri, no, it's not a joke."

Derek and Bri stood facing each other on opposite sides of the deep pile rug. Bri in his usual M&S navy chinos and round neck jumper. Derek in a coral A-line midi dress with delicate white flowers on it, some sandals and third attempt make-up that had taken him ages to apply. Clearly, he wasn't going to get a job at Max Factor, but he thought the light brown eyeshadow followed by some bronze shading and the peach-toned lipstick looked pretty damn good. YouTube tutorials were game changers, as he had discovered that week.

Bri bit his lip. "I don't understand, Derek. If it isn't a joke, what the hell is going on, mate? Why are you dressed as a bloody woman?"

*He called me mate—a good sign. He is still here, in my living room—another good sign. Time to tell the truth.*

"Can I get you a drink first, mate? And please take a seat." Derek gestured towards the sofa and started making his way to the kitchen. He was overwhelmed with panic, with relief, with an excruciating desire to be accepted. He wasn't sure if he was going to cry.

"I'll have a beer. Make it two."

In the kitchen, Derek took the opportunity to try and calm down as he turned the oven off. The food was ready. Hopefully, Bri's appetite had not completely dissolved.

Derek grabbed four beers with shaking hands and headed back to the lounge. Bri was sitting down, Des at his feet, leaning against him, demanding attention. Bri was stroking him. *Great*, thought Derek, *he's relaxing*. But as soon as he saw Derek come back in, his body language stiffened again.

Bri looked Derek up and down. "What is all this, mate? I don't understand. Why the hell are you dressed like that?" Bri shook his head, perplexed. "Who is bloody Debbie? Are you gay?" The questions frantically poured out of him. "Do you want to be a woman, mate? Bloody hell, is this why Brenda left you?"

"Bri, I know this is a lot to absorb."

"It is, isn't it? It's why she left. You want to be a woman."

"Bri, Bri, please, one question at a time. Please let me explain. I know it must be weird for you seeing me like this." Derek was on the verge of tears, knowing it could all go so wrong.

"You're not kidding. This is just madness, Derek."

"I wanted to tell you, well, show you because you are my lifelong friend, and if I can't be myself with you, who can I be myself with?" Derek's voice trembled. *Don't cry, don't you dare cry*.

"It's why Brenda left, isn't it? Cos you're one of them."

"Bri, stop bringing Brenda into this. This isn't about sexuality, mate. I just know that I feel alive when I am Debbie. That I feel like me."

"Feel alive? Eh, are you going to go on stage and parade around with your cock and balls tucked in?" Bri was laughing, and Derek wasn't sure if it was with him or at him.

God, he had rehearsed this conversation a million times. It had sounded so good in an empty room. Now, it felt as if there were a chance Bri would be carted off to the local psychiatric hospital for assessment.

Bri necked his second beer.

"I'm still me; I'm still Derek. Most of the time, I like being Derek. I just also like to be Debbie sometimes. An alter ego; a different personality. Someone who I feel free being, where I feel creative, beautiful and happy."

"So, you don't want to be like this all the time? No chopping your bits off? Hey, you aren't going to come to the pub like this, are you?" Bri fidgeted slightly on the sofa.

Derek laughed an awkward laugh. "No. No sex change, Bri, and no, I don't want to be a woman or dress as a woman constantly, I just want to express myself and be Debbie when I want to. It's complicated, I know that. It's been a lot for me to understand, never mind anyone else."

"This is a lot to absorb, Derek. A big bloody shock. Friggin' hell, you'll be saying you're vegan next."

Derek started laughing again, this time not awkwardly.

"Mate, this is intense. I don't know what to say. I've never known a drag queen."

"Bri, I'm not a drag queen or gay or whatever you think. It's just something I like to do. I don't know—a hobby or something. Like someone who likes to go on motorcycles."

"Mate, it's nothing like bloody motorcycles." It was Bri's turn to laugh now. "Anyway, I'm starving. Can Debbie cook better than Derek?"

"Well, dinner is ready, so you can decide for yourself."

"Well, it at least smells as if Debbie knows her way round a kitchen," replied Bri.

Derek felt as though the dumbbell on his chest had been lifted. He was far from safe, but Bri was still here, and he hadn't called him that word that hurt Derek the most: a pervert.

Bri walked to the kitchen, and Derek followed, slower than usual due to his heels.

Over dinner, Derek told Bri everything. That he had fond memories of wearing his mother's clothes as a child. The smell of them, tinged with her perfume and body lotions, the feel of the materials. The colours, choices and styles being so much more varied and interesting than men's.

"So, it's your mam's fault, eh?" Bri winked.

"It's no one's fault. It's just the way it is. Like you supporting Sunderland AFC," he joked.

"Aye, this is premier league shit right here, Derek, mate."

Derek explained that it wasn't something he did all the time, and over the years he had smothered his feelings. But he was sick of not being himself. Wearing women's clothes now and then didn't make him a bad person. He shared how Brenda used to call him names, say he was a pervert and not a real man. The resentment Derek felt and, ironically, Brenda being a controlling bitch that had led to the final straw in the marriage. There were the odd nods of what could have been understanding from Bri, mixed with the odd eyebrow raise.

"Brenda never mentioned it to Eileen. She would have told me."

"She was ashamed of me, Bri. She bullied me, used it against me. Don't get me wrong, the marriage had been dying for ages. She made me dislike and resent her. This was just the tipping point really.

"I just want to be myself, and part of that is being Debbie if I want to. I'm not saying I'm going to turn up at work or the match or The Spitting Feathers like this. I just want to dress up in my home if I want to. At first anyway."

Derek explained that he had thought long and hard about not hiding Debbie anymore. People would judge, of course, but in some ways, it felt as if the society today was more tolerant of difference. Christ, he knew there was a load of intolerance with certain things such as religion and ethnicity, sadly, and that ignorance was an epidemic. But he also saw progress in issues. Folk no longer stared at disabled people, gay people holding hands. Someone could have purple hair and no one would look twice. Well, that was how he perceived things. He saw role models in the world of transvestism, such as Eddie Izzard being a great campaigner and even going to Labour Party campaign events in women's clothes.

"I understand. It's just a lot to take in. I thought I knew you. You should've said something to me, mate, you know you can trust me." Bri looked to the floor before looking back at his lifelong friend.

"I do trust you, Bri, I just had to get things clear in my own head first. I don't want this to change our friendship. You're a massive part of my life."

"You're always going to be my mate. Whether you're Derek, Debbie or whoever, you're still the same person.

It might take a bit of getting used to, but I just want you to be happy."

Derek's eyes began to tear up. "Thanks so much, mate, your words and acceptance really do mean the world." He hugged Bri, a tear landing on his shoulder. Bri patted his back firmly but comfortingly.

"Less of the waterworks, mate. What's for pud?"

# 7

# New Networks

## Derek

Derek woke the next morning feeling light of burden. The relief of speaking to Bri and him meeting Debbie had been massive. He hoped and prayed Bri wouldn't change his mind about being okay with the situation.

It was time to future plan. Brenda would be back from Tenerife soon. They would have to talk and look at the practicalities of separating. These two weeks had given Derek thinking space. He was still a little angry with her, resentful even, but he wasn't a vindictive man. He just wanted to be amicable and try and move forward, maybe even as friends. Twenty-eight years together was a long time, and there had been good times—he had to focus on some of those to ensure he didn't turn bitter over the entire relationship. What was done was done. He didn't expect Brenda to change. He didn't even want her to.

Part of Derek felt lonely. He didn't miss Brenda per se, more the company, the presence of someone on the sofa next to him, even if conversation was strained. Someone cooking for him, someone sharing food with him.

He had lost weight and couldn't decide if he was pleased or not. Of course, he should be pleased—he was decidedly rotund and needed to lose a few stone. He felt lighter and looked a bit trimmer, but he certainly didn't want to lose his appetite.

As he got ready for work, Derek started daydreaming about the big shop he needed to do the next day. It had been a real treat last time, daunting, no doubt, and bloody expensive, but it had felt like an adventure. He had made a few new recipes, from the simple to the more extravagant, which had been a delight. Yes, he would buy plenty more ingredients and keep up with his culinary education.

And Derek did just that the next day, back at Foodways. List in hand, bags for life in the trolley, he went trundling into the supermarket with a similar awe to that he'd had on the last visit. He spent a little more time perusing the homeware and clothes departments, seeing items he hadn't noticed last time: candles, bedding, ornaments and gifts. Shoes and bags.

He ventured into the food aisles, enjoying making small talk with fellow customers. Asking the odd question, folk were just as helpful as last time. He noticed flyers with recipes on at the bottom of one of the vegetable aisles. *What a marvellous idea*, he thought, grabbing a few. He had been looking online for recipes, alongside checking out forums for crossdressers (which were a complete minefield, he had found). But having handy flyers to pop in the kitchen drawer and refer to would be a welcome addition.

Eventually, he reached the checkouts. Still full of enthusiasm and energy, he loaded the conveyor belt and exchanged pleasantries with the checkout operator, noticing her sparkly nail varnish.

Wishing her a good day, he pushed his loaded trolley off, passing the noticeboard with information for locals again. He stopped and had a quick look. An advert for a badminton club, someone advertising their dog grooming services, the local school doing a choir for the community. An idea popped into his head, followed immediately by a "don't be daft". He dismissed it, pushing his trolley off again.

Derek packed his car with his many bags, travelled back home and unpacked before doing his usual walk with an ever-eager Des. He had decided to stay in this weekend and do some much-needed deep cleaning and, of course, cooking.

After getting back home with Des, he popped some bread in the toaster. Two slices wouldn't be enough for his appetite.

"Posh eggs on toast, I think," Derek said, thinking of the spinach, eggs and mushrooms he'd just bought. He looked down at Des. "Not for you, Son."

Fifteen minutes later, Derek looked down at his masterpiece with a big grin. "I'm a natural."

Sitting in the silence, the thought came back into his mind. Was it silly? Would anyone really be interested? *I guess I won't know if I don't try. Nothing ventured and all that.*

He polished off his posh eggs on toast and went into the sideboard drawer for a pen and paper. Even better, there was a scrap of card in there that he could cut. *Best do a draft on the paper first*, he thought.

**Do you enjoy cooking? Would you like...**

*No, that's not right.*

**Do you enjoy cooking and eating? Would you like to meet other...**

*Greedy buggers*, he thought, laughing. *Maybe not.*

**Would you like to meet fellow foodies for nights of cooking and eating?**

*No, how about...*

**Cooking and company? If so, contact Derek to join *Dine in With Me.***

*Not sure if that is copyright; need another name.*

**To join The Dinner Club, call, text or email on...**

"Then, my details go in there," he said as he filled in his contact details. Way-hee!

**Do you enjoy cooking and eating? Would you like to meet fellow foodies for nights of cooking and company? If so, contact Derek to join The Dinner Club...**

"Bloody marvellous, Des," he announced as Des tilted his head, looking lovingly at his owner.

What a great way to make new friends, try out his recipes, have others cook for him and perhaps introduce Debbie. Derek felt a rush of excitement. He wanted to take it to Foodways there and then and put it on the noticeboard.

So, he did just that.

Barbara, the customer service rep at Foodways, advised Derek that the noticeboard was free for the first month, then five pounds a month after. Perfect. Derek placed his card on the board, right next to the school choir notice. He stood back, a warm glow of satisfaction flowing through him. Now, all he had to do was wait.

# 8

# *Life Before Death*

## Eddie

Eddie couldn't remember a time when he woke up and didn't feel that wave of sadness. Was it loss? Emptiness? He wasn't quite sure. But he was sure that it felt as persistent as his morning piss. His alarm went off, and he sighed. God, the urge to roll over and bury his head under the duvet to hide from the world. How he wanted to pack up, run away like a leaf in the wind, never to return. But it wasn't an option. He had his little Willow; his reason for living. It was hard, it was definitely hard, more hard than easy this last year and with no great signs of relief. But Willow—his natural cure and forever a reminder of the reason behind his depression—needed him.

Willow was almost three when her mummy died. Luckily, she had memories, although, at times, Eddie wasn't sure if that was a good thing or not. She slept with a photo of herself and Issy cuddling and smiling. Willow was her double.

Eddie had always been focused on his job in accountancy. He had studied hard when younger, and once graduated, he had started with the firm Hendersons, working his way up in the finance team to Company Finance Director. It was a good job; a job Eddie could do with ease.

He had met Issy at work when she'd started as the HR manager five years ago. Eddie didn't believe in love at first sight—well, if he did, he would never admit it. However, the morning Issy joined Hendersons, Eddie knew he had to be with her. She'd walked in, a little apprehensively, but even with first day nerves, she'd had an aura around her which could light up the sky. A warm smile, illuminated eyes, bouncy voice and equally as bouncy hair. That hair, wow, that hair. He could see her, standing there, that stunning red, wavy hair. Thick, shiny hair you wanted to bury your face in, hair that always smelt of apples or peaches. Eddie smiled a sad smile as he recalled the day in his head.

Issy had been introduced to the teams in each department. He had watched, eager like a child waiting for a film to start, nervousness increasing as she neared.

"Eddie Sansom, meet Isabelle Montgomery," said the director, George.

"Morning, Isabelle, lovely to meet you," he stumbled.

"Please, call me Issy, and great to meet you too," she said, reaching out a hand for him to shake.

Her warm slender hand, her light pink nails, he didn't want to let go. He wanted to keep chatting, looking into her Indian Ocean blue eyes. Eyes that could light a dark night. He was mesmerised. Instead of words, a stupid nervous laugh came out. *What a dick*, he thought.

"Well, it was nice meeting you. Hopefully I can find out more about the finance team over the week," Issy said, breaking the silence.

"Oh, yes, of course. Just give me a knock when you're settled in."

And with that, his siren was whisked away by George to meet more of the staff as he stood for a second, watching in a trance until she was out of sight.

That was the beginning, that Monday, in June, five years ago. The day that changed his life.

By the end of the working week, he had become infatuated with Issy. She was like a rainbow in the office, full of presence, beauty and colour. He couldn't keep his eyes off her. He resented having meetings that week—it meant he couldn't sit in his office with his blinds open and look out to where she sat. Her posture was graceful and slim, like a dancer. She would rise from her seat and walk across the office to a colleague, the drinks machine or kitchen as if she were skating on ice. Her presence was magnetic. She was his perfection, and he couldn't stop thinking about her all week. Stealing opportunities to speak to her, he rehearsed dialogue, not wanting to look too desperate or too interested. After all, he didn't know her relationship status or even sexual preference.

Did she like him? It was hard to tell. Issy was one of those people who was just genuinely nice.

Halfway through week two, he couldn't stand it any longer. Action had to be taken. Eddie was never known as a big socialiser with his work colleagues. Matt and Andy were his closest colleagues, and they had a few pints after work every couple of months, but Eddie didn't go on the bigger nights out. There was always a complete twat making a fool of themselves or someone copping off with someone they shouldn't. He couldn't be arsed with it and wanted his sexual endeavours to remain outside of his work circle. That was until Issy appeared.

"Couple after work Friday?" he asked Matt and Andy that lunchtime. Another guy, Joe, was eating lunch with them. Joe was the biggest social butterfly going, so Eddie already knew it would be a yes from him.

"Yeah, why not, it's payday Friday as well," said Matt. The others nodded. "I'll ask around and see if a few fancy meeting in The Boston Blues."

*Perfect*, thought Eddie. That afternoon, as he watched Issy waltz over to the water cooler, he dashed out of his office and hurried over, trying to be casual.

"Afternoon, Issy, how are you today?"

"Oh, hi, Eddie. I'm great thanks, how are you doing?"

"Yeah, all good here thanks. A few of us are going for one or two drinks after work Friday. It's just at The Boston Blues pub over the road. You're welcome to join if you're free. No worries if you can't make it." God, he hoped he didn't sound desperate.

"Sounds lovely, yeah, I should be able to make it," she said before floating off.

Was that a yes or a no? Should be able to make it. That had to be at least a sixty-five percent chance of making it. Had he sounded casual enough? Damn, should he have complimented her? Bugger. He had rehearsed compliments to her hundreds of times. "You look well today, Issy." "You're looking radiant, Issy, surely you must do modelling part-time." *What level borders creepy?* he pondered as he walked back to his desk.

Friday afternoon came, and he hung on her every movement that day, counting down the minutes. Then, 5 p.m. came. Staff started packing up and leaving the building. Matt came to his office.

"Come on, mate, need to get a seat. Andy is getting the round in."

Quick spray of Hugo Boss and Eddie was out of there, Matt practically dragging him.

Eddie saw her from the corner of his eye, talking to Jean from HR. She had a floral dress on, which came down to just below her knees. She looked beautiful, although, to him, she would look stunning in a bin bag. She didn't turn around as they left, not noticing their departure in the large office.

Taking a mouthful of his first pint, the anticipation was intense. That nervousness you get when you're going on holiday. That kind of excited but something could go wrong feeling. Bugger it, he would just get pissed if she didn't come in and then feel sorry for himself, no doubt. Then, when his mother asked him on Sunday, as she did every bloody week, if he had met a special someone yet, he would say, "Yes, but she isn't interested, so stop bloody asking!"

Then, it happened: she walked in. She actually walked in, followed by Michelle from her team. He felt his face light up, realised Matt caught him and felt a blush rise in his cheeks.

"Oh, aye, you old dog," Matt joked. He was so transfixed, he couldn't even answer.

That night, he got much-needed time to talk to Issy. To find out about her, her family, hobbies, history and learn more about the chocolate box that was her wonderful personality. In the pub full of people, he felt there was no one else in the room, or even in the world. As he ensured her and Michelle got into their taxi that night and he gave her a peck on the cheek, he'd known she would be the woman he would marry or else love did not exist.

# 9

# The Three Musketeers

## Eddie

Over the next few weeks, Eddie plucked up the courage to ask Issy out alone via taking small steps first. He had got to the point of asking if she wanted to pop out to the shop for lunch together. Sometimes, Michelle would hang around, not getting the bloody hint, and come along. Other days, he watched for her going to the staff kitchen and rushed along after her, orchestrating it as a coincidence.

"Any plans for the weekend, Issy?" he asked that Wednesday on their lunch break.

"I'm going to my friend's Friday night for a girls' night in and seeing my folks Sunday. Apart from that, the usual cooking, gym, housework. What about yourself, Eddie?"

"Hmm, much the same. Well, not the girls' night in obviously." He blushed, and she giggled. "Do you fancy going for a cuppa on Saturday in town? Or maybe a stroll around the park? Only if you have time, of course."

"That would be lovely, Eddie," she replied, smiling. That smile—it could melt icebergs.

"Oh right, erm, great. Yeah, that's smashing. Let me take your number, and we can arrange a meeting time."

Numbers exchanged, Eddie tried to focus on his breathing. He was sweaty from the anxiety of preparing himself to ask her out and the anticipation of her response. Now, he felt faint with excitement. *For God's sake*, he thought, *she will think you're a right prick.*

For the last five minutes of his break, he couldn't remember a word she'd said. He was in a trance, dreaming about Saturday and looking into her Indian Ocean eyes. He thought it would be the best Saturday of his life. And it was. And every Saturday after that as Saturday soon became their day. Issy was his oxygen; being around her was better than life itself. He fell, quickly and eternally. She was his life, his soul mate and his best friend. Everything was so easy with her.

His family loved her—how could they not? His friends told him he was punching above his weight and welcomed her into their group with respect for dropping her standards and taking him off the shelf. Saturdays together became full weekends together, and just before Christmas that year, Eddie told her he loved her and asked her to go on holiday with him. She agreed, and they booked Rome for the spring.

When they got back from Rome, four months after their first Saturday together, Eddie asked Issy to move in with him. They were a perfect match. Eddie knew it was the way love should be: happy, easy, equal.

Happiness kept flowing, and within six months of moving in, he had proposed, and they were wedding planning for the next spring. They had everything to look forward to: new adventures, growing old together. Then, Issy announced she was pregnant. Not planned, and a massive shock to them both, but Eddie was elated. He knew Issy was his true love, and she would be the best mother in the world. So what if it was earlier than they would have planned? It's not like they hadn't talked about children, and they were both in their early thirties.

Issy was just starting to show at their March wedding. She was five months pregnant and more beautiful than ever. Willow was born in the summer and was a vibrant baby from the start.

Eddie's life was magical; it was the stuff of romance films. *The Three Musketeers*, he called them. They had over two and a half blissful years. Years of memories, milestones for Willow and ongoing love. They planned their future and relished the simple things: a stroll in the park, a trip to the beach, bath time with Willow, date nights, cooking together. So in love. So lucky.

And then she died. His Issy, his soul mate, his true love, his best friend. Gone. Wiped out by a drunk driver one night as she was driving home from a night out at the theatre. No chance to say goodbye. No chance to prepare. No more adventures.

Eddie, thirty-six years old. Eddie, a widower. Eddie, a single dad. Eddie who was nothing without his Issy.

The waves of sadness had been drowning him ever since.

# 10

# *A Fraying Rope*

## Eddie

Eddie had once asked his friend Paul about grief. Paul had lost his mother seven years earlier. Paul had said that sometimes it felt as if his mother were on holiday, and then sometimes it felt as if he had not seen her for a lifetime. Eddie felt exactly like that about Issy. He still hoped she was just on holiday and would bounce through the front door like a puppy with a new ball, high on the simple pleasures of life. His head hurt. His heart hurt. He hurt for himself, for Issy and for Willow. Everything really hurt.

In the early days, he would go to the crematorium and talk to her gravestone every Saturday morning whilst Willow was at his parents'. Then, he would attempt the weekly shop. Shopping as a widower felt like trying to get out of quicksand, with every aisle absorbing his energy. There were times where floor staff or strangers would ask if he was ok as he stood staring at toothpaste or sweet potatoes, sometimes on the brink of what felt like hysteria or a complete meltdown. That saying: you can be lonely in a room full of people. My God, was it true.

There were times he bought things that neither he nor Willow liked. Things that Issy used to eat, products she used to use. That Mexicana cheese she'd loved eating straight from the fridge, Assam tea bags, deodorant that smelt of honey and cream. He just couldn't let go.

The three of them used to go food shopping. Another thing he'd taken for granted. Another thing he would surrender anything to have again. To see her face as she rooted through the bananas, ensuring she picked up every shade, from grass green to yellow—before speckles, of course—so that their fruit would last them all week.

A true carer; a selfless, nourishing partner; a magnificent mother. Wiped out in an instant by someone who'd never know exactly what she meant to everyone.

Eddie felt the tears start; he wanted to sob so hard, rock the pain away, scream and yell at how unjust it was. He wanted to kill the man who took her—the murderer. He wanted her back. He needed her back. Willow needed her.

He still talked to Issy every single day. Most of the time, he actually expected her to answer. Forgetting for a split second that she had been snatched away from him for eternity. His Issy. Gone. Dead. Saying or thinking the word made him want to run to the toilet to throw up. In the early days, he had. The grief had been overwhelming. It still was. He wondered if he would ever cope again. How did people do it? Then, there was the anger. The fire of absolute rage that had been burning in his gut with ferocious energy for so long. The need for revenge. The wishing bad things on the murderer and his family. Which had turned to realising that two families had been ruined. Not that it made anything any easier.

He was holding on to a fraying rope. The only fibres left were the fibres of Willow.

Every day, he saw Issy in Willow. Some days, it was magical. Other days, as disgusted as he felt in himself, he resented Willow. She emphasised his grief on days he felt weaker. Despite this, he knew if Willow wasn't around, he would have taken his own life. Willow: the only fibres in his rope. Much of the time, he wanted the rope to snap, and for that reason, he had to swallow the resentment.

They say time heals. It doesn't. It gives us better ways of managing grief, but it never dissolves the pain. We simply become used to the void in our life. We smile, in time, with fond memories rather than breaking down or suppressing them. Eddie knew this. Friends had told him. The counsellor that he'd had one session with had told him.

In his darkest hours, days and weeks, he knew he had to keep going. For Willow. For Issy's memory. He knew she would've been devastated seeing him deteriorate and give up. In those early days, he would sit at her grave, come rain or shine. His parents, Connie and Robert, would end up having Willow for the full day on a Saturday as he lost himself in the grief he muted all week. Willow would bound back home at teatime with a new toy or some tat from his mother, returned to a father with red, puffy eyes.

Of course, his mother and father were supportive, and in those early days, more fibres in the rope, but a mother knows when her child is failing, even her thirty-odd-year-old child.

"Eddie, Son, this can't go on."

It didn't help. Highlighting the obvious just didn't help. Grief had him paralysed. The disintegration of his future had him frozen. Moving on felt like an unachievable battle.

Connie witnessed her son deteriorate for a few more weeks, questioning when to step in with insistence. Within the month, she had moved in "temporarily" to help. Eddie felt like a failure, but part of him was so grateful that his mother was helping to save him from drowning.

He stopped going to the crematorium every week, and instead, Willow, Connie and himself planted a tree in the back garden. An acer tree—Issy had loved them. They got a bench and put it next to the tree, and Willow chose an ornament of two meerkats to go alongside. Eddie figured that Issy wouldn't be at the crem, as it was always cold there and she had hated the cold. Plus, she had no memories there. He rationalised that she was always with him and Willow and always in their home, where all their happiness had been. He still went to the crem—there was some kind of duty he felt—but it became fortnightly, then monthly.

Instead, he used the time to try and conquer the housework as Willow spent time with Momar and Grandpa, then in the afternoon, he would take her swimming, to the park or to soft play. Was it hard? Most certainly. Was every second tinged with sadness? Most definitely. But he would continue to live for Willow. For Issy.

# 11

# Another Saturday Morning

## Eddie

Eddie dropped Willow off at his parents' at 9 a.m. She was full of excitement for a soft play party that afternoon for one of her nursery friends' birthdays. Willow had insisted on dressing as Buzz Lightyear, her most recent favourite Disney character. He looked at her in the rear-view mirror as he drove the six miles to his parents', chuckling to himself as she sat in her car seat, chuntering away to her Belle doll.

Eddie pulled up at his parents' and got his little Buzz out of her seat.

"Grandpa," she shouted, seeing Robert and running up the drive, into his arms.

"Right, little one, you be good for Grandpa and Momar, ok?"

His little Buzz nodded.

"Love you, Bubba," he shouted to her as she rushed inside. "See you in a few hours, Dad. Thanks."

Back in the car, Eddie started on his usual route to Foodways. Radio on, adverts playing before "Time After Time" came on by Cyndi Lauper. A song he had always liked, and a song that seemed to have been on the radio a disproportionate number of times since Issy had died. Maybe it was just coincidence, but he always seemed to hear it when he was thinking of her. The lyrics indicating the reoccurrence of memories and of lost love.

For God's sake.

He changed the radio station. Tom Walker: slightly better, albeit still depressing.

Eddie couldn't help but think about Willow and how difficult he found being a single dad. He adored his daughter, he truly did, it was just so bloody hard sometimes. He couldn't be Mam and Dad when he couldn't even be Dad properly. He wondered if he would ever heal from this torment.

"Don't you dare cry. Don't you dare," he shouted to himself. It was so painfully unfair.

With the tears held back, Eddie arrived at Foodways.

It had been around four months of Eddie doing the weekly shop alone. He had become more skilled, and the process had gradually developed to be a tiny bit less painful. He got a few smiles from regulars and greetings from staff. It wasn't much but it meant a lot to him. He would often sail up the aisles, wondering what people's stories were. How many had lost a spouse? How many were struggling? How many of these strangers walked up and down the aisle, picking up bits of food as they crumbled inside, broken, scarred, lost and lonely?

If only we saw what was in the hearts and minds of people, rather than just their outer shells, the suits of pretence, the costumes of make-believe. People desperate to stay afloat.

But today Eddie felt ok as he wandered up and down the aisles, his trolley getting fuller. Dare he say he felt happy? Willow made him happy. He allowed himself to feel it but often felt a sense of guilt for any other rare and fleeting happiness. Like he was somehow cheating on his grief for Issy.

As he put his shopping on the checkout conveyor, the cashier smiled at him. "Morning, would you like a hand with your packing?" he asked.

"No thanks, but thanks anyway."

He scanned Eddie's items, commenting on bits and pieces here and there. Once he was done, Eddie paid and pushed his full trolley away.

He strolled in the direction of the exit, contemplating whether to get a drive-through cappuccino. Glancing at the noticeboard, the school choir caught his eye. *What a lovely idea*, he thought. His little Willow would love that in a few years' time. They often sang together. He noticed another advert, for a dinner club. Sounded a bit like *Dine in With Me.* "Cooking and companionship" sounded lovely to Eddie.

Everyone he knew had this everlasting look of pity when they spoke to him, as if he were a wounded dog. The elephant in the room. New friends would be great; they would see him as Eddie and not Eddie the widower. Of course, it was part of his identity, a bloody monumental part, but he wanted to also be just Eddie, and he couldn't. Well, not in his current circles.

*Maybe in the future*, he thought, pushing away again and deciding a drive-through cappuccino and pain au chocolat were definitely on the menu.

# 12

# *Bran flakes and Banana*

## Florence

Florence looked over to her side table as she did tens of times each day and smiled. There she was with her beloved Ernie, on their wedding day in September 1958. She was twenty-one years old in the photo, Ernie was twenty-three. It had been love at first sight when they'd met fifteen months earlier in the summer of 1957 on a trip to Blackpool.

Ernie had been working there at the time—he was a long-distance lorry driver, gaining work exporting goods around the country. He'd stayed an extra night, convincing one of his pals to come on the trip from Newcastle.

Florence had been visiting Blackpool with her older sisters, Lydia and Elizabeth. They'd travelled there every year for one weekend a summer since she was sixteen. Born in Ashton-under-Lyne in Manchester, it wasn't too far on the coach, and it was something the sisters had looked forward to all year.

She was walking along, linking Lydia with one arm and eating an ice cream. The three girls were giggling as they absorbed the warm summer sun.

She saw him from a distance, on the promenade. He noticed her too, stopping conversation with his friend Jimmy and staring at her. Their eyes followed one another as they passed.

They were about thirty metres past each other when Ernie came running back. "Er, hi, erm, I noticed you there. The name is Ernie. Pleasure to meet you," he announced, holding out his hand.

Blushing, Florence took his hand. "I'm Florence. Pleasure to meet you too, Ernie."

That was it—the meeting they'd talked about all their married life. The story they'd told their children and grandchildren.

The day in Blackpool ended with their first date that evening, dancing at the Blackpool Tower. And they continued to dance their whole marriage, even though Ernie never really got the hang of it.

Florence moved to Newcastle, a young twenty-year-old, to be with Ernie. He got a job on the shipyards, and she worked in the local sweet factory until she became pregnant with Veronica. And then she became pregnant with William two years later. She never lost her accent, but she gained another family, more friends and her happy ever after. Well, for thirty-six years anyway.

Ernie had had a massive heart attack when he was only fifty-nine. And then she'd become a widow.

Florence had been alone since. When she said alone, she never truly meant alone, as she had her family and her friends, who she'd continued to dance with for another ten years before hanging up her dancing shoes. But she didn't have her Ernie; her beloved.

Now, as she sat in her recliner, aged eighty-two, looking at her wedding photo and eating her bran flakes and banana, she realised she had to make the most of her time left in the world.

With health problems and age creeping in, she had two lovely carers who came each morning to see her. She could manage most things: cleaning herself, washing herself, feeding herself. Her mind was intact, even if her body was failing. Jessie came five mornings a week, Lucy two. They would help her out of bed if she was struggling, make her breakfast, do a little housework and ensure she had her meds. She enjoyed her thirty-minute call, and the carers seemed to enjoy her company also.

Once a week, William took her food shopping. He worked long hours with his own security business, so she didn't see him much. When he wasn't working, he tried to see his grown-up children, Shaun and Sophie, and Sophie's children, Evie and Scarlett, who were just toddlers.

Veronica lived in Canada, so contact was a weekly telephone call and visits over twice a year. Before she'd turned eighty, Florence would fly out once a year. It was too much for her now, so she had to rely on phone calls, summer and Christmas visits, and greetings cards, which she always treasured.

Still, Florence counted her blessings, most of the time. Recently, that had changed, and she was searching for more fulfilment. She had rejoined the library, and William took her at the weekend, after their trip to Foodways, where she got two books out. She was thoroughly enjoying reconnecting with literature. But she longed for more, especially now. She wanted company, new people to get to know and talk to, and not bloody old, moaning people.

# 13

# *New Beginnings*

## Derek

Derek had planned his menus for the next week and had decided to make lasagne that Sunday. *Bloody hell*, he thought as he finished grating what seemed to be a full block of cheese. No wonder he had lost a little weight—Brenda used to make lasagne all the time and Derek would often have seconds with another portion for work the next day.

He carried on, following the recipe from the card he had picked up at Foodways. Helping himself to a beer as he cooked, radio on, he was enjoying his newfound interest.

Des watched his every move, keen to respond swiftly if any scraps came his way.

Bri had text for a bit yesterday. Debbie wasn't mentioned, and it was just like old times. Derek hoped it would remain so the next time he saw him. He didn't want their friendship compromised, and he hoped, after Bri had digested meeting his alter ego, things would still be as they were. Time would tell.

After what seemed like hours, the lasagne was bubbling away nicely. Derek was almost salivating. Pulling it out of the oven, he inhaled his creation. It looked delicious. He had prepared a mixed salad to go alongside it.

Serving himself a large portion, he piled some salad on the side, got another beer and went into the lounge, Des like glue to his side. "You're a greedy bugger, Son," Derek said to Des. "You're like a bloody fly on shit."

Sitting down and switching on the TV, he noticed *Dine in With Me* was on. "Nice one." He left it on, hoping for more inspiration. Derek felt a little excitement washing over him in the anticipation he may have his own version of *Dine in With Me* in the coming months. The mood quickly altered when Derek noticed a text on his mobile from Brenda.

***Derek, I am back from my holiday. We need to talk. I will come around on Wednesday night at 7 p.m.***

His heart sank. He wasn't ready for his bubble to be burst and to have to face reality, whatever that may be from Brenda. The remainder of the night was tinged with nerves.

Wednesday night came. Derek had taken Des for a longer walk, trying to calm himself and predict the conversation with Brenda. Poor Des was worn out, and when they got home, he retreated straight to his basket.

Ten minutes later, the doorbell rang. Without waiting for an answer, Brenda let herself in with a "Hi, Derek". He looked at her, eyes wide, mouth open.

"Derek, it's still my bloody house. I am entitled to come in when I want," she sneered.

"I know, I know, Brenda." Why did she always reduce him to a pushover? Looking at the woman he had been married to for so many years, he wondered how the personality he had fallen in love with had all but disintegrated, exposing an unpleasant stranger.

"Listen, Derek, I've had time to think. I don't know what the hell went on before I went away. I don't know if you're having a breakdown or a late midlife crisis with all this pervert stuff." She looked at him, shaking her head as if he were a silly schoolboy.

"Brenda, for the love of God, will you stop referring to me as a pervert? You make me sound like bloody Jimmy Saville, for crying out loud."

She puffed out a laugh. "Derek, don't be so dramatic. You aren't a woman yet." She walked a few steps towards Derek, placing her hands on her hips. Derek sensed her patronising impatience. He was determined to stay assertive.

"Piss off, Brenda. It's you that ruined our marriage. You and your ignorance and constant put-downs. Dressing up never made me not love you. Your vile attitude and bullying ways made me stop loving you." Derek was shaking with nerves, adrenaline, fear, pride.

Brenda sniggered. "Bullying ways? Who the hell do you think you are, Derek? Shirley friggin' Bassey having a diva strop? I have come back here to give you a second chance and you go on like this. Well, I'm not putting up with it."

She stepped closer to Derek, and he instinctively edged backwards. Brenda's finger came towards his chest, pointing aggressively. "You have a long, hard think. Have a good search in your brain for any other woman who would put up with this... this weird carry on. It's sick, and you are lucky to have me."

Brenda stormed out of the house, slamming the door behind her.

It wasn't long after Brenda left that Derek heard his phone ring. Withheld number—just her style.

"What now, you mental cow?" he screamed down the phone.

There was a slight pause.

"Erm, hello. I think I have the wrong number; I am looking for Derek."

It wasn't Brenda.

"Ah, ever so sorry, you caught me off guard. This is he, erm, this is Derek. Sorry."

"Oh, hello then, Derek. My name is Florence. I saw your advert in Foodways, and I would like to know more. I'm not quite yet a mental cow." Florence giggled.

# 14

# Sweet William

## Florence

William had called to collect Florence at midday, as he did every Saturday. William, like his mother, was a creature of habit. The time worked well for Florence. Her Saturday morning carer call always came around 9 a.m. Florence would get up at 8:30 a.m. and get ready before Jessie or Lucy arrived.

That morning, it had been Jessie, her favourite. Of course, she was very fond of Lucy and even Annie, who sometimes filled in during holidays or sickness. But there was something about Jessie she loved. Jessie had the warmest heart and a wise mind for a young girl of twenty-seven years old. She had worked in the care sector for over six years and had a natural affinity with the older population. Jessie would tell Florence about her own grandmother, who she helped out a great deal and who had partly brought her up following her mother's death. Florence felt very certain that Jessie's mother was watching over her, immensely proud of the intelligent, caring and beautiful woman she was.

Each morning she came, Jessie often stayed a little longer if she could, having a cuppa and talking to Florence. She felt like a friend, a granddaughter and a carer all in one.

About a year ago, Florence had taken a turn for the worse whilst going to the toilet early one morning. She had collapsed on the floor, and Jessie had found her two hours later during her call. Jessie had called the ambulance and held Florence's hand as she'd cried in pain and relief that her guardian angel had arrived.

*In our increasingly aging population, carers, paid and unpaid, do so much more than what is often financially recognised*, Florence thought. She was very lucky to have Jessie and Lucy.

Her Saturday morning call was over by 10 a.m. It gave Florence time to read the daily newspaper she got delivered as well as get herself ready for William's visit.

"Only me, Mam," he would shout as he opened the door.

They always had a cuppa and a snack before they set off. Usually, some crumpets, a toasted teacake or jam on toast. William would cut her toast into triangles, which always made her heart swell. That was how she'd always cut William and Veronica's jam sandwiches. She missed being able to look after people, the warmth of gratitude on their face, the love and authenticity of a thank you. Yes, Florence most definitely missed looking after people.

That Saturday, they had a toasted teacake each, smothered with butter and apricot jam. William had brought her some flowers: her favourite sweet Williams. She used to tell him she named him after the flowers. The beautiful rustic nature of them, the dark colours, they were art to her, and when William brought them, they had an extra sprinkling of love over the petals.

She saw the worry in his eyes. She had told him that week that she was having tests at the doctors' surgery. She had minimised, of course, but he had asked about her diabetes that Wednesday night on the phone, wanting to know what was happening. She had lied and said she would find out in the next few weeks.

He asked about the next GP appointment, wanting to accompany her and speak to the family doctor, Dr Dunn.

"William, stop bloody fussing. It will be fine. I will update you after my next appointment, when the results are in and Dr Dunn knows what the options are. Until then, please don't fuss. It won't help anything, Son." She deliberately said the last line holding his hand, looking in his eyes, in an attempt to reassure him. She could do without him stressing.

William talked about his week at work—he had been travelling across the region and down to York, reviewing contracts. Florence was so proud of William. He worked hard. She wished he would find a nice woman to settle with. He had divorced Gina over ten years ago, and although he'd had a few short-term relationships, none had lasted longer than a year. William was fifty-seven now, and she thought he worked too much. How would he ever meet a woman with his lack of free time?

Florence had liked the last girlfriend, Vicky. She had been around for about a year. William had been on holiday with her, talked fondly of her and then it had come to an abrupt end. William hadn't disclosed details, only that "she wanted me to commit further, and I wasn't ready". Florence didn't pry, but she was disappointed. All a parent wants is to see their babies happy, even if they are in their fifties.

Half an hour later, they pulled up at Foodways. Florence's mobility wasn't too bad on the whole, although she knew it would deteriorate. Foodways could take up a lot of time, and although she relished her weekly shopping trip with her son, it often took it out of her, so she liked having the trolley to lean on as William fetched things from the shelves and crossed off her list.

Florence knew where everything was in the supermarket. She ate a varied diet, with limited foods she disliked. Any evenings she cooked for herself, she still tried to cook some meals from scratch. Every single

Sunday, she had herself a roast dinner, without fail, although some were now ready-made if she was having an off day.

During and after the war, the plates didn't always have meat and sometimes no gravy, but her mother would always cook veg, and if no meat, they would have homemade broth to start. Florence may have a slight addiction to ginger nuts, but she loved her vegetables.

At the checkout, William did his usual of placing all the items on the conveyor belt and packing them once they were scanned. He was methodical in his approach, and Florence felt reassured each week that the eggs would not get crushed and her bread would not get squashed. All packed and paid for, they made their way towards the exit.

"Hang on, Mam, I need to nip to the loo," William said, hurrying off.

Florence dawdled along, leaning on the trolley. She was tired now. She stopped at the noticeboard. She often looked at it, seeing if there were any book clubs and admiring what was going on in the community to keep spirits and camaraderie up. She didn't like big groups herself. She'd always been a little shy but liked the idea of a small gathering. Of course, there had been opportunities over the years. She hadn't taken many but always had her dancing and sometimes went to the film club at the library. But now, it felt like a really good time.

Then, she saw it, on cream card, in black, large, clear writing:

**Do you enjoy cooking and eating? Would you like to meet fellow foodies for nights of cooking and company? If so, contact Derek to join The Dinner Club.**

A smile crept over her face. A dinner club. It sounded perfect. Surely, a dinner club would be a small, intimate, friendly group. A few people coming together for food and chats, cooking and company, exactly how the advert said.

It didn't say where the club was or what it involved, but for the first time in a long time, Florence felt excited and intrigued. She got her mobile phone out and took a photo of the advert.

William had made her get a smart phone last year. Although she believed it should be renamed "stupid phone", as that was how it made her feel. She was only just getting to grips with it now after eight months. She could now call and text without a problem, take photos and even use the calendar and calculator. That was more than enough for her.

"What's this?" William enquired from behind her. She hadn't heard him approaching.

She put her hand on her heart from the small jump. "Just an advert for a dinner group, Son. I quite like the sound of it and want to find out more."

"Ah, good for you, Mam. As long as it's not a cannibal pervert trying to lure people to his home."

"William, will you pack it in."

They laughed as they left.

"Right, let's drop these off, put your freezer stuff away, then head to the library, eh, Mam?"

"Perfect. What would I do without you, Son?" Florence replied, squeezing William's arm.

# 15

# Dinner Call

## Florence

Florence had decided socialising with strangers was probably not a good idea. William was right that the man in the advert could be some lunatic pervert inviting people around to kill them. Or perhaps a thief who wanted to groom people into giving over their belongings. However, by Wednesday morning, Florence had convinced herself that she needed to contact the chap on the advert for The Dinner Club, even if it was just to enquire. There was something about a chance to share recipes and enjoy a good meal that appealed to her.

She had spoken to Annie and Lucy about it on Monday and Tuesday. Both had said it sounded ok and she should at least enquire. Florence wanted Jessie's view the most, but Jessie had been on leave until that morning.

Florence was sitting in her usual chair—a recliner that had cost her almost one thousand five hundred pounds but was worth every penny. She had spent as much time in it as possible for the eight months she had owned it. Resting on the arm of it was her heat pad, which she plugged in most nights, relaxing in her own little, heated heaven. Florrie hated the cold; it was the one thing she couldn't stand. Well, that and mayonnaise.

Jessie opened the door. "Morning, Florrie, it's just me."

"Ah, love, I am so pleased to see you," Florence replied.

Jessie was the only one allowed to call Florence "Florrie". She disliked it, but from Jessie, she loved it. "Flo", on the other hand, she would not tolerate. She was a distinct disliker of name shortening.

"How are you, love? Did you have a nice few days off?"

"Yeah ta, Florrie. I took me grandma out and I decorated her bedroom for her. A lovely lemon—it looks clean and tranquil. She was over the moon. How have you been? Any news from the doctor?"

Florence had told Jessie about the tests. She hadn't gone into detail, saying they were general wellbeing tests. She knew that Jessie suspected more though. Jessie was very experienced and knew a lot about conditions from her work as well as from her studies at college. Florence knew she could utilise her skills in the future when she was ready to disclose more.

"No, love, I am going back on Monday, so should find out more then."

As Jessie made Florence's breakfast of bran flakes and banana and a mug of tea, Florence updated Jessie on last night's *Family Guy* and the risqué goings-on of Peter Griffin. She laughed, retelling the episode, and her infectious giggling and excited description made Jessie laugh in sync. Florence then brought up the advert she had seen in Foodways.

"Go for it, Florrie, it could be great for you. New friends, someone cooking for you, you helping out. Eating together. You should definitely at least find out more."

That was all the reassurance Florence needed; she trusted Jessie implicitly.

Twenty-five minutes later, Jessie left, giving Florence a kiss on the cheek as she always did.

That evening, cosy in her recliner after her soaps had finished, Florence made a note of the contact number and name of the chap from the photo on her phone.

*Here goes nothing.*

She rang the number, using a trick William had taught her of putting one-four-one in before the number. Apparently, it meant the caller didn't get your number. *Best be safe*, she thought.

It rang a few times, then an answer.

"What now, you mental cow?" was screamed down the phone.

Florence got a shock and held her breath momentarily. She took her phone away from her face and looked at it for a second, not knowing quite what to do. Returning the phone to her ear, she spoke, "Erm, hello. I think I have the wrong number; I am looking for Derek."

She was about to hang up but then the voice changed completely, as if it were someone else, to a gentle, soothing voice.

"Ah, ever so sorry, you caught me off guard. This is he, erm, this is Derek. Sorry."

"Oh, hello then, Derek. My name is Florence. I saw your advert in Foodways, and I would like to know more. I'm not quite yet a mental cow." She giggled.

# 16

# Dinner Club Conversation

## Derek

Derek was cock-a-hoop as he walked to The Spitting Feathers, his hands inside his pockets—his first enquiry about the advert for The Dinner Club had come in. A woman called Florence who described herself as a pensioner who enjoyed good food. Perfect. Derek would have never dreamed of such an adventure in the past. Any dreams he'd had had always been squashed by Brenda. She pissed on everyone's rainbow. *Well, not anymore*, he thought triumphantly.

Poor Florence had had an abrupt beginning to the phone call she'd made to him. Derek, of course, had apologised profusely, but he was conscious he didn't want to scare an elderly woman. Saying that, weirdos came in all forms these days. For all he knew, she could be some mad Peter Sutcliffe type masquerading as an old woman. Bloody hell, he could be attracting absolute lunatics with his advert. He had read about some crazy cannibal who'd recruited people to a group and ate them. Christ, he would have nightmares tonight. They may have thought it was a secret message for some S&M dominatrix club or a swingers' night or something weirdly perverse.

He laughed to himself. Ironic, given Brenda frequently liked to refer to him as a pervert.

*I'll run it by Bri in a second*, he thought, opening the door to the pub.

"Afternoon, mate." Bri got out of his usual seat at The Spitting Feathers and gave Derek one of those man hugs, grabbing his hand and patting him on the back of the arm with the other. This was a popular but not every time greeting from Bri. Derek felt it symbolic. They hadn't seen each other since Debbie had come to tea. To Derek, he felt, or at least hoped, that it was Bri's way of showing his acceptance.

"Hi, mate, nice to see you. I'll get a round in," Derek said, already making his way to the bar.

He returned a couple of minutes later with two pints and four bags of cheese and onion crisps. Bri looked at him, then at the crisps, raising his eyebrows.

"I haven't had lunch," said Derek defensively.

Bri shrugged, deeming this an acceptable explanation, and changed the subject. "How's your week been, Derek? Heard from Brenda at all?"

"No, not since Wednesday when she came round, had a go at me and left, almost taking the front door off its bloody hinges as she went."

"She rang Eileen yesterday, then was texting her. It must have taken her a few days to calm down. She told Eileen she's filing for divorce and that you aren't normal."

Derek felt himself seethe. "Not normal? She's the one who isn't normal. She's some kind of bloody sociopath," he said, trying not to raise his voice too much and draw attention. He wasn't even sure what being a sociopath entailed, but he felt it was a strong enough insult.

Bri laughed. "I could have told you that, mate."

"How dare she, Bri, how bloody dare she go around saying I'm abnormal. How dare she blame our marriage breakdown on me and play the victim. You should have heard her the other night, Bri, calling me horrendous names, making me feel like a bloody deviant." He could feel himself welling up. Tears of anger or upset, he wasn't sure.

"I know, mate, I know. She's bang out of order. She's wanting a reaction, and she's wanting sympathy from people. Eileen wasn't giving her the lickings of a dog, mate, don't worry." Bri smiled warmly at Derek. "We're team Derek all the way."

"Thanks, mate, you are one in a million," Derek said as he reached for a packet of crisps.

"Maybe you need to have a think about things though: the house, Des, all that. If I know Brenda, she isn't going to just walk away from it all." Brian kept his voice low as one of the regular customers walked past, nodding in their direction.

Derek nodded back. "Yeah, you're right. She won't just go quietly. I need to chat with her, see where she's at with things. Maybe I should seek some legal advice." He scratched his head; there was a lot to consider.

"Good idea, mate. Our Maurice got fleeced to high heaven from that bitch Emily. It can all go very wrong," Bri warned.

Derek opened the crisps, shoving his hand into the packet and stuffing them in his mouth. Food had forever made him feel better when he was emotional. He knew he had to start facing reality and the even nastier side of Brenda that was likely to present itself. Chomping on the crisps, they felt like a crunchy blanket of satisfaction. Within a few minutes and well into his third bag, he had calmed down.

"So, I put an advert on the noticeboard in Foodways."

"Yeah?"

"For a dinner club."

"What, like a soup kitchen or something?" Bri asked curiously.

"No, mate, I'm not homeless yet, you daft sod." Derek laughed. "It's more like a social get together. I guess a bit like a book club but with food instead of literature." Derek tapped his stomach and grinned at Bri.

"Excellent idea, mate, sounds like it'll suit you down to the ground," Bri replied, nodding.

"I got the idea from that programme, *Dine in With Me*. Have you seen it?"

"Oh yeah, it's always really nosy buggers who love the sound of their own voice."

Derek laughed; Bri was pretty accurate there. "Well, this will be different. I'll be informally interviewing people, and they have to be the right mix. I want to keep learning to cook, Bri, and I want to cook for people. But I also miss getting cooked for. And to be honest, I'm starting to feel lonely." Derek moved his gaze to the coaster his pint was sat on and picked at the exposed edge. He didn't want pity from Bri, or anyone, irrelevant of his loneliness.

"Listen, mate, you know you can always come to our house. Eileen loves to cook. Me, on the other hand, you would have to settle for a Pot Noodle." Bri chuckled,

"I know. I appreciate how much of a good friend you've been, especially, you know, from the other night." Derek still felt a little shame mentioning Debbie. It would take a while to get over what Brenda had instilled in him. *Small steps, Derek, small steps*. He picked up another bag of crisps, opening them and offering Bri one before he continued.

"I want to do something for me, Bri. For years, I've had to dance to Brenda's beat. She's never wanted me to succeed in anything and always resented me doing anything without her. I want to try this, boost my confidence and make new friends."

"As long as you don't forget the ones you already have." Bri nudged Derek playfully.

"Of course I won't. You're stuck with me, mate. Fancy another pint?"

"You know me. I'm not one to say no to that." Bri said, picking up his glass and draining the last mouthful.

# 17

# Cooking Companions

## Derek

That evening, Derek made himself steak in a Diane sauce, with roasted veg. The Diane sauce wasn't the best, but for a first attempt, he was satisfied. He mopped up the sauce with wedges of tiger bread.

He had told Florence he would ring her in a few days to arrange an initial meeting. He had wanted to get off the phone quickly, given the borderline abusive first encounter. She had passed on her number, and Derek had written it on his magnetic to-do list that lived on his fridge freezer.

He walked into the kitchen and dialled the number, Des following, assuming it was supper time.

"Hello," said a warm, gentle voice.

"Oh, hello, is that Florence?"

"It is. Hello, Derek."

"Ah, you saved my number. The outburst didn't put you off the other day?" he nervously enquired.

Florence laughed. "No, it takes a lot to put me off something I'm interested in, and I can be just as fierce when the situation requires."

Derek smiled to himself. He liked Florence already, and she most definitely didn't seem like a Peter Sutcliffe impersonator.

"That's good to know, Florence. I'd really like to meet you and see if we can look at developing The Dinner Club. You're the only person to get in touch as yet, but the advert's only been up a week. How about we arrange to meet for a cuppa in three weeks' time and then if others have got in touch, they could join us?"

"Sounds lovely, Derek," replied an enthusiastic Florence.

"I think it's important we meet and that it feels like a good fit for us all. And also to make sure all is above board and safe," said Derek, deciding using the Peter Sutcliffe analogy wouldn't be a wise move.

"Good idea. Better to be safe than sorry."

"Ok, so how about Saturday the twenty-fourth? We could meet in Foodways Café? Seems appropriate."

"Yes, definitely. My William takes me shopping each Saturday afternoon, so I will be there anyway. Can we make it about 1 p.m., please, Derek?"

"That works for me. I'll look forward to seeing you. I'll save your number and text you on the morning to say what I'm wearing. It'll be like a blind date." He winced, regretting the words as soon as they came out. He didn't want to come across dodgy in any way. "I meant like a friendly date," he added in nervously.

Florence laughed. "I don't get much excitement these days. I shall look forward to your description, and don't forget the flowers. Goodbye, Derek."

Standing silently for a moment, he felt a wave of happiness. His advert had been a success. Even if it was just Florence and himself, it had been a success. He'd done it.

For the next three weeks, he would research more recipes, ready for his first meeting and food discussion with Florence. Along with researching forums for crossdressers and cooking new foods, of course. His nights would be filled.

# 18

# *Sofa Surfing*

## Cara

"You arsehole," Cara screamed as her pitiful belongings were thrown out of the window of what she had called her bedroom for the last three weeks.

She had met Taylor—DJ Bounce, as he was known—at a club, following an argument with her friend, Caitlyn, whose sofa she had been sleeping on for over a month. Cara had flirted outrageously with Taylor. Christ, it was an Oscar nomination worthy performance. It had worked, and she'd gained a bed for the night. It meant she'd had to have sex with him, which had repulsed her, but he didn't know that. It also meant she'd had somewhere to stay for three weeks, and she'd managed to avoid most intimacy with Taylor due to his DJ shifts and her attempts to stay engaged with college, plus the odd cash-in-hand shifts at Amici's Italians.

But now it had all turned to crap. She had been suspended from college for going in drunk and swearing at the lecturer. Taylor knew she had stolen forty pounds from him, and he was furious. He'd immediately kicked her out. Cara was desperate to go back to Caitlyn's, and forty pounds would help seal the deal until Cara was paid next week. Caitlyn had forgiven her and was happy to put her up for a little longer until Cara got sorted with a place of her own.

Collecting her meagre belongings off the ground, she sobbed half angry tears, half tears of defeat as she marched away. It took her around an hour to reach Caitlyn's. She pressed the buzzer to the flat and waited.

"Hello, who is it?"

"It's me, Caitlyn. It's Cara. Can I come in, please?"

"Come on up."

Once inside, Cara ran up the three flights of stairs, still clutching her belongings. The door to flat nineteen was open, Caitlyn standing there. Cara ran into her arms, clothes jammed between them and spilling onto the floor.

"Woah, Cara, it's ok," Caitlyn said, holding her best friend closely as she sobbed.

At twenty years old, Cara sometimes felt as if she were eighty and sometimes felt as if she were eight. Rarely did she feel anything between.

Cara had entered the care system at the age of eight, after an early childhood surrounded by substance misuse, domestic abuse, mental health issues and neglect. Her mother had been on the scene, albeit towards the end more in body than spirit. Cara didn't know her dad. Apparently, he had wanted nothing to do with her. Her mother, Kate, had been twenty when Cara was born—the age Cara was now. Kate had received a council house, Sure Start and parenting programmes, and for a few years, she'd managed. Then, she'd got into a bad relationship and had started drinking too much. Maybe she resented Cara for stealing her youth, maybe she just couldn't cope. Cara would never know.

Kate deteriorated, having short-term relationship after short-term relationship. She would focus on her own need to be loved, with Cara, a toddler and then starting school, on the back burner. Social services got involved when Cara was six years old, after her teachers caught her eating out of the bin at school. Before that, Cara had consistently gone to school tired, pale and unkempt. But no one had done much about it. *The world is always too busy to notice me*, thought Cara. And she'd got used to it.

Cara remembered her early years of bed wetting and searching for clean clothes in their cold and dirty family home as her mother lay passed out on the sofa, an empty bottle of vodka on the floor. Sometimes, there would be strangers coming and going.

"Mam, Mam," she would call out. There would be no answer, a groan or sometimes a "Mam's not well, Cara, she needs to sleep."

Cara had known no different. But as she got older and things with Kate got worse, she had to fend for herself more and more.

For the next eighteen months, she was on the Child Protection Register as a child at risk. Social services worked with Kate to try and help her to parent. Cara was taken to new groups and activities outside of school to encourage socialisation and to have fun like most young children. Reading and crafts were her favourites. She also met weekly with a social work assistant, Caroline, who she absolutely adored. She wished Caroline was her mother on so many occasions it hurt. Cara remembered Caroline always smelt faintly of apples mixed with flowers. She found out later that it was a DKNY perfume and saved up to buy it when she was sixteen, a reminder of Caroline.

All the time social services were involved, Cara continued to try and support her mam, cooking for them and pretending Kate made the meals to Caroline. She remembered on some days, mainly at weekends, Kate would go out for hours on end. Cara would sit on the sofa and eat cereal out of the box or eat a packet of custard creams, waiting for what felt like an eternity for her mam to return. In the back of her mind, scared she never would.

Kate would come in drunk or crying. Or both. Sometimes, she would bring a stranger home. Cara would hide in her room, worrying both for herself and her mam.

Things came to a head when Cara was almost eight years old. As usual, Kate had been drinking vodka. Cara was hungry and wanted to cook something for them both. She decided on egg sandwiches and put some oil in a pan, warming it on the hob. She hadn't done it before but had seen her mam do it and thought it seemed easy enough. Cracking the eggs into a bowl and picking out numerous pieces of shell, she smiled, thinking how proud her mam would be of her.

She then carefully placed the eggs in the oil, waited for them to start bubbling, then turned down the heat. She had seen her mam do this. Five minutes later, they looked done. The bread was buttered, and Cara even got the tomato sauce out. Cara lifted the pan off the hob. She hadn't anticipated the weight of the pan full of oil, and within a second, the pan dropped, splashing on the floor and against her right arm as it fell.

Cara let out an almighty scream, followed by a flow of tears. Her arm bright red, her face ashen, Cara felt certain she was going to vomit.

The scream had alerted the neighbour in the flat next door, Jeffery. He was banging on the door, asking if everything was ok. Kate, now awake, opened the door in a drunken haze.

An ambulance was called, and Cara was taken to hospital, where she received treatment for second-degree burns. She never returned to her family home.

# 19

# Fleeting Love and Further Trauma

## Cara

For the next eight years of her life, Cara had been in and out of foster care.

Her first placement after the burn incident had been an emergency placement with a lovely lady called Rebecca. Cara remembered sobbing and sobbing, yet somehow feeling at ease with this strange new woman. She'd felt like a warm blanket and always gave Cara an "it will be ok" smile that she could still see now if she closed her eyes and really concentrated.

Those initial few weeks with Rebecca helped Cara manage her distress enormously. And, God, the food! Cara felt like a queen. She would have hot porridge with golden syrup and sliced banana before school. And, for the first time, like the other kids, she had a snack to eat at breaktime. Some raisins or a biscuit or a Cheestring. Then, when she came home, it would be a hot meal like pasta and vegetables or a roast dinner or fishfingers, chips and beans—still one of her favourites now.

And even after that, she would have a pudding. Slices of Swiss roll, apple pie or sponge cake, sometimes in custard. Rice pudding with jam swirled in, Angel Delight, ice cream, yoghurt or fruit. She was even allowed supper if she wanted it. A crumpet with cheese or jam on, a slice of malt loaf or a few biscuits and hot milk.

She could never eat more than a few mouthfuls in the first few days. She remembered being sick on a few occasions and having stomach pains. She would put the rest of her meal in her pockets, regardless of what it was, worried about the next time she would be fed. It seemed too good to be true, and Cara was certain it would end.

Rebecca caught her after the first few days, stuffing toast dripping in butter into her trouser pocket. They had a discussion. It didn't all make sense to Cara, but her portions became smaller for the remainder of the time, and Rebecca left snacks out and about for Cara to have at any time.

Those few weeks of introduction to full and nutritious meals literally transformed her life. But the biggest transformation came not from the food but the affection. Cara felt nourished by love. Rebecca, this warm, smiley, nurturing woman who just wanted to see Cara smile. For so long, Cara had been the parent, her childhood snatched away from her by adult responsibilities and neglect. Cara loved Rebecca for her mothering, allowing her to not worry about adult issues and just enjoy the innocence and simplicity of childhood.

Cara put on half a stone in those few weeks, just about making the lower end of what her BMI should have been by then. For all she missed her mam dreadfully, she developed a deep love for Rebecca, and for the first time in her life, felt looked after.

She would go to school in clean clothes and would have a daily shower or bath. She'd sit in the bath for hours, rubbing the bubbles over her skin and even playing with the ornamental rubber ducks. Rebecca used to have to call to her to get out before she turned into a prune. She would put on clean, soft pyjamas and get into a bed that didn't reek of urine from the night before.

Cara didn't feel cold. Until that point, she'd always felt cold, even in the summer. She remembered wearing her tatty coat for bed to try and keep warm through the winter. When Kate wasn't drunk, she would give her a hot water bottle. To this day, Cara had a hot water bottle most nights—a bit of comfort, a positive association.

During her time with Rebecca, the boys and girls at school stopped calling Cara names. They were still not noticeably nice to her, but at least she lost the "tramp" and "stinky" tags in those few weeks. It made Cara feel invincible, as if she were a celebrity, when in reality, she was simply not getting abused.

Caroline came to take her for a McDonalds. It was nice but Cara still missed her mam. After a week, she got to see her at a community centre. Caroline was there in the corner of the room. She looked as though she were working, when in reality, she was watching.

Kate seemed disinterested and didn't smile when Cara told her about Rebecca. Nor did she smile when Cara told her she missed her. Cara left feeling rejected and confused.

Cara didn't stay at Rebecca's long. She was what is known as an emergency placement, so she only had kids staying for a few weeks before a longer-term placement was sought.

The day Cara moved, she was inconsolable. Even her beloved Caroline couldn't soothe her. She sobbed in the passenger seat as Caroline's car drove away and Rebecca closed her front door. Uncertain and frightened for her future, at seven years and eleven months old.

The next eight years and one month of Cara's life were spent in foster placements. Throughout this time, she experienced fleeting love and further trauma. Her first long-term placement provided some happy memories. She was in a home with a married couple, Sonia and

Craig, their own birth son, Toby, and another foster daughter. Marie, the foster daughter, was eleven, and even through the pain of being separated from her mother and Rebecca, Cara had a flame of hope that she would make a friend, if not an older sister in Marie.

Toby was five years old, and Sonia and Craig were unable to have more children, so they fostered. Marie had been with them for some time, and it was thought they may adopt her. Cara, however, never felt like a permanent fixture. Marie was a talented, clever girl. Academically, she thrived despite the adversity she had encountered in her formative years. She was also a beautiful dancer, and in the eighteen months or so that Cara was with Sonia and Craig, they nurtured and invested in Marie's dancing—something that seemed to be a coping mechanism for Marie and an obvious natural talent.

Cara, on the other hand, had no natural talents. Academically, she was behind. Not surprising given she'd spent her childhood scavenging the house for food, washing dirty clothes and putting her mother to bed. She'd had no time for homework, hobbies or books.

Now, as an adult, Cara looked back in disgust and distress as to why she had never been saved. Had it taken authorities two years to take her away from harm because she meant so little to anyone? A pale, quiet, smelly little girl who no one noticed. Every time she saw something in the media around child neglect, she would be filled with rage and heartbreak. Heartbreak for the victim, the child, but also heartbreak for herself: the child no one rescued. The child whose story was never told. The child who grew into a damaged adult.

Life with Sonia, Craig, Marie and Toby continued. Cara tried desperately to fit in and find something she was good at to impress her foster parents and make them love her. Were they unkind? Certainly not. Yet, throughout her placement, she always felt like an afterthought. Invisible.

Like Toby and Marie completed the couple, and Cara was an extra that they could take or leave.

They were never cruel. She couldn't pretend they were. She just never felt particularly special or wanted. They were nice enough, but something was just missing. It wasn't like it had been for those short weeks with Rebecca. They didn't make Cara feel like Caroline did. Cara had experienced fleeting love—she knew how it felt. It wasn't that. No. The love Sonia and Craig had for her just didn't hit the mark.

The foster placement ended after eighteen months. Cara never knew why. By this time, she was nine years and five months old. She was taken to live in the next county with a woman named Shirley. Wonderful, soft, warm, cuddly Shirley. Shirley who lived in the cosy cottage and had land with horses and chickens. Apple trees and potatoes grew in the back garden, and there was space to play and run as Cara soaked up the summer sun. Wonderful, soft, warm, cuddly Shirley.

Luckily, she was close enough to attend the same school, so had some level of normality and routine. Cara had a best friend by this point, for the first time in her life. She and Ethan were inseparable. She also had a few girl friends. None of massive significance, but she was invited to play with some of the girls and to birthday parties.

Cara was the only foster child with Shirley. In fact, there were no other children there at all. Just the farmyard animals and Zak, the Red Setter. Cara felt love again. More importantly, she felt accepted. Shirley would feed her with love, both in her stomach and mind.

Cara was told she was pretty, that she was a good girl, that she was clever. When she brought homework home, Shirley helped her with it, supporting Cara's learning and understanding. When Cara got the odd certificate or positive feedback at school, she would tell Shirley and be rewarded with a treat and a cuddle. Cara could still feel those cuddles. Those warm, big-bosomed cuddles which always smelt like talcum powder. The soothing sensation of being nurtured that radiated through Cara in those moments was her benchmark for love, just like the love she had experienced with Rebecca and the feelings she felt for Caroline. The fear was always there that it would be taken from Cara, ripped from her heart, like it had been before.

Almost three years of Shirley, Cara, Zak, the horses and the chickens. Years where Cara started to improve at school and even excel in some subjects. Where she started to make more friends and feel included. Where she started to see herself as an ok child, not a rubbish daughter, not a smelly, stupid, worthless girl. At twelve years old, these messages were key.

Then, *he* arrived. Joe. Shirley had met him at a school reunion, and they had clicked, keeping in touch. As per policy, she advised social services of her new relationship. They had no reason to worry: Joe managed a mechanics in town and refereed under-16's football for the boys' club. He had a clean DBS criminal record check and was seen as great with kids. This may have been subject to gender, as Cara was to discover.

Joe soon moved in. Cara was heartbroken. She wanted Shirley to herself. After a childhood of being second best to vodka and substances, sometimes even third in the pecking order after the latest man her mam would pick up, Cara didn't want to share Shirley with anyone. The hostility towards Joe just fuelled his reasons to persecute her.

It began as comments when Shirley wasn't in the room.

"You must do as we both say, otherwise Shirley will give you the heave-ho."

"She's got me to think about now. She loves me more."

Such comments penetrated Cara's paranoid mind. Love with Shirley seemed too good to be true. Maybe it was.

Joe would make snide comments to Shirley in front of Cara, making them out to be jokey.

"You've never been a parent, Shirley, you don't see you are too soft with her."

"Children need boundaries and levels of conformity. Especially wild girls like Cara."

Shirley never questioned why Joe's ex-wife had taken his two children to live in Australia. He simply claimed that the lifestyle was better there for kids, and he writes and visits once a year.

On her thirteenth birthday, the physical abuse started. Shirley was running late purchasing Cara a lovely birthday cake. Cara returned from school, and Joe was in after giving himself the afternoon off.

"I am the boss, after all," he would say to justify his part-time hours.

Cara had been desperate for Shirley to be in. Her heart sank when she realised it was just her and Joe. His comments and attitude towards her had soured more of late. Cara was biting her tongue frequently, and hatred was building in her towards this greedy, lazy pig of a man.

"Well, Cara, now you are thirteen, you will have to start doing more around here to earn your keep. We aren't made of money, and you cost a bloody fortune." He smirked as he said it.

"Shirley knows I help out where I can," Cara replied defensively.

"Not enough, Cara. You are always on that bloody phone, talking to that faggot friend of yours. You need to start helping out more. Maybe get a little job."

"Don't you dare call Ethan that. Who do you think you are? On the scene for a year and you think you own the place. You're a lazy, fat prick, Joe. That's what you are." She instantly regretted the words coming out. But it was too late. His face was red, anger seeping out of his pores.

"You little bastard child. You whore's baby," he screamed at her, his face becoming a deeper shade of fury.

Then, he grabbed her by the arm, pulling it. It felt as if it were going to come out of the socket. He dragged her to the back door, opening it as she kicked and screamed. Holding her with one hand tight around her arm, he used the other to slap her right across the face. Cara would have fallen if he weren't holding her up with his hurtful, tight grip.

"Get the hell out of my house," he screamed in her face as he pushed her out of the back door, slamming it behind her.

Cara could only watch, shaking, her ears ringing from the words and assault.

# 20

# *Practice Makes Perfect*

## Derek

Derek was getting increasingly serious about improving his culinary skills. He'd even looked into a catering course that was starting the following January at the local college. The cookery programmes he was watching on TV now extended beyond *Dine in With Me*. He meant business.

He had ventured into baking and had made an apple and cinnamon crumble. A few eyebrows were raised when he took it into work; his colleagues weren't yet used to the new chef Derek. Everyone had a piece though, and Jeff even had seconds.

"Ten out of ten, mate. I could eat this every day," said Jeff, shovelling it in his mouth.

Derek wasn't too convinced by his scoring. Jeff would eat food that was almost excrement. Those nasty, dirty microwavable burgers in buns. The ones Derek always thought smelt like how a rat pulled out of a muddy, pissy puddle, then nuked would taste. Des's food smelt delectable in comparison. In fact, those burgers made Des's colossal turds smell edible. So, he took Jeff's compliment with a pinch of salt, or should that be sugar?

"Tasmin, love, how did you find the crumble?"

Derek had respect for Tasmin; after all, she cooked a bloody lovely steak and kidney pie. Her corned beef and potato pies were also super tasty, and even the cheese, onion and potato pies warmed up and served with plenty of tomato sauce were a festival for the taste buds.

"It was lush, Derek, I really enjoyed it." She smiled. "You should definitely make more puddings."

Acceptance, validation, positive feedback. Derek couldn't wipe the grin off his face for the remainder of the day.

It was almost two weeks before he would meet Florence and his dinner club would become a reality. He felt like a child excited to go to Disneyland. With this and his continued research around cross-dressing, finding out he wasn't the freak Brenda branded him as, he did indeed feel as though all his wishes could come true.

That evening, Derek arrived home from work and did his usual walk with Des. It was almost October, one of Derek's favourite months. He loved the autumnal colours and the changing of the leaves. He didn't see it as the foliage dying, he saw it as new beginnings. And this year, he could really relate.

Back home, Des fed and some pasta on the boil for himself, he was weighing up whether he could have a quick shower before tea when there was a knock at the door. Opening the front door, Susan from next door was stood there.

"Hi, Dekka, I took this parcel in for you earlier." She kept her eyes on him, waiting for words.

"Ah, thanks, Susan. That's really kind of you." Inside, he was fighting not to add, "Stop calling me friggin' Dekka, you daft, annoying cow." Instead, he forced an awkward smile.

"Been splashing the cash, eh, Dekka? A present for Brenda to try and win her back? See, you men can't live without us. We are the glue that keeps your species together," she said, chortling.

"Yes, whatever you say, Susan." Derek took the parcel, smiled and abruptly shut the door. "Absolute deluded bat," he muttered. Brenda must have been bloody gossiping about him.

He placed the parcel on the kitchen table. All over the packaging was "Fashion First"—a renowned stockist of women's clothes in the town. Derek hadn't analysed the possible scenario a nosy neighbour may conjure up when he'd ordered some clothes for himself. He felt a flutter of resentment towards Brenda yet again.

The pasta was sticking to the bottom of the pan when he returned to it. Derek let himself seethe a little more towards Susan and Brenda for his sticking pasta as he stirred it, muttering rants under his breath.

He had prepared some Bolognese the night before using Quorn mince. He had announced this to anyone who would listen at work that day, as if he had been awarded an MBE from the Queen herself. People hadn't seemed as impressed as he'd hoped.

"Nice one, Derek. I think it tastes like the sole of me trainers, personally," Jeff had piped up.

Derek had shaken his head. Why do people do that? Say "it tastes like", followed by something they had never and would never bloody eat. Then, he'd thought about Jeff's rat burgers and changed his mind.

Lucy at work was a vegetarian, so she'd been naturally impressed by his preservation of the cow. Little did she know he had a fridge and freezer full of farmyard friends but had just been testing the taste of Quorn out.

As he ate his pasta, allowing Des a few scraps, Derek started to mellow from parcelgate. He knew he needed to gain thicker skin against what people thought.

"You are only this big," he said, holding his thumb and forefinger a few inches apart, looking at Des. He smiled, a silent tear falling from his eye.

"I miss you, Arthur."

His phone beeped in the other room. Getting out of his seat at the dining table, he picked up his cup of tea and strolled into the lounge, Des following.

An email. Derek got quite a few emails each day. Some from the forums and websites he had signed up to, some from Asian chicks and Bitcoin, which he had most definitely not signed up for.

The email was from an address he didn't recognise. He clicked onto it.

***Hi there,***

***I saw your advert in Foodways for the dinner group. Sounds like a great idea. Can you tell me more?***

***Thanks in advance,***
***Eddie.***

Derek read the email again and again, a feeling of excitement enveloping him. He thought of a Nelson Mandela quote that always made him feel positive: "There is no passion to be found playing small—in settling for a life that is less than the one you are capable of living."

And with that in mind, he composed his reply to Eddie.

# 21

# *Life Is for Living*

## Eddie

It had been a long week for Eddie. Willow had been poorly with a virus which saw her temperature soar. Eddie had thought the worst, of course, resulting in a trip to A&E. Willow was fine, but rest was prescribed, along with Calpol and monitoring of what looked like a viral infection. Eddie catastrophised—he couldn't help it. He panicked regularly about losing more of the people he loved.

In times of deep, dark distress, he would look at the quote he'd had laminated in a moment of strength inside his wardrobe. Placed next to a photo of his Issy, it read: "Death ends a life, not a relationship." It was from Mitch Albom, an author who Issy had loved. His books had made her cry happy tears and reflect on life. Eddie had managed to read one of his books, but it had taken him eleven months, as he'd struggled to remain focused.

He dreamt of Issy that Thursday night. He fell asleep out of exhaustion after watching Willow sleep the night before, worried she may stop breathing. God, he loved it when he dreamt of Issy, but he would wake, often sobbing, realising it wasn't real. Then, he would feel that familiar kick in the stomach and the bile almost rising into his mouth.

In his dream, Issy looked beautiful. He always thought she looked stunning in her jogging bottoms and one of his old hoodies, but wow, did she look something else in his dream. She was standing in the doorway in a black lace dress. Her long, wavy red hair lay over her shoulders, with a mind of its own.

He turned where he sat, watching her in the doorway. She was holding a tray full of little cakes. She walked over and placed them on the table. For the first time, Eddie realised there were people sat at the table. Issy sat next to him. Placing her hand briefly on his shoulder, he desired to freeze time and feel that moment for eternity. Then, she faced the man opposite and started talking to him. The woman next to him joined in. Eddie could see these new faces, but he didn't know who they were and couldn't quite make out what was being said.

Then, he woke. He shut his eyes, willing sleep to return so he could try and re-join his dream. Desperate for another few dream minutes with Issy. But it wasn't happening.

"Shit," he shouted, crying. Would it ever stop hurting?

2:22 a.m. It was always about 222 or 2222. Eddie had researched this online when he had started seeing these numbers several times a day. It had felt more than a coincidence. It transpired that these numbers were linked to angels and the spiritual realm. Of course, the numbers could mean much more, but his discovery had only seemed to increase the numbers being an ever-present part of his day. He sobbed, holding the pillow where her head should've been. He lay there for four long hours until his alarm eventually went off.

The next day at work, six people commented on how tired he looked. He told them Willow was poorly. It was the truth. People stopped caring about grief that wasn't their own. They lost interest. Grief was timebound if it wasn't personal.

He left early that Friday. Picking Willow up from his mother's, they drove home together, Willow a little brighter with the discussion of Princess Jasmine. They passed Foodways, and he remembered the little cardboard advert with the neat writing, talking about a food club or something similar.

His heart raced. Was it a sign from his Issy? The dream, the strangers.

Parking up, he scooped Issy into his arms.

"Come on, baby, we need some more magical medicine."

He put her down and walked into Foodways, holding her hand. He took a photo of the advert, knowing he had to get in touch.

After putting Willow to bed that night, he sat with a glass of red wine and emailed Derek.

After sending the email, he finished his glass of wine and went to bed, leaving his phone downstairs.

The next morning, he woke with that heavy head feeling. Questioning for the hundredth time why he'd drank red wine at all, he got up and strolled into Willow's room. She was lying there innocent and cosy, clutching her picture of her mummy. Eddie's heart cracked every single day.

He had perfected the morning routine since Issy had died, and now it was more often enjoyable than challenging. Willow was such a good girl. Not only did she have Issy's kindness and compassion, she showed sensitivity way beyond her years. She was so patient and loving, reassuring and selfless. He could feel the tears. *For Christ's sake, just one day without crying, please*, he pleaded.

"Right, Buba, breakfast time," he sang in an attempt to not only distract her but dupe himself out of his sombre state.

Willow had porridge, while Eddie opted for cornflakes. He picked up his phone and checked his emails as Willow tucked into her breakfast. He noticed a reply to the dinner group advert.

*Evening, Eddie.*

*Thanks ever so much for your enquiry. The Dinner Club is something I thought of to meet fellow foodies and hopefully enjoy company and friendship while learning and sharing new culinary skills. I see this as similar to* Dine in With Me—*without the £1,000 prize, sadly!*

*I am still at the point of collecting contact details from people interested and arranging an initial meetup locally to have a chat about the idea.*

*Do let me know if this sounds like something that would appeal to you.*

*Thanks,*

*Derek.*

Nice. He liked the tone and content of the email. This guy seemed a sound bloke. A smile crept onto his face, and for the first time in a long time, he felt as though he had done something right.

# 22

# It's a New Day, and I'm Feeling Good

## Derek

The night before, Derek had gone to bed positively giddy, over the proverbial moon that he had received ANOTHER enquiry about his dinner club. Him. Derek. Almost a pensioner, a nobody and freak according to Brenda, was doing something now. He was showing the world his idea. And it was a bloody good idea.

He had dreamt of crème brulée and Eton mess, stuffing his face like Augustus Gloop. Then, he had woken early, taken Des for a chirpy walk, singing as he went, and came back with plenty of time to get to work.

On his 11 a.m. cuppa break, he sat with Jeff, talking about the match. His phone beeped, letting him know he had an email.

It was that Eddie, saying he liked the sound of The Dinner Club. *Bloody marvellous*, Derek thought as Jeff chuntered on about the fantasy football league.

This Eddie man only wanted to meet up for the initial meeting. Two had become three. Derek, Florence and Eddie. It had a ring to it.

"Jeff, I'm gonna nip outside, buddy. Make us another quick cuppa, will you?"

Derek dashed outside, into the peaceful autumn air to compose his reply.

***Hello again, Eddie.***

***I am pleased you like the sound of the club. It would be great to meet you. I have already arranged a meeting with a lady interested in finding out more.***

***I definitely want it to be the group's club and not just mine, so would welcome input. The initial meeting is in Foodways Café on Saturday 28th at 1 p.m. I hope you can make it. I will hang around the entrance of the café, hopefully not looking too dodgy.***

***Look forward to meeting you.***

***Have a good day,***

***Derek.***

Hopefully, the dodgy comment would be taken in humour.

"Three custard creams, please, Jeff," he shouted, returning to the canteen.

Muse's "Feeling Good" was on the radio. Derek sang along, smiling. He was most definitely feeling good.

# 23

# *That Woman*

## Violet

"For the love of God, Violet, do you have to bloody cremate everything?"

Violet sat across the table, barely four feet away from Ben, yet his words didn't even register. She had stopped trying to listen to him a long time ago. She heard every word but listening was pointless. She could never win, and words always meant something different each time they poured out of his abhorrent mouth. Violet had been on the receiving end of "not listening" dozens of times over the years. Now, it was as if her spirit couldn't stand listening anymore as her soul slowly eroded like cliffs from the salty sea.

"I followed the instructions, Ben, mine is fine," she said in deflated monotone.

"Well, you must be stupid as well as useless then," he sneered. "How am I meant to eat this pigswill when you could tarmac roads with it?"

He picked up his plate, and even though she knew what was going to happen, she made no attempts to avoid it.

Smash and splat. The sounds, the sensations. She had heard, felt, seen and smelt this event so many times before. Another plate broken on the floor. Another pile of food smeared onto the beautiful porcelain kitchen floor tiles. More brown marks splattered up the white paintwork. More sprays of food landing on Violet. Her face, clothes and hair full of raindrops of gravy and herbs.

Strange how she had stopped flinching as much as the pain had become so much more than physical. This had led to more abuse. She would receive the odd kick, pushing her off the dining table chair, a quick hair pull as he stormed off, a shove against a piece of heavy furniture. Yet, her body, just like the not listening, had stopped reacting like it used to. Was it giving up? Maybe. Was it just her becoming accustomed to the behaviour? Most likely. Or was it because her heart that had once been filled with love and hope was now torn and dead?

Flinching, crying, pleading, speaking—it never changed anything.

She hated this bastard man. This cruel, spiteful, abusive excuse of a man. She hated him with every cell in her body and prayed he would drop dead. That he would die and be eradicated from her existence. That his sick, vindictive, perverted, sinister heart would explode and he would be gone. God, did she pray.

"No other man would put up with you, Vi. You're a complete nightmare. The lads all think it. Always moaning and bloody nagging. And you're a lazy bitch, sponging off me instead of working full time. Aye, you're bloody lucky to have me, Vi. I suggest you be a little bit more damn grateful that I put up with you."

And on that parade of verbal diarrhoea, Ben got up and left, heading off to the local pub as he did eight out of ten times he had a go. The other two didn't end that way.

Violet sat and sobbed. She cried for the monster Ben had become, when twelve years earlier, he had been a gentleman, courting her and charming her. She cried for the doormat she had become, the target, "that woman" who put up with anything. She cried because she needed a way out but had no energy, her mind too depleted to think of options.

That night, she cried, no idea that the next day would be the start of her new chapter.

# 24

# Wednesday Dreaming

## Violet

Ben had come in a little after 11 p.m. the night before. She had heard him clattering around downstairs as she'd lain in bed. She hadn't been to sleep yet. She never did when he was in one of his moods. Not after that time three years ago. Even to this day, he would protest it was a mistake.

"It was a drunken mistake, Vi, you don't half hold grudges. Why can't you see the funny side of it?" he would say over and over, trying to dissolve the severity and make excuses for his vile behaviour. It was always a bloody mistake, a misunderstanding, a reaction to provocation, an overreaction from Violet.

They had argued that night. Violet couldn't even remember what about, as arguing was such a regular part of their life, even then. But that night, he had called her a fat bitch. Even at just under ten stone, he'd still called her fat. She had shown weakness and cried. These days, she didn't cry. Well, certainly not in front of that monster. He had stormed off to the pub. He had a few borderline alcoholic friends, one of which always seemed to be propping up the bar in the local, The Flying Scotsman.

When Ben had come home that night, Violet was asleep. That had been her second mistake that night after crying in front of him. She woke to water on her face, but it wasn't water. Ben was urinating on her face, a smirk spreading across his mouth, in the light of the summer night sky. She shot up in bed, that heart-racing adrenaline you get when you are woken abruptly running through her.

"Ben, what the hell?" she shrieked.

"You aren't even worth my piss," he slurred drunkenly at her.

She had tried so hard over the years, for he hadn't always been a monster. Violet had analysed her own behaviour, gone through the motions with Ben. She had denied his abuse, minimised bullying behaviours, blamed herself. Christ, he had blamed her enough. She had made excuses for him, and he had made excuses for himself. She had asked him to get help. The cycle had gone round and round, repeating itself with no interventions.

Around two years ago, he had said he was going to seek help. Violet had given him a list of services, including his doctor, anger management counsellors and relationship counsellors. She'd felt hope as Ben agreed to explore options. A week later, she had reminded him, and he had said he would do it next week. The next week passed. Nothing. Then, the next. Violet had mentioned it again. He'd told her to stop being a "nagging bastard" and he would do it in his own time. That her "stinking, selfish, ugly attitude" was half of the problem, and if she would back off, he would be ok.

Violet never asked him to seek help again. The last two years had been about her trying to be a better partner but failing. She couldn't win. She could be the most beautiful, tolerant, understanding, selfless person in the world, and Ben would still abuse her. The penny had dropped around eight months ago that Ben was never going to change. The problem was Ben, not her, and it was a problem she had to address and find a solution to, alone.

What could possibly justify his behaviour? Ben had called her names for years, messed with her head, made her feel inadequate, stupid and unattractive. Made her feel grateful to have him, with all his despicable ways. He had physically assaulted her. Over the last year or so, he had even raped her on several occasions, always saying he was just "joking" or that he knew she wanted it and for her to stop being such a prude. Violet had lost every ounce of dignity on the first time, so she'd thought. He had continued to abuse and rape, and she had reached despair.

The only person that knew of her situation was Rosie, her closest friend. They had met at work, and Violet saw Rosie on most of her shifts. They'd have lunch together when they could or a cuppa after or before work. Ben went to darts at The Flying Scotsman each Tuesday, and more recently, each Thursday as well, always out for a good few hours. Violet would sometimes visit Rosie on these nights, confide in her and feel the weight of her burden lift slightly. Rosie was kind and caring, compassionate and empathetic. She never told Violet what to do but offered possible solutions for her to consider.

Violet was so grateful she had Rosie. There were times in her darkest hours where she felt Rosie was the only person in the world who loved her.

That Wednesday, Rosie started her shift at the same time as Violet. They had arranged to meet for a cuppa an hour before clocking in. Violet arrived at Foodways at 9 a.m. Rosie was waiting by the kiosk, talking to Fred, who had worked at Foodways for almost twenty years.

"Morning, me little lovely," he said to Violet.

"Morning, Fred, how are you?"

"Aye, not bad, pet. Better for seeing your pretty face."

Violet blushed. Daft as Fred was like a father, his comment had been innocent and meant to make her feel better. She just wasn't used to it. Well, not from men.

Rosie gave her a hug, enveloping her like a fleece dressing gown covering you with warmth and comfort.

"Your hair looks nice today, Vi," Rosie said as they walked towards the café.

Rosie always paid compliments—another thing Violet liked about her. Kindness came so naturally to her.

They ordered their usual: two teas and a toasted teacake to share. Sitting in their regular seat, Rosie examined Violet's face. She saw through the mask of pretending she was ok; she knew Violet so well.

"What did he do, Vi?"

"He started last night, Rosie. It was probably my fault, as tea was overcooked. It was the usual swearing and name-calling. Then, he threw his plate at the wall. He went to the pub, and I spent all night wondering what was going to happen when he got in." Violet was cracking; the tears would start soon.

Rosie grabbed her hand. "It's ok, take your time. No one is around."

"He got in after eleven. He was downstairs for a bit, having a takeaway. Then, he came upstairs, into the bedroom, saying my name. I kept still, pretending to be asleep."

The tears started, as expected. Rosie handed her a serviette and rubbed her arm.

"He got in bed and started pulling at my pyjama bottoms. I said no, but he wouldn't listen, Ro, he just wouldn't listen. He said he has needs and I'm frigid and need to start being more loving. That I'm lucky he still wants to have sex with me and wasn't shagging other women. I couldn't stop him; I was too scared."

Tears streamed down Violet's face as Rosie tried to hide her expression of sorrow and anger.

"Honey, this can't go on. He won't stop hurting you. I love you, Vi, and I want you to be safe and happy."

Violet knew she was right and bowed her head. She felt emotionally exhausted, embarrassed and helpless, wondering how she could get out of this nightmare.

"What would I do without you?"

Rosie had been her rock for so long now. Patient, caring Rosie, who always put her own worries at the bottom of the pile to listen to Violet's. *It isn't fair really*, Violet thought. Her only hope was that it wouldn't always be like this and that there would be more positive conversations in the future.

It was 9:45 a.m., fifteen minutes before their shifts officially started. Violet knew she had to go and sort her tear-stained face out and take some deep breaths. Customers don't give a damn about the checkout operators' problems, they just want their salad and chicken scanned and to be on their merry way. Soon enough, Violet was behind her till, waiting for the first customer.

Her morning dragged. She had worked in Foodways for almost four years now, so she could conduct the routine from the greeting through to taking payment and wishing the customer a good day, with little concentration. For the next three hours, she went about this routine robotically, all the while daydreaming about a future without Ben. If only.

Her half hour lunch was from 1 p.m. Violet didn't feel hungry. She decided to go for a walk instead to get some fresh air and thinking space. The harsh lighting in Foodways always induced a headache if she had been emotional that morning, her eyes feeling as if she were looking into a bonfire. The fresh autumn air would do her good.

After collecting a cuppa, she started towards the entrance. She glanced at the noticeboard on the way out. The lost poster for Henry the lurcher was gone, hopefully because he'd been reunited with his human parents. There were a few new adverts, including a recruitment advert for local taxi drivers. Then, she saw it, handwritten on cream card, in neat writing:

***Do you enjoy cooking and eating? Would you like to meet fellow foodies for nights of cooking and company? If so, contact Derek to join The Dinner Club.***

Violet smiled to herself. *What a lovely idea*, she thought. She couldn't remember a time when she'd cooked and received compliments. In fact, she couldn't remember a time when she'd cooked for anyone other than Ben. Her friends didn't come around much, as Ben made people feel uncomfortable. He would make snide comments, pretending he was joking. Or he would hang around and try and join in the conversation but dominate it. He would then complain to Violet that her friends didn't like him and made him feel uncomfortable in his own home and how dare they do that. It simply wasn't worth the verbal abuse, sometimes physical abuse that inviting her friends over came with.

Ben would say her food tasted like dog crap. That she was the worst cook ever, and he was better off making things himself. That she only worked twenty-eight hours a week and he worked forty-eight, yet she still couldn't produce an edible meal at the end of the day with all the free time she had.

Violet had always enjoyed cooking. She remembered, when her mother was alive, making homemade casseroles, soups and pies. Baking cakes with her mother, then as she became poorly, taking them to her in a feeble attempt to stop the cancer devouring her. Her mother would always be so grateful, even though she never ate more than a single, obliged bite. Violet yearned for her mother and for some gratitude.

She spent the remainder of her break walking around the nearby housing estate, stealing glances into people's front rooms, wondering who lived there, what their story was. The day had an almost winter chill to it. She zipped her coat right up and clasped her takeaway cup with both hands, enveloping the warmth of the liquid inside. She dreamt of walking into one of the newly-built homes and transporting herself into someone else's life. Someone else's happy life, someone else's safe life.

# 25

# *Terrible Teens*

## Cara

The teenage years are hard enough. For Cara, they were unbearable. After that first incident on her thirteenth birthday, things got worse. Joe never apologised. Instead, he embarked on a subtle campaign to make Shirley dislike her. Shirley, who had always put Cara first, was love blind. She had waited so long for a partner, someone to love and to love her. It was more important than the love of someone else's damaged child.

It was insidious, calculated and clever. Joe orchestrated his poison in the right doses, at the right times. He used clichés and teenage issues to solidify his dislike for Cara and to casually turn Shirley against her.

Cara knew soon into his campaign that she was doomed. It was just a matter of time.

She had been labelled as ungrateful on her thirteenth birthday. It hadn't been discussed in detail but Shirley was quiet around Cara for a few days. She wasn't quiet around Joe, indicating whose side she was on. She never asked Cara her side of the story, and Cara never got a chance to explain.

Joe began giving Cara a more frequent smirk, reminding her who Shirley loved more and that she was on borrowed time. Cara wanted to sink a knife into him on more occasions than she could remember. Within a number of months, she loathed the air he breathed. She resented every cell of his being and prayed bad things would happen to him. The hostility kept her awake at night and robbed her of concentration at school, which led to underperformance and more problems at home. She was trapped in a vicious circle of spite and jealousy.

It was the October after her birthday, and Shirley was out for her closest friend's birthday meal. Cara had tried to stay at a friends' that night, but it was a Wednesday, so no one was interested. There was nothing on after school, but even if there had have been, it would only have killed a few hours. She knew Shirley would be out until near midnight. Cara planned to get home and go straight to her room. She would sacrifice tea in order to keep away from Joe.

Cara got home at around 5 p.m., after dawdling about after school.

"Where the hell have you been? I was worried about you," he faked.

Cara made a "pfft" noise, rolling her eyes. It was her immediate reaction, and as soon as it was out, she shuddered.

"Are you taking the piss, Cara? You have some nerve. We've taken you in, looked after you, put up with you. I tell you I was worried, and you respond with a sarcastic remark. You are one cheeky bitch, you really are."

"Sorry." Cara bit her lip and dashed upstairs.

It was quiet for an hour or so, then as she went to the bathroom, she heard Joe.

"Cara, come down here."

"I'm busy."

"I said, come down here!" his voice roared. Cara felt sick.

She crept down the stairs, body tense. He was sitting in "his chair", four empty cans by his feet and an open one in his right hand.

"Cara, you need to start realising we can get rid of you at any time. You aren't our problem, and your bloody lack of gratitude for all we do is becoming tedious."

She looked at the floor.

"You are turning into a nasty little bitch, Cara. I am trying to help you here. You came from feral, and I am trying to teach you some fucking respect. You walked all over Shirley; you won't walk all over me. If you don't start behaving, I will make sure she gets rid of you."

Cara felt as though she would faint. Like the blood was draining out of her body and the room was starting to spin. She grabbed the sideboard as she took some deep breaths. She'd had a few years of happiness with Shirley. How stupid she'd been to think it would last.

Over the next few months, Cara started to save money from a paper round as well as packs of sweets she frequently stole from the shop and sold on at school. She knew what she had to do. She had to leave. It was just a matter of time before Shirley and Joe got rid of her anyway. She had to take control.

Seven months after that night in October, now aged fourteen years and three months, Cara ran away. She ran away two more times in the next six and a half months, before she was eventually moved back to her final foster care placement for the remaining fourteen months of her children's services involvement. A service that specialised in supporting runaway and missing children got involved. Yet another professional who would float in and out of Cara's life as quick as the wind changed direction. She was assigned a support worker, Leah. Cara would express how she didn't feel wanted by Shirley and Joe to Leah. Mediation would take place. Joe would say she was wanted and that she was just at a "difficult" age. Shirley would say she loved Cara, but Cara knew it wasn't true anymore. It was all pointless.

One of the times she ran away, she went to Edinburgh and sat begging at the train station. She was approached by a man, who turned out to be almost thirty. He said she could stay at his, so she went with him. She said she was sixteen years old. At his flat, which was more of a squat, Cara was sexually exploited and raped. She was fourteen years and nine months old. To this day, she had only told one other human about her experience. She still got flashbacks. Flashbacks of him touching her, grabbing at her clothes. Her saying could they just talk instead. Him saying he wasn't a charity and that she owed him for the hospitality. The smell of his stale breath, his weight bearing down on her. The searing pain in her genitals as he forced himself upon her. The absolute feeling of raw emptiness after, and the sensation of her downing two litres of cider, hoping he never woke up again.

Her first sexual experience and one that haunted her.

# 26

# *Penny Dropping*

## Violet

For the rest of the week, Violet had avoided Ben where possible. She had purposely worked a few late nights to avoid him. Her love for him was diminishing, replaced by ever-growing disgust. She knew in her heart he would never change. It was just a case of building her courage to leave and, of course, finding somewhere to go to.

Each morning that week, she had chatted with Rosie and had gained comfort and reassurance from her. It had given her strength to realise that things had to start changing, and the change certainly wasn't going to come from Ben. Ben would never leave her, despite his frequent outbursts of saying he could do better or claims some woman at work or at the petrol station—even the neighbours, for God's sake—apparently fancied him.

"Stevie Wonder can see clearer than that arsehole," she had scoffed with Rosie on Sunday's overtime shift.

"He's got the dreamer's disease, that's for sure, Violet. Daft pig."

They howled as they had their cuppa; it was just the tonic Violet needed.

On her break, she headed off for a stroll and some fresh air. Walking past the noticeboard, her eyes clocked the advert for The Dinner Club again. She had looked at it a few times that week. Despite her curiosity, she knew she couldn't do anything like that. Ben always told her she was a "crappy cook" and had "a personality like cardboard". Why would anyone want to spend time in her company and eat her food?

"Hi, beautiful," shouted Fred across the kiosk.

"Going for a quick fresh air break, Violet?" asked Henry, the security guard, smiling.

"Hi, Vi," Sarah from the pharmacy said, coming in as Violet walked out.

Three people in a matter of minutes, all speaking to her, smiling genuinely. At least, it looked genuine to her. Maybe she didn't have a "personality like cardboard".

Violet was only outside for three minutes before she decided. She was going to do it. It could be the boost she needed to start a whole new chapter in her life. A new beginning, with people who didn't know her. People who couldn't judge her because they didn't know.

She stood in front of the noticeboard for the last five minutes of her break and emailed Derek.

# 27

# Sunday Roast

## Derek

Derek liked Sundays. They were always pleasantly uneventful with Brenda, but there was something about the mundane routine that was satisfying.

Sundays would involve a cooked breakfast—a treat Derek looked forward to most of the week. Then, some housework, the odd job and a leisurely stroll with Des. Sometimes, they would stop off for a posh coffee and a slither of cake. Happily boring and usually one of the few days in the week where Brenda seemed to be more civil with Derek, even borderline kind at times. Where conversation was relaxed, normal and not filled with snide digs aimed at belittling him.

Sundays were simple, some would say dull, but a day Derek enjoyed. Most Sundays, he also enjoyed Brenda's company, so not surprisingly, this was the day where he would experience fleeting bouts of missing her as loneliness crept in.

His Sundays since Brenda had left had followed most of this routine. Some elements had taken longer, as he was alone now, so the housework had to be done a little through the week, and he had a newfound responsibility to keep on top of chores. But Derek had adapted his routine and felt it worked. He was enjoying cooking and baking new foods on Sundays, which was good practice, given the meeting for his first dinner club discussion was less than a week away.

That Sunday, he made lamb tagine and homemade bread, following a recipe he had googled. The smells danced up his nostrils as he prepared the feast. The spices, colours and aromas were a delight, and he was almost salivating waiting to try it. His homemade bread, a shop-bought mix, had a comforting, hearty aroma as it baked in the oven. Derek loved a bit of stodge; carbs were his favourite, and he'd already promised himself that he'd make the loaf of bread last until Wednesday. He had frozen soup from his midweek cooking session to enjoy for the next few nights with the bread. He would not succumb to sitting in the kitchen, smearing butter over it and eating slice after slice.

Two hours later, he sat in his armchair, belly full and content. His life had changed the last few months, more than it had in the last few decades, but he had let the storm pass and was now feeling the calm. Brenda was still being vicious, and Derek suspected she was hoping he would come begging. But Derek had been given space and time to readjust to being alone and to solidify his decision that breaking up was the right thing. He knew there would be a point when divorce had to be mentioned, discussions of finances and legal processes, but he wasn't in the market for another wife, partner or even lover. Derek just wanted to love himself and feel happy in his own skin. It was all he had ever wanted, and it was Brenda's mission to prevent it.

Derek went upstairs to get showered and ready for bed, already thinking of pudding. He checked his mobile, which had been on charge. A text from Sue at work reminding him the lottery syndicate money was due tomorrow, and a new email.

He clicked the email:

***Hello, Derek.***

***My name is Violet. I saw your advert in Foodways. Actually, I have seen it every day this week, as I work there! Anyway, I think it is a brill idea, and I would love to find out how to sign up.***

***Thanks ever so much.***

***All the best,***

***Violet x***

"Get in!"

Violet sounded lovely; a warm and friendly soul. Derek was elated.

Bloody hell, what with Florence, Eddie, Violet and himself, that was four possible members.

He quickly replied to Violet, anxious to encourage her to join the group:

***Hi, Violet,***

***Thanks ever so much for your email. We would be delighted for you to join the group. In fact, we have our very first meeting at Foodways Café next Saturday, 1 p.m. I hope you can make it and look forward to meeting you.***

***Much thanks,***

***Derek.***

Derek was flabbergasted. In that moment, he felt as though The Dinner Club could be the pinnacle of his new life.

# 28

# Trapped in a Nebulous

## Eddie

It was Saturday morning, the day Eddie was meeting Derek, the organiser of The Dinner Club.

Eddie still had his regular Saturday morning commitments but knew he had plenty of time. He hadn't got this far in his career without excellent organisational and time-management skills, even as a grieving widower and single parent to a princess-obsessed, energetic little madam.

"Pancakes are ready, Willow."

The princess-obsessed madam had less energy this morning. Eddie had taken her swimming after nursery last night. Willow loved the water. She was a fearless, natural water baby. She was a delight to watch. There was only one thing missing: Issy. He hoped, somewhere, she was watching over them and seeing all the tiny and monumental developments in their wonderful little girl.

Eddie yearned for the day when activities with Willow wouldn't be overshadowed by the void that Issy had left. Would it ever happen? The paradox of his happiness, the fleeting escapism filled instantly with cutting reality. It hurt like hell, and it was bloody unfair.

"Buba," he shouted up the stairs. He heard her little footsteps on the floorboards. Then, he heard the radio. His secret message from Issy was on once more, delivered by Cyndi Lauper. It was as equally comforting as it was distressing.

Eddie was trapped in a nebulous of pain, grief and love. His heart hurt, raw and angry, just as it had the day she'd died. He wanted to remember, to bathe in the memories of their love, their laughter, their secret times, but he couldn't. The recollections felt distant, out of reach, tarnished by tragedy. He couldn't sense them and feared he never would.

Willow's happy footsteps entered the room.

"Hey, baby, you hungry?"

"Yup."

Her little face lit up, so innocent, so easily pleased. He wanted to bottle those feelings for her forever. To protect her from anything that could possibly ever hurt her in the future: bullies at school, boyfriends or girlfriends, social media, societal pressures, adolescence, break ups, exams, more death. The joy this three-foot bundle of smiles and sticky fingers gave him was immense, but he also thoroughly understood why people chose not to have kids. In fact, why they chose to never get close to another human or even animal. Loss and grief. Only one thing we can be certain of is that we and others will die.

Eddie was on the brink of tears. Then, his Willow wrapped her arms around his leg, and his heart flourished for a moment. He looked down, she looked up, her happy little face still sleepy. She was his heartbeat. He had to get better for her. He had to live for her. He wouldn't let grief beat him.

After breakfast, it was time to get Willow ready to drop her at his parents'. Eddie watched his daughter stuff random toys into a bag. For some reason, she loved to pack bags. He found them almost daily, stuffed with teddies, princesses, crayons, paper and jewellery. Anything she could get her hands on would be packed into a bag and carried around at any available opportunity. Her mother had liked handbags. Maybe it was Issy's way of ensuring Willow was always prepared. As much as you can be prepared with a plastic backpack containing Princess Belle, a toy car, drawing paper, socks and a teddy.

Twenty minutes later, they arrived at Connie and Robert's. Connie was eagerly watching for them out the window and went straight to the front door when she spotted them. Willow began waving manically.

"Hi, Mam," Eddie said as he got out the car.

Reaching into the back to let Willow out of her car seat, he was half-deafened by her shrieking.

"Momar!"

*Bloody hell, the lungs on this one*, Eddie thought as he smiled at his mam.

"She's excited to show you what's in her bag this morning."

"Ooh, let's get you inside, Willow-woo, Grandpa is waiting."

"I will be back around two-thirty."

"No rush, Son, we have plenty planned for this little lovely."

Eddie's heart melted as his mam hugged Willow. In so many ways, he and Willow were extremely lucky. He just had to try to remember that on the days, hours and minutes he felt the injustice of the world.

Eddie had three hours to get his weekly housework done, grab some lunch and head to Foodways for his 1 p.m. meeting. He calculated he would need a good half hour at home to psyche himself up for it. He was confident at work; people came to him with queries and he was most definitely an expert in his field, but out of his comfort zone, and this was out of his comfort zone, lack of preparation could be catastrophic. He would get there early, have a coffee to calm his nerves. Actually, make that a tea—coffee could work as a laxative for him on a nervous stomach.

Eddie made a start on the housework. An hour and a half later, he was finished. The place smelt wonderful and gleamed. Doing housework was almost a workout in itself. A quick cuppa and a sit down was needed before jumping in the shower and getting ready to go to Foodways.

Eddie arrived at Foodways at 12:35 p.m. He entered the supermarket and walked along to the café. Purchasing a pot of tea, he sat a few seats from the café entrance so he could monitor the comings and goings and hopefully spot Derek easier or make it easier for Derek to spot him. It was like some weird, cringey blind date.

He expressed a light chuckle; Issy would have thought this was a hoot. Him sitting there with a pot of tea, worried about needing a poo and waiting to meet a man about cooking. Bizarre. Jesus, that could even be the start of a story about a serial killer.

Eddie reached for his phone from his now off jacket pocket, to scroll on social media and hopefully relax himself.

Adam had put up a new photo and status from the night before: "Mad night with this stud". The photo was of him licking his friend's cheek in a nightclub.

*For God's sake, he's thirty-two years old*, thought Eddie. At times, it was as if Eddie were working with kids. Adam wasn't doing much to challenge that view. He would mention something casually in the office on Monday.

He continued to scroll, seeing images and updates of families, pets, nights out and day trips. Social media could depress you chronically or uplift you immensely and absolutely nothing between. He shut the Facebook app and opened the BBC News one.

As he read the latest political embarrassment, he heard a voice:

"Are you Eddie?"

Eddie looked up. An older, chunky man stood there with a warm smile.

Eddie got out of his seat and held out his hand. "Yeah, yes, I'm Eddie. You must be Derek."

Still smiling, Derek took his hand, giving a firm handshake. "Great to meet you, Eddie. Can I get you another cuppa?"

# 29

# *Carpe Diem*

## Florence

William arrived at 11:30 a.m. that Saturday morning instead of his usual noon. He didn't seem very impressed with the disruption to routine, even when Florence insisted it was a one-off.

Florence had crumpets with melted cheese on ready for his arrival; she knew that would soften him up, and she was right. Florence still liked to look after William in ways she could. He was still her baby, albeit a big baby. Their roles had reversed, like so many parent and child relationships do in time. Florence had become the cared for and William the carer, but she would still do her bit, and food was a way of showing her love.

Over the years, Florence had loved to cook. Ernie had had a big appetite and Florence liked nothing more than seeing him and the children full and content. They never had the same meal twice a week. Even when times were tough and money wasn't always in abundance, food was always the heart of the home. Florence made sure her family had a full belly and plenty of cuddles. They lapped up her homemade delights: cottage pie, roast dinners, sausage casseroles, fish pie, mince and dumplings, homemade broth. And the puddings, Florence always had a sweet tooth and would make homemade rice pudding, rhubarb crumble, apple pie, ginger sponge and custard.

Then, as times changed and different food became popular, Florence would make chicken tikka masala, creamy pasta bakes and quiches. Food time was family time. She missed it. She missed the laughter and chat food created. The warmth, the joy on someone's face from a new taste, the compliments on her food. She yearned to look after people, even though she needed a level of looking after herself. The desire to nurture never does disappear.

Florence handed William the plate of golden crumpets, the cheese melted over the top, inviting a big bite.

"Thanks, Mam," he said, giving Florence a kiss on the cheek.

They ate their crumpets, had a cup of tea and were ready to go fifteen minutes later. The plan had already been discussed earlier that week: William and Florence would do their weekly shop, as per usual. William would then put the shopping in the car if time permitted, then go back to the café with Florence until she met her guest, ensuring that he wasn't some deranged pervert trying to groom pensioners (William's words but it had crossed Florence's mind). William would then leave, and Florence would text when her meeting was over so William could come and collect her. Simple.

"Mam, talk me through the plan again, please."

"Bloody hell, William, I feel as though we should be in a James Bond film with all this detail." Florence giggled.

"It isn't funny; I'm being serious." William looked at Florence, eyes fixed sternly on her, no sign of a smile from her playful reference to James Bond.

"I know, Son, I know, sorry."

Florence went over the agenda of the operation again, satisfying William's nerves, and then they got to putting it into action, as they were soon at Foodways.

All shopping purchased, packed and put in William's car, it was 12:50 p.m. *Good timing*, thought Florence, smiling to herself.

William walked her back into the supermarket and towards the café. They stood at the entrance for a minute, looking around, studying the patrons and wondering if any could be Derek. There was no male sitting by himself.

Derek had text the night before as promised, describing what he was going to be wearing. Florence got her phone out of her handbag and scrolled through her messages.

"Here we go. 'I will be wearing a maroon jumper and dark blue jeans. I wear glasses and will sit near the entrance of the café if I am there before you.'"

Florence looked again at the customers. She spotted a man meeting the description, sitting with another man.

"William, I think that is him," she said, pointing.

"What, with another man?" He lowered his voice and shook his head. "Mam, I don't like this, two men meeting a pensioner, Christ almighty."

Florence tutted. "William, stop being daft. Not everyone is a deviant."

And with that, Florence strutted over, with a sheepish William close behind.

"Erm, afternoon, gents, I'm Florence." She looked quizzically at Derek.

"Florence!" he exclaimed, jumping up. "A pleasure to meet you. Please, please, take a seat. And will this chap be joining you?" Derek glanced at William.

"Oh no, William is my son. We've been shopping together. He just wanted to make sure I wasn't stood up." Florence smiled.

"I see, very wise. Nice to meet you, William." Derek advanced his hand and shook William's. "Florence, dear, this is Eddie. He is joining our discussion today."

"Lovely to meet you, Florence." Eddie smiled, and Florence returned it.

"Righto, I will get you a drink, Florence. What's your poison?"

Florence laughed. "A pot of tea would be wonderful, thanks."

Satisfied that his mother's company appeared to be of the non-deviant nature, William turned to Florence.

"Text me when you're done, Mam. Enjoy."

# 30

# *Breaktime*

## Violet

It was just after 1 p.m., and Violet was desperate for the loo. Her break was late, and her bladder knew it. Violet dashed to the toilet, where she relieved herself and put on some lipstick, before rushing down to the café.

It was now 1:10 p.m. Violet arrived at the café, out of breath and probably looking more than a little neurotic. She scoured the customers, searching for someone meeting the description Derek had sent to her the night before.

*Crap*, she thought; there were too many people, and she had no idea if he would be alone or not. She groaned defeatedly, then immediately told herself off for not absorbing, reflecting and looking for solutions to the barriers. She always thought the worst—another trait Ben had projected onto her that she disliked about herself. Then, she spotted him. Well, someone who could be him. She darted into the café and straight over.

"Derek, Derek, please say you are Derek." She blushed as she said it, still catching her breath, which was rapid from rushing and nerves.

"You must be Violet." A warm face smiled at her.

"Yes, yes, it's me. So sorry I am late; I couldn't get off my till. Lovely to meet you."

"You had the shortest travel time and you're still late," a man sitting opposite said, chuckling. He also had a welcoming smile, so Violet felt confident it was in jest.

"Violet, take a seat and let me introduce you to the group. This is Florence," Derek said, nodding in Florence's direction.

Violet looked at the elderly lady sitting next to the cheeky man and smiled. "Great to meet you, Florence."

"Likewise, dear."

"And this fine, young man is Eddie," Derek said, gesturing towards Eddie with another nod.

"Nice to meet you, Violet."

"You too, Eddie."

"Let me get you a drink, Violet. Take a seat." Derek moved out of the way for her to sit. Still feeling a little overwhelmed, Violet gladly took the seat and rested her shaking legs.

"Thank you, Derek, a coffee would be lovely."

Derek went off to get Violet's drink as the remaining three sat there, looking at each other in silence.

"Wow, well, this is us then, I guess," Violet advanced, trying to fill the awkwardness. She hated silences. Well, unless with Ben, as she couldn't stand to listen to him. Saying that, most of the time he was silent, he was plotting something unpleasant.

"Yeah, we are either all a bit mad or this is a brill idea. I can't quite work out which," said Eddie.

Florence smiled and nodded. "Toffee, pet?" Florence held out a bag in Violet's direction. Violet took a toffee, with a thank you.

Derek returned with a coffee and about sixteen sugars. "Sorry, not sure how you take it," he said, sliding the sugars and some milk towards her.

"Thanks." Violet replied, gratefully picking up two sugars from the mountain in front of her.

Derek got comfortable in his seat and then addressed the group. "Right, folks, this is us then. The first four members of The Dinner Club. Hopefully, you're all hungry to find out more. See what I did there?" He laughed at his joke.

All nodded in agreement, giggling at his pun. Violet liked him; he was like a cringey dad.

"Ok, well, I guess it may be useful for us to talk a little bit about ourselves. Kind of a little introduction, maybe? Does everyone feel ok with that?"

Another look around, and another round of nods.

"Perfect, I'll start then, since I dragged you all here." Derek beamed. "I'm Derek, I'm sixty-three years old and very recently separated. I work local, for Cartington's, where I've worked for many happy years. I have a loyal dog, Des, and I have always, always loved my food." Derek patted his stomach as the group continued to listen.

"Since my separation from my wife, I've been cooking more and decided to try and learn new recipes. Never too old to learn, eh? The inspiration for this group came from watching *Dine in With Me* the week of my separation. Not sure if you've seen it?" he asked curiously. Eddie shook his head.

"Anyway, as time's gone on, I have been enjoying cooking and learning new skills, but it has been lonely, and I want to share my cooking with others as well as meet new people. And, of course, I like being catered for. So, that's why I put the advert out, exactly as it said, for cooking and company. And that's me, I guess. Thanks all." Derek breathed out a satisfying sigh, as if he had given a speech at the Oscars.

Violet smiled. Derek seemed so proud of himself; it was heart-warming. She loved how he had turned the negative of a relationship breakdown into a positive opportunity to meet new people and learn new skills.

"Violet, would you like to go next?" Derek said. Everyone was looking at her.

"Erm, yeah, sure, why not," she responded, nearly choking on her coffee, caught off guard. "So, I'm Violet.

I work here in Foodways on the checkouts. I live local, just down the road, with my partner, Ben. We don't have children. My life is really boring, to be honest." Violet laughed, but sadness tinged her insides. "I wanted a new hobby and new friendships. I want to feel a bit more energised, feel the excitement of a new pastime and have something to look forward to." Violet paused and swallowed; she could feel emotion blocking her throat. She took a breath and looked at the group. Their warm, expectant faces helped her composure. "I don't see my friends that much—I guess everyone is so busy. But I do love cooking and used to cook lots with my mam when she was alive. So, I guess when I saw the advert, it ticked the boxes for me. That's why I'm here."

"Thanks for sharing, Violet, that's great. Florence, my dear, would you like to go next?" said Derek. His eyes lit up when his mouth smiled—the true sign of a genuine smile. Violet felt at ease, even after talking about herself to three strangers.

Florence nodded confidently and began to talk. "My name is Florence, and I am eighty-three years young. I know, I don't look a day over sixty-five." Florence gave a cheeky grin. "I'm a widow and live in a bungalow down on Western Way. I have two grown-up children, William and Veronica, three grandchildren and three great-grandkids. My eldest, Veronica, lives in Canada with her daughter and grandson, but my William lives local." Florence turned to Violet. "He brought me here today. Made sure Derek and Eddie here weren't some sort of perverts before he left the café." Florence chuckled, and Violet burst out laughing. Violet loved how elderly people often had no filter and said what they thought without trying to be diplomatic or politically correct. Eddie playfully rolled his eyes, and Violet noticed Derek playing with the sugar sachets on the table. He seemed slightly distracted, or maybe it was just unease from the conversation.

"I used to cook lots, even after my Ernie died. My health isn't what it used to be, and part of me has given up on cooking. I want to reignite that part of myself, cook for others and eat with others. I want to make new friends, share stories and laughs. I want to feel alive again, appreciated and to feel part of something."

Violet could see tears welling up in her eyes. When she looked at Florence, she saw a lonely woman who had so much love to give.

Violet replied, "Florence, that sounds lovely, and I'm certain you will. I, for one, would love to get to know you more."

A relief, a smile, a little glow swept over Florence's aged face.

"Last but not least, Eddie, would you like to introduce yourself?" prompted Derek.

"Hi, yeah, erm, I'm Eddie. I live local also, on the Ford Estate. I work in Finance, and I have a daughter called Willow. She keeps me very busy. I need to learn to cook better, for Willow's sake. And meeting new people is never a bad thing."

Violet smiled; she saw the way Eddie's face lit up when he mentioned his daughter. He never mentioned the mother, but Violet imagined them to be the perfect family. Two good-looking parents, a beautiful daughter, perhaps a dog. Plenty of money, a posh house, holidays and nice cars. The ideal lifestyle.

The sound of Derek's bouncy voice brought her back from her daydream.

"Smashing. Well, it's marvellous to meet you all. What do you all want the group to involve? I obviously have my own ideas, but this needs to be a club for us all, everyone equal, everyone appreciated." Derek clapped his hands together, excited with the prospect. "I could jot down a few ideas?" he suggested, getting a notebook and pen from his jacket pocket. Derek looked at the group, wanting confirmation as he held the pen.

"Sounds great," said Violet.

It was the green light Derek needed. He continued, "So, firstly, the purpose of The Dinner Club."

Everyone nodded towards Derek.

"I saw it as us meeting up as a group, taking turns at people's houses, the host cooking for the group. No prize like on the tele, but good company and an evening of cooking for others or being fed."

"Sounds perfect to me," Violet said, feeling more relaxed in the company of strangers than she had in her own home for a long time.

"It doesn't have to be Michelin Star grub, just a way to try out new recipes or your signature dish and to enjoy an evening of good company. No rummaging around each other's underwear drawers like on the tele either, mind."

"Mine would scare you all off," said Florence. Violet smiled; she loved the edge to this pensioner. *How refreshing*, she thought.

"Well, we all have our skeletons, Florence. Does that sound like what you all thought it would be?"

"Sounds great to me," said Eddie, followed by the others echoing their approval.

"Fantastic. So, we need to agree on how frequently we meet, then I think we need some rules. Without wanting bureaucracy, I do think it is important so we are all on the same page, singing from the same hymn book and all that."

The group decided to meet once a fortnight initially. Some expectations were also agreed on, that Derek would circulate via email.

Violet glanced at her watch. *Bugger*.

"Sorry, I have to get back to my shift," she said, standing from her seat. "Thanks so much. It's been great to meet you all though, and I'm excited to see you all again next time."

They all said their goodbyes to Violet before she dashed back to her shift, wondering for a second if that was a bounce in her step.

# 31

# Dinner Club Expectations

## Derek

Derek had driven home, window open, music blasting, singing his heart out to *Phantom of the Opera*. Yes, he'd received a few strange looks at traffic lights, belting out "Music of the Night", but he'd felt magnificent, liberated, powerful and in control. His favourite musical soundtrack had been the perfect way to celebrate.

Now—after a dinner of roasted veg, steak and chips—Derek was on his laptop. He had three tasks:

1) Check the forum for any messages around cross-dressing.

2) Type up The Dinner Club expectations, and circulate.

3) Ring Bri.

They hadn't met that afternoon, so Derek was hoping he would have time for a few pints tomorrow.

Derek logged into the forum. He had a message from wearwhatiwant54.

***Hi, De1958,***

***Nice to see you in the group.***

***From your public post, I thought you may appreciate a private message. It's always a bold step telling people about cross-dressing, and there are different things people want when it comes to it.***

***For example, mine was always at home only, but now I go to friends' on occasion dressed as Paula. Sometimes, I even dress as Paula on nights out, depending on where we are going.***

***At first, I think people felt awkward, but it was their own feelings, not mine, that were the problem. My friends are in their 50s, so perhaps less compassionate to diversity than younger folk these days. But I persevered, and they were fine in the end. Well, all apart from one, my friend's husband, who's a prick anyway!***

***I have also made some new supportive friends through Paula.***

***Please ask any questions; I know what you may be going through,***

***Peter/Paula.***

The message from Peter had helped Derek feel some validation. He had been struggling that week, really needing the perspective of someone who understood. Derek wanted Debbie to be involved with The Dinner Club. He had talked about being non-judgemental in the group expectations. *People always say they are non-judgemental, but we all judge*, he thought. He would adapt the words to try and enforce the importance of acceptance. Florence, Violet and Eddie seemed like a pleasant bunch; he had warmed to them all and no alarm bells had rung. He hoped, he really hoped, that this could be the start of something fantastic.

He opened a document and started to type:

**<u>The Dinner Club Expectations</u>**

1. All members to have a voice within The Dinner Club.

2. Any changes to The Dinner Club diary dates to be given with as much notice as possible.

3. Hosts to take responsibility for communicating plans with the group members.

4. Members to respect each other's homes.

5. All members to be accepting of people in the group, treat each other equally and support one another.

6. Members to host on a bi-monthly cycle (review if needed).

7. All members to bring a bottle of wine/non-alcoholic fizz to each event.

8. Hosts to serve a minimum of two courses.

9. First Dinner Club to be held on Tuesday 20$^{th}$ October (Derek to host).

10. All members to have fun and enjoy an evening of food and good company!

And there they were, the expectations of The Dinner Club. He emailed them to Florence, Violet and Eddie, requesting they check them and feed back. It was all coming together.

Heading into the kitchen, he heard his mobile ring. Rushing back into the lounge, he picked it up. It was Brenda.

"Err, hello, Brenda, to what do I owe this pleasure?" He tried not to sound too sarcastic but knew it would have come across as that.

"Derek, we need to talk. We've both had our huffy time, and now we need to talk like two adults. I can come over tomorrow?" She sounded serious. Derek knew Brenda had a point. He had been avoiding things, enjoying his ignorant bliss, knowing they had to talk rationally at some point.

"Yeah, that's fine, how about teatime? I could make us something to eat."

"Ha, well, I hope you can manage more than a Pot Noodle." She had to be snipey; she just couldn't resist.

"I'm managing fine, more than fine, but you can always eat at Linda's, Brenda. I was just trying to be civil."

"No, food would be nice, yes. I will be over at six." No apology, obviously. Derek let it go.

"Ok, see you then, Brenda. Bye."

# 32

# *The Weirdness of New*

## Eddie

Eddie sat in his car for fifteen minutes before collecting Willow. He needed some thinking space, time to absorb the weird yet slightly wonderful hour he had just spent in the company of three strangers. He could imagine the conversation in the office on Monday morning:

"What did you do at the weekend, bud?"

"Well, I met three strangers in Foodways Café to talk about a cooking club."

Eddie laughed. It was bizarre, something he had never thought about doing before, yet there was something really soothing about the last hour. The welcome Eddie had felt from them all. The fact they didn't know him and they weren't going to ask the same questions everyone in his life always asked:

"How are you bearing up, Eddie?"

"Does Willow talk about Issy?"

"Is there anything I can do?"

These questions were asked day in, day out, to the point Eddie wanted to turn and scream, "Piss off". It was unbearable. Carrying grief, people constantly infiltrating his thoughts.

There were days where for a few solitary minutes, sometimes even a full hour, his tired brain wasn't absorbed with thoughts of Issy, of loss, all the never agains. Then, some arsehole who meant well would send a text:

"I heard Paloma Faith on the radio, and it reminded me of your wedding."

"Just got sent a photo of Willow off your mam. She's so like Issy."

On and on and on.

People meant well, he knew that, but he wished to God they would back off.

"Here if you need to talk."

"Thinking of you."

He didn't want to fucking talk. People don't know what to say around grief, so they try, and fail, to comfort.

He remembered a time Issy's friend Anna sent the "I know what it feels like" line. He'd snapped and told her she didn't. How could she possibly have known how he felt? She hadn't lost her husband, the parent to her child, the love of her life, her best friend, her better half. He'd been offended that she'd even tried to compare.

He resented people trying to make it about them. He knew that was part of grieving and that others were certainly grieving for Issy, he just didn't have the mental capacity to give a damn. He wondered, almost daily, when the time would come that he wouldn't be consumed with thoughts of Issy. He wasn't even sure if he wanted this time to come. He was frightened of ever forgetting her. Which, right now, sounded ridiculous, as he had thought of very little else since she'd died.

Some days, he forgot she wasn't here. He would find something out and want to tell her, then realise she had gone. He craved normality, but his normality was Issy, so it would never be obtainable.

He raged at the injustice of the world and wondered about the man who'd killed her. He couldn't comprehend how people coped with death. He'd survived but certainly wasn't thriving. Maybe this small group of what seemed like lovely and different people could help in a small way.

He had deliberately not mentioned Issy in his introduction. Quite honestly, he had felt as though he were back at college, having to introduce himself nervously in front of a class of forty eager students. He didn't want to be seen as the widower. Florence had lost her husband; she'd been upfront about that, and something had ignited in Eddie around common ground. But still, there was always that pity he'd experience when he told people about Issy. A shock of loss that isn't so prevalent when loss is in older age. Maybe he was overthinking, maybe Florence would help and understand. He was surrounded by pity in his life and wanted to be seen as Eddie, not Eddie whose wife died.

He would mention it in time, of course he would, but this group, for him, almost felt like part of his recovery. A desperate attempt, influenced by a dream he was clutching to, to try and grasp some normality. For his tired, traumatised brain to stop tormenting him about things he should have said or could have done. To finally stop poisoning himself with hatred towards the man who'd ended Issy's life. So he could be a better dad to the only thing keeping him going ninety-nine percent of the time. So he could recover.

# 33

# *Help at Hand*

## Florence

Florence waited on the seat outside the supermarket for William to collect her.

"Well, no perverts or murderers." She laughed as she got into William's car.

"Mam, you can never be too sure. I don't want you served up at someone's dinner party," William said, squeezing his mother's hand protectively.

"They were a lovely bunch, Will, really nice people," Florence replied, squeezing back.

"That's great, Mam. It will do you good to have something extra socially. They will enjoy your company too. Just take it easy."

"You're right, Son," Florence said, content as she fastened her seatbelt and placed her handbag on her lap.

William dropped Florence off at her bungalow. He had put her shopping away already. He was a good lad, and Florence was proud of him. She was proud of Veronica too, of course, and the grandchildren, but William did so much for her, and he was a lovely, gentle lad. He had all the positive qualities of his father.

After making a cuppa, she sat in her recliner, three ginger nut biscuits by her side, and started thinking about her new group. She was looking forward to going to the others' homes to be catered for. Meeting once a fortnight was enough to have something to look forward to but not too onerous. She was worried about her turn to cook. She did have a drop-leaf table that she could put up and chairs she could bring in from the bedroom, so that would be fine. It was the preparing and cooking, serving and hosting that might be too much for her.

Florence didn't want to acknowledge it as a barrier but her health was going to deteriorate. Already, she struggled to do some things. That was why Jessie and Lucy were so essential. She had thought seriously about asking Jessie to help. Jessie would get paid, of course, from Florence's allowance, and she thought Jessie may also enjoy it, learning the recipes Florence had brought her family up on. She would ask her in the morning.

Florence thought the group members seemed pleasant. It was nice to have Derek, who was in his early sixties, then the two younger members. Four felt like a good number, and Florence hoped it wouldn't get much bigger. They would have to sit with lap trays at her bungalow if the group did grow.

Ernie would have laughed at the idea but would have loved the element of having a free meal. He'd always loved his food. Hearty, traditional meals. Florence missed cooking them, and The Dinner Club would be the perfect opportunity to cook again. She may even name a dish after her beloved.

Florence felt excitement, happiness and opportunity. Things she hadn't felt for a while. For a few seconds, it took her away from her reality. The reality she was keeping secret, ignoring and avoiding for as long as she possibly could.

With that thought, she got up and went to the kitchen to look for her old nineteen-sixties recipe books.

# 34

# *Focus*

## Cara

Cara had been back sleeping on Caitlyn's sofa for three weeks now. She was growing increasingly intolerant of Caitlyn's boyfriend, Rhys, who had recently moved in. His routine included playing computer games, walking around in boxer shorts with a bowl of cereal constantly in his hand, and waking her up in the early hours four nights a week when he came in from his job at Harlem Club in town.

Caitlyn was a good friend, someone who Cara could rely on, someone who cared. But there was a fine line, and Cara didn't want to cross it. Last week, Cara had started looking for a full-time job. After insomnia crawled over her one night, she'd had a few hours in the dead of night thinking about her past, her present and her future. She had always been resilient and determined. She wouldn't be here still if she wasn't. But some part of her felt that her life being crap and chaotic, lacking focus and true happiness, was allowing all the people who had abused her, let her down—the systems, the individuals—to continue neglecting and mistreating her.

She realised she had the power to change it; her and her alone. It could be worse. She could be on the streets, addicted to drugs and alcohol. She knew she had demons that had to be addressed. She still had bad coping mechanisms, food being one of them. But surely acknowledging it was the first step to recovery.

Cara needed routine, focus, a purpose. A reason to get up in the mornings and keep going. She had managed a few short-term jobs in the past. She'd worked at the local shopping centre over the Christmas period since she was eighteen and had worked in the Italian for about four months, on a casual basis, cash in hand. She knew she had some transferable skills.

Last week, she had started her job search, looking online in the library and in the local free paper. She had updated her CV—completing some positive steps had given her a sense of achievement. Caitlyn had supported, praised and encouraged her. Cara had lapped it up. She absorbed praise like sunrays.

Scouring jobs had helped Cara identify jobs she could do with no problem from her previous experience. It had also helped her discover new opportunities. Ok, so she had little chance of getting the job of "Animal Welfare Officer" with the local animal sanctuary that she would have loved, but there were other possibilities. By the end of the week, she had applied for six jobs and felt confident she would get at least a few interviews. For the first time in a long time, Cara believed things could be looking up.

Rhys woke her again at 2:15 a.m. that Friday morning.

"For fuck's sake," she muttered to herself.

He wasn't even drunk, yet he was clattering around as though he were Mr Bean roller skating around the room. Part of her thought he did it on purpose to make her realise it was his flat. It wasn't his flat, it was Caitlyn's, but Cara omitted to tell him that. She heard the usual noise of the cereal being poured into the bowl as the packaging rustled. Then, the fridge opening, milk pouring, lid on, put back, fridge closed. Cutlery drawer pulled open, spoon taken out, clanging against the others on its removal. The cupboard door shutting, footsteps into the bedroom. It was enough to put Cara off cereal for life—she resented it as much as she resented Rhys for waking her. She knew they were doing her a favour, but she just wanted a bloody normal and easy life. And so what if the cereal was getting the blame at this point in time?

Cara woke when Caitlyn got up for work. It was 7:45 a.m. Despite being woken in the night, Cara felt refreshed. She did her usual of offering to do any jobs and run errands whilst Caitlyn was at work. This was Cara's way of contributing to the household, making her feel both wanted and useful—two things she had never felt much of in her life.

"If you could fetch some bits of shopping, Cara, that would be awesome. Some bread, milk, bananas and a few of those cheap pizzas, please. I'll leave a tenner for you."

"No bother at all." Cara smiled.

Cara pottered around the flat, cleaning. She had always liked cleaning. When she'd lived with Kate, she'd done most of the housework, finding it therapeutic. It was one of the only healthy coping mechanisms she had. Cara knew when she eventually had her own house, it would be spotless. She dreamed of that day, matching bath and hand towel, fluffy cushions on her sofa, a hallway rug. Clean, welcoming and always smelling of candles.

At 9:30 a.m., she headed to the shops. It was a short, enjoyable walk to the town centre. Cara passed a bus stop full of pensioners who smiled at her. She smiled back. She knew what it was like to feel lonely and the power of a kind "hello" or a genuine smile.

Taking her phone out of her pocket, she checked social media—same rubbish and people self-promoting. She checked her emails. She had two from some of the job applications she had made last week. Rejection emails probably. She tapped into the first one, Premier Pizza offering her an interview next week.

"Get in," she shouted, a grin spreading across her face.

The second was from a finance company in town: Hendersons. Another invite for an interview.

"Oh my God." Cara looked at her phone again, double checking as she did a little victory dance on the spot. This job was one she really fancied but didn't have loads of experience in. It was for a receptionist assistant/post room assistant.

Cara could feel herself getting emotional as she approached the shops. Even this, a simple interview, an acknowledgement that she just may be good enough, was a huge deal to her. She just wished she had more people in her life to share the exciting news with.

# 35

# *Peace Meal*

## Derek

Derek's stomach had been full of knots since waking up, in anticipation of Brenda's visit that evening. He wondered what Brenda would say. Would she want to come home? Sell the house? Divorce? Try again? Bloody hell, he was winding himself right up.

He turned the radio in the car on as an attempted distraction. He couldn't avoid Brenda forever; sitting down and talking was inevitable. There had been ample time for them both to consider their future and think about what they wanted. It just felt so hard. A full lifetime of each other. They'd been each other's comfy slippers, good and bad habits, companions, lovers and best friends for many years. Of course, there were factors making him want her back, but it was little to do with the Brenda he'd had to tolerate towards the end of their marriage. The Brenda he'd fallen in love with was long gone, eroded over time like the banks of a river. He no longer wanted to hide behind desire, keep secrets and feel wrong. It wasn't fair on either of them to inflict misery on each other. It was just hard. Breaking a habit was hard. Being lonely was hard. The unknown was hard. And it was exceptionally hard taking those comfy slippers off and putting them in the bin.

Derek arrived home from work, Des the time-telling dog waiting for him.

"A quick walk tonight, Son, before Mam comes over. Not sure if you've missed her, mind."

They walked around the block, Derek thinking again of his future. He certainly didn't want to fall out with Brenda permanently. He wanted them to be civil for mutual friends, for their history. It wasn't as if another woman had been involved. *Actually...* Derek thought, laughing to himself. Seriously though, things could have ended with more hostility.

He hoped tonight would be amicable, but if there was any name-calling from Brenda, any fat references, pervert references or anything he now realised was bullying, he would ask her to leave or he would leave if needed. It was still her house—something else they needed to sort out.

Once the pair were back in the house, Derek started cooking for Brenda and himself. He'd decided on spaghetti Bolognese made with vegetarian mince. He had perfected it over the last couple of months. It was healthy, tasty and quick to make. Brenda had never made it before, so he felt confident in showing off his skills.

Derek flitted from feeling like Gordon Ramsey to Frank Spencer. He was halfway through, getting into the swing of it, even singing as he browned the onions and mushrooms and made his tomato-based sauce, when the doorbell went.

*Bollocks. Here goes*, he thought, turning down the hob and rushing to the front door. Luckily, he had none of those first date nerves and therefore no need to check what he looked like before he answered the door. However, after a day of his guts churning, he did feel he may have to dash to the toilet with explosive diarrhoea at any given moment. He opened the door, and there she was, standing there. The woman who he'd shared three decades of his life with, the woman who in more ways than imaginable felt like a complete stranger. It could have been anyone at the door in that instant. Then, she opened her mouth. One word and it came flooding back.

"Derek," she almost tutted, making her way into the hallway.

"Hi, Brenda."

Brenda passed Derek her coat.

"Dinner is almost done. Come on through."

"I will, given it's my house." She smirked.

*Don't bite*, he thought, following her into the lounge, fingernails digging into his palms.

"Drink? I have some merlot. Or a soft drink?"

"Merlot would be nice, thanks." She softened slightly, indicating she was impressed with him making an effort.

"Smells nice, Derek, what you making?"

"Spaghetti Bolognese. Should only be five minutes or so. I'll just get you some wine."

Des came strolling in, looked at Brenda and walked over to her. It looked almost forced, as if he were dragging his feet along in obligation rather than desire.

"Des, my baby, look at you. Come here, Son. Think he's missed me, Derek," she said, looking at Des, who was now looking the other way but exploiting the hand that stroked him. "But have you, Derek? That's the question."

"Must check the food. Two mins, Brenda." Derek scurried away like a child out of the school gates at home time.

Bugger, why was she asking that? Bloody hell, what did she want him to say? He could never win when they lived together; he had no chance of saying the right thing now. Avoidance—that would be his strategy.

"Do you need any help, Derek?" Brenda shouted from the next room.

He wanted as much space as he could get; a chance to gather his thoughts. "No. No ta, Bren. Just get to the dining table, it will only be a sec."

Brenda was taking a seat just as Derek came in with a bowl of salad and crusty bread. He returned a minute later with some more wine and a jug of water.

"Lovely, you've clearly put some thought into this, Derek."

Ah no, did that make her think he was trying to romance her? Derek felt his stomach churn again. *Bloody hell, not the runs as I'm trying to serve dinner*, he pleaded. What a time to have gut rot. He opened the window and took some of the night air in, breathing deeply. Des strolled in, on the hunt for any food that might come his way. *He's worse than the bloody seagulls and probably not much bigger than the ones around here*, thought Derek.

Derek served the food. Plenty of Bolognese and some oregano, a little sprinkle of chilli flakes and some fresh parsley on the top. He had to admit it looked the biz to him, and he knew it would taste delicious. One of the tips from Tasmin at work had been to crumble half a veggie stock cube in the mix. Derek had experimented last time, and his mouth had been like a party. As a man brought up and married into meat and two veg principles, he was rapidly embracing the expansion of his taste buds, creativity and alternatives. The veggie mince being a firm favourite.

"There you go, Bren, I hope you enjoy." He placed her plate down. He couldn't help but notice the smile on her face.

"Where have you been hiding all these years, Derek? This looks fantastic."

"Bon appétit," he said, tucking in. This would either settle his guts or he would be darting up those stairs in the next five minutes.

"So, how have you been the last few months, Derek?"

*Well, Brenda, it's been a shitting delight being away from your twisting, suppressive, critical, quite frankly vicious face, mouth and mind. I have felt a new lease of life. I have learnt to cook, can quite adequately look after myself and Des. I have made some possible new friends through a creative initiative I had. I've bought some women's clothes, experimented with make-up and let Debbie out from where she'd been locked away for years and years. I've lost weight and gained sanity. And I might be lonely but I only miss the part of you who died many moons ago.*

Of course, he didn't say this. Instead, he said:

"Yeah, I've been ok. It's been strange, but I think we've both managed, haven't we? I know we have to make some decisions, and I just want it to be amicable, Brenda."

"Well, you've clearly learnt how to cook, Derek. I'm impressed." Brenda laughed.

"Vegetarian mince as well," he said, pointing to her plate.

"Well I never. Very healthy. Are you dieting?"

"No, not as such, just trying new things."

"Sounds as if you're coping fine without me." There was a sulkiness to her voice. Derek felt a pang of guilt, then tried to remember her cruelty.

"It hasn't been easy at times, Bren, but we weren't happy. You know that."

"Of course I know, Derek; it was me who left, after all."

*She has to try and make out she's in control*, he thought. Maybe she was, had been—he didn't really care. All Derek wanted was to continue to be happy and to maybe salvage something, even if it was just remaining civil.

"I don't regret our marriage, Derek. I just think we maybe want different things. But it doesn't make it easier for me. I felt as though I was never enough for you. You always seemed to be searching for more. It was exhausting. And this whole cross-dressing thing was becoming too much to bear."

Derek looked down at his plate. It was pointless going over old ground again. How many times over the years had they had this heated discussion? He'd told her over and over it didn't make him not love or not find her attractive, even though over the last few years, her personality had become the ultimate repellent of any sexual urges he'd ever had for her. He just wanted to wear women's clothes now and then.

The times she had caught him when she'd come home early, she had been disgusted, and Derek had felt like a naughty schoolboy.

"You look like a hippo in a leotard."

"Dame Edna looks more feminine than you."

"You look like a fat old man in drag."

Derek could feel himself getting irate. He sipped his wine. "Well, you must be happier without me then, Brenda. You look well, and you've been on holiday. You seem to be doing ok yourself." Derek spoke slowly, trying hard to remain calm and in control.

"Yes, yes, I am, Derek. I did always love you, you know, I just didn't like you at times."

*Friggin' touché*, he thought.

"I think we both thought that at times, Bren," he said diplomatically.

"We are still young enough to have another life, maybe meet someone else. We shouldn't stay together because of our history. Even if we do miss each other now and then."

"You're right, we can't stay together out of fear of loneliness." Derek thought he would entertain her shitshow of emotions and need to feel she had the upper hand.

"So, you don't want me back, then?" She looked up, expectant. Christ, she didn't want him but of course he had to still want her. Brenda had rejected Derek, the real Derek, for so long, but she still wanted him to need her.

"I think we're better off as friends, Bren, we've grown apart. I don't want you out of my life altogether." It was only partly a lie. He'd wanted to stay amicable.

Brenda drank the remainder of her wine. "I feel the same. Maybe we both need to think about what to do going forward: practicalities, finances and stuff." Her voice began to sound more assertive; the earlier softness had been swallowed along with the wine. "Linda is happy for me to stay there, she likes the company, but I can't be there forever. We should both have a think and then discuss again." Brenda looked away from Derek as silence began to fill the room.

"Erm, yeah, sounds like a good idea, Bren." Derek didn't really know what else to say. The conversation had quickly turned very procedural on the demise of the last three decades of being "Derek and Brenda". It felt a little surreal. Certainly not a bad thing, but surreal all the same.

Ten minutes later, Brenda was out the door. Dinner eaten, no pudding wanted, a goodbye to Des, a "goodnight" to Derek at the front door and then she was gone.

Derek returned to the lounge, sat and cried. Tears of sadness or tears of elation, he wasn't quite sure. But he sat and cried.

# 36

# *Monday Morning Memories*

## Violet

Violet had woken early, feeling energised. It was her day off, and she had plans. Yesterday, she had received the group email from Derek with The Dinner Club expectations. She was thrilled it was becoming a reality. Meeting the group on Saturday had been a big step for her, and she had really warmed to Derek, Florence and Eddie. The group felt pleasant, comfortable, natural.

Violet had refrained from telling Ben. He liked to pop everyone's balloon. She already knew he would tell her it was a waste of time or make a nasty comment about her cooking. He wouldn't be able to help himself. It would be impossible for him not to twist it and sour in his usual spiteful manner. She would keep it secret as long as possible. It was something for her and her alone.

Derek had asked the group via email to confirm they were happy meeting once a fortnight in the first instance, suggesting a Thursday but enquiring what days of the week were best for them. Violet was keen on it being a Tuesday or Thursday, when Ben was at the local darts club. Thinking of excuses when he was at home would be dangerous.

Violet admired Derek's organisational skills. It was a quality she prided herself on trying to demonstrate. Years ago, Violet used to work in home care, travelling around, supporting those in need. She always remembered a wonderful, older ex-navy veteran she used to help. His name was John. He was a cantankerous old sod at times, but he got used to Violet, and she became very fond of him. He used to look forward to her almost daily visits.

"You know what I like about you, Vi? You plan well and always do what you say you're going to do."

John had been right—she had. She liked to think she was honest, transparent and had integrity.

Ben had changed all that, turning her deceitful and closed as well as dissolving her ambition. She'd been studying health and social care at college when they'd met. Although she'd had no idea at the time, Ben had sabotaged her dream. He had changed her over the years into someone she didn't recognise. Someone who, at times, she strongly disliked.

In the early days when Ben changed, it started with name-calling now and then. He would call her "ugly", "a slag", "thick". He would tell her she wasn't clever enough for college and that he needed her looking after their home and caring for him with how hard he worked. That they needed each other.

How would she cope without his income? She would never pass her exams due to how "thick" she was. Plus, why would she want to work in a hard discipline when he earned so much? He would make sure she had money. She could stay at home, look after the house for them both and raise their children.

None of that happened.

She knew he was a bully. She knew she was a doormat. Some days, she knew she deserved more, better, equal love. Some days, she felt everything was her fault. Ben told her she was useless; couldn't even produce any children for him. She had rotten eggs inside her. She was not fit to be a mother.

"Who else would want you?" he would scream in her face. He was right. Who else would want her?

The abuse worsened as Ben became more and more frustrated with the fact they couldn't seem to conceive.

She remembered the first time he'd physically hurt her. It was a Thursday night, and he had been at the local, coming in late. Violet had left his dinner to warm up. He had shouted her downstairs even though she had work at 8 a.m. the next day. She had got up without a fuss—she'd never won an argument with him sober and would certainly never win one when he was drunk. She heated up his food as he talked about his night with the darts team.

"What the fuck is wrong with your miserable face, Vi?"

"Nothing, I'm just tired." She was calm, trying to defuse any tension. She smiled and served his dinner, sitting opposite him.

"You are one miserable bitch, Vi. I don't know why I put up with it. The other lads tonight were talking about their lasses, saying they are spot on, good mams and all that. Then, there's you. Miserable, disgusting, a pathetic excuse for a woman. You've let yourself go, and you can't even give me a son or daughter. Useless.

Violet felt as if a knife had been plunged into her heart. Ben knew how to hurt her the most with words. She instinctively moved her hand to her chest as she began trembling.

"And your food tastes like shite."

He threw the food across the room. Violet ducked slightly, trying to make herself disappear. If only she could. She looked to the corner of the room, away from Ben's eyeline, and let out the breath she had been holding for what felt like forever.

Ben got up from his seat, pushing it back so it crashed to the floor, and stormed over to where Violet sat, frozen in her seat. He grabbed her face, his eyes almost bulging with rage and his mouth sneering.

"Don't dare look away from me, you ugly bitch."

He grabbed her cheeks hard until she let out a whimper. She could feel his hardened fingertips and raggy fingernails in the flesh of her face.

"Get out of my fucking sight," he bellowed in her face as spit flew from his mouth.

There was never an apology for that or subsequent incidents. Violet hated herself as a woman for thinking it but she thanked God that she was unable to have children with Ben. Would Ben have abused their child also? Probably, given he was a bully. Violet struggled to look after herself most days, how could she have looked after a child in a household with Ben. What had happened to her, to Ben, that Violet even thought that way? She wasn't living, she was existing in an endless cycle of torment. Her only escape in her toxic life was Foodways. Bloody Foodways, her sanctuary. It felt like a joke. A cruel and sick joke at that.

Suddenly, Violet didn't feel so energised. Her reality was that she thought some stupid meal with three new people would change her life. Ben was right, she was stupid. In that moment, at 6:15 a.m. on a Monday morning, as she sat at the kitchen table with a cuppa, Violet hated herself more than she or anyone else ever could.

# 37

# *Winning Wardrobe?*

## Cara

Cara sifted through her miniscule wardrobe, trying to find something to wear for her interview that Wednesday morning. She had so few belongings. Most of the things she had were of sentimental value and stayed in her backpack. Over her short life, she had never really completely settled anywhere since being taken from Kate.

Looking into her pathetic wardrobe, she reflected on never feeling secure or truly accepted anywhere. Living like a stray dog that no one really wanted. Never feeling part of anything, never feeling understood, never feeling cared about for long. She sat on the floor and cried. There was no one to comfort her; there never was. But there was fire in her belly. A determination to change her life.

Jeans, a black T-shirt, a red T-shirt, a checked shirt, a grey jumper, a black hoody, some leggings, three vest tops, a black blouse, the joggers and vest she was wearing now, a pair of trainers and some flat Chelsea boots—that was the sum of her entire wardrobe. Could she wear jeans for an interview? She tried them on with the blouse and boots. She looked neither trendy nor smart. She screamed with frustration. She had given Caitlyn fifteen pounds yesterday and had twenty left until Friday. She would get some bread and milk later in the week, so she needed five pounds for that and about eight pounds for travel to her interviews that week. That left around seven pounds spare. She would go to the charity shops in town to see if there were any smart trousers and perhaps a colourful top.

Pleased with her plan, Cara headed to town. She walked into the first charity shop and started rummaging. At a size eight and five foot one, it wasn't always easy to find adult clothes, but she had the bonus of fitting into some children's items. Cara smiled at the elderly woman behind the counter. The elderly woman smiled back.

Cara was desperate to make a good impression. It was a massive deal, both of the interviews were important to her, but the one tomorrow at Hendersons was a real opportunity for her.

Sifting through the clothes, she found a nice black blouse with polka dots on in her size. She took it off the rack, moving to the next.

"How are you getting on, dear?" another older woman asked warmly as she approached Cara.

"I have a job interview tomorrow, so want to look smart." Cara beamed at the woman like a child would to a parent, displaying their latest artwork from school.

The woman nodded. "Well done. It's important to make the right impression. Shall I help you look?"

Cara was delighted; a second pair of eyes would be perfect. "Yes, please, that would be great."

She resumed her search, the shop assistant now at her side, chatting away.

"These are nice, dear."

Cara looked over as the shop assistant held up some black trousers. "Yes, they look ideal."

"They certainly do. Let's put these to one side for you to try on."

Ten minutes later, the pair had an armful of items ready for Cara to try. Three pairs of trousers, a skirt and four tops. Cara was excited but had to remember her budget.

She tried them on as the shop assistant tidied the rails, waiting to see if an opinion was needed.

Cara opened the curtain. She had black trousers and a floral, sheer blouse on.

"You look so pretty and very professional," said the shop assistant.

"Thanks, I like it too."

The next outfit wasn't a hit. Cara looked like a frumpy middle-aged woman in the skirt, and the spotty blouse highlighted her lack of shape and bust.

The next outfit was some checked trousers and a black jumper.

"Very smart, dear, you suit that."

Cara tried the last pair of trousers on and the last top. Both a little ill-fitting.

It was narrowed to two outfits: the black trousers and floral shirt, and the checked trousers and black jumper. Cara decided to go with the first outfit. It only cost her six pounds eighty.

"I'll tell you what, dear, let us throw in the jumper for your seven pounds, and *when* you get the job, you can come back and give us a few quid donation, eh?"

Cara's face lit up. Someone believed in her. Someone she had met less than twenty minutes ago truly believed in her.

"Thank you so much, that's amazing, thank you."

"You're welcome, dear," the shop assistant said as she bagged up Cara's outfit. "Good luck with that interview. Knock 'em dead."

Cara left the shop, cradling her new clothes.

# 38

# *Interview Panel*

## Eddie

It was Wednesday morning, and Eddie was irritated that he had interviews for most of the day. God, at times, he couldn't stand people. More and more, he was noticing the bad qualities duplicated in folk; qualities he strongly disliked. Incompetency, sloppiness, those always after self-promotion, stupidity, falseness and greed. He feared he would come across many of these and more in this day of tedious interviewing. How hard was it in life to come across genuine, nice, kind humans? People who made mistakes and apologised, people who did what they said they'd do. He bloody hated interviewing.

His mood wasn't helped by a creeping feeling of guilt he'd developed over the last few days. He was struggling and wasn't sure what had triggered it, but little Willow was getting the brunt of it. He just couldn't be bothered with her and had been shouting at her for silly reasons. Last night, he had made her cry, again, and she'd asked why he didn't love her. Hearing this from his baby had felt like his heart had been pulled out and stamped on. He had embraced her ferociously, despising himself and apologising over and over in his head to Issy. She would have been so disappointed.

He'd arranged for Willow to stay overnight with her momar and grandpa last night, after as much apologising and soothing as he could manage. He'd left her happily getting chased by Grandpa round the dining table, shrieking and giggling as he pretended to be a shark.

"I just need a break, Mam. There's lots going on at work. I'm tired."

Eddie wouldn't dare tell his mother that his mind was dissolving in acid. That his heart was about to stop beating through the pain of his grief. That on more days than not it felt suffocating. That his depression and loneliness was like climbing Everest with a toothpick. That some days he wished he could run away from it all, from everyone, even from Willow. That trying to ask for help left him voiceless. That he never felt he would ever get better. No, he couldn't dare tell his mother.

"No bother, Son, you know we love having her. Just look after yourself, love."

Eddie had driven back home, drank a third of a bottle of whiskey and sobbed until 2 a.m.

And now he had to entertain a load of morons all day, with phoney answers and overpowering perfume. Repeating himself over and over and listening to the same monotonous crap four times from four carbon copies, lying and desperate to impress.

Eddie, Danielle from reception and Martha from HR were interviewing. The role was for an assistant receptionist/mail room assistant. A dogsbody role in reality, but Danielle needed help, and it would increase productivity.

They had short-listed four candidates. The first one was due at 10 a.m. That was enough time for Eddie to have a coffee and check his emails.

9:40 a.m. arrived, and Danielle knocked on Eddie's office door, opening it without waiting for a response.

"Ready?"

"Danielle, it's nine-forty. We don't need to go and sit in a small room for twenty full minutes for no reason. I will see you in there in ten minutes minimum," he snapped.

Danielle rolled her eyes, turned and walked away without uttering a word. Eddie heard her angry heels as she strutted off.

At 9:52 a.m., Eddie walked into the interview office. Danielle had Lindsey from HR covering reception. He clocked the first candidate waiting in the seating area, a glass of water in hand.

"So, we have Pamela Blackhall first. Worked in admin for years, so quite experienced. Maybe wanting to wind down to retirement. I will nip to the loo, then get her on the way back," said Martha

"Thanks, Martha," replied Eddie.

"I hope we find someone decent. I need someone who will take instruction, is a quick learner, personable and will get on with the job," said Danielle. She had obviously forgiven him for his prickly response earlier.

"Agreed. Sounds like the perfect colleague. Fingers crossed, eh." Eddie faked a smile.

Martha returned with Pamela, and introductions started.

"We'll take it in turns to ask questions, Pamela, then there'll be a chance for you to ask questions at the end," said Martha.

Danielle started. "What do you think the role entails?"

"Well, it's helping with the running of the business. It's the front of house, dealing with the public, keeping the ship sailing. It's nothing I haven't done before. I've had many years of working in admin, up to management."

"What skills and characteristics do you have that would make you suitable for this role?" asked Martha.

"My experience is vast," Pamela began. "I could probably do this job with my eyes shut. As I said, I have many years in this field. Over thirty years. I have had to change with the times and systems; I have seen many new developments over the years. New ways of working and technology. Some good, some bad. I've helped ensure the smooth running of the core of services. Without correct admin, services fail. I'm organised, methodical..."

Eddie started to switch off. He found Pamela a little abrupt for his liking. Spikey, as Issy would have said.

Danielle asked a question about admin priorities and duties, Martha asked about teamwork and then it was Eddie's turn to ask the last question.

"Pamela, give us an example of something in your life you have had to overcome. What was it, and how did you manage it?"

"I will keep it professional and give a work example. My recent job was temping for Office Solutions. My role before that, I'd been in for seven years. They then employed a new CEO. He had ideas—ideas above his station, in my opinion. A young executive thinking he knew everything."

*Uh-oh*, thought Eddie, *here we go*.

"Well, he actually had a lot to learn but wouldn't listen to any of the staff who had been there the longest and knew the business."

*Meaning you*.

"He wanted to implement new-fangled policies, meditation at work, standing desks and other daft things. He made my working day very challenging, and I became unhappy. By the end, it felt personal, so I raised a grievance. It became a stressful few months, and I ended up leaving. I didn't want to pursue it any more. Although it meant I didn't have a job, I didn't sacrifice my integrity or backdown from my viewpoint about processes, so I see that as a positive."

*Bloody hell*, thought Eddie, *sounds like she could be a right workie ticket.*

"Thanks for sharing that, Pamela. That's us done. Do you have any questions for us?" asked Martha.

Pamela then proceeded to ask questions around process, length of time other staff members had been there, annual leave entitlement and progressions. Once she was done, Danielle saw her out.

"Jesus, I'm knackered already," Danielle said, chuckling as she came back in.

"That was intense," added Martha.

"Very. Not sure you could manage her, mind, Danielle. She was like The Baroness off *The Chase*."

They all laughed.

"Clearly very experienced but would never take instruction from me, and there's definitely more than meets the eye with the job before last. Bet they were trying to get rid of her."

"I don't think the customers would warm to her, Danielle. She seemed abrupt and quite frankly a little scary," Eddie commented.

The next candidate came and went, with little enthusiasm from the panel. Then, it was a break for lunch. After lunch, the next candidate seemed promising but very nervous.

"Maybe it was just interview nerves," stressed Danielle.

"Perhaps. Well, we have one left, Cara Whittle, so let's leave it open, and we can reflect after this."

Martha went to get Cara as Eddie stretched his arms, relieved it was almost over.

# 39

# *Filters and Fantasies*

## Cara

Cara tried her outfit on for the twelfth time, just to make sure. She stood, looking at her reflection in the full-length mirror in Caitlyn's room. The outcome of today could mean a complete change of direction in her life. Would she employ herself? She wasn't sure. Her mind swung from confidence to the worthless messages that haunted her brain.

*It will just be an act. Thirty minutes or so of acting like I'm the most confident person ever, playing my best in the hope of getting the leading role*. She had to give it her all, she just had to.

She put her pyjamas back on. She would have something to eat, jump in the shower and aim to get to Hendersons half an hour before her scheduled interview.

Opening the fridge, she picked out a yoghurt and peeled off the lid, daydreaming about having a job, a career. Playing a part in society and working as part of a team. Feeling useful, achieving something and helping others. She could have what she'd always wanted: a little house of her own, to learn to drive, feel happy enough in herself to have a relationship and make new friends. Things she promised herself she would never, ever take for granted.

She ate her yoghurt in silence, thinking of answers to possible interview questions. Caitlyn had spent some time helping her prepare. "Just be yourself, Cara," she had said.

She would go in, act confident and hopefully say the right things, whilst trying to be true to herself. She had life experience and skills, she just had to make sure they knew that by the end of the interview.

Less than an hour later, Cara was on the bus, travelling to Hendersons. It was on the other side of town, and as the bus followed its route, Cara fantasised about how she would spend her first wage. She would get some new clothes, maybe some from town but also the charity shops. She would buy some nice toiletries instead of always scrounging Caitlyn's or using cheap soap that never seemed to lather properly. She would get some new make-up and get her hair cut. Cara wasn't the girliest of girls but she yearned to feel she looked nice and not scruffy. She would fill the fridge for Caitlyn as a thank you and take her out for a posh cuppa somewhere.

*Crap, you've done it again, putting the pressure on. What if they think you're useless?* She let a sigh out.

Five minutes later, she was at her stop. Cara could feel the nerves starting as she thanked the driver and stepped off the bus. Her legs were a little less stable, her heart beating a little quicker, her temperature rising ever so slightly.

*Deep breaths*. She had arrived early specially to calm herself. One of the counsellors she had seen as a teenager had talked about tapping therapy and pressure points in the body. Cara had always remembered this. She wasn't sure if it was bollocks or not, but she often used it in times where her nerves overwhelmed her and she feared she would crumble, wanting to shout "piss off" or run away. She had never conquered her distress tolerance or regulated her emotions effectively.

Sitting on a bench close to the Hendersons building, she used her learnt method to calm herself. With twenty minutes to spare before her interview, she walked in and took the lift up to the office reception. She was greeted by a friendly face as she exited the lift.

"Hi, I'm here for the interview," she said, approaching the desk.

"Hi, welcome. You must be Cara Whittle?"

"Yes, that's me."

"Great, take a seat, Cara. Someone from the panel will be out to collect you soon."

Five minutes later, a woman came through some double doors and headed towards the lift. Cara couldn't tell if she was an interview candidate or just worked there. Cara massaged between her thumb and forefinger, humming a tune in her head. With her breathing more regulated, she opened her eyes just as a lady came smiling towards her.

"Cara?"

"Yes, that's me," Cara said as she rose from her seat slowly, conscious that her legs felt like jelly.

"Lovely. I'm Martha. Pleased to meet you. Do come with me."

Cara followed obediently.

Martha led her to a small office, where two other people sat at one side of a row of tables, an empty seat on the other. The tables dominated the room, making Cara feel immediately intimidated. A kind voice broke through the creeping feeling of overwhelm.

"Please, take a seat, Cara. We'll do some introductions and then ask you some questions. There will be time for you to ask any questions of your own at the end."

"Thank you," Cara replied nervously. Sitting down, she started regulating her breathing again and took a sip from the glass of water placed in front of her. She could do this; she knew she could.

"So, I'm Martha, HR manager; this is Danielle, our receptionist; and Eddie, our finance director." Cara looked at all three as they were introduced, trying to absorb their names and roles. Martha was middle aged and had a schoolteacher look about her, but Cara felt a warmth from her. The receptionist had smiled momentarily before looking back to her paperwork. She didn't look much older than Cara. The guy, Eddie, was all suited and booted and looked very serious. The vibes were definitely different to those she'd experienced at the restaurant she had worked at.

"Hi, nice to meet you all," Cara said quickly.

"Let's crack on. What do you think the job role entails?" asked Danielle.

Cara took a deep breath. She knew her voice would start out shaky but hoped her nerves would settle as she got into it. "Well, I think it sounds like a really exciting role, and I imagine no two days are the same. I assume it would be helping at reception, taking instruction from yourself or other colleagues to complete duties, answering queries and providing help to visitors as well as anyone in the company." Cara observed the panel scribbling away, making notes. "I think the mail room side of it would be making sure mail is organised and distributed quickly and keeping the place tidy. Generally, helping out where needed."

"Thanks, Cara. What skills and characteristics do you have that would make you suitable for this role?" asked Martha.

"I'll be honest, I haven't done much in the form of similar jobs, as such. However, I have experience in working with people, customer service, defusing difficult situations, being organised and multitasking. I'm a good communicator, and I like the satisfaction of helping people." Cara looked at the panel, trying to gauge their interest. "I have no problem taking instruction and will always go above and beyond. This role really appealed to me, as I think I could learn so much. I see this as a career development opportunity." Cara paused, wondering if her admittance to lack of experience in similar jobs had already blown her chances. But she wanted this. And she was ready to put herself out there to get it.

"I haven't been given many opportunities in life, and I have had to be independent and strong." She looked across at the three strangers. Martha and Danielle were making notes on their paperwork, Eddie was looking at Cara. He still looked serious and business-like to her but there was something else, as if he was really listening to what she was saying. "That's where my determination comes from. What I really want in the workplace is to feel part of something, help others and know they will help me also. I want to have positive role models around me, and I want to be a role model for others. I'm a hard worker, I just want a chance." Cara looked at Martha, who smiled kindly.

After what felt like an eternity, Eddie asked the last question. "Cara, give us an example of something in your life you have had to overcome. What was it, and how did you manage it?"

Cara held in a sarcastic laugh, realising it wasn't appropriate. She wasn't on *The Jeremy Kyle Show*, although her story would most definitely fit in there. God, how much should she filter? She didn't want them thinking she was unstable or for them to feel sorry for her. Pity was offensive. She took a sip of water, needing a second to gather her thoughts. She heard Caitlyn's voice in her head: "Be yourself, Cara." Stuff it. If she was the right person, she was the right person.

"I have actually had to overcome a lot of barriers in my life. I was put into care when I was eight years old and spent eight years in foster placements. Some were great and I thrived, others not so great and I struggled. It made me grow up quicker than I probably should have had to. It made me recognise what I value and think is important in people. We aren't all lucky enough to have both parents, sometimes even one parent. But it's the quality of love we give, not quantity. I will always remember the people who showed me love and kindness, who cared for me as a child and who have supported and appreciated me as an adult. Those people have given me the strength to overcome barriers. I don't give up, and I try to always believe and to hope."

The room went silent for a few seconds, and Cara's heart sank. No one could seem to make eye contact with her. Had she said too much? Went too deep? These people probably thought she was some crazy, drug-fuelled problem.

Then, Eddie croakily spoke, "Thanks, Cara, for being so refreshingly honest. It takes a lot to share such personal experiences. For what it's worth, you definitely come across as a strong, young woman who should be proud of herself." His serious face softened for the first time since she had entered the room.

Cara thought she may start to cry. This man she had never met before saying such a nice thing. *Deep breath, deep breath*.

"Thank you," was all she could muster.

"Ok, thanks, Cara. That's our questions asked. Anything you want to ask?" said Danielle.

Thankfully, given the emotional charge in the room leaving her brain unable to think properly, Cara had written some questions down. She got out her notepad and cleared her throat.

Once the questions were done being asked and answered, Eddie got up to see her out.

"What you said was really powerful. Thanks again for sharing, and I hope you didn't feel put on the spot," he said, looking at Cara as he saw her into the lift. She sensed kindness in his voice as his business-like body language she had seen most of the interview relaxed.

*Maybe he was in care himself,* Cara thought as she headed down in the lift.

All Cara could think about in that moment was that she desperately wanted that job, that opportunity, that recognition of her potential skills. She willed with all the power she had that they thought she was good enough.

# 40

# *Reflections*

## Eddie

Eddie spent the rest of the day thinking about what Cara had said. The bit about some people not having any parents and love being quality, not quantity. A twenty-year-old saying something he should have realised a long time ago. Despite the death of her mam, Willow still had Eddie and his love, and Eddie kept Issy's heart in his, so part of his love for Willow came from her.

His grieving, his depression, his lack of interest was punishing Willow. It was stopping love conquering all. It was stopping Issy shining through. He was perpetuating his heartache by letting it affect him and Willow.

Eddie's friend Paul had once mentioned the analogy of grief and an injury. That we may fall and break a bone or gain an injury through a sport, and it may always be there—the scar, the twinges, limps—but we keep going and going. We still play football or dance. Our injury adds to our performance and determination.

Grief is like this: our heart may never heal, it will always be scarred, but the person lives on in that scar, and we continue to experience life, even with our wound. We never forget, we never fully recover, but we heal as much as we can and carry our scars. And our scars make us who we are.

It was just all so much easier said than done.

The panel had all agreed Cara was the right person for the role. She was honest, friendly, not pretentious and, most importantly to Danielle, she would take direction. She seemed like a nice fit for Hendersons. Eddie was drawn to her wise young mind, and he thought he could learn a lot from this resilient young woman. Of course, he didn't admit that to the panel.

Tomorrow was the first dinner club. Eddie had mixed emotions about it. Although confident in character, this was something new, something different, with not yet familiar people. Change made him nervous. Pre-empting what they may ask him made him nervous. Rehearsing what he would say made him nervous. But within this, there was a flicker of hope, a flame of adventure, positivity, recovery.

The first session would be at Derek's house. It made sense, as it was Derek's idea, after all. Eddie liked what he'd seen so far of Derek from their initial meeting.

Eddie wondered what may be on the menu. Derek had sent out a group email at the start of the week asking if anyone had dietary requirements, allergies etc. He hadn't asked if there was anything people didn't like. Eddie thought this was a good thing. Connie always said she didn't like cheese because she'd had it once when she was four years old or something. Bearing in mind that his mother was now sixty-four and had refused to give cheese, any type, another chance in around sixty years. Eddie would try anything, even things he wasn't keen on. It would be part of the experience. His tummy rumbled at the thought.

# 41

# *Dinner Club Premier*

## Derek

It was Wednesday night, and Derek felt discombobulated and tired. The first dinner club was tomorrow night, at his house. The pressure was on. He now wished he had taken tomorrow off work as he had dithered all day between ideas for the final menu. Sitting earlier that day, drinking his morning coffee and eating his toast with a generous lashing of lemon curd, he had pondered on how being part of a couple for so long affected people's decision-making skills. Had he relied on Brenda for so long that making assertive, concise decisions was perhaps harder than he'd anticipated? He had no one to bounce the everyday queries and ideas off—the blue trousers or the black ones? White or red wine? Italian food or Indian food?

The menu clarification wasn't the only thing preying on Derek's mind. He needed to be Debbie tomorrow night. It was symbolic, and it had to happen on the first dinner club or he feared it never would. But it could destroy everything: the happiness, the confidence, the purpose he had felt these last four weeks. He had only met these three people once. A few extra communication encounters via email. They could all be mass bigots. They could laugh at him. They could be appalled and disgusted. And he could be judged. Again.

Derek stared at the fireplace from his favourite seat, Des at his feet as he made a list of what he needed to do before his guests arrived tomorrow night. Terror was pulsing through him, leaving him clammy and dizzy.

"Deep breaths, you dafty."

He had sent an email to Florence, Violet and Eddie earlier in the week, checking they had no dietary requirements or allergies. He had chuckled to himself, betting that one would come back vegan, one would be allergic to nuts and one would be gluten and lactose intolerant. All came back saying they had no dietary requirements, although Florence had stressed, "Too much pastry plays havoc with my indigestion."

Derek had settled on his menu and had ensured all the ingredients were purchased by Tuesday night. At chez Derek's, or should that be chez Debbie's, the menu for Thursday evening's dinner club was:

***Starter***

*Mediterranean Vegetable Stack and Homemade Ciabatta*

***Main Course***

*Hunter's Chicken, Sweet Potato Fries and Asparagus*

***Dessert***

*Homemade Chocolate and Raspberry Brownies*

Derek had to remember not everyone ate one more potato than a pig like he did, meaning he needed to be mindful on the night to not shovel ten tonnes of food onto everyone's plates. Brenda could put it away for a woman of average size, but he imagined Violet and Florence didn't quite have the appetite of a WWF wrestler.

He would, of course, make extra in case people wanted more, doggy bags and all that. He would take any leftovers to work the next day. He hated waste, especially in this day and age where there were families who couldn't afford to feed their children and people who went to bed hungry.

Maybe that could be a discussion point tomorrow night. Not to get too political. He did not want politics taking over his first dinner club but brief views were always interesting.

He was without doubt, however, that the number one thing his guests would want to talk about would be Debbie. The elephant in the room (hopefully not literally). He wasn't sure if anyone would actually ask questions, but he would bet his bottom dollar that they would most certainly want to ask. Well, the evening would entertain them, if nothing else.

# 42

# *Confession*

## Florence

Instead of feeling her days were a little unfulfilled and, of late, worried about her future, Florence was very much looking forward to the first dinner club tomorrow night. Derek, the person she'd warmed to the most, was hosting. Maybe he was the one she felt more at ease with because he had taken the lead, she wasn't sure, but there was a little twinkle in his eye which she found magnetic. He had a spirit, a spark, something about him. He was warm, cuddly and had a kind smile. Florence hoped he was also pretty nifty in the kitchen and that she would get a satisfying, flavoursome meal.

Florence's stomach rumbled at the thought of food. It was late afternoon, and she hadn't had any lunch, unable to stomach it. She had been to the doctors'. William had taken her but stayed in the waiting room, thankfully. She had lied to him and felt dreadful for it. Florence knew she would have to speak to William about her health, but she had to process it all in her own head first. William thought it was about her borderline diabetes, and Florence was happy to keep it at that.

Using her walker, she went into the kitchen. Florence could manage without her walker, sometimes with just sticks on good days, but her arthritis was flaring up at the moment and she felt a little weak. *Tipping Point* would be on in thirty minutes or so. She would have a ham sandwich, prepared by Jessie that morning, and then get ready for the show. She thought that Ben Shephard was just so lovely.

When Florence had spoken to Jessie about The Dinner Club earlier that day, Jessie had asked, "These people are ok though, aren't they, Florrie?"

*What is it with people these days? Society has us thinking everyone is either a pervert, robbing drug addict or a terrorist. To think that my mother, and even I, used to leave our front doors unlocked in the sixties and seventies. Everyone took the time to get to know each other back then. No sense of community spirit nowadays. Too many buggers out for themselves. And everyone thinking the worst in people, which often turns out to be true, sadly. Ernie would have hated it. Although he always said he would prefer a house full of animals over humans.*

"They seem fine, love. Very nice folk, and I felt comfortable with them."

"Well, that's good, Florrie. You must tell William when you are going to the first one though. Will you be ok going alone?" Jessie asked with concern as she handed Florence her cup of tea.

"Yes, love, I'm going to get a taxi. I did want to ask you though, Jessie, if I got an extra few hours organised through my payments, do you think you could help me with the preparation, cooking and serving on my night to entertain, please, love?"

Jessie smiled. "It would be my honour, Florrie; I can't think of anything better."

"You're a good girl, Jessie, I am lucky to have you," said Florence, looking the other way, her voice breaking with emotion.

"What's up, Florrie? Hey, what's wrong?"

Jessie rushed over to Florence, who was sat in her recliner chair. Florence was crying.

"Nothing, love. Nothing, honest. I'm just being silly," Florence said as she tapped Jessie's arm in a failing attempt to pretend she was ok.

"Florence Lawson, stop telling fibs. What's wrong? I'm not going until you tell me, so you better, else I will be late for Muriel, and it will be your fault," she joked.

Florence looked at Jessie as she knelt, holding her soft hands, with absolute care and compassion in her eyes. And she told her. She told her the truth in the bravest way she could.

# 43

# *Thursday Night Escape*

## Violet

The first dinner club was tomorrow evening. Violet found herself drifting into daydream mode whilst at work, between conveyor belt dumps of weekly shops and the odd colleague asking if she had any bags for life. She felt the excitement of looking forward to something—a feeling she hadn't experienced in a long time. It was a little bit of the unknown, a little bit of being able to be whoever she wanted to be for those few hours, a little escapism and enjoying a meal. Ben couldn't allow her to eat one single meal without ruining it with his poisonous tongue. Violet's relationship with food had soured as it had with Ben. She had lost passion for something she'd loved as a child and enjoyed with her mother. She wanted that desire back.

Violet, however, was already panicking about when she'd have to cook for the others. Luckily, The Dinner Club was on a Thursday, one of the nights Ben went to the local, so she knew she would almost always have the house to herself. But she couldn't risk it and decided she would ask Rosie if she could use her place when it was her turn to host. Any wind of The Dinner Club and she knew that Ben would sabotage it with satisfaction, like a lion capturing its prey. She shuddered.

As for her fortnightly trip to one of the other members' homes, it would be coordinated when Ben was out. She may get an intense level of interrogation if caught, but if he was out enjoying himself, as he was each Thursday, he didn't much care what she was up to.

She would say she was starting to go to Rosie's to learn how to cook. Given he accused her almost nightly of serving "dog shit off the pavement", "the neighbour's dead budgie" or "a plate of rats from the sewers", she clearly needed to learn how to cook properly.

She was quickly snapped out of her seething by a customer approaching the checkout.

"Alright?" he enquired, hopefully not seeing the snarl on her face from her thought process.

"Morning there, how are you? Need a hand packing?"

"No ta, I'm good thanks. It's bloody cold out there, mind. You're in the right place."

He smiled, and Violet smiled back. They continued small talk as she scanned his purchases. She enjoyed natters with the customers. Sometimes, although they never knew it, they helped her. A compliment; gratitude; a warm, soothing smile.

Violet's shift was soon over, and she drove home, thinking about what she could wear the following night to Derek's. Pulling up on the drive, she had narrowed it down to three possibilities. She didn't wear much make-up—just mascara for work, eyeshadow, bronzer and a bit of lip gloss—but she would make an effort and enjoy herself doing so.

Cuppa made, Violet went upstairs to try on her potential outfits. She had a few hours to herself before Ben got in. She would pick her clothes, put a wash on and hoover, then a quick shower before she started tea. Violet had a real knack for managing her time effectively. It reduced reasons for Ben to twist and become abusive, so she had learnt to multitask and ensure household chores were done before she relaxed.

Opening her wardrobe, she saw so many items that she never got a chance to wear due to never going out. Many items were almost ten years old.

She and Ben used to go out, but she'd gotten so sick and quite frankly frightened of his unpredictable behaviour when drunk that she'd started making regular excuses to stay in, encouraging him to go out with his friends. Then, when he'd joined the darts team, she hadn't had to make excuses anymore, as he hadn't wanted to go out with her. She wore some of her dresses when they went to couples' nights, which, thankfully, were only a few times a year. She would always offer to drive. He would, of course, criticise her driving but at least she remained sober for her protection. She was sharper and more alert when sober; alcohol made her vulnerable to abuse, defusing the situation and getting away if she needed to.

She saw the red lace dress, the one she had loved so much. She had bought it on a shopping trip with her mam. Her mother had always loved her in red, and Violet had felt like a film star. She'd worn it early last year on a night out with people from Ben's work. He had chipped away part of her forever that night, but worse, he had ruined her love for that magical dress. Ruined something that she had such cherished memories of with her mother, turning it into something disgusting and degrading. Violet put her hand on the dress and let out a sob.

"Oh, Mam, I wish you were here."

Violet moved on to a classic black dress. She had bought it years ago, but it was timeless. Tight enough to show her curvy figure but not too tight as to feel revealing. A definite possibility.

Then, there was her floral, long-sleeved midi dress in cobalt blue. She always felt comfortable in that, and the colour brought out her blue eyes.

Lastly, a striped jumpsuit that hugged her in all the right places and made her feel tall and slim.

Violet slipped on her outfits, feeling glamourous and pretty. Ben never paid her compliments, not anymore. He used to back in the day. He used to make her feel like the most beautiful woman on the planet. What had gone so wrong?

As the years passed, he had stopped telling her he could look into her eyes forever and that her smile made his heart feel whole. Instead, he'd tell her she had let herself go and was repulsive. Where had her Prince Charming gone?

Violet stood, looking at her reflection in the mirror, wondering who she even was now. She was a ghost of her former self. Ben had made her this way, and she had let him. Her thoughts flipped instantly from feeling pretty and positive. She hated herself, she hated her reflection, she detested who she had become.

Violet cried. Long, hard sobs of despair for everything that had happened, everything that once was and all the things she would never get from the abuser Ben had become.

# 44

# Social Butterfly

## Florence

It was the night of the first dinner club, and Florence couldn't wait. She'd impatiently watched the clock all day, wishing the hours away like a child waiting for their birthday party.

Jessie had been off work yesterday, so Lucy had been round. Of course, Florence loved Lucy, you couldn't not, but she wasn't Jessie.

Being a carer was hard, Florence could see that, no one could deny that. What they tolerated, the endless tasks they had to complete for so many vulnerable people. All for minimum wage. It was quite frankly obscene in Florence's opinion.

"They need to give you all a bloody pay rise, love. I'm going to tell your boss," Florence would say.

Day in, day out, her carers and their colleagues would walk, drive and cycle to local people's homes, feed them, cook for them, bathe them and put them to bed. Making sure they took their medication, cleaning up and chatting to them. Giving something priceless to the ageing population who had given society so much through the years.

Florence often talked about how lucky she was to have her carers, but she still felt the pain of loneliness. As she climbed into bed each night, the empty side always seemed so big. She would look over to the bedside cabinet that felt a million miles away from her and wish with all her being that she would see her Ernie's mug of cocoa resting on its coaster, like it had done for so many years. She would read, trying to tire herself out, and always kiss his photo goodnight, which was preciously resting on her bedside cabinet.

"Goodnight, my love, please visit me in my slumber," Florence repeated every night, willing Ernie to enter her dreams. A sign, a thought, a feeling. Anything. The flame of her love for her soulmate had never dulled. Decades later, she still felt the crippling void.

The tiny, miniscule things we all take for granted were the things she missed most of all. Cups of tea made by Ernie, which had always tasted so much nicer than her own. The way he would put her slippers on her feet and help her into her dressing gown, even though she was more than capable of putting it on herself. She missed goodnight kisses; the way he used to hold her hand, always kissing it before letting their hands drop between them; that absolute look of love in his eyes. Anyone who knows true love knows that look, and it's the most beautiful interaction you can have.

She missed seeing him in his favourite jumper, the feel of his beard, the sound of his laugh. She missed making his packed lunch and always putting a toffee in. She missed watching him read, the concentration on his face. She missed listening to him singing songs and not knowing the words as she chuckled. She missed sitting next to him on the sofa, their crocheted blanket on their knees as they sat in content silence. She missed so much.

The carers made a massive difference. Undoubtably, no one ever did or ever could replace Ernie, nowhere close. It would have been like trying to fly to the moon by flapping your arms. But her carers gave her a love that helped heal her heart a little. Yes, they were paid, but it was so much more than that. They were her friends, like grandchildren, they looked after her in ways Ernie would have. They made her smile, they made her laugh, they loved her stories of old.

Lately, Florence had felt a sensation in bed at night. She had told Jessie about it a few months back. A kind of pulling on her shoulder.

"I think it's my Ernie, Jessie, I really do. But I'm not ready to go, love," she'd said.

"You're tough as old boots, Florrie, you will outlive us all." Jessie had laughed.

It had happened again this week. Florence sat thinking about it, waiting for the two hours to pass until the taxi would come to take her to Derek's. She carefully dipped her third ginger nut into her tea, cautious not to slop any on her clean royal-blue blouse. She had bought the blouse especially for this evening.

Blue was her favourite colour. Royal blue in particular. She wore it with some smart navy-blue trousers and her St. Christopher necklace that always hung around her neck. It had been her Ernie's, and she'd worn it since the day he'd died. It protected her, her Ernie protected her, and she would wear it until the day she joined him.

"I love you, Ernie."

*Tipping Point* was about to start. Florence watched it every day, crossing her fingers for the contestants and occasionally swearing at the screen when they lost. She would always have her cuppa and some biscuits to keep her going if she wasn't ready for dinner. Tonight, she would have to wait a little longer for dinner. She knew it would be worth it and that she would be in for a treat. No matter what was on the menu, the company would satisfy her.

# 45

# Pre-dinner Nerves

## Eddie

It had been a productive day for Eddie at Hendersons—something he was grateful for as a distraction. He was ridiculously nervous for the first dinner club. He felt utterly stupid for feeling such a way. Eddie could stand in front of hundreds of people and present on behalf of the company with ease, but for some insane reason, the thought of this second meeting with three strangers sent him into a cold sweat. It didn't help that Eddie feared he would have to confess all about Issy and then end up with a side portion of pity as his main course was served.

Martha had rung the interviewees from the latest round of recruitment. Eddie had made a strong case for the young girl, Cara. She showed promise and personality. He'd expressed his opinion to Danielle and Martha that he believed she was the right person for the role. Not that he'd had to convince the panel—both Danielle and Martha also felt she was the right candidate. There was something about her; something that resonated with Eddie.

Martha had fed back that Cara had accepted the job, that she'd been surprised but very grateful. Eddie was pleased and liked her humble response. He was certain she would fit into the team well, and Eddie always liked an injection of new ideas and visions to Hendersons.

The day flew by, with Eddie only managing to grab a quick sandwich at lunchtime, meaning he was hungry by the end of the day and looking forward to being fed.

Willow was spending the night at his parents'. She had packed her usual collection of bags, with things certain not to be needed.

"Bubs, what's all this in these bags?" Eddie had said. He'd known not to say the word "rubbish". He had recently got that wrong, leading to a sobbing fit from Willow for referring to her belongings as such.

"It's stuff I need, Dad. I need to take it all to Momar's and Grandpa's," she confidently replied.

Eddie peeked into the bag. The bag was indeed full of rubbish. Two pairs of tights, a jewellery box, some wellies, three teddies, Buzz and Woody, Princess Belle, a few dressing-up outfits. Another bag seemed to be almost full of underwear and nightwear.

"Willow, honey, you are only going for one night. You really don't need all of this stuff."

"I *need* it all," she pleaded, looking up at him.

"I don't think you do, bubs."

"I can't leave it. What if someone takes it?"

"Who's going to take it? Willow, you can't take your whole bedroom with you every time we leave the house."

Willow burst out crying, grabbing Eddie's leg, pleading to take her three bulging bags alongside her overnight bag.

Eddie took them. He couldn't cope with another meltdown.

Eddie would have to address her incessant bag packing soon—it was moving on to bags for life now, which were slowly disappearing from the hallway cupboard.

Derek had advised the group to get to his house at 7 p.m. Eddie lived about a fifteen-minute drive from Derek. He would take his car this time, maybe just have one drink. He could handle his drink; what Eddie couldn't handle were the emotions that often came with him drinking in excess. Taking the car was definitely the right move for this evening.

After a quick shower, he faced the obvious dilemma of what to wear. *Bugger*, he thought, *I should have organised this already*.

He stared at his wardrobe. He didn't want anything too formal, but at the same time, it was important to make an effort. Jeans and a T-shirt would not suffice. Eddie raked through his wardrobe, trying to find something that hit the mark but didn't look too intense. Chinos—they were a safe bet. He pulled out a navy-blue pair. Moving over to his shirts, he pulled out a small checked one in a light blue and white gingham design. Perfect. He would wear a jacket over the top and take it off once at Derek's. A pair of desert boots would finish the outfit nicely. *Wasn't that hard*? he thought smugly.

# 46

# *Showtime*

## Derek

Derek was home by 1:18 p.m. that afternoon. He was a man, or maybe a woman, on a mission. Much of the prep had been done the night before, and the house was clean but homely.

The food was not his main concern; his main concern lay with the reaction his dinner guests would have to Debbie. It was a bold move; these three people were strangers. But that was half of the reason he had to be Debbie—she had to be accepted as part of Derek from the off. He had to take a chance without trying to sneak her in like the dirty secret Brenda made her out to be. He wanted transparency, he wanted acceptance. But most of all, he just wanted to be himself.

Debbie's outfit had already been chosen: a black dress with red roses on. This was one of his favourite prints, pretty but not too stereotypical.

Derek had been watching some tutorials on YouTube for make-up and had found them to be quite addictive. What with that and the forum, he was spending most nights with his laptop on his knee. It was a whole new world. He had been talking to Peter/Paula, wearwhatiwant54, for the last few nights. Peter sounded similar to Derek in a lot of ways, and Derek felt reassured and less alienated by their chats. Maybe people weren't as judgemental as Derek thought.

He remembered when Arthur had come out in the early nineties. People were less tolerant then, and there was still the stigma and fear of HIV/AIDS, as Freddy Mercury hadn't long died.

"Bugger 'em. I live my life for me, no bugger else. When bad things happen, you find out who really cares. Your true friends will be your number one fans and will never give up on you. They will inspire you, pull you to your feet when you fall, cheer you on as you struggle and carry you on their shoulders when you can't take any more. They don't care what you eat, where you live, your job or who you share your bed with, as long as you're happy. Friendship can be made in an evening and last a lifetime. I'm doing it for you, mate. For everything I want to be that you were."

Derek looked out of the window, reflecting on his fond memories of his precious friend. There was a bird on the tree directly outside. It looked at him before flying off. Derek's eyes followed the bird as it flew into the sky, free. He wiped a tear from the corner of his eye.

# 47

# *Hunger*

## Florence

*At last*, Florence thought as she saw the taxi pull up outside her bungalow. She had the front door open, impatiently waiting. Time dragged for someone whose routine was so dictated by the clock.

She had placed a few toffees in her handbag, which she had dipped into twice already.

She hobbled out, using her walking sticks, as a familiar taxi driver climbed out and opened the passenger door for her. *What a gent*. It was Davey, a regular taxi driver to the row of bungalows where Florence lived. He was a typical Geordie chap, happy, friendly and a little bit cheeky.

"Evening, love, how are you?" he enquired, a chirpy, warm smile on his face.

"Better for seeing you, pet." She beamed as she got into the car. "Want a toffee?" Florence asked as she belted up.

"Aye, why not, thanks, Florence," he replied, taking one from her hand. "Where to, my lovely?"

Florence gave Derek's address, explaining what her evening hopefully had in store.

"All through an advert in Foodways? That's smashing, Florence, good on you."

Florence felt a jolt of confidence. It was a big deal, and she could have easily not bothered, in her eighth decade of life, with deteriorating health. But no, she wanted this adventure, and an adventure she would make it.

"Thanks, pet," she said, smiling to Davey.

Seven minutes later, she arrived outside Derek's. Paying Davey and handing him a few extra toffees, she thanked him, telling him she hoped to see him later when she returned home.

"Quite possibly, Florence, it's dead in town tonight. Enjoy."

And there she was, standing at the bottom of a semi-detached house with a basic garden and two plant pots with Buxus shrubs, one either side of the front door.

"Here goes nothing," she said, making her way up the drive. Reaching for the doorbell, Florence rang it twice and waited patiently for her host to answer.

Thirty seconds later, the door opened.

A person stood there who wasn't Derek. "Oh, sorry, I think I have the wrong house," she blurted out, bewildered and wondering which house she was meant to be at. But then she looked harder, and the face half smiled, an awkwardness in the expression.

"Evening, Florence. It's me, Derek," said the person, who was certainly not the Derek Florence had met before. But it was definitely Derek's voice, quieter, with croaky nerves.

Florence's eyes widened as she quickly glanced Derek up and down. "Oh my, oh, hello, Derek. Now, this is a surprise."

Florence was struggling to make sense of who stood before her. It was Derek, yes, it was most definitely Derek under that lovely dress, wig and make-up. It was Derek, but certainly not as she remembered him.

"Come in, Florence, please, come on in."

Florence nodded as she went into the house, bemused but also intrigued. She turned to look at her host and gave a quick smile, sensing his nerves.

"Let me take your coat. Tonight, your host will be Debbie, but you can still call me Derek, if you want."

Florence wasn't sure what to say or do. She hadn't seen this in real life before. It definitely didn't offend her, it just felt a bit surreal. She was certain, however, that she had to make Derek feel comfortable. It was his home, and this must have taken a lot of guts.

"Oh, excellent," she exclaimed. "Lovely to meet Debbie," Florence said as she gave a smile of reassurance to her host.

The smile was returned, followed by a tiny glimpse of what looked like relief.

# 48

# Debbie's Dinner Club Debut

## Derek

Derek was ready half an hour before his guests were due. He had prepped the food as much as possible and would do the finishing touches when everyone arrived. He paced the lounge, a glass of wine in his hand. After spraying deodorant for the fourth time and still sweating profusely, he opened the dining room windows for some cold air.

"Bollocks, bloody hell, bugger," he swore as he circled the lounge, expecting that with each profanity he would either calm down, get drunk enough not to care or storm upstairs to change out of Debbie's clothes and into his chinos and jumper.

Derek had that nervous gurgling in the pit of his stomach and the sensation of a tennis ball lodged in his windpipe. Breathing felt like he had run a marathon, his heart beating as if it were screaming to squeeze blood around his body. His vision was blurry, and it wasn't the wine. God, he was about to have a panic attack.

He sat and focused on the ornament on the fireplace that spelt the word "HOME". Arthur had once talked about panic attacks he'd experienced whilst in the midst of substance misuse. It was different to alcohol withdrawals, the delirium tremens, as Arthur used to say, referring to the medical terminology. It was the reality of his situation, the sobriety of his truth that would cascade upon him and make him feel as though he were having a heart attack. A nurse had told him that to stabilise his breathing and focus his vision, as well as prevent further escalation of anxiety, finding something to look at and concentrate on was vital. A poster, picture, a word or number, a brick or shape. Anything, as long as the eyes stayed focused on that object until the breathing stopped accelerating and normal functions resumed.

Derek focused on the ornament, trying to regulate his breathing as he did so, looking at nothing else but those four, white wooden letters.

What felt like hours but was barely minutes passed. Derek felt his heart tension ease, he felt less nauseous and sweaty, but he kept focused on the letters a little longer.

"It's going to be ok. It's going to be ok. It's going to be ok," Derek repeated, still looking at the ornament.

Then, the doorbell went, earlier than expected. Instead of spiralling into another panic, Derek got straight up from the sofa and headed to the front door, willing himself to be brave.

"What's the worst that could happen?"

He reached the front door, pausing just before his fingers grasped the handle. Pulling his hand back as if the handle were on fire, he squeezed his hands together in anxious anticipation. He couldn't leave her out on the doorstep all night.

Derek repeated his mantra again—"It's going to be ok"—as he opened the front door to Florence.

"Oh, sorry, I think I have the wrong house," Florence said, a bemused look on her aged face.

Derek tried a smile as he looked at Florence, willing her recognition and a positive response. A few seconds of silence felt painfully long before Derek cleared his throat and could manage to speak. "Evening, Florence.

It's me, Derek," he said gently, lacking the confidence he had mustered on rehearsals for this very moment.

"Oh my, oh, hello, Derek. Now, this is a surprise," she responded, clearly slightly flustered by the sight before her.

Derek wasn't sure if Florence was going to stay or leave, but he certainly couldn't have her standing there in the cold any longer. "Come in, Florence, please, come on in." Derek moved to the side, gesturing Florence in.

Florence slowly entered the hallway, nodding, with a smile. Derek turned, and they were facing each other once again. Another few seconds of silence as Florence looked at Derek with a level of fascination a child would display.

Derek straightened his shoulders, clapped his hands together and said, "Let me take your coat, Florence. Tonight, your host will be Debbie, but you can still call me Derek, if you want." Derek tried his utmost to sound calm and confident. On the contrary, he felt he may collapse with nerves at any point, and his legs felt like utter jelly.

Florence held his gaze, her eyes friendly as the shock subsided. "Oh, excellent. Lovely to meet Debbie."

Derek let out a breath that could have filled a hot air balloon. Florence must have noticed his tension.

"It's ok, son, don't worry. Erm, I mean, it's ok, Debbie. Derek. Bloody hell, you know what I mean." She laughed, putting her hand to her mouth and shaking her head. She handed Derek her coat, touching his forearm with gentle reassurance. Derek smiled softly, the relief from the build up to this moment overwhelming him.

"Ah, pet, I couldn't care if you dress up as a purple giraffe, as long as you're happy, love. Life is too short. I just got a bit of a shock, pet, that's all," Florence said, noticing the relief on Derek's face. "Debbie's a nice name. I worked with a Debbie once—she was a bloody gem and gave the best cuddles in the world. Apart from my Ernie, of course."

Derek chuckled, holding back the tears.

Des came trotting in, alerted by the guest and potential attention.

"Oh, and meet Des, my four-legged son."

Des came over for a sniff.

"Hello, boy, aren't you a handsome chap?" Florence gave Des a head rub, and his tail started wagging ferociously.

"He is a right bloody flirt. Come on in and take a seat. What's your poison?"

"Oooh, I could murder a shandy, please, love."

"Coming right up, my lovely." And with that, Derek went into the kitchen, grinning like a Cheshire cat.

# 49

# *Hungry for Company*

## Eddie

Eddie had been pacing the lounge for seven minutes. Why was he so nervous? He wasn't even hosting. Then, it clicked. Not only had he not been to a social event with new people since Issy had died, but there was something ridiculous about this whole situation that instilled an absolute need for acceptance for Eddie. Acceptance from three strangers he was very unlikely to see again if he didn't go tonight and stopped shopping in Foodways.

He thought back to the dream where he'd been with Issy at a dinner party. Her hosting and enjoying the company of people he didn't recognise. His feelings about the whole scenario seemed symbolic. Eddie wasn't sure how much he believed in life after death, signs and all that. He wasn't sure if it was just desperate desire for something, some fantasised level of communication from a loved one that had passed, or whether it was a complete fact and those blind to it would never see it. Whatever it was, he had some scale of comfort from what may have been coincidences over the years. There was something different about this whole situation, something normally so out of his comfort zone but so utterly compelling. It felt weird, really bizarre, but something he was absolutely drawn to continue.

"Get a damn grip, man," he said, shaking his head with disbelief at how preposterous he felt.

He snatched his keys off the side table, checked he had his phone and left the house. Straight into his car, he started the engine and the radio blasted as he reversed off the drive.

It only took twelve minutes for Eddie to reach Derek's estate. His heart started to beat faster, an internal heat overcoming him. He opened the window, slowing down to look for the street signs. Then, it came on the radio: Cyndi Lauper's "Time After Time".

"For God's sake, Issy, you are such a bugger." Eddie let out a laugh of reminiscing tainted with heartbreak. This was why he had to believe in signs. It was her way of saying he was doing the right thing tonight, that all would be ok. That she was by his side and forever in his heart.

Eddie turned onto Derek's street. He found the house number, stopping a few doors down. He switched off the engine, leaving the keys in to hear the end of the song.

"I love you, my darling," he said after the song finished, rubbing his wedding band. And with that, he got out of his car and walked two houses down to Derek's.

Eddie knocked on the door, bottle of wine in hand. It was quickly opened by someone Eddie assumed was Derek's ex-wife or new girlfriend.

"Hi there," he said.

"Hello, Eddie," the mysterious woman replied.

His brows furrowed at the deep voice. A split second later, after adjusting to the hallway light from the darkness of the autumn evening, Eddie realised. It was Derek. In drag. Wearing women's clothes, a wig and, to be fair, quite good make-up.

Eddie started to laugh. "Nice one, Derek, I didn't get the email saying it was fancy dress."

"Err, come in, Eddie."

Eddie walked in, chuckling.

"I will take your coat. And it isn't fancy dress, Eddie, I'm hosting tonight as Debbie. She is someone I dress up as now and then, nothing sinister, just something that I feel comfortable with. I hope you aren't offended. I'm happy to answer questions about it, perhaps when Violet gets here also."

Eddie noticed how nervous Derek seemed and immediately felt awful.

"God, Derek, I'm sorry, I didn't mean to sound as though I was taking the mick. Honest. I guess I just wasn't expecting this. I'm not offended at all, each to their own. I'm sorry, mate."

Eddie blushed. He truly felt like a prize prick. He knew people came in different shapes and sizes, had different preferences and inclinations. He always tried not to judge, stare or snigger. He didn't care who people fancied... well, as long as it wasn't animals—that was sick beyond comprehension. And those freaks who married bridges and monuments and weird objects like that—he certainly had judgement on that. But what people looked like and who they wanted to go to bed with wasn't of his concern.

He used to play five-a-side about a decade ago with the local pub team, and someone there, Mark, was a transsexual, becoming a woman after years of therapy and treatment. Some of the lads took the piss. Mark had said he'd always loved football but had always felt he'd been born in the wrong body. Eddie had chatted to him a few times, some really insightful conversations, and Eddie completely empathised and understood Mark's perspective. He never once found it funny. On the contrary, he found his plight really sad, and when Mark became Eva a few years later, Eddie had been over the moon for her.

"Brought some wine for those not driving, Dere... Debbie." Eddie handed it to Derek, with a nervous smile.

Entering the lounge, Eddie saw Florence and felt a little relief that the spotlight would be taken off him.

"Hi there, Florence, lovely to see you." Eddie went over and gave her a peck on the cheek.

"Oooh, I haven't had a snog off a handsome man for years. Don't go telling your wife." Florence winked at Eddie. Eddie's heart sank. He was nowhere near ready to tell the truth. Luckily, a dog bounded towards him, cutting the topic off.

"Oh, shit," he swore, startled. "God, sorry, Florence, I didn't mean to swear." Christ, this wasn't going well. He had been here less than five minutes and offended two people already, and now a dog was licking his hand.

"Ah, I'm not easily offended, son. My words can turn the air blue at times." Florence chuckled.

"You little minx," Eddie replied. They both laughed.

Then, the doorbell rang.

# 50

# *The First Supper*

## Violet

Violet walked up the driveway to Derek's house, a flutter of nerves in her stomach. Ben had been ok that day. Of course, he hadn't been nice as such, but he hadn't been horrendous either. He had returned from work and grabbed a sandwich, as he always did before the darts. Violet had prepared some food to warm up for him when she got home. Ben usually came in around 11:30 p.m. on darts nights. Violet knew she would be back before then.

Luckily, he'd left by 5:45 p.m., giving Violet an hour to enjoy getting ready. Granted, she didn't want to look like she was going for a night out on the town, but she wanted to feel pretty for once, rather than her usual frumpy or plain in her putrid Foodways uniform or jeans and a jumper.

She'd opted for the blue floral dress—it seemed appropriate yet a bit glamourous. Slipping on the dress, the material had felt luxurious against her skin. She had put some of her favourite body cream on and sprayed lots of expensive perfume. She felt a million dollars already. As she'd pulled her tights up, she'd wondered when she'd last felt good about herself.

There had been times in the past where Ben had been wonderful, loving and caring, especially in the first few years of their relationship. Even though he could have a temper and say the wrong thing, he could also be her ideal man. When the abuse became more frequent, Violet had held onto these times, with ever fading hope that he would love her more and abuse her less. Maybe he'd been acting, maybe he'd just got sick of her, maybe it *was* her. He had told her enough times that it was her fault. Deep down, Violet knew he was never going to return to the man she'd fallen in love with. That man was long dead, replaced by a monster who had broken her heart countless times. Did she hate him? Loathe him? Resent him? To a degree, most definitely. But paramount to her feelings about her relationship was that she had just had enough. She was deflated and exhausted. She didn't want to be a walking ball of hatred, wishing bad on Ben and wanting to seek revenge. She just wanted to not hurt. She wanted to be loved and love back, without physical pain or mental anguish.

Violet needed to find herself again and gather the strength to start over. She had started her new mission. It would take time, but she had started it and that was the main thing.

Violet reached Derek's front door and rang the bell. It didn't take long for him to answer. But he wasn't how she remembered him. Before her stood Derek in a dress, wig and with make-up that looked better than hers. Her mouth opened, and she felt her eyebrows rise. She looked at Derek as he bit his lip, almost willing her to speak.

"Oh, hi, Derek, erm, you look great." Violet smiled at Derek, not sure if this was fancy dress or Derek's choice of attire for the evening. Derek's face lit up at her positive response.

"Come on in, Violet, my lovely." Derek took her coat as she entered. "You look beautiful."

Violet blushed. "Thank you, Derek. You look rather stylish yourself."

"I'm glad you think so. I'm hosting as Debbie this evening, but you can call me Debbie or Derek."

"Well, nice to meet you, Debbie," Violet said, considering this the politer option and wanting to let Derek know she would accept him as whoever he wished to be.

She didn't know the history, no doubt he would tell them in time, but she could imagine this must have been a huge deal.

Derek showed Violet into the lounge, where she was greeted by Florence, Eddie and a very friendly dog.

"Hi, everyone." Violet crouched to stroke the friendly dog, grinning. "Ooh hello, baby, what's your name?"

"This is Des," said Florence. "He's a right flirt."

"Well, hello, Des, aren't you lovely?" Violet scratched behind Des's ear as he leaned against her leg, content in the fact he would receive masses of attention that evening.

"Violet, love, what do you want to drink? We have wine, beer, gin, juice, tea, coffee," Derek called from the kitchen.

"A wine would be lovely. Just a small one, thanks."

The three started chatting as Derek served the drinks and finished off the starter.

Violet had a feeling she would enjoy the company just as much as the food that evening.

# 51

# *Acceptance*

## Derek

Derek's guts were churning but he also felt elated from the tsunami of relief that had washed over him. *Thank you, God*, he thought. He had been accepted by the guests. Debbie had been accepted. There had been a slight dodgy moment with Eddie, but once Eddie had realised it was serious, he'd been lovely. The smiles and support as his guests had arrived had meant more to him than he'd thought it would.

This was a massive deal. He had never unveiled Debbie to strangers. Hell, he had only ever unveiled her to Brenda and Bri, and half of his experiences had ended in aggression, shouting, name-calling and distress.

He was determined to make this night a success. All guests had a drink, he had Michael Bublé on the CD player and Des was keeping them entertained.

"Grub's up, everyone." Derek showed his guests to their seats before bringing the starter in: Mediterranean vegetable stack and homemade ciabatta.

"Here you go. I hope you all like it."

"This looks delicious, Der... Debbie," said Florence.

"Did you make this bread yourself?" asked Violet.

"I did. I have a weakness for bread. Used to have a bread maker a few years ago. Gave it to St Oswald's shop in the end, as it was becoming an addiction."

"Bread is my weakness also, mate, I love a bit of tiger bread and butter," said Eddie. They all expressed their approval, agreeing there was nothing better.

The four munched away, chatting like old friends, the atmosphere relaxed and warm.

"Top up, anyone, before I get the main course sorted?" asked Derek.

"Yes please, love, another shandy for me. I intend on being hungover for my carer in the morning." Florence laughed.

"Do you have carers every day, Florence?" Violet asked. "I used to do care work myself for a short time. I loved it."

Derek smiled as he listened in to the conversation. He wasn't surprised about Violet's revelation—she came across as sweet and caring.

"I bet you were a great carer, pet." Derek could tell Florence was smiling as she spoke. "And yes, I have them every morning. Two lovely girls who feel more like family. I couldn't be without them.

"I had a stroke last year, and social services sorted me out a care package. Well, them and my William. At first, I was reluctant. It felt as if my independence was being taken away. I'm a stubborn old bugger and fiercely independent, so it seemed a big deal. But as soon as I met Jessie... She was my first carer and still comes most mornings. Her and Lucy.

"But my Jessie is like my guardian angel. I had a funny turn a few months back, and she found me and saved me. I love her to bits. I know I will need them more in the future, and I am so thankful to have such good girls looking out for me." Florence's voice wavered, filled with emotion and gratitude.

"Aw, bless you, Florence, that's so lovely. I bet they love coming to visit you. I know I would if I was still a carer."

"Why did you stop doing care work, pet?"

"It wasn't through choice, more circumstances," replied Violet, sadness apparent in her voice. Derek wondered what those circumstances could be. Maybe they'd find out at some point.

"Well, I'm sure you do a great job at Foodways anyway, love, they are lucky to have you," Florence commented.

"Here we go, everyone, main course is served. We have hunter's chicken, sweet potato fries and asparagus," Derek announced, carrying in two plates. There was a unison of ooohs and ahhhhs as the hungry faces stared at the plates.

"Ladies first," Derek said, placing the plates in front of Florence and Violet.

The delicious aromas wafted up the guests' noses, all eager to tuck in.

Derek returned with the remaining two plates. Then, there was a minute of silence as they all took their first mouthful.

"Bloody delicious. That asparagus is cooked to perfection," Eddie said. "Florence, I am sure you never did this, but in the eighties, my wonderful mother used to nuke all vegetables to the point they all tasted the same and lost all nutritional value. These days, I like my vegetables al dente and retaining some nutrients." He chuckled.

"My mam used to do that too, Eddie, it must have been an eighties mother thing." Violet laughed.

"I couldn't comment." Florence giggled.

Derek smiled. They were getting on like a house on fire, new friends that felt like old friends coming together over food and conversation. But there was an elephant in the room, and it had to be discussed.

"Is everyone's chicken cooked to their liking?" asked Derek.

"Oooh yes, wonderful, succulent and tasty," said Florence. "Chicken is my favourite. I get the Wilkins Farm meals delivered. Greg, the driver, brings them every week. They're delicious, but there is nothing like a meal being made for you, is there? I sometimes say to Jessie that I think I would eat a pile of horse manure if someone served it to me."

The guests burst out laughing, Eddie nearly choking on his sweet potato fries.

"God, Florence, I've never met anyone like you," Eddie said, coughing.

"Ooh, Derek, Debbie, I didn't mean your food tasted like horse crap, erm, manure. It's nothing like it. Not that I have eaten horse manure to compare but, well, you know what I'm trying to say."

They all howled again.

"Florence, love, you should be on stage," said Derek.

Florence's face lit up as she soaked up the attention from her new friends.

*Bite the bullet*, thought Derek.

"So, folks, I guess you want to know a little bit more about Debbie?"

"That's up to you, pet," said Florence.

"No pressure at all," added Eddie.

"No, no, it's fine. I think it's important you all understand. You see, I've never done this before."

Florence touched Derek's hand, a comforting sign of friendship and acceptance.

"I've had this feeling for years. A feeling I have had to swallow and supress for more years than I can remember. I just want to be myself, it's really as simple as that, and part of being myself is dressing up as Debbie now and again. I don't want to live as a woman, I don't want to get me bits chopped off, I just like women's clothes, make-up, how dressing up makes me feel. I am still Derek and like who Derek is, I just want to be Debbie sometimes. A little escape, my alter ego, whatever you want to call it."

"Sounds fair enough to me, mate. Good on you. Too many of us go around feeling we can't be ourselves, smothered by society's expectations. I get it, on a different level, I really get it," said Eddie.

"Thanks, that means a lot. I have only ever shown Debbie to my best mate, Bri, and my soon-to-be ex-wife, Brenda. You can probably imagine it didn't go down well with Brenda, and that was the biggest problem in our marriage. Well, that and she's a right cow." Derek snorted.

They all chuckled.

"Pet, you be whoever the hell you want to be and let no one stop you. The right people will support you; the rest can bugger right off."

"Well, I think it's great, and you put me and my façade of a life to shame, Debbie. But that's for another day," said Violet.

"And mine," said Eddie quietly.

"Just shows, we all carry secrets, and maybe we should just be our bloody selves," stated Florence.

"I am just so grateful you've all been nice about this. It means the world to me, folks, it really does. Part of the whole dinner club idea was so that I could be myself. It may not be that Debbie is at each one, but I wanted to be me after years of feeling I couldn't."

"Aw, son, it's ok. We will always accept you and each other. We are a good little team." Florence held Derek's arm.

"Now, where is this pudding you've promised us?"

# 52

# New Horizons

## Cara

Cara figured she had slept for around four hours in total. What with Rhys coming in from work, the discomfort of the sofa and nerves for starting her new job that Monday morning, sleep had not been forthcoming. She only hoped adrenaline would see her through the day. Cara had spent hours the day before preparing her outfit and packed lunch. Not that there was much to do, her wardrobe being so limited.

Caitlyn had said she was proud of Cara. Those words meant the world to her. She wouldn't screw this up.

She left with plenty of time, purchasing a weekly bus pass, leaving herself with very little until she got paid, but another step towards being organised, in her mind.

Arriving at Hendersons for 8:30 a.m., she took some deep breaths and walked in. Danielle, who'd been one of the people interviewing her, was sitting at the reception desk.

"Oh, hi. Morning, Cara." Danielle got up and shook Cara's hand. "Great to see you. Cuppa?"

"That would be lovely, thanks."

"Come with me, and I'll show you around. We have fifteen minutes or so before it starts to get busy."

Cara followed, already feeling important. Danielle showed her where the toilets were, the kitchen area and talked about how everyone put two pounds in a month for tea and coffee, milk etc. They had a sports and social club, and any leftover money from the tea and coffee fund went towards summer and Christmas events.

Danielle pointed out fire exits and different departments to Cara, giving a history of Hendersons as she went. The place was huge. There was a lot to take in, but Cara felt privileged to have the opportunity to be part of what sounded like a great company to work for.

Teas sorted, they returned to the reception desk in time for colleagues to begin coming in. As they arrived and signed in, Danielle gave introductions. Cara tried to remember the first few names, then they became a mass of different faces, the names dissolving rapidly in her memory. Crap, how would she remember everyone?

As if reading her mind, Danielle chipped in, "We have an electronic directory of all the staff, their roles, department and a photo of each of them. You'll get used to everyone, but you can have a browse as part of your induction." She smiled at a grateful Cara.

People streamed in, some permanent staff, some for meetings. Martha, who'd also interviewed Cara, came in, chatting and congratulating her. Then, Eddie turned up, who'd also been on the panel. Cara felt a little intimidated by him, remembering he was a big boss who seemed to know his stuff. He dressed powerfully and had a tall stature.

"Ah, nice to see you, Cara, welcome to the team." He smiled, and Cara felt a little less self-conscious.

"Thanks, and thanks for picking me, I'm really happy."

"That's what we want to hear. I am sure you'll feel at home in no time. Anything I can do to help, just let me know."

Maybe Cara had him wrong and he was a big softy.

The day flew by. Danielle helped Cara find her feet, and Cara spent time reading over policies and getting to grips with some procedures. Danielle had worked at

Hendersons for a number of years and seemed to really know her stuff. At the end of the day, Cara thanked her for her help and told Danielle she appreciated her knowledge.

"You're welcome, Cara. I think you are going to be a great fit at Hendersons, and I think we will make a perfect team."

Cara left Hendersons and got on her bus home, cosy in her own blanket of sheer happiness for the whole journey.

Cara's next day at work went just as well, and so did the rest of the week. She relished in keeping Caitlyn up to date and planned what she would spend her first wage on at the end of the following week. Whatever was left after outgoings, Cara would keep to start saving.

Cara couldn't stay on Caitlyn's sofa forever. She knew their hospitality would come to an end soon. Rhys was becoming progressively short with her, and Cara was becoming increasingly annoyed with him and his disturbances, especially now she had an important and responsible job. Cara wanted some independence and a bedroom to call her own. It would take time to save for a deposit, admin fees and a month's rent upfront. They didn't make it easy. She also worried about needing a guarantor—there was no one who could vouch for her except Caitlyn, and Caitlyn wasn't in a financial position to offer such a role. A few barriers, but Cara was an Olympian in overcoming hurdles. She would find a solution.

On her second day at Hendersons, she had gone into the kitchen area for lunch. Most people went to the local shops to get sandwiches, salads, pastries and takeaways. Cara could only imagine the amount of money they must spend a day. Some of them always had a takeout cup of coffee in their hand as well. Two days of cuppas, lunch and, for some, cigarettes would be more than what Cara spent on a whole month's worth of food costs and household contributions to Caitlyn. It boggled her mind, although she imagined some of them were on mega bucks. Still, seemed like a bit of a waste.

She was pondering costs and savings as she picked at her homemade cheese and cucumber sandwich. The lunch half hour was good for her, helping her to focus and actually sit and eat something. Her appetite was poor, and she had never enjoyed food as a social event. Other than the odd cuppa and cake with Caitlyn, food had always been something that had made her anxious. Before her time in foster care, she'd never been fed much, her school meal often being her only meal of the day. She'd searched bins for food in the early days until her stomach had got used to feeling empty, or she would drink juice, diluted to the extreme, to fill up.

Food became a frantic rush to get something in her mouth or something her mam may have given her after both being in tears for hours. In foster care, she used to ask to eat alone or in her room. The foster carers got it, well, most of them. Food wasn't to be enjoyed, it was survival, a function. Cara spent the first eight years of her life associating it with utter desperation, anxiety and pain. It lingered into her foster care days, after the flourishing of her first placement with Rebecca and then being taken away again. Her stability with Shirley, until Joe came along, couldn't even help her conquer her food demons.

Now, as an adult, she ate very little, had a bad nutritional input into her body and knew nothing about cooking. She began nibbling on her sandwich as she heard, "Hello".

"Oh, hi, Eddie," she said, looking up at him.

"May I?" he asked, gesturing to the seat next to her.

"Of course, yeah." Cara smiled. Eddie sat down, getting out his packed lunch. Cara told Eddie how she'd been wondering how much people spent on their lunch each day.

"Ha, I think these types of things too. Not to mention the smokers and the cost of tabs these days. Then, some workers go to the pub after work. They must have more money than sense."

Cara laughed. The two of them sounded like a pair of miserable old sods.

"I hate waste. I never throw any food away, not that I buy a lot. We had nothing when I was little, maybe it's that," Cara said, immediately feeling she had overshared.

"I don't like waste either. I have a daughter and try to instil that in her. It's an environmental issue, as well as cost, and we shouldn't waste anything if we don't have to."

Cara raised her eyebrow. Clearly, she'd underestimated Eddie as a person and judged him all wrong. "I bet you don't buy from charity shops though, do you? Not with the smart suits you wear," Cara asked, half poking fun at Eddie.

"Well, no, actually, I don't, but I do donate to charity. Does that even it out?" Eddie smirked at Cara; he was enjoying the banter. "You have a wise head on your shoulders, Cara, just what this business needs. You will go far."

Cara blushed. She'd always struggled with compliments, and this was no exception, but at the same time, Eddie seemed like someone she could talk to with ease. Something she would never have predicted on first meeting him, especially not with the barriers she always put up against men.

"How old is your daughter and what's her name?" Cara asked, trying to move away from her awkwardness. "Sorry, tell me if I'm being too nosy."

"Not at all. She's four, and her name is Willow. She is a little character, keeps me on my toes. But she has a lovely nature, like her mam."

"And dad," Cara added.

Eddie smiled. "I hope she has all my good points and none of my bad."

"Is that her on your phone?" Cara said, indicating to Eddie's mobile on the table, lit up by an incoming message.

"Yeah, that's her, I took that in the summer. We went to Richardson's Farm in Northumberland. She loved it. Have you been?"

"No, I've not been. Ah, Willow is so pretty. You and your wife must be very proud," Cara commented.

"Yeah. Yeah, we are. I am anyway. Willow's mam isn't around. Well, not in body anyway. She died a year ago..." Eddie trailed off, his eyes glazing over.

Cara's mouth dropped, struggling for words. And then they all came at once. "Oh God, I'm so sorry about your wife. I didn't realise. I would never have brought the subject up if I'd have known. You must think I'm a right nosy cow. I really am so sorry." Cara could hear the trembling in her own voice. Why did she always put her foot in it?

"Cara, don't worry. Honestly. And thanks, it was horrendous, for me and for Willow, but we're working through it. It's nice that you asked—people these days just seem to want to talk about themselves."

"Erm, want some flapjack?" Cara opened her snack and pushed it towards Eddie, like some sort of awkward apologetic peace offering.

Eddie pulled off a chunk and put it in his mouth, smiling. "Good choice. Issy used to always put flapjacks in my lunchbox."

# 53

# *Food for Thought*

## Violet

Violet got in from Derek's before Ben came home, warmed his tea up for his arrival and got her pyjamas on. He never asked what she had been up to, so she didn't have to lie. He was in a foul mood though. The darts team had lost, and one of the many negative things about Ben was that he was a bad loser.

She was expecting the worst—an assault, name-calling—but that evening, he only made a few nasty comments, blaming her in some warped way for the other team beating his. She took it and didn't speak back. She wasn't prepared to antagonise him; her night had been too nice to let him burst her balloon.

Violet went to bed as quickly as she could, leaving Ben to unwind in front of the TV. As she lay in the dark, the dull sound of the TV downstairs in the background, she reflected on the wonderful night she'd experienced. It had been beautifully bizarre and something about it had felt like that feeling when you get into a hot bath filled with bubbles. That soothing sensation. With a little bit of unexpected pleasure thrown in. The food had been magnificent, homely, comforting with a touch of restaurant flair. Derek, as Debbie, had been something else, in a positive and inspiring way. Violet had a real fondness for him.

As for Florence, well, she was the grandma anyone would want. Funny, loving and considerate, with a sprinkling of naughtiness—the key ingredients of the best grandmas. A natural tonic who'd had everyone laughing.

Then, there was Eddie. A bit of a dark horse. He was intriguing, kind and intellectual. Violet predicted he would be a right gent and a real family man. She was looking forward to knowing more about him and the others.

Violet felt warm inside, like the gooey chocolate brownie Derek had made for pudding.

Next fortnight, it was to be Eddie's turn to cook, followed by Violet and lastly Florence. Violet couldn't wait to talk to Rosie about something nice for a change rather than what a bastard Ben had been.

"It must be bloody awful to feel you've been born in the wrong body or that you just want to be who you want to be, dress how you want and not feel judged," Violet stated to Rosie before their Saturday shift. "Let folk be who they want, I say, it's none of our business, and think about how you would feel," she added.

Rosie nodded. "You're right. It must be really hard for people, but it's nice he felt he could be authentic with you lot."

"In fact," Violet continued, "the Derek and Debbie thing has got me thinking. He was so brave, and here I am, living a lie, pretending I'm happy in my horrendous relationship. Letting a man abuse me. Not being myself." Violet looked into her cup, then back up at Rosie. "I can't go on like this, hun, I can't stand him, and I'm scared of him, Rosie."

Rosie's expression softened. "He won't change, Vi, it's gone on too long. I'm pleased this Deb thing has made you think. Maybe it's time to look at your future and you being you, like you said."

"I think it just might be, Rosie, I just need to get the strength to start the wheels in motion."

Rosie hugged Violet, their shifts about to start. "I love you, Vi."

"I love you too, you soft arse."

Violet made her way to her checkout as the shop started to fill with the usual Saturday morning shoppers. Rosie was two tills away. Customers were far and few between at first, picking up after an hour or so, and she scanned away, sharing jokes with some of her regulars. And then she looked up, taking a breather from a long queue of customers, and caught herself blushing as a familiar face approached her empty till. Eddie.

"H-h-hi, Eddie," she stuttered.

"Morning, Violet, I thought I would look out for you. How are you?" He smiled, placing his items on the conveyor belt.

"Oh, I'm fine thanks. How are you?" she replied, scanning the first of his items.

"Good, all good, ta. The other night was great, wasn't it? So much more than what I was expecting." Eddie let out a little laugh.

"It was that," Violet agreed. "I really enjoyed getting to know everyone a little, and the food was so tasty. Florence is such a darling; I can't wait to see her, and you all, again." There was that blush again. *Why am I blushing? For God's sake.*

"Yes, it was lovely, exceeded my expectations. I'm looking forward to hosting next time. Will be nice to continue getting to know everyone."

"Mind you, no getting your wife to do the cooking and you passing it off as yours." Violet chuckled.

"Erm, well, no chance of that." Eddie bit his lip. "Actually, Violet, my wife isn't around. She died a year ago. She was killed by a drunk driver."

Violet felt the colour completely drain from her face. *Oh no. Oh God.* "Oh, Eddie, I am so, so sorry. I just assumed. I am so terribly sorry for your loss. I don't know what to say."

"It's not your fault. Don't apologise. You weren't to know. It's not as if I told any of you. I guess I wanted to be Eddie first before being Eddie the widower," he said, sighing.

Violet felt tears trickling down her face. She knew how to silent cry—years of practice with an abusive man had perfected her silent distress.

"Bloody hell, I didn't mean to make you cry, Violet, I'm so sorry," Eddie said as his hand reached out to Violet's across the checkout.

"No, no, I'm sorry for crying. I'm just so sad for you. I can't believe it," Violet said, squeezing his hand. She felt electricity at his touch but now wasn't the right time to dwell on it.

"Are we just going to keep apologising to each other?" Eddie laughed, desperate to lighten the mood.

"I want to give you a cuddle and comfort you, but I can't because I'm at work. And because we don't really know each other." Violet finished scanning and fumbled with her sleeves, smiling awkwardly at Eddie. "But please know that if you ever want to talk or want help with anything, I'm here. Sorry, that's a stupid thing to say, offering help. No one can help, I guess." Violet sighed. "God, I'm apologising again, sorry."

"Thanks, Violet, and thanks for the Guinness World Record conversation of how many times two people can apologise. Seriously, I appreciate it. Best get this shopping home now though. I have a greedy little monster waiting for her Saturday treats." And with that, Eddie paid and left, wishing Violet a good day.

Violet couldn't bring herself to share the usual banter with her next customer. After they went, Rosie called her name. Violet turned.

"Bloody hell, who was that dish? It looked as if youse were having an intense conversation," Rosie asked, excitedly.

"It was Eddie, one of the men from The Dinner Club."

"The crossdresser?"

"Shhh, Rosie, and no, that's Derek. Eddie's the one with the daughter and wife. Well, so I thought." Violet looked around for approaching customers. Seeing none, she continued. "He just told me she's dead." She felt herself filling with tears again.

Rosie gasped. "Christ, it's like bloody *EastEnders*, this dinner club."

A customer approached Violet's checkout, and she served the woman in her usual pleasant manner, but her head felt foggy and her heart felt heavy. Heavy with sadness that Eddie had lost his wife, the mother of his child. Devastated that a child was now without her mother. Violet scanned the items, wondering why she had such an overwhelming urge to help Eddie and why someone who until very recently was a complete stranger felt like so much more.

# 54

# *The Truth*

## Florence

Florence told William of her fate, sharing what she had just about got her head around herself. She told her distressed son what Dr Dunn had informed her of her stage 4 bowel cancer and the treatments available to her. She told William again the results of the colonoscopy and what the hospital had fed back to the doctor.

Florence wasn't shocked; she'd known this was coming, after initial denial. She had tried to protect William, but he'd needed to know. He needed to prepare.

Florence had a low pain threshold. She often wondered how she'd managed to give birth. These days, she couldn't even tolerate a headache. She knew invasive, exhausting treatment that wouldn't produce a solution, just a temporary extension to her life, was a definite no. She wasn't frightened of dying, well, not really. The last few weeks, she had done very little but think about it and gain some level of acceptance about the inevitable.

Granted, it was very different for William. This was the first he had really heard. He'd known about her appointments but Florence had covered them up as follow ups from her stroke, and general checks. Florence had kept it secret to absorb it herself, to gain strength for her children, grandchildren and great-grandchildren.

"Mam, you have to try; you can't just give up." He sobbed, grabbing her hand as he looked at her with pleading eyes.

She tenderly touched her son's cheek and replied, "Son, there's no point; it's not guaranteed to do anything except give me a few more months of suffering and invasive treatment."

William let go of his mother's hand and dropped his head into his hands.

Florence kissed her precious son's head and tilted his face gently to look at her again. "It'll take away my quality to extend my quantity, love." She spoke softly, letting the intermittent silence be time for William to absorb the news.

William looked at his mother, his protector all his life. He needed time to process the inevitable.

Florence had told Jessie, who was distraught. She loved Florence like a grandmother, but Jessie had much experience of death, sadly, and she was a resilient young woman.

The last few weeks, Florence had been talking to her Ernie. No, she wasn't scared. How could she be truly scared when her Ernie was waiting? Florence had so much to live for, but she had so much in the afterlife waiting for her also. She had to swallow the fear, for William and Veronica and the kids now.

"Mam, I just don't understand. There must be something..."

"Come on, Son, let's go home and have a cuppa, and we can talk then," Florence said, soothingly touching William's shoulder.

# 55

# *Cause for Celebration*

## Derek

"Mate, it sounds like it went great. Good on you," said Bri, picking up his pint of beer as the friends sat in The Spitting Feathers.

"Honest, Bri, it was better than I could have ever dreamed. They are such a nice bunch, and I could really be myself with them," Derek replied joyfully as he opened a packet of crisps.

"You aren't going to come down here as Debbie, are you, mate? Not that I mind as such, but I think the lads would rip it out of you." Bri fidgeted in his seat.

Derek wasn't sure if he was using others as an excuse. But he knew it was a great deal to take in, even more so for a bloke of their generation. *The young ones today seem much more tolerant*, he thought, *Florence being an exception.*

"No, mate, I don't think so. I don't want to start parading around as a woman. I don't want to be a woman. I just want to wear women's clothes and kind of become someone else, an actress, for a few hours. It's always been in the privacy of my home. I'm not sure if I ever want to venture out into a public place as Debbie or if I would be brave enough, but it's not on my radar right now."

Derek observed the relief in Bri's eyes.

"Makes sense, mate. Listen, there may be questions I want to ask, I don't really understand it all. I hope you don't mind. I'm still Bri, and you're still my mate, that won't change. I just want to understand what's going on in your head."

"I know, Bri. Another pint?"

Two hours later, Derek was back home, sitting with Des, looking lovingly into his eyes and contemplating what to have for tea. He was still elated at how his food, and Debbie, had been received last week by his guests and genuinely couldn't wait for the next Dinner Club. Derek was already thinking of recipes for his next turn. But for now, it would be something less elaborate.

Shuffling into the kitchen, he opened the fridge. There was a fresh pizza he had bought from Foodways that morning. Derek had looked out for Violet but hadn't seen her. *She's a lovely lass*, he thought, taking the pizza out the fridge.

Peeling off the packaging, he could smell the fresh herbs. The toppings looked like gems in a rainbow on dough.

"Bloody hell, Son, I'm Hank Marvin now," he said to Des, who was close to Derek's side, always on the scrounge.

He popped the pizza in the oven, then returned to the lounge. Des followed him, an obvious sulk in his movements. Derek had already intended on turning his laptop on and messaging wearwhatiwant54.

***Hi, Peter/Paula,***

***Hope you are doing good.***

***Thanks so much for your supportive message. It gave me the confidence to introduce Debbie to strangers this week. I had only ever introduced her to two people, so it was a massive deal for me. The***

***strangers are new friends, it was only the second time we'd met, so we don't really know each other. Anyway, they came to my house, and there I was, Debbie! They were bloody marvellous and made me feel on cloud nine. They really supported me. I hope everyone is as accepting as they are in the future. Have you had similar experiences, or has it been more difficult? You don't have to answer, I know I'm being nosy.***

***Thanks so much for your encouragement, it was just what I needed.***

***Gratefully,***

***Derek***

Send. Derek smiled. He went to check on his pizza and heard his phone beep. *Bloody hell, that can't be a reply already, can it?* he wondered, rushing into the lounge. Opening his emails, he realised it was Brenda.

"Friggin' emailing, who does she think she is, Steve Jobs?"

Then, he read the email, and it started to make sense.

"The bloody..."

It was a meeting with a solicitor to look at divorce proceedings and equity. Derek sighed. He'd known it was coming, known it had to happen. Christ, he wanted it to happen. But that bloody woman had some psychic way of always pissing on his rainbow.

Derek returned to the kitchen; his food was ready. He grabbed a can of pop despite craving something stronger. Cutting his pizza, he heard another beep from his phone.

"For crying out loud, what does she want now?" he said, hissing through gritted teeth. He gathered his plate and drink as he stomped back into the lounge. Derek was relieved to see it was a message from Peter/Paula, and his mood switched in an instant from anger and worry about Brenda to positivity about Debbie.

*Derek/Debbie,*

*Great to hear from you and great news about introducing Debbie to your new friends. I bet that was a relief; it was a relief for me the first time. I had a lot of negative responses when I first came out. For me, it wasn't just sharing Paula, it was also admitting that I was gay, so for some people, it was just too much to absorb. Others had guessed I was gay, but Paula was a shock. Most people were accepting and asked questions.*

*Some people were cautious, and it didn't really get discussed for a long time. The sexuality seemed a lot easier for people to accept. Maybe it's a societal stigma thing. No one is really bothered about sexuality, apart from a minority of ignorant b@*$ards, but the transvestism holds more stigma, and people struggle between that and transgender. I don't think it's necessarily discrimination from people, sometimes just them not knowing. It needs to be discussed more in the media, awareness raising, but that's a whole other subject, Derek.*

*Sadly, some people distanced themselves from me. At first, I was devastated. Now, I'm grateful. I don't want such people in my life. But at the time, it was a big rejection, and I felt very low.*

*I've made some great new friends from the scene, some gay, some straight, some bisexual and some who don't want a label and just want to be who they want when they want. C'est la vie!*

*I'm so pleased my message helped, and I hope this one does as well. Please let me know. And don't take any crap, ha!*

*Px*

*What kindness and encouragement*, Derek thought. Just what he needed to read. It was a shame Peter had lost some friends on his journey, but Derek figured they were probably not real friends in the first instance. He imagined Peter to be confident, with swagger and many friends. Derek didn't aim big, he just wanted to be happy and healthy.

He went back to the email from Brenda. The appointment was on Thursday night, after work, 5 p.m. The same night The Dinner Club was at Eddie's.

*Bloody hell*, Derek thought. He couldn't miss either. If he asked Brenda to change it, she would play funny buggers and persecute him. Instead, he would take a change of clothes to work, go to the solicitors', then on to Eddie's. He would ask Bri to pop in to his on his way home to let Des out into the back garden to do his business. He may even ask Eddie if he could leave his car there overnight—it would be a certainty he would need a drink after the meeting with the solicitor.

# 56

# And It All Came Flooding Out

## Eddie

Mopping the chicken casserole sauce up with a wedge of bread, Eddie stopped his conversation with his mother to compliment her on the meal again. "That was delicious, Mam, it really was. That sauce gives it a whole new kick."

"Glad you like it, Son."

Connie had come over for the evening, armed with dinner. Connie visited once a week, always with supplies. It was her way of checking on her big baby and her four-year-old grandbaby. Eddie appreciated it more than he let on.

Eddie had been updating Connie on The Dinner Club's first meal. He hadn't mentioned it before, just to make sure it was something he wanted to keep up. But now it involved her and his father, due to babysitting duties, Eddie felt bound to confess. Connie was elated.

"Son, I'm so happy you are making new friends, meeting new people and doing something for yourself. Although, it sounds crackers from what you've said."

Eddie laughed. "I know, Mam, but honest, it was great. I can't remember the last time I enjoyed myself that much.

It's totally different to going down the pub with the lads and playing squash with Duncan. I was so nervous, but the group are lovely. I would never have met them in real life, if you know what I mean, but I think we all just clicked. And, Mam..."

"Yes, Son?"

"Since last Thursday, I've told two new people about Issy. And each time, I didn't break down. In fact, I felt a little lighter." Eddie beamed.

Connie rushed around the table to hug her son. "Ah, that's fantastic. I'm so proud of you. That's such a big deal." Connie let go of him and put her hands to her face, shocked at her son's transparency after burying his head for so long.

"And it's these new people that have made you open up, Son? Is it a support group or something?"

"You know, Mam, I think it might well be that. And I really think by me opening up, I've been able to really help and support one of them."

At the end of last week at work, following the intense conversation with Cara the day before, Eddie had made an effort to check she was ok. She was only a young lass, after all, and he worried he had burdened her and been unprofessional. It was clear from her interview and a few snapshot conversations that Cara herself had a history, maybe a current situation. He didn't want her to feel uncomfortable.

"Well, the first week's almost over. How's it been?" he asked, walking into the staffroom as Cara made herself a cuppa.

"Hi, Eddie, it's been great. It's like my dream job," Cara said proudly.

"Wow, that's good to hear. Seems Danielle is impressed with you as well," Eddie said as he dropped a teabag into his cup.

"She's been lovely. Everyone has. They are all so nice." She took a sip of her own hot drink.

Eddie nodded; it was important new staff felt welcomed. “Yeah, we are a canny bunch. Got much planned for the weekend?”

“No, not really. I’m skint until payday next Friday. So, just staying in and watching TV.” She gave a nervous laugh at the end of her sentence.

“Are you local?” Eddie enquired.

“Yeah, just in Byker. I’m staying with my best mate at the moment. It’s not ideal, but once I’ve had a few monthly pays, I’ll look for somewhere for myself. One step at a time, eh.” Cara looked at the floor, as if she had said too much. She took another sip of her drink, moving her eyes from the floor to the liquid.

Eddie sensed her unease. It sounded as if Cara had problems of some sort, in the past or now. “Sounds like a plan, and you’ve done great here this week, so be proud of yourself.”

Eddie watched a smile appear across Cara’s face, like a child with a new toy. And she really did look like a child. There was something about her big eyes and nervous body language that mirrored the way Willow was around strangers the first time. With her petite frame and lack of make-up, Eddie thought Cara could easily be mistaken for a girl of fourteen. What was her story? There was something about her that he was drawn to, some vulnerability, this young girl who at times looked like a wounded deer and other times had the spirit of a lion.

“Have a good one, Cara,” he said.

“You too, and thanks, Eddie. Thanks for helping me this week and making me feel important.”

# 57

# *Perspective*

## Violet

"Well, what did you say to him, then?" Rosie asked.

Violet had spent all week planning a conversation in her head whilst daydreaming on her till about a future free from Ben. She was still reeling from what Eddie had said last week. She felt so sad, heartbroken for him and his daughter, heartbroken for herself that she was in a loveless relationship. Eddie had lost the love of his life without warning, and here she was with a bastard of a man who showed her no love and who she couldn't stand. She was missing out on the love that everyone should experience.

Violet had fantasised about telling Ben to piss off and leaving him. Of course, in her head, it was all very glamourous and she was in control. Her hair flowing and her make-up perfect as she left him speechless, packing her car and driving away with her middle finger up. In reality, Violet knew far too well that any departure would have to be done on the sly. Ben was a violent bully, and she had gathered some information over the years about domestic abuse. She knew that when people leave their abusive partners, they are most at risk of serious harm, even murder. She had to be careful. She had to be safe. It had to be final.

There was a lot involved, and Rosie was a big part of the plan. She had been for a while, but now it felt to Violet, for the first time, that the plan could become a reality.

"C'mon, what did you say?" Rosie repeated.

"Well, I asked him if he ever thought about us splitting up. He said, 'Why? It'll never happen. No one else will have you' and laughed in my face. The prick. So, I said, 'But do you not think you'd be happier with someone else?' The arrogant bastard said, 'Yeah, more than likely, if I could be bothered to find someone. Tell you what, Vi, I'll start looking and let you know how I get on'. Then, he went to the bathroom, laughing." Violet shook her head, letting out a sigh.

"Jesus, does he have a magic mirror or what? I mean, Vi, he's repulsive, inside and out." Rosie laughed uncomfortably.

"I know he is. I've known for a while. Then, later on, he asked why I was talking like that and if I was shagging someone at work." Violet bit on her thumbnail. "Then, he said if I was, he would kill me and kill them. He was right in my face, Ro, inches away from grabbing me." Violet stopped talking, her hand went back towards her mouth as she recalled the conversation in her head. Rosie grabbed her friend's hand, squeezing it in gentle reassurance.

Violet went on, "I was really frightened. I had to kiss him to calm him down and said I dreamt he left me as an excuse. I don't know how he didn't see me shaking, Rosie." There was a moment of silence. Violet nibbled at her half of the toasted teacake as both the women reflected on the reality of Violet's circumstances.

Rosie looked at her friend, compassion in her eyes. "Ah, Vi, he won't ever leave you, unfortunately. These types of scumbags never do. But now you know what you need to do and, hun, you're as strong as they bloody come. I'll help, I promise. You can do this. I want to see my Vi sparkle again." Rosie rubbed Violet's arm.

"I know, Rosie, I will, I promise. I'm so lucky to have you. Come on, time to do our thing."

Just over two hours into her shift, Violet spotted the same familiar face from last weekend strolling up the checkouts. It was Eddie. She turned around and looked at Rosie, who very blatantly pointed him out as if Violet hadn't seen. Violet sniggered. Eddie caught her eye about ten metres away and waved. He was coming over.

Violet smoothed her hair down and straightened her posture as much as she could in her checkout booth. *What are you even doing?* she asked herself, catching what she had just done.

"Hi, Violet." Eddie's eyes were tired but happy, a hint of a smile in them.

"Morning, Eddie, nice to see you." And she really meant it.

"And you. How are you? How's your week been? Looking forward to Thursday?"

"Oh yeah, I can't wait. Are you buying the ingredients now? And I'm good thanks, are you?" Violet felt flustered; it was hard having in-depth conversations whilst scanning shopping and thinking about how ghastly she must look in her Foodways uniform.

"Some of it, yes, it will be nice to cook for more than me and the little one."

The first Dinner Club had mainly been small talk and then getting to meet Debbie, leaving little time to ask questions about each other. Violet realised she knew very little about Eddie and now found herself wanting to ask him loads. At the same time, it was as if she had met him months and months ago—a similar feeling that she had with Derek and Florence.

"I bet you're great at your job. You look the type: smart and liked by everyone." *Ah, hell, what a stupid thing to say.* "I, I mean you've clearly worked hard, you know," she stammered, lowering her head.

"Well, thanks, Violet, that's very kind. Not sure it's entirely true but very kind of you. Likewise, I know you do a grand job here." Eddie grinned.

Violet beamed; his smile was infectious. It had a slight lack of symmetry to it that was endearing. As Eddie popped his debit card in the machine, Violet wondered if he was deliberately taking his time or if it was just a man thing. He was handsome, there was no denying that. He had that mid-thirties look where men's faces start to have that more mature appearance: slightly weathered, wrinkles forming, the odd grey hair in their beard. Signs of living, of struggles and happiness. It was attractive.

Violet snapped out of it as Eddie took his card from the reader.

"Well, thank you, Violet. I look forward to seeing you on Thursday. Have a great weekend."

"Yes, definitely, I can't wait," Violet replied a little too quickly. *God, I sound desperate.* What was she even playing at? *For crying out loud, his wife is dead. He's heartbroken. He was just being nice*—something Violet was certainly not used to from a man.

Yet, she couldn't help but watch Eddie until he was no longer in sight.

# 58

# *Heard*

## Cara

Cara left the office that Friday like a giddy teenager planning their prom. It had been the best week ever at work. She had felt like part of the team, included, welcomed and supported. Danielle was ace and so good at her job. Cara knew that with her mentoring, she could be just like her one day.

She had made friends with Stevie, a lad who was four years older than her. He had talked about gigs and the local comedy club. She'd had loads of chats with Deena, another lass in her twenties. Then, there was Sue, who had worked at Hendersons from the start and was the go-to person. And, of course, she'd got to know Eddie a bit more, who'd made her feel comfortable and had that trendy dad appeal.

Cara's task for that weekend was to do some budgeting, work out her salary each month and her outgoings. She could explore how much surplus she could save to move out of Caitlyn's as soon as possible. She knew Caitlyn would always look out for her, but she had heard Rhys talking about her needing to go soon. Cara was kind of getting in the way. She was used to feeling like that. She wanted her own bedroom and space to put her belongings. She wanted to feel professional—a wardrobe in a bag, using other people's cosmetics and a poor sleep each night on a sofa wasn't the best approach to achieving that.

Cara stayed on the bus, passing her usual stop for Caitlyn's. The bus continued for a couple of miles before Cara got off. Walking along the high street, she popped into the florist. Cara had a look around even though she knew what she would buy. It was always the same, and they always looked so pretty. Candyfloss pink roses, just like the ones that used to grow in the garden all those years ago. For all the bad memories, she had some good ones from childhood, and they still felt vivid and comforting. Cara spotted the perfect bunch. Picking them up, she inhaled their fragrance. She carried them to the jolly shop assistant, —a new employee she hadn't seen before during any of her frequent visits, —who commented on their beauty.

"They're for someone important," Cara said, staring off into space for a second.

"Well, I'm sure they will love them," replied the enthusiastic assistant.

Cara nodded, collected her change and left the shop to walk the five minutes to her destination.

She hadn't visited for a while but knew where the plot was off by heart despite the cemetery going back for what seemed like miles. She soon reached the spot. She stood silently for a few seconds, as if in a trance, her feet rooted to the ground, eyes struggling to focus on the headstone, still somehow unable to accept reality.

"Hi, Mam, I've brought you some flowers for your birthday." She placed them at the bottom of the gravestone.

"Sorry I haven't been for a while. Things have been a bit mad. But I've got a new job. I'm proud of myself, Mam, and I hope you're proud of me."

Cara sat on the ground, staring at her mother's headstone. For all the years Kate had neglected her, putting men, alcohol, drugs and herself before Cara, there had still been some hope for Cara that her mother would step up and be a mother. That something would just click into place in Kate's head and she would reach out and embrace her daughter, her baby. That she would see that no man was more important than her own flesh and blood. That she could get help for her addictions and mental ill health. That Cara could be part of the solution. Cara had so much love to give, always waiting to give it. Even after the ultimate rejection of her own mother, followed by repeat rejection in foster care, abuse and fear, the sexual abuse she had experienced, the loneliness, the desperation, the trauma, the distress. Even after all of this, Cara had still had hope.

But then Kate had died. Cara could never have her acceptance now. She could never have her mam, a proper mam who would love her unconditionally. All the unanswered questions, all the what ifs, all the never agains gone. Cara never got to say goodbye.

It was an overdose: a cocktail of prescription drugs, alcohol and heroin. Found by a neighbour after three days. The only evidence of Cara ever existing was a birthday card Cara had sent her mam on her twenty-eighth birthday and a handful of photos.

Cara stared at the headstone; a life etched into the marble.

"Everyone's really nice, Mam. They've made me feel welcome, and I'm going to stick at it. In a few months, I will have my own place. A new start." Cara's voice was quietened by the early winter wind.

When Kate had died, four years ago, Cara had promised herself her visits to the cemetery would be filled with talking. Her mother had known nothing of her adulthood. She'd never sent cards, never replied to letters. Never heard or never listened—Cara wasn't sure which. Now, it was her time to talk and Kate's time to listen.

"So, I'm going home now to look at my finances," Cara said proudly, getting up off the ground.

"Happy birthday, Mam."

# 59

# *Food Glorious Food*

## Eddie

It was Wednesday, the night before Eddie's hosting debut. Willow had been bathed and was in bed, tucked up with her toy of the week, Sebastian the lobster from *The Little Mermaid*.

Laptop open, Eddie had a beer in one hand and a big bag of crisps in the other. He had started jogging home from work—exercise had always made Eddie feel good and he had neglected his fitness of late. The crisps were totally counteracting his efforts, but still, the intention was there.

Eddie's week had been filled with thinking and a mixture of emotions. Talking to Connie last night had helped relieve his mind, and for the first time in a long time, Eddie was being positive. He was looking forward to seeing the group tomorrow night. The nerves he'd felt for the first visit had dissolved. Instead, he felt prepared.

Willow would be staying at his parents' like last time, and he was going to work for 7 a.m. to finish by 3 p.m., giving plenty of time to prepare. All ingredients had been bought, and Connie had offered to pop over and give the place a quick clean during the day tomorrow. It didn't need it in Eddie's opinion, but he knew his mother wanted to help out, so he gratefully accepted.

Eddie typed in everyone's email addresses and began his group email:

***Evening, diners,***
***Looking forward to seeing you all tomorrow.***
***The menu is as follows:***
***Starter: Pâté and Melba Toast***
***Main: Indian Feast***
***Dessert: Lemon Posset***
***Dress code: Perfect as you are!***
***Your host, Eddie x***

Eddie prepared the table, got the crockery out and marinated his meat for the curry. The rest could wait until tomorrow afternoon.

Eddie's alarm woke him up at 6 a.m. It was pitch black outside and cold; colder than most late Novembers.

Robert was coming over in forty-five minutes to get Willow ready for school, taking her overnight bag and at least one extra bag of rubbish that he'd seen Willow packing before bed.

Eddie got up and had a quick shower. He wasn't running this morning. He was keen but not that keen. Getting out the shower, he put his dressing gown on and poked his head around Willow's door.

*Christ*, he thought. There were four bags on the floor. He'd have to speak to her about this bag packing, as it was definitely expanding. Eddie made a mental note.

He was downstairs having breakfast at six-thirty, when he heard the familiar, frantic footsteps that he loved so much.

"Morning, bubs, you're up early." He greeted a sleepy Willow with a hug. She smelt divine: of sleep, warmth and that little Willow smell she had. He wished he could bottle it.

She spotted his toast. "I'm hungry, Daddy."

"Are you, my little mischief maker?" Eddie joked. "Well, take a seat, madam, and we will see what is on the menu this morning to choose."

Willow clapped her hands and smiled. So easily pleased. Eddie adored the naivety of his daughter, that Nutella and banana and toast and porridge made her the happiest creature in the world each morning. He wanted to protect her forever, keep her in her banana bubble where the only thing that mattered was that her toast was cut into triangles.

"I love you, honey," he said, looking with adoration at her chubby, rosy face.

"Love you, Daddy." She beamed up at her breakfast hero.

Eddie prayed that Issy was watching them, right there in the kitchen at 6:36 a.m.

# 60

# *Spice Girl*

## Florence

"What do you think the Indian feast constitutes, love?" Florence asked Jessie that Thursday morning.

"Sounds bloody lush, Florrie. I bet it's curry, pilau rice, naan bread, onion bhajis, samosas, the works. Can I come?"

"Ooh, I hope it's not too spicy."

"Ask for a glass of milk instead of a shandy, Florrie," Jessie joked.

"You little bugger," teased Florence.

"Anyway, what did the doc say this week, Florrie? Did he try to change your mind about the treatment?" Jessie's tone changed; she was visibly concerned.

"No, pet, it's my choice, and I've made my decision. He just wants to monitor me. I have to see the social worker, look at a care package and any changes I might need."

"Ah, Florrie, I don't even want to think about it. I hope it's a long way down the line. You mean the world to us." Jessie held Florence's hand.

"I know, love, and my life wouldn't have been as long as it has if it wasn't for you, my angel."

Jessie smiled at Florence, a genuine, loving smile.

"Best get you a cuppa and your brekkie. I'll give you a little extra in case you don't like that curry tonight."

Florence's nieces Sheila and Carole came over that afternoon, bringing carrot cake and plenty of chat. Florence had a great time and of course managed two slices of cake and a few cups of tea. That would keep her going until she went to Eddie's.

She then managed to have a little siesta in her recliner chair that afternoon, her heat pad on her back and her fleece blanket over her knees. When she woke, it was time to get ready and get her taxi to Eddie's. Jessie had helped pick Florence's outfit that morning. A navy-blue skirt and a lovely red blouse, with her navy cardigan on top. Florence got ready, squirting her perfume and putting her expensive foundation on.

"Who's that beautiful woman?" she joked to herself, looking at her reflection in the bathroom mirror. The foundation and matching powder had set her back over sixty pounds early last week. Carole and Sheila had taken her into town, where an assistant at the beauty counter in the department store had given her a makeover. Florence had felt like a film star, so naturally she'd had to treat herself to the products. If tonight wasn't an occasion to showcase them, she didn't know what was.

Ready with time to spare, Florence patiently waited. Davey pulled up five minutes later. Florence quickly pocketed a few extra toffees, just to keep him going on his rounds, grabbed her handbag and walking sticks and opened the front door.

"Evening, me dear," said Davey as he came to help her down the path and into the taxi.

"Hello, pet, nice to see you."

"Off on the pull, are you, Florence?" Davey teased.

"Oi, cheeky!" Florence tapped his arm playfully. "Actually, a handsome young man is cooking for me."

"Oh aye, what's that all about then?" Davey chuckled.

"It's my Dinner Club, pet, once a fortnight from now on. I've been looking forward to this all week."

"Well, I hope you have the best night ever, Florence."

Davey's taxi soon pulled up at Eddie's house, and Davey helped Florence out. After saying their goodbyes, Florence rang the doorbell.

Eddie opened the door, looking handsome and happy.

"Florence, wonderful to see you, come on in." Eddie helped her in, taking her coat and making sure she was ok. *A true gent*, thought Florence, *just like my Ernie was*.

"You look a picture, Florence, you really suit red."

"Thanks, son, you look rather dashing yourself. Your wife is a lucky lady."

Eddie's welcome smile dropped slightly as he stammered an agreement and gestured towards the lounge. She took a seat and was given a cup of tea. *Save the shandy for the meal*, she thought. She had been the first to arrive, and she sat enjoying the jazz music on the CD player, and the smell of the cooking food as she waited. Eddie kept popping in to converse and check she was ok, but for those few minutes before the others arrived, Florence soaked up her surroundings, feeling peaceful and lucky.

# 61

# *Change Is as Good as a Rest*

## Derek

Thursday came round quickly. Derek left work at 4:45 p.m. and drove the four miles to the solicitors', Marsden and Co, parking outside, with five minutes to spare. His hands were trembling. He had asked Jeff's advice at lunch.

"What will happen, Jeff?" he had said, hoping for some reassurance.

"Well, the greedy bitch will want to rinse you, mate. That's what Maggie tried to do. Greedy cow she is. Luckily, my pension is crap, else she would have been after that. She was entitled to half of the ISAs in my name, my bloody money. Then, the house sale, what a nightmare that was. I don't envy you. Just don't let her bloody rinse you."

Derek had taken a deep breath, wishing he had never asked.

The receptionist greeted him as he walked into Marsden and Co. "Evening, sir, can I help?"

"Hi, I am here to see Alison."

"Name, please, sir?"

"It's Derek. Derek Morgan. Like the character in *Criminal Minds*." He chuckled.

Brenda strolled in, trying to look like an executive in her trouser suit. "Derek." She nodded coldly.

"Hi, Bren." Derek took a seat.

"I'll let Alison know you're both here." The receptionist smiled.

Ninety minutes later, they came out of Marsden and Co feeling deflated, emotional and wanting to get away from each other. Their divorce would go ahead with no objections. Brenda would be entitled to a proportion of Derek's work pension, and Derek would buy Brenda out of their home. Brenda would struggle to get a mortgage not working, and she claimed the house had "unhappy memories", whatever she'd meant by that.

The valuation and process of buying Brenda out was instructed, and they would reconvene with Alison in just over a fortnight. Derek would have to remortgage, as he didn't have that type of money. His wage at Cartington's wasn't especially high, and he had outgoings, more now, paying solo. But he wanted to stay in the house, he just had to work a few things out. Christ, he was ready for a drink. He would give Bri a call and update him, then drive over to Eddie's, hopefully to be greeted with a strong drink.

# 62

# *The Perfect Evening*

## Violet

"That Eddie's fit, mind, and I think he likes you." Rosie winked.

"Rosie, he's lost his wife, and I am in a relationship, albeit a toxic one."

"Well, some flirting would do no harm, and I am confident you will be away from that arsehole Ben in a few months anyway, Vi, or I will kill the swine myself." Rosie impersonated an evil laugh, and they both giggled.

"I know, I'm in the zone, Ro, I know I'm getting stronger, and I will know the right time to go. The Dinner Club is just the boost I need. What with that and you by my side, I can take on the world." She held Rosie's hand, smiling affectionately at her friend.

"Now, go home. Go and get ready. I'll come pick you up later." Rosie grinned as she shooed her away.

Violet arrived home that afternoon with plenty of time to get ready. It was Eddie's night, and she had first date nerves. There was something about Eddie that made her giddy with excitement. She felt guilty—he was a grieving widower, and she was with Ben—she had meant what she'd said to Rosie. But still, there was just something about him and talking to him that made her feel good.

Talking to her as an equal, paying compliments, it was so alien to her. She knew she was looking too much into it, but she would relish in the feelings it was giving her.

Ben did his usual Thursday routine of coming in from work, having a snack and getting ready for the club. Violet was relieved. She wanted to get ready in peace, have a glass of wine and enjoy her anticipation. Rosie had offered to drop her off at Eddie's, partly out of being curious or nosy, Violet had thought, but Rosie had also claimed to be going to legs, bums and tums at her gym at seven-thirty, which wasn't far from Eddie's estate, and advised Violet it was "no bother".

Violet poured herself a glass of wine. She had picked up a single-serve bottle from work. If she left some wine in the fridge, it would set Ben off. He would either quiz her on why she was drinking or drink the rest himself and no doubt use it as an excuse to be abusive. Violet had learnt survival skills the hard way.

After showering, she smothered her skin in body lotion, absorbing the fruity smell and seeing the shimmer on her soft, peachy skin. She had chosen her red lace dress to wear. It showed a little more cleavage than what she was used to, but it was very classy, so Violet felt it was bold but not inappropriate.

She took time applying her make-up, studying her face. Wrinkles had crept around her eyes the last few years, and tiredness, both physical and emotional, was visible on her face. The older she got, the more she looked like her mother, which was a comfort. She knew exactly what her mam would say about Ben and about her outfit tonight. Applying her eye make-up, she added some of the sparkly eyeshadow from the palette Rosie had bought her for her birthday. She would just put a little clear lip gloss on—no need for lipstick, she wasn't going to The Oscars.

She finished off the wine and straightened her hair. Sliding on her black heels and grabbing her black clutch bag, she looked in the full-length mirror. Violet smiled. While her self-esteem could be rock bottom most of the time, she knew deep down she wasn't the fat, ugly, disgusting bastard Ben told her she was. She knew her body wasn't the best and maybe her boobs were a little saggy like Ben claimed, maybe her tummy was a little podgier than she would like, and maybe she had more wrinkles than other women her age, but Violet knew she was a kind and decent person. It was only Ben who thought otherwise.

She remembered a quote Rosie had sent to her once, by the great Roald Dahl: "If you have good thoughts, they will shine out of your face like sunbeams and you will always look lovely."

In that moment, as she heard the toot of Rosie's car horn outside, looking at her reflection, that's exactly how Violet felt.

# 63

# *Canapés Confession*

## Eddie

Eddie heard laughing outside as the doorbell sounded for a second time. As Florence sat happily, tapping her foot to the music, cup of tea in hand, Eddie went to open the front door.

"Ah, two for the price of one," he joked, opening the door to both Derek and Violet, who had arrived at the same time. "Come on in."

"Evening, Eddie," Violet said, entering the house.

*Wow, she looks amazing*, thought Eddie. "You look lovely, Violet."

Violet smiled kindly and thanked Eddie.

"And, Derek, where is Debbie tonight?" Eddie enquired.

"A long story, mate, I will tell you all once I've had a beer, please. I'm bloody gasping."

Eddie welcomed them into the lounge, and both went over to greet an elated Florence.

"Hello, my lovelies. Ooh, come here so I can have a cuddle." Florence embraced them both, and neither Derek nor Violet seemed to want to let go. Eventually, the cuddlefest finished, and Eddie grabbed a beer from the kitchen for Derek.

"Wine, beer, gin, soft drink, Violet?"

"White wine, please, Eddie. I got a lift here, as I fancied a drink."

After getting his guest a drink, Eddie asked everyone to follow him through to the dining room. They all took their seats, impressed with the table layout and decoration.

Starter was served: pâté and melba toast. They all tucked in, passing round the crackers.

"So, Eddie, I noticed a photo of your beautiful wife and daughter in your lounge. Where are they tonight? And is this really going to be your own cooking?" Derek chuckled.

Eddie noticed Violet wince. She'd made that same joke too.

"Actually, Derek, Issy, my wife, died a year ago." Eddie said it flatly; he'd almost mastered saying the words and totally detaching the meaning over the last year. People hate saying the word "dead"—it feels so final. Eddie had struggled at first, like most people. But in the first few months in particular, when he'd lost Issy, it had felt like something he said as much as "hello". Strangers mentioning partners, wives, mothers. Friends, family, colleagues asking. Over and over. "She's dead. She died. She's gone," he would repeat. Eddie had learned that they were words, not feelings. He could now say it, say his wife was dead, without feeling grief flowing through his veins like anaesthetic.

"Oh my God, Eddie, I am s-so dreadfully sorry," Derek stammered, turning red.

"Derek, it's ok, honest. I knew someone would ask; it's a beautiful photo." Eddie had an instant flashback to where the photo was taken, Hyde Park in the Summer on a visit to London. A trip where they'd talked about their future. The future that wasn't to be.

Eddie looked at Derek, then his other guests. "I wanted to tell everyone, but I wanted you to know me as me first. Since Issy died, I've been "Eddie, Issy's widower", "Eddie, whose wife died". It was refreshing to meet new people who met me as Eddie and got to know a little bit about me, as Eddie, initially. But to tell you all now, in my home, in mine and Issy's home, it feels right."

Violet wiped her eyes.

"I can't lie, the last year has been horrific for me. For Willow. For us all. I didn't get to say goodbye, I didn't get to remind her how much I love her and that she was the best mam in the world. I don't have my last birthday card from her, I don't have the sound of her voice on my voicemail, I struggle to remember what her cuddles feel like and the smell of her hair." Eddie stopped and took a deep breath. He had struggled to talk to some of his life-long friends like this, to tell them of his pain. Looking at his dinner guests, people he had known less than a month, he saw sincerity in each of their faces as they listened compassionately.

"But through all the heartache and the voids that are in our life every day, knowing I had that love from her and loved her back helps to keep me glued together. I was lucky in so many ways, albeit for not as long as I would have liked." Eddie looked down at the table and rubbed his beard.

"Oh, son, that's beautiful. She will be watching over you, so proud." Florence, sitting next to him, held his hand tightly. She was visibly upset.

Eddie looked around the table, mustering a smile, "Sorry, everyone, I didn't mean to upset you." He held Florence's hand back, squeezing it gently.

"You are amazing, Eddie. Willow is so lucky to have you." Violet smiled.

"Eddie, I'm so sorry you lost your wife. I'm sure I speak for us all when I say you're inspiring, and we're here if you need to talk," Derek said sincerely.

"Love never existed until I met Issy. She made me experience, in our short years, what some people will never experience in their long life. I've had more good days than bad recently. I feel her around us, and I'm grateful." Eddie noticed Florence nod as she dabbed her eyes with a serviette.

"I guess you feel that too, Florence, with your Ernie," Eddie said gently as Florence continued to wipe her eyes.

She nodded and touched her chest. "I carry him here, son, always in my heart," Florence replied. "And you carry your Issy's heart in yours, and in your little girl's."

The table was quiet for a few seconds, a silent reflection, a shared understanding of love and the fragility of life.

"Thank you. All of you. Anyway, let's have a toast before our main, eh?" Eddie lifted his glass, as did his guests. "To love. Love that never dies. And to new friendships." He took a gulp of his drink before placing the glass down. Eddie got up from the table and headed into the kitchen, wiping his eyes as he walked.

For the rest of the meal, Eddie tried to lighten the conversation. They talked about favourite holiday destinations and where they would love to visit.

"I've always fancied Vegas," Derek announced.

"I went to Vegas on a stag weekend about ten years ago. It was unreal, like nowhere else on earth. They have escalators in the street, I mean, in the actual street. It's mental. Everyone drinks alcohol twenty-four seven, and the casinos have no daylight, so you can never tell the time of day inside. There is something seedy yet phenomenal about the place. I think you would love it, Derek. RuPaul even has a residency now, I believe," Eddie said and then bit his lip, wondering if he should have said the last bit.

"Sorry, mate, I hope that didn't offend. I'm not sure if drag queens and crossdressers are the same thing?"

"Actually, I like RuPaul, although a tad over the top for my liking. I'm not a fan of looking like a peacock. A simple dress and a bit of make-up does it for me." Derek laughed, and Eddie knew he hadn't offended him.

"And no, they aren't the exact same thing. Drag is more of a flamboyant act, whereas, to me, cross-dressing is more of an urge, more private or at least less of a performance. I think a good comparison would be theatre and pantomime. Cross-dressing is theatre and panto is the exaggerated, animated and over the top version of theatre."

"That's a great analogy, love, makes a lot of sense." Florence nodded.

"Where is your favourite place, Florence, and where would you like to visit?" Derek asked.

"Well, I went to Austria once with my nieces. It was lovely. Of course, I love Canada, more because our Veronica and the family being there than the place itself. And Manchester will always feel like home. I think I would have liked to have gone to Italy; it always looks so beautiful on the TV. Seems romantic. I wish my Ernie and I could have gone." Florence looked into the distance.

She looked back at Eddie, and he saw sadness in her eyes. *Time doesn't heal, it just helps us to adapt to voids*, he thought, rubbing her arm gently as she gave a grateful nod.

"You should go, Florence; you should plan it. Do all the things your Ernie would have loved. He'll be there by your side, I'm certain," Violet said, looking fondly at Florence.

Florence laughed sadly. "Maybe in my dreams, pet, maybe in my dreams."

"And you, Violet, where is your favourite place and somewhere you've always wanted to go?" Eddie smiled at Violet. She was shy but Eddie felt she was coming out of her shell.

"I've only ever been abroad once, to Nice with my childhood friend Alice. We were nineteen, and I really enjoyed it. Beach, shops, museums, bars, plenty to do. I haven't been away since I've been with Ben." She looked at the table, then looked up again. "He won't fly and says holidays are a waste of money. I would love to go to Spain, Italy as well, the Greek islands, the whole world." Her eyes lit up as the dream danced in her mind.

They chatted through pudding about childhood and school. The group was fascinated with Florence's stories of childhood in the nineteen-forties, during the war and post-war. They felt like a group of old friends sharing memories and stories. Eddie glanced at them all as Florence talked and felt a wave of happiness. For the last hour of talking and getting to know each other, he had found himself constantly smiling and laughing. He couldn't remember feeling like that since Issy had died. Everything was always shadowed by sadness, tinged with loss, grief, resentment and distress.

As he went to get his guests another drink, Eddie felt a kick of guilt. He had never enjoyed himself like that with Willow, not since Issy had died. He'd had nice times with her, laughs and fun, without a doubt, but he had never let go completely and really enjoyed himself, even for a minute. He'd never felt one hundred percent happy. Until tonight.

Eddie felt sick with guilt, panicky that he would never be the dad he needed to be. That he would forever not give his whole self to his daughter. That he resented her. He placed his hands to his face. Then, he felt a touch on his shoulder.

"Eddie, are you ok?"

Violet. He turned and saw the concern etched all over her face.

"Oh bollocks, yeah, sorry, Violet. I just feel a bit weird, but I'm fine." He faked a smile.

"Weird in what way?" she enquired.

"Erm, I'm not sure. I think I just feel strange having such a nice night. Talking about Issy but then for the first time in so long, actually letting myself go, having a laugh and feeling happy. Not tense and guarded, like I usually am.

It's weird. Alien, I guess. But nice," he said, nodding with his realisation.

"Well, it sounds like a positive thing for you. You deserve to be happy, Eddie," Violet said with tenderness in her voice.

"Thanks, Violet, I will get there, I really will."

Violet helped Eddie with the drinks, then they returned to the dining room. Florence and Derek were chuckling away together.

The drinks were flowing when a mobile started ringing. It was immediately clear who the phone belonged to, as Violet's expression changed, and she jumped up from her seat to get her phone from her bag, glancing at her watch.

"Shit!" she shouted through clenched teeth. Eddie had never heard Violet swear before. She retrieved her phone as it rang off.

"Violet, is everything ok, love?" asked Derek.

"Sorry for swearing. I have to go. I didn't realise the time. I need to book a taxi immediately."

Eddie was concerned and confused at the panic in her voice.

"I'll take you home, Violet, if you need to go right now. I've only had the one beer, and that was four hours ago. Florence and Derek can keep chatting. That's ok, folks, isn't it?" Eddie frantically looked at Florence and Derek, who both nodded their agreement. He didn't know why but he sensed something was really off with Violet's situation, something more than just a time she promised Ben she'd be home by.

"No, no, I can't expect you to do that, Eddie," Violet said.

"Look, Violet, you seem upset, and we're concerned, so please let me take you home. Come on, let's go, we're wasting time." Eddie grabbed his coat, indicating he was serious.

Violet followed sheepishly. "Sorry, Florence. Sorry, Derek. All is ok, I just have to get home. I've had the most amazing night, thanks, see you soon," she blurted out as she followed Eddie to the front door.

Eddie couldn't believe how quickly the night had gone—time flies when you're having fun and all that. But now, his attention was completely on Violet.

"Is everything ok?" Eddie asked as he drove her the ten minutes back to her house. He didn't want to pry but her reaction in the house had been out of character from what he knew of her.

"Yes, I just need to get home. It was Ben. He'll be worried where I am."

"Did you not tell him you were coming to The Dinner Club?" Eddie glanced at Violet for a second, who was sat in the passenger seat.

"No." Her voice trembled. "He wouldn't understand, so I just thought I wouldn't say anything. He plays darts at the pub every Thursday, so I knew I would be home in time for him not to find out. I just lost track of time. I can be so stupid sometimes. He would have been worried, that's all."

"I don't think you're stupid," Eddie mumbled.

He stopped at a set of traffic lights and looked at Violet, who was shaking and looking the other way.

"Violet." He touched her arm. "Violet, look at me, what's going on? You're shaking like a leaf."

Violet turned to face him, tears rolling down her face.

"What the hell? Violet, please, I'm worried, what's going on?"

The lights turned green, but Eddie didn't move. There was no traffic behind him.

"Please, I need to get home. Please, please drive. It's bad enough already," Violet begged.

"What's bad enough, Violet? Christ, you're really worrying me now. If I drive, will you please talk to me?"

Violet nodded, wringing her hands together.

"I can't hear you, Violet, and I'm still worried," Eddie prompted.

"God. Eddie, please, I can't talk about this. I don't even know you." Violet's voice rose in pitch.

"Violet, I know, but you are in my car, and you're visibly upset, concerned, scared, I don't know, but whatever it is, it isn't the Violet we had tonight. Do you trust me?"

Violet nodded.

"So, talk, please. I don't need details; I just need to know you're going to be ok."

'It's, it's," she stuttered. "It's bad, it's complicated. I don't know what to say."

"Is it Ben?" Eddie asked. Violet nodded again, crying uncontrollably now.

"Violet, I'm pulling over."

"No, no, please, please no," she screamed. "Just get me home, please, Eddie. You don't know what he'll do."

"Eh? What will he do? What the hell will he do, Violet?" he shouted back anxiously, somehow protective of this near stranger.

"He can be a bit stuck in his ways, a bit nasty when he's had a drink. He's not going to like seeing me dressed up, wondering where I have been. Because I didn't tell him. And I'm dressed up. I never dress up. I never wear this much make-up. God." Violet grasped the sides of her head, shaking it manically.

Eddie took a deep breath, trying to calm his temper, which he could feel starting to soar. "Violet, has Ben hit you?" He was pretty certain he knew the answer.

She paused. "Once or twice," she replied, focusing on her knees.

"Fucking bastard!" Eddie hit his steering wheel with his palm and then felt immediately terrible when he noticed Violet flinch. He despised bullies, and wife-beaters were the scum of the earth. How anyone could hurt someone like that, he didn't know.

"Eddie, it's fine. I am going to leave him someday, hopefully soon. It's fine, I get through it, most of the time."

"It's *not* fine, Violet. Domestic violence is *not* fine. Bullying is *not* fine. How dare the scumbag hurt you." Men like Ben made him sick to his stomach. Violet was such a lovely woman. No one deserved to be bullied, but Violet? No way.

Violet stayed silent.

"Listen, Violet, I'm sorry, I am probably way out of line putting my opinion in. But, Christ, you can't hit someone, regardless." He placed his hand on her knee. She shifted awkwardly in her seat. "Violet, I don't want to take you there to him."

"Eddie, you have to, or drop me off now and I'll walk the rest. It's nothing to do with you," she said, suddenly cold.

*Is she seriously defending her bully of a partner?*

"I... I... what will he do tonight?" Eddie asked exasperatedly.

"I don't know," Violet replied quietly. "Listen, we're almost at mine. Please drop me at the end of the road. If you park outside and he sees you, it will make things worse."

"No way, Violet." Eddie couldn't help himself.

"Eddie, please. You aren't helping."

They pulled up at the end of Violet's street.

"Listen, take my number, Violet, please text me so I know you're ok."

"Alright, yeah, sure."

Eddie said his mobile number aloud as Violet tapped it into her phone, her hands shaking.

"I'll wait here for a few minutes just in case you need to leave, is that ok?"

"Thank you, Eddie, you're a good man." Violet opened the car door and started getting out.

"Violet," Eddie said. She turned to him, half in the car, half out. He grabbed her right hand and held it. "Please take care."

And then she was gone. Eddie sat in silence, waiting, somehow knowing she wouldn't come back to his car irrelevant of what she'd have to go through that night.

"For fuck's sake, why did I let her go?" He sighed, his head in his hands.

# 64

# *Breaking Point*

## Violet

Violet opened the front door, holding her other keys to be as quiet as she possibly could. She edged the door open slowly, like a newborn parent does whilst going into the bedroom. She took her heels off before she stepped in, desperate not to make the slightest noise on the tiled hallway floor. Pulling the keys out of the lock with a surgeon's precision, she stopped for a moment. The house was in darkness. For a second, Violet felt relief and she basked in it, almost laughing as she turned the hallway light on. He obviously hadn't even got home yet and was probably ringing to say he was having a lock-in at the pub.

Violet put her bag on the stairs, along with her keys. She felt immediately lighter. But then she turned and saw his shoes, there by the coats. He was in. Panic rose in her body. She felt her heart beating faster, hearing it in her ears, her head. Her whole body felt as if it were vibrating like a speaker in a nightclub.

He must be in bed. Hopefully asleep. Perhaps passed out. She didn't know what to do. She could say she hadn't felt well and had gone for a late walk. It sounded far-fetched, but she hadn't taken the car and he would have noticed this, so maybe he would believe her. Yes, she would say that. It was half believable. Perhaps.

Violet decided to get some water, then get changed in the spare room in case he woke up when she went into the bedroom. There were some baby wipes in the kitchen, so she could take her make-up off there and then creep up the stairs, straight into the spare room. She could deal with whatever he had in store for her in the morning.

Violet turned the hallway light off. Ben would probably be drunk, but she didn't know for sure and didn't want any extra stimulus.

The lounge blinds were open, so she began walking through the house, aided by the light from the streetlamps coming in. A second later, a light flicked on. Her eyes darted across the room to where Ben was sat in "his chair", next to the table lamp.

"And where the fuck have you been?" He looked at her with fury in his eyes. Violet clammed up immediately. She knew that look, and she knew what that look meant.

"I said, *where the fuck have you been*, Vi?" he shouted. "And *what the fuck* are you wearing?"

Violet remained frozen with pure terror.

Ben started to get up from his seat. Violet knew what was going to happen. She turned and rushed out the lounge door, grabbing her keys off the stairs. Violet felt a sear of pain as Ben grabbed her hair and pulled her back from the door that she was so close to opening. She screamed.

"You are going nowhere, you slag," he spat. "Now, stop your lying mouth screaming, Vi, or I will shut it for you."

Ben grabbed her arm and dragged her back into the lounge, pushing her into the sofa. She couldn't look at him; she didn't want to see the pure evil in those eyes.

"Now, answer my questions or it's going to get a hell of a lot worse." Ben stood over her as she slumped onto the sofa, trembling.

"Where the fuck have you been and who with, Vi? Are you shagging that bloke from Foodways? The pervy security guard? I will fucking kill him, Vi," he warned.

"I've been to Rosie's, that's all." Violet's voice trembled as if she were on stage in front of hundreds.

Ben laughed, unconvinced. "Why are you all tarted up, then?" Ben grabbed her cheeks, smearing her lip gloss all over with his thumbs.

"We were going to go out, but we just put some music on and shared a bottle of wine instead. That's why I didn't hear your call." She swallowed.

"I don't believe you. You're a *dirty fucking liar*," he hissed.

Then, she felt it. The blow, followed by the strange sensation of blood flowing from her nose, onto her red dress. Wiping the back of her hand across her upper lip, she then brought it down and stared at the blood covering it. What had her world become? What type of awake nightmare was she living in? Not even living, just existing. What had become of the woman she had been? Replaced with a shell of herself, a doormat, a mug, a victim.

"We can do this all night, Vi, all night, you lying whore, until you tell the truth."

Violet's dress was becoming a darker red as blood continued to flow from her nose, saturating it. She couldn't feel it, partly due to the shock, fear, the wine she'd had at Eddie's, maybe even because she now felt pain differently. She didn't know. What she did know was that Ben meant what he said, and he would torture her all night if he had an excuse to.

"Ben, I was with Rosie. Honest. Exactly what I said. I dressed up because we were going to go to that new pizza place for the special in town. But we couldn't be bothered, so put nineties dance tunes on and had a few glasses of wine instead. That was it. I just wanted to wear a dress. Here, ring her and ask her. She will tell you."

Violet and Rosie had talked many times over the years, more so in the last six months, about safety planning. Rosie categorically knew that if Ben ever asked if Violet had been with her, to say yes, then speak to Violet to give her the heads-up as soon as possible.

Ben looked at the phone. "You better be telling the truth, Violet. I'm not having you making a mug out of me. Do you hear me, bitch? I'm not having it."

"It's the truth, Ben, I love you, I'm not interested in anyone else. Never will be."

She witnessed him soften immediately, as if he were two different people, Jekyll and Hyde.

"I love you, please, Ben, I'm sorry, I should have called and told you. It won't happen again. I know you were just worried."

Vomit rose in her gullet. Apologising, taking the blame and professing her love were survival tactics. Darwinism in domestic abuse. She hated this man standing in front of her. Every last cell of his vile, sick, poisonous body. Hate was almost pumping through her body, wrapped around the blood in her veins. She wished, in that moment, with every part of her, that the sick bastard would drop dead. But she had to survive; she had to get through this night. The way to do it: lie and placate him, like she had done many times before, diffusing the situation.

In the early days, she'd meant it. She had loved him, wanted him to change, get help. She'd wanted to be a better partner. Now, her love, hope and excitement for their future were dead. In that moment, as blood slowed to a drip down her face, she could only think that her two choices were for Ben to be dead or her to be gone.

# 65

# Emotional Evening End

## Eddie

Eddie returned home to a chirpy, giggly and quite tipsy Derek and Florence after dropping Violet off. They were having a right old time, Florence showing Derek how to do the waltz in the lounge, with Derek holding her up. Eddie smiled and clapped as he entered the room, greeted by a curtsy and bow. But inside, he was raging with anger from the snippets of information Violet had disclosed in the car journey.

"Eddie, son, is all ok with Violet? We've been ever so worried what with her rushing off and all that." Concern was etched into the lines on Florence's aged face.

"Yeah, all's ok, she was just a little worried that Ben was locked out." He hated himself for lying and covering for a monster, a disgrace of a man, but it wasn't his place to tell Florence and Derek the truth.

"Ok, pet, as long as all is well." Florence seemed satisfied with Eddie's explanation. "Well, I will book my taxi now you are back. Derek, perhaps we can share one since we are going in the same direction."

"Perfect, dear, I will give them a bell," replied Derek. "It's been a wonderful night, Eddie, just the tonic I needed. If this was *Dine in With Me*, you would be in the lead." He warmly patted Eddie's shoulder as he went into the hallway to order the taxi.

Ten minutes later, the taxi arrived.

"You're a good lad, Eddie, you have a good heart," said Florence as she hugged him.

Eddie wasn't sure what she meant but thanked her anyway. Then, they were gone, giggling as they got in the taxi. Eddie chuckled—it was as if they had known each other for years. Then, without anyone left to take his mind away from Violet's situation, the fury returned.

Violet hadn't made contact, and it had been over thirty minutes. He had asked her to let him know she was ok. Filled with anger and concern, he made a cup of tea, although he most definitely wanted something stronger. Carrying his cuppa up to bed, he was far from tired, wired from the adrenaline and worry.

After what felt like a lifetime of tossing and turning, Eddie grabbed his phone off his bedside table. Screw it. If she wasn't going to text him, he'd just have to email her.

# 66

# *Change*

## Violet

Listening to Ben snore, Violet fantasised about putting a pillow over his face. He had made them a pot of tea once her nose had eventually stopped bleeding. He'd even taken a packet of chocolate digestives out of the cupboard to take upstairs. He'd apologised with his usual, "You provoked me, Vi, by not talking to me. You put ideas in my head", "I love you and don't mean to hurt you", "I only hurt you *because* I love you so much", "It won't happen again, Vi".

Violet had played along; she'd had to play along. Unsure as to whether her nose was broken, she'd lain in bed, praying he would pass out, fearing the worst that he would want to "make up", which meant rape her.

Luckily, he had passed out. Violet lay silently crying. After an hour of analysing, thinking and planning, she looked at her phone. Crap, she hadn't contacted Eddie like he had asked. He didn't have her number, but she had four emails flashing on her app. She clicked on her emails. Three were from Eddie, increasing in urgency.

12:10 a.m.

***Hi, Violet, I didn't get your number but just checking all is well? Eddie***

12:32 a.m.

***Hi, Violet, me again, I hope you are getting these. Just let me know all is ok, please, a little worried. Thanks. Eddie x***

12:58 a.m.

***Violet, I am worried about you, please let me know you are ok, no matter what time you get this, ok? From Eddie x***

Violet felt awful that she'd dragged a complete stranger into her mad life that resembled something out of a gossip magazine.

It was now 2:15 a.m. She would text Eddie, let him know all was ok. He had already been saved as "Marnie". She didn't know what to say. Should she lie? More lies? If she told the truth, it became real to more people. After ten minutes of typing and deleting, she sent:

***Hi, Eddie, it's Violet. Sorry, I didn't mean to worry you. Thanks so much for your kindness and concern tonight. Sorry if I ruined the night. I'm going to be ok. I've made a decision to start the wheels in motion to leave Ben. I already knew it had to happen, but now I definitely need to do it. Thanks again X***

Violet's phone was on silent. She felt guilty after sending it. Eddie had enough on his plate, he didn't need to be worrying over someone he had only met a handful of times. Hopefully, the text saying she was leaving Ben would reassure Eddie she was going to be ok. Within seconds, she got a reply.

***Violet, I am so pleased you're ok. I wanted to drive over and check. Has he hurt you? Are you sure you're***

***ok? I can come and pick you up if you need to leave. x***

Violet started crying again, overwhelmed that a practical stranger was so concerned about her wellbeing. Eddie's nature—well, what Violet knew of his nature—made Ben look even more vile.

***No, honest, I'm fine. He won't hurt me again, and he's passed out now. I'll have a few days of him being lovely, apologising and making excuses. That's his pattern. The few days will give me time to do some planning x***

She sent it, deciding that telling someone meant she would have to stick to it. She couldn't change her mind or let Ben change her mind. No. She couldn't back down, under no circumstances.

Violet thought about the way Eddie had talked of his wife tonight. She had never experienced a fraction of such love. Ben's words were poetic, but no feelings resonated with her. She yearned for love like that: true, pure, magical love. She had to leave Ben. She had to leave the man that she not only didn't love but actually feared and hated.

She text Eddie again.

***Oh, and, Eddie, thank you from the bottom of my heart for caring x***

It didn't take long for a response to come through.

***Anytime, Violet. Get some sleep. Text me if I can help in any way or if you need to talk X***

Violet deleted the text conversation; she couldn't risk Ben reading it. Placing her phone on the bedside cabinet, she pondered on her future until sleep conquered her.

# 67

# *Abundant Abuse*

## Eddie

Judging from Violet's messages in the early hours, she was ok now, but it sounded as if something bad had happened. Now wasn't the time to ask details, and it wasn't Eddie's place. Christ, he was a crap agony uncle and wasn't used to these types of dilemmas. His family weren't the "this is how I feel" type. Even when they'd lost Issy, it had been all practicalities and not much on the side of emotional impact. But he would still try his best to be there for Violet.

He would never have laid a finger on Issy, and they'd never had arguments or cross words. Yes, they'd bickered, but they'd never fallen out. He couldn't imagine it any other way. And it wasn't about luck, it was about respect.

His head was thumping due to lack of sleep. Who the hell was this scumbag Ben anyway? All he knew was that he was a darts-playing bully. He would text Violet later today and hopefully see her at Foodways as he did his weekly shop the next morning.

Eddie had spent the whole morning at work totally distracted. He was doing some online research about domestic abuse and was, quite frankly, appalled at the facts, figures and real-life stories he was coming across.

"Morning, Eddie, how are you?" Cara asked as she entered his office with a handful of mail, a smile on her childlike, pale face.

"Hi, Cara, I'm not bad thanks. How are you doing?"

"Yeah, I'm good thanks, having a great day." She pulled something out of her mail trolley. It was a flapjack. "I got you this. I know you said last week your wife used to get you them for your lunchbox." She coyly handed it over. "It's a thank you for making me feel welcome here."

Eddie swallowed the lump in his throat, taken aback. "Thanks, Cara, I'll enjoy that with my cuppa." It was a simple, inexpensive gift, yet such thought had gone into it.

Cara beamed. Handing him his mail, she enquired, "You got a busy day today?"

"Actually no, for once." He laughed. "I'm doing some research, perhaps from a HR perspective but also for my own knowledge, about domestic abuse." He sighed. "I can't believe how prevalent it is, especially for women. You just don't think about these things until you or someone you know experiences it, I guess."

He saw Cara's face and instantly regretted bringing it up. It was as if she were back in time, eight years old all over again.

"You ok, Cara?" he asked.

"Oh, yeah, it's just that I grew up with some domestic abuse. Well, when I was really young. My mam had many relationships with proper dicks." Her eyes widened and she brought her hand to her mouth. "Sorry, sorry for saying dicks."

Eddie smiled. He wanted to laugh but it was far from appropriate.

"I'm sorry to hear that, Cara. It must have been hard for you, as well as your mother. I hope she is with someone nice now." Eddie said it as a comment rather than a question.

"No, she's dead. If she weren't, I think she probably would still be with an arsehole. It's all some people know, I think. And some women just let people walk all over them all their lives, one person, then the next, targets, doormats, or they just don't seem to think they're worthy of anyone respecting them."

Cara's eyes started filling up. Eddie got up from his chair and walked around his desk to where she was standing, placing his hand on her shoulder.

"Hey, listen, your mam, wherever she is, would be mega proud of you, ok? You've got your whole life ahead of you, and you've done absolutely great here so far. You are now part of the furniture."

Cara let out a small laugh.

"You told me, that first week, about your plans and dreams. Keep planning. Keep dreaming, Cara."

Without any warning, Cara hugged him like a child would their parent. Instinctively, Eddie placed an arm around her as she clung on. He knew it wasn't quite appropriate in the workplace but also knew Cara needed a hug more than anything else in the world in that very moment.

# 68

# *Hungover*

## Florence

"Florrie, it's me. Morning."

Florence startled at the sound of Jessie's voice. Jessie said the same thing each day as she opened Florence's front door.

Florence never slept in unless she was unwell, and although technically Florence was unwell, she wasn't necessarily feeling the impact of it just yet. So, that meant one other thing: Florence was hungover.

"Where the bugger are you, Florrie?" Jessie called, walking through the bungalow.

Jessie entered the bedroom. "Florrie, are you ok?" There was urgency in Jessie's voice as she rushed to Florence's bedside.

"Oh yes, pet, I just slept in. Put the kettle on, love, I'll be through in a few minutes."

"Ok, as long as you're ok," replied Jessie, reluctantly leaving the room.

Florence's mouth felt dry, like parched soil in the summer sun. Her head was thumping; she hadn't had a hangover for over forty years. Last night had been such a lovely night: the company, the conversation, the dancing with Derek. The drink had just flowed. And now, trying to get out of her bed, an eighty-two-year-old Florence was well and truly paying for it.

It took five whole minutes for Florence to get out of bed and sheepishly enter her lounge, still in her pyjamas. Jessie brought her breakfast, a pot of tea and tablets to her, shaking her head in a humorous manner.

"Late night last night, was it, Florrie? You dirty stop-out."

"Erm, yes, pet. It was. But a bloody good night." Florence became alive with her memories, clapping her hands together and tilting her head back as she giggled.

"I bet, you little bugger. You're hungover, aren't you? Too many shandies." Jessie winked.

"Actually, I was on the white wine in the end."

"Good on you, Florrie, good on you."

They both laughed.

Jessie stayed for another twenty-five minutes before grabbing a few toffees from Florence, giving her a hug as always and then leaving. She'd made sure Florence was left comfortable on her recliner chair, with some juice to rehydrate, some paracetamol and a packet of ready salted crisps from the cupboard—the "best solution" Jessie could find for a hangover.

Florence felt rough, but it had been worth it. She hadn't enjoyed herself like that in years. Her body was aching heavily, but she wasn't sure if that was the beer and wine or the little bit of dancing she'd performed with Derek. He had held her up at most points, but she had felt like her former lifetime as she'd attempted to show him how to dance the waltz, the two of them laughing as Derek had tried to get the rhythm. It had felt like old times, her trying to teach Ernie as he'd faked interest, just for her benefit.

Florence believed she had connected with all the others so well and genuinely felt as though she had known them for years. That's why she knew there was more than meets the eye with Violet scurrying off. She hoped she was ok. Maybe she would email her later on and check. Until then, it was repeats of *Midsomer Murders* and an easy day.

Florence looked to her side, to the photo of Ernie. She could almost picture him laughing at her.

"I know, I know, I'm a daft sod, my love." She chuckled.

She simply couldn't wait until the next Dinner Club.

# 69

# *Payday*

## Cara

It was the final day of Cara's second full week at work, and it was also payday. She had checked her online banking first thing that morning and had been elated to see the money in her account. She had budgeted and planned how almost every penny would be spent. She'd earned more than expected, so had already allocated a little extra towards moving out of Caitlyn's. It was becoming increasingly harder with Rhys's shifts for Cara to get a decent sleep for work the next day. Cara wanted to be diligent and focused. She didn't want to turn up to work after five hours of sleep, exhausted, it subsequently affecting her performance.

Her job was her everything, and she craved being able to have normal routines such as getting her packed lunch ready for work and having a bath at the end of a hard day.

She had been looking at bedsits to let in the local free paper each morning on her way to work. The cost of a bedsit and the oncosts of utilities and shopping were just about doable with her wage. Bits of furniture could be bought over time. But the bond, admin and sometimes guarantor were the stumbling blocks. Cara wouldn't give up though, and every spare penny would go into her house fund.

However, Cara was more concerned that she had just hugged one of the bosses. She didn't know what it was about Eddie, but there was something that she gravitated towards. She wanted to spend time with him, listen to his stories and advice. She wanted to tell him things and ask him questions. He always seemed to say the right things. Although her hug had clearly taken Eddie by surprise, he'd held her back and hadn't told her off. But now she was worried about boundaries and that Eddie may think she fancied him. She couldn't lose that job. The last few weeks had changed her life. The motivation, the purpose, the people. For the first time in forever, Cara felt she had a positive future and that she would be happy through her own merits. She was angry with herself, thinking she may have risked it all by needing some affection, something she, ironically, normally couldn't stand.

She would have to apologise, to try and amend the situation. She would wait until the end of the day and tell him she would never do such a thing again. Cara was embarrassed of her neediness.

It was soon lunchtime, and Cara went into the staff kitchen, taking her usual seat. She had started reading again—something she used to love but hadn't had the headspace for in the last few years. Becoming absorbed in a good book was her version of an escape, almost becoming the characters, feeling and thinking them. She was reading a book by Matt Haig, one of her favourite authors, as she picked at her cheese and pickle sandwich and crisps.

"I've read that."

Cara looked up. It was Eddie. *Shit.* She would have to deal with cuddlegate now.

"You enjoy it?" Cara asked nervously.

"Yeah, it was great. I like all his stuff. Different but really good."

Eddie took a seat next to her. Clearly, the reading was over.

"Look, Eddie, I am really sorry I hugged you. I am sorry I overstepped the boundaries and hope I didn't make you feel uncomfortable." She felt herself blush.

"Ah, don't worry, I just don't want people talking, you know?"

"I totally get it. I just feel as though I can talk to you; you're a nice bloke. There aren't many around."

Eddie was smiling, but she sensed unease. *Ah no*, she thought, *he really thinks I fancy him.*

"You're like a nice dad."

Eddie raised an eyebrow. *God, I've called him old now*.

"Not that you are old enough to be my dad, but you know." She wasn't sure he was buying it. He was a good-looking man. Some would find him very attractive.

"And I'm gay, Eddie, so I don't fancy men. Although, you are a nice-looking man."

Eddie's facial expression changed completely to the shock of revelation. Then, he started laughing. The tension was eased. Cara started laughing alongside him.

"I'm so relieved. But I don't want to be old enough to be your dad either." Eddie grinned.

"Fancy some flapjack?" he said, halving the gift she had presented him with earlier that morning.

"Yes please," Cara replied, taking the flapjack and relaxing into her seat.

# 70

# The Fallout

## Derek

"Mary, mother of Jesus," Derek called out as he woke that Friday morning. Surely, he had been abducted in the night and steamrolled. No one could feel like that. What the hell had Eddie done to them? Then, he remembered and groaned. He had drunk two bottles of red wine almost to himself. For half an hour or so at the end of the night, it had been just him and Florence, and they'd been dancing as well as swigging the wine.

"Bloody hell, I didn't realise I was that drunk," he mumbled. He felt a weight next to him. Cringing as he turned over, he was faced with Des's marble eyes staring back at him.

"Des, you sneaky little bugger." Derek laughed. "Taking advantage of your dad being tipsy and coming up here to bed. Well, what a brass neck you have." Derek stroked Des as he told him off in jest.

Last night had been amazing. Derek felt proud of his achievement of getting four strangers together who gelled so well. Last night and the first Dinner Club had been exactly what he'd envisaged in his mind when he'd embarked on the concept. Eddie's food had been divine, and it had been great to get to know each other further. Derek would have liked to have gone as Debbie, but at the same time, it had allowed the group to get to know

Derek, and they would get to know more about Debbie in time.

Derek had a real soft spot for Florence. She was one hell of a woman. With such interesting life stories and such a character, he couldn't wait to see her again. Eddie was a lovely gent, who had experienced such a loss. Derek admired that he could talk about it, and he spoke of Issy with such love. It was tragic, and Derek felt instantly sad for Eddie and his little daughter. Then, there was beautiful Violet, quiet and endearing. She was gentle and a great listener. She was the one Derek felt he needed to get to know better. He wasn't sure what had happened last night with her rushing off home. Hopefully, all was well.

The Dinner Club had most definitely achieved what Derek wanted. It could only get stronger. No one else had contacted him in the four weeks the advert had been up, so after the initial meeting at Foodways, Derek had not continued with the advertising of the club. He felt four was a nice number, and the mix of people, bringing their own characteristics, had so far provided the perfect ingredients.

It was 7 a.m., and Derek had to be in work by nine. He wasn't sure if he would make it. After dragging himself out of bed and downstairs, he knew there was one sure way of helping his recovery. If it didn't work, nothing would. A big, greasy fry up. All that dancing had made him ravenous. Eggs, bacon, sausages, mushrooms, hash brown and beans. It took double the time to prepare than usual, but Derek forced himself to get motivated. Hunger conquering hangover. Once cooked, he gathered two slices of bread. Was there anything better than mopping up egg and bean juice with a slice of bread and butter? Des sat near him, salivating despite having scoffed his own food ten minutes earlier.

Derek felt half better already after his breakfast and a quick Berocca. He would have loved to go back to bed and to watch some TV, but instead he dragged himself upstairs, travelling slower than a sloth. Then, into the shower he went, singing as he washed, letting the water invigorate him from his hungover trance.

After quickly getting dressed and a ten-minute walk with Des, he was ready to leave for work. It was 8:30 a.m. Derek was a little concerned he was stinking of alcohol and could be over the limit. He rang Jeff.

"Morning, mate, don't suppose you could pick me up this morning? I'm a bit worse for wear."

"You been on the pull, you dirty dog?" Jeff enquired. He had such a way with words.

"No, you daft sod. I had my group last night, The Dinner Club. Too much red wine. Sorry, I know it's a little out your way. I will buy your lunch as a thanks."

"You're on, Derek. I'll be there in fifteen, you plonky."

Derek sat back in his armchair. Time for another coffee to try and shake this hangover.

As he sat waiting for Jeff, Derek reflected on the day before, prior to his wonderful night at Eddie's. The appointment at Marsden and Co had been infuriating, but sadly, something he'd been expecting. How the hell was he going to buy Brenda out? He had no idea what the house was worth, but he didn't want to be remortgaging at his age, for Christ's sake. Plus, the interest would be phenomenal—they were robbing swines, those mortgage folk. He would need to sit and do some calculations, work out his income and expenditure and how much he could afford to pay out each month. Maybe Brenda would be satisfied with a monthly income from Derek rather than a big payout. He needed the house valued. He would ring some estate agents on his break today. *What a bloody carry on*, he thought.

# 71

# *Safety Planning*

## Violet

Violet woke up later than usual. Then again, she had gone to sleep later than usual. Ben had left for work. He would have sloped out this morning in an attempt to metaphorically lick his wounds. Ironic, given Violet had what she thought may be a broken nose. She touched it gently. She let out a yelp, like a wounded animal, quickly followed by tears as pain seared through her.

She felt disappointed in herself, ashamed that she had put up with Ben all these years. But within her, there was a flicker. It was the flame of her freedom, and this was the time to fuel it. It was the straw that broke the camel's back, *or the bully that broke his partner's nose*, she thought with painful sarcasm.

She lifted her head off the pillow. Yelping again, her head felt heavier than a hundred bricks, and there was ringing in her ears that made her brain throb. Violet sobbed. She felt like a deer that had been knocked down on a country road. But she had to get up; she had to start planning her escape.

She picked up her mobile, wanting to ring Rosie before Rosie's shift started. She had four text messages off Ben.

***Let's forget last night, just don't do that to me again. You had me worried.***

***Everything will be ok, I promise.***

***I love you, Vi, you're my world.***

***Do you love me?***

"Go to hell, you horrible bastard!" she screamed at the phone.

She rang Rosie.

"Hey, honey, how are you? Hungover from your Dinner Club?" Rosie's cheery voice asked.

"Not quite, Ro, something happened when I got in," Violet said, her voice shaking.

"What did that prick do to you, Violet? What the hell did he do now?" There was panic in Rosie's voice, but she couldn't reply, she just sobbed down the phone.

"I'm coming over, Violet, give me half an hour. I will be there soon. I love you." Rosie hung up the phone.

Violet lay there in silence. There were no words. Nothing to change what had happened, nothing to erase it, nothing that could make her feel better. It was the beginning of the end and everything the end signified.

She struggled out of bed, wincing. Her head was sore from where Ben had pulled her hair and from the impact of her swollen face. Her arm and side were sore from where he'd grabbed and pushed her. A bruise was emerging on her leg where she'd been pushed into the side of the sofa.

She entered the bathroom and looked in the mirror. She gasped. She looked as though she had been set upon on a night out by a gang of violent thugs. Her nose resembled that of a boxer's after a vicious match. There was black starting to form under her eyes. There was blood around her nostrils and above her lip. Her nose had to be broken—she could tell from the size of it alone. She wasn't sure how but there was also a cut to her head.

She couldn't break her eyes away from her reflection as silent tears fell. Staring. Staring at that image. That case study image. That magazine article image. That TV advert image. That image of a victim. A victim of domestic abuse. A battered woman. A woman lucky to be alive. A woman who might not be so lucky next time.

She had some witch hazel in the cupboard. Saturating some cotton wool pads, she delicately placed them on her face. It didn't sting, but even the lightest pressure hurt. How the hell could she go to work tomorrow like that? What was she going to say to colleagues and customers? People would just automatically ask, "What's happened to you?" Make-up could never cover that up.

Violet felt sick with worry. What was she going to do? She went back to the bedroom and straightened the bed. Another text from Ben came through.

***Are you awake?***

Violet knew she would have to text him back and pretend all was ok. She had to play the short game for the long gain. His violence knew no bounds. She had to act as though she had forgiven him. Forgiven him for being a sadistic monster, a savage beast and bully, just for a few days whilst he would be on his best behaviour. It was essential she pretended all was forgiven and they were both to blame, even though the thought of it made her want to vomit. No, she couldn't let her plan be known. It was paramount she acted, and her performance wouldn't be for long.

***Yes, just woke up. I agree, we need to pretend it never happened and make sure it doesn't happen again.***

She was shaking with fury and fear.

Two minutes later, he responded.

***Yeah, we'll both behave better, and I shouldn't have done what I did. It won't happen again, Vi, I love you.***

***Love you too.***

*You evil swine*, she thought.

The doorbell went. Rosie was going to get a fright seeing her, but she needed Rosie's help and she couldn't wait. She needed to ask Rosie if she could stay at hers until she got sorted. Ben didn't know where Rosie lived, only the estate. It was safe, and she could give Rosie some money to help her out.

Violet opened the door slowly in case the neighbours were around.

"What the hell, Violet?" Rosie grabbed her own face, bursting into tears.

"Shh, Rosie, please. Come in," Violet said anxiously.

"Violet, what has he done to you? Oh, Vi." Rosie edged inside and immediately reached out to hug Violet.

Violet flinched. "Gently, Ro, please, gently."

"I will kill him, Vi, what has he done?" Rosie cried, holding Violet's hand looser than she probably would have liked to. "What has that sick bastard done?"

"Come on, let's have a cuppa. I need your help, Rosie; I really need your help."

Rosie followed Violet into the kitchen. Violet updated her on last night's incident, from having a lovely night, to the missed phone call and everything after. Rosie kept shaking her head and reaching for Violet, distressed that her friend had endured such violence and trauma.

They grabbed their cuppas and made their way to the lounge.

"So, I need to leave, Ro, in the next few days. He'll be on his best behaviour for a good three days. It's his pattern. I need to leave on Monday, when he is at work. I need to get what I can and just leave. But I need somewhere to stay, just for a short time."

"God, you can come to me, of course you can. You know that," said Rosie adamantly, not having to even think about it.

"Thank you. I'm going to get documents together today and stash them in the spare room so they're ready to go. Then, on Monday, if you can come over with the car, we can load them up when he is at work and just go."

"Yeah, for sure, Vi. I can take some bits with me today to get started, if that's easier? Things he wouldn't notice are gone."

Violet nodded. "That's a good idea. I can get my mam's stuff out the loft. It's up there for safekeeping after he burnt one of my photo albums. I couldn't risk him destroying anything else of my past." Violet started to cry again.

"He's beyond vile, Violet. You are one hundred percent doing the right thing. People like Ben never change." She grimaced as she examined Violet's face. "I think we should get your nose checked out though, Vi, it looks broken. Will you go to the walk-in centre? I'll come with you."

"Yeah, I'll go. Just give me ten mins to get ready, and I will bag some belongings up and get my memory box from the loft as well," said Violet.

And with that, a plan had formulated. Not just a plan that had been in Violet's head for the last three years. A real, obtainable plan. The wheels were in motion. Her flame felt a little stronger. She had hope, she had support and determination amongst the dissolved confidence. She could do it. She could start living and not just existing. More importantly, she could start living without fear.

Tears fell down her face as she hugged Rosie. These weren't tears of sadness though, these were tears of relief.

# 72

# New Perspectives

## Eddie

It had been a strange day for Eddie. He had been absorbed with thoughts on the safety of Violet. Having thoughts about a woman who wasn't Issy felt alien to him. Then, there'd been the hug and subsequent conversation with Cara. Everything had been so intense. He was looking forward to a quiet night in and seeing Willow. They were going to make pizzas for tea and watch a Disney film for the hundredth time. She would fall asleep on the sofa after fighting to stay awake. Then, Eddie would carry her to bed, inhaling her little Willow sleepy smell of warmth and bubble bath. He smiled at the thought. How he adored his baby: her innocence, her simplicity, her unconditional love. He hadn't been the best dad, he knew that. He had resented Willow, had been angry with her, had wanted to run away from her. There was no point denying it, even though it now made him feel physically sick. But surely it was part of grieving? Recently, he'd started trying harder to be a better dad. He was slowly turning a corner.

The rubbish thing for Eddie was that it had taken The Dinner Club to do that. Strangers had changed his ways in just a few weeks. He felt weak for not trying hard enough in the past, but it wasn't going to change anything. The worst thing of all was that for the last seventeen hours, he had thought so much of Violet's safety that for the first time since Issy had died, he realised he hadn't been consumed by thoughts of her. Violet getting beaten up had distracted him. It had given him determination to try and help, to make sure she was ok. A focus out of a bad situation. Eddie acknowledged that he needed more focus, less dwelling about loss and more remembering positives. It made him realise he had to keep trying harder for Willow. He couldn't wait to clock out and go and see his little girl.

Eddie had spent the day wanting to check in on Violet, concerned, but he was conscious Ben may be around. The research he had done had worried him more, but he now felt adequately informed in case Violet did need someone out of her circle to speak to. Maybe he would email her—that probably felt safer than texting for her. He knew from his research that many perpetrators of domestic abuse intercepted their victim's phones. He should probably do it now before Ben finished work. Although he wasn't even sure what his job or working hours were. It was silly really—he was somehow feeling compelled to support a complete stranger. He tapped a quick email.

***Hi, Violet, how are you today? Just checking in, hoping you're ok. Anything I can do, remember I'm here x***

Adam popped his head into Eddie's office. "Coming for a pint, mate?"

"Not tonight. I didn't see Willow last night, so best get home. But thanks and enjoy," Eddie replied.

"No bother, mate, have a good weekend."

It was 5:30 p.m. by the time Eddie logged off his computer. Eddie was often one of the last in the office and often did extra at home. Fifty-hour weeks seemed to come with senior management. He collected his belongings and left the office. He hadn't expected to stumble across Cara packing up her stuff.

"What are you doing working so late?" he asked, approaching her.

"I've enrolled on a health and safety course that Danielle showed me. I was just doing a little of it now, as I don't have a computer where I am staying at the moment," Cara replied, smiling.

Eddie felt sorry for her. It was so often patronising to pity someone, but Cara had something she radiated that made Eddie root for her. She was like the runt of the litter, the wounded puppy, the flower that refused to die all winter. It was as if her heart had no home and her mind had no peace. Christ, maybe there was something he saw in her that he saw in himself. She seemed lonely and lost.

Being late November, it was cold, dark and rainy outside.

"Which way you heading, Cara?" he asked as they stepped inside the lift.

"I'm staying over at North Bay, on the Forestwell Estate."

"Ah, yeah, I know where you mean. Want a lift?"

"Oh, don't worry, I have a bus pass." Cara seemed proud of herself.

"It's awful out there, and I'm kind of going past that way to pick Willow up from my parents' anyway, it's not a bother. And now I know you don't fancy me..." He nudged her playfully. Cara immediately turned bright red.

"Ah, God, Cara, sorry, I was joking, I didn't mean to offend or embarrass you."

"No, it's ok. Erm, yes please, I would appreciate the lift." Cara looked up at Eddie, smiling. He saw that wounded, lost animal in her eyes again.

In the car, they got chatting about Cara's plans for the future.

"I want to do as many courses as I can. I struggled at school, maybe 'cos I was never in a foster placement for very long, so I never felt settled anywhere. Then, college wasn't for me. So, it's great I can do courses."

Eddie agreed, sensing how utterly excited Cara was by the thought of Basic Health and Safety and An Introduction to Customer Service.

"And your first pay today, although obviously not your full month," said Eddie.

"Yeah, it's great, and more than I thought. I'll put some to one side. I need to leave where I'm staying as soon as I can."

Dread fell over Eddie. *Please, not another one*. "Cara, you aren't at risk where you are, are you?" he asked with a serious tone.

"Nah, nothing like that. It's just that I'm on my best friend's sofa and don't have a room. I'm outstaying my welcome, and it's not ideal for anyone. Plus, her boyfriend is pissing me right off." Eddie sensed Cara's face screw up, realising she'd sworn in front of him again.

Eddie laughed. "Well, hopefully you'll be out of there soon."

"Yeah, I just need to try and save, but it will take me a good few months. All the extra fees they want is shocking. I'll hopefully not get chucked out by Caitlyn in the meantime; otherwise, I'll be camping out in Hendersons," Cara joked.

"Well, it would make the commute quicker," Eddie joked back.

# 73

# Broken Hearts Heal

## Cara

It was Thursday, and Cara felt sad it was almost the end of the working week. She wondered, as she sat in the kitchen for her lunch break, just how many people have that feeling. Are people living for the weekend? Do they wish their days away, caught in a rat race? Do they hate their jobs, hate their colleagues and surround themselves with nine-to-five misery? Cara didn't know. But what she did know was that these few weeks at Hendersons had changed her life.

For the first time since being eight years old, she felt she had a purpose, a place, an identity. She felt useful, needed and, most important of all to Cara, she felt appreciated—a feeling she had never truly experienced.

Even on her average four hours' sleep a night due to being disturbed and her mind being consumed with new courses, processes and childlike excitement, her adrenaline kept her engaged at work. She always felt a little deflated when 5 p.m. came around. Danielle and the others at Hendersons were lovely. They said hello, asked how she was. Lots of it was small talk but said with such warmth. This young woman who had been called a "miserable child", a "problem teen", a "nightmare" couldn't keep the smile from her face.

Cara and Eddie had lunch together most days. It was a bizarre yet beautiful friendship, and, each day, one of them would pull a flapjack out to share.

Eddie strolled into the kitchen. "Hi, lunch buddy." He smiled, taking a seat.

There was definitely something dadlike cringeworthy about Eddie, but Cara liked it.

"Any plans for the weekend?" he asked.

"No, not really. I was thinking of visiting the cat and dog shelter to see if they need any volunteers at weekends, then keep doing some research for flats."

"Wow, that sounds great about the cat and dog shelter, what a good idea. I would love to do that, but I'd bring them all home." Eddie laughed.

"Well, I have no fear of that, do I?" Cara rolled her eyes.

"Shit, sorry."

Cara smirked. "Did you just swear?"

"Umm... flapjack?" said Eddie, grinning as he handed her half.

# 74

# The Last Lie

## Violet

The X-ray at the walk-in centre had indicated Violet's nose had a fracture. The nurse had asked what had happened. Violet had lied, of course, saying she'd been at a children's party the night before, she'd been bending down and a child had stood up and banged into her face. Violet was an A-star liar; she had fine-tuned her deception capabilities. Living with a monster makes you do that. Violet was ordered to monitor it and to try to keep it from being exposed to further trauma. Her eyes were becoming increasingly black. *It will take a make-up masterclass to camouflage this tomorrow*, she'd thought as she'd left. But she knew she couldn't take tomorrow off. She had no sick pay left, and it was the first Saturday in December, so it would be far too busy for them to give her a day off.

The afternoon was spent sorting what she could in the house. Documents, photos, toiletries, things Ben wouldn't notice. She gathered them and put them in a bag, then transferred the bag to the loft. She started piling some of her wardrobe clothes in a drawer, making it easier to pick straight out and place in bags. She arranged some things in her wardrobe, putting things she would just leave if needed to one side.

That night, after eating tea brought home by Ben and when he'd eventually fallen asleep, she text Eddie. It was nice to have someone who cared. Of course, Rosie did, but it was different from a man. A man who seemed the polar opposite of Ben. He seemed to say the right things without prying. It was hard for Violet to be honest, even to Rosie. She felt ashamed that she hadn't left after the first time, the tenth time or even after the fortieth time. But she was going to leave now, and as they say, better late than never.

# 75

# Distraction

## Eddie

Eddie picked Willow up and squeezed her tight, spinning her around and blowing raspberries on her neck as she giggled with delight. He had missed his little bubba. Connie smiled, watching the moment of affection.

"Thanks, Mam, we will see you in the morning," he said as Connie left. Turning to Willow, Eddie used his best excited voice. "Right, my little bubs, let's make some pizzas."

"Yay, yay, yay," Willow replied, running round in circles and clapping her hands.

They sang and danced as they prepared their pizzas, Willow attempting to make a face with her toppings. Eddie put their pizzas in the oven, and they watched them cook through the oven door. Then, they ate their pizzas, washed down with fizzy pop.

Willow handed Eddie her last slice. "Daddy, this is for you to make you big and strong and happy," she said with the concern of an adult.

"Thank you, baby," he replied, smiling and commenting on how hers tasted better than his as he polished it off.

An hour later, Willow had been bathed, had her pyjamas on, had talked about her day and had fallen asleep in bed as Eddie had read *The Tiger Who Came to Tea* for the third time that week.

Eddie kissed his lifeline on the head and went back downstairs.

He opened a beer and sat on the sofa, grabbing his phone from the coffee table. Violet had messaged.

***Hi, Eddie, I'm not going to lie, I have had better days! But I'm going to be ok. Thanks for caring x***

Eddie wasn't sure how to take it. Did she want him to ask what her plans were? Was it interfering? Was it even safe to text her?

***What are you going to do, Violet? Sorry, I don't mean to be nosy, I've just been thinking about your safety today x***

Was he overstepping the line? Perhaps. He hoped Violet saw him coming from a perspective of concern.

***I'm going to leave him, Eddie. I'm going to stay with my friend. He's destroying me; I can't stay. I'll text later when he's asleep, sorry, can't talk now. Thank you for caring x***

*Bollock*s, thought Eddie, it really must have been bad for a long time. He knew, from his research, there are often multiple incidents before someone leaves an abusive situation. Violet deserved better; no one deserved that.

Eddie spent the next few hours channel hopping and having a few beers. He checked his phone every now and then, wanting to hear from Violet, wanting to text her, knowing he couldn't. He was woken by the sound of his phone. Nearly midnight. It was Violet.

***Hi, Eddie, sorry I couldn't text earlier. Anyway, how has your day been? X***

Eddie felt calmer now he'd heard from her again. He quickly replied, knowing she might not have much time.

***Not bad for a Friday, thanks, pleased it's the weekend. Willow and I made pizza for tea. She gave me her last slice x***

***Sounds lovely, Eddie, and Willow sounds like such a lovely little girl. She is so lucky to have you as her dad x***

Eddie smiled to himself as he read the text before replying.

***Ah, thanks, Violet, I think I am the lucky one. I just want to make Issy proud x***

***You will do that every day, Eddie. I can guarantee x***

***So, you are definitely leaving Ben? x***

He wondered if he'd overstepped here, but it was playing on his mind.

***Yeah, he won't ever change. I've been a mug, putting up with it, thinking he'll change, believing him, thinking it's my fault. He doesn't love me, he can't, he wouldn't do what he does if he did. I can't live like this anymore x***

Eddie felt calmer still with the relief that she seemed definitely ready to leave.

***No one deserves to be abused, Violet. You seem such a nice person. He doesn't deserve you x***

***When you talk about Issy, you describe true love. The way you loved her, the way she made you feel, your clear love for her still. I've never had that with Ben. I've never felt the most important things: appreciated and loved. I've never felt adored, that I am his everything in an equal way. I've been with him so long that he's become my bad habit. I want to feel I'm someone's everything instead of worthless x***

Eddie paused for a moment, remembering his words and the emotions he'd felt about his own wife.

***Life is short, Violet, I know that more than most. Don't ever settle for something that's wrong. You can do this, and you can start over, wherever you want x***

***Thanks, Eddie, you're a good man and a good dad. Night x***

Eddie could only imagine the strength it had taken Violet to survive in her relationship and the determination to now try and leave.

***Night, Violet. Always here if you want to talk or meet for a cuppa x***

Was that last bit too much? He didn't want to look patronising, and really, she probably had friends to talk to. There was something about Violet that drew Eddie to her. Perhaps it was the potential that she could have a new life. Maybe it was hope for her, something inside him willing her to be ok. Maybe, like Cara, there was something he saw in Violet that he saw in himself. Some damage, some need to emotionally recuperate, to be rescued from her own tormented mind. Maybe she was a distraction from his own grieving. Eddie didn't know. What he did know was that for the last twenty-eight hours, his thoughts had not been consumed by Issy, and he had not felt like running away, screaming, crying, killing the man who'd killed Issy.

# 76

# *Exposed*

## Violet

Violet had got out of bed extra early. Partly because she wanted to spend as little time with Ben as she feasibly could until she escaped, partly because she was swollen and bruised and knew she needed to attempt a magic trick with her make-up application.

She got to work at her usual "meet Rosie" time. Rosie was already waiting at their seat in the café. Rosie saw her coming and dashed over.

"I've not stopped thinking about you, Vi. Look at your beautiful face, the swelling. Ah God, Vi, he's an absolute monster."

"Shhh, I know, I know. Is it that obvious? My face, I mean," Violet asked.

Rosie looked away. "It's not good. I think you'll have a few questions and funny looks today. How many layers of bloody foundation have you got on?"

The friends sat in their seat, sharing their teacake, a cuppa each. Violet cherished these moments. The things that Violet would remember until her last day. The little things that felt like monumental things.

Violet started crying. "I'm scared, Ro. I'm scared about my future. What Ben will do when I leave. About being alone, starting again. I don't know how to do it. Trusting another man. That's if another man would even want me.

Damaged goods, unable to have children—not much to offer, have I?"

Rosie took Violet's hand in hers. "Hey, don't you dare put yourself down, Vi. That excuse of a man has done enough of that. In a few months' time, you'll be wishing you did this years ago. You can stay with me for as long as needed. We can sit all night and eat teacakes and talk absolute crap. You are bloody beautiful, Vi, inside and out. It's only you who doesn't see it. You will need a shitty stick to keep the men away, I can guarantee."

Violet went from sobbing to half laughing, half crying. Rosie always knew what to say.

"Now, stop bloody crying, your eyes are black enough without the mascara-running, Alice Cooper look."

"*Rosie*," Violet snorted.

"C'mon, love, let's go to the loos, clean you up, then you'll hold your head high and scan a few hundred chickens, some potatoes and some tampons. Then, you'll go home and do a little more sorting, ready for Monday."

"Thanks, Ro, what would I do without you?"

"Well, you would have a full teacake each Saturday. C'mon," Rosie said, leading the way to the loos.

Ten minutes later, Violet was at her till, ready for her 10 a.m. start.

"Christ, Violet, what the hell has he done to you?"

Violet startled and looked up. Eddie was stood there, without any shopping, his mouth gawping.

Violet grimaced—she hadn't wanted Eddie to see her like this. But she'd somehow known she would bump into him at some point today. "Eddie, please, be quiet, I'm at work," she pleaded, feeling somewhat more exposed than before.

"Sorry, sorry. Shit, Violet, has he broken your nose?" Eddie raised his hands to his own face in shock. Violet thought he would probably pass out if he saw her without make-up.

"It will be fine; I just have to be careful. It's fine, Eddie, honest."

"You have to be careful? It's that monster bloke of yours, he's the one who can't be careful. What type of lowlife does this to a woman?"

Eddie's irritation was making Violet light-headed. Luckily, the shop wasn't too busy, but floor managers were lurking around. She didn't want to draw attention to herself, and here was Eddie, looking frantic, with no shopping, at her till.

"Eddie, please, I am at work, and you are at my till, with no shopping. I can't talk. I get a break at twelve, we can talk then?"

Eddie nodded. "I'll be there."

He walked off, rubbing his head and face. Why did he care so much, and why did she like that he cared so much?

Violet was self-conscious about Eddie seeing her face again. All morning, customers had commented. It wasn't their fault, but as she'd scanned their shopping and made excuses as to why her face looked so bruised and swollen, all she could think was how insensitive and nosy people were. Or maybe it was just that they had never been punched in the face by someone who was meant to love them. She wished now that she hadn't come into work. After her break, she would be scrutiny to a further few hours of "What's happened to you, pet?" and "Ooh, that's a pair of shiners". Telling them to mind their bloody business and have a nice day wasn't really a phrase that would catch on as the strapline for Foodways.

As each hour passed, it felt an hour closer to her freedom. Violet had never been in prison, but this was her own incarceration, to which she could not wait to be freed. She was exhausted, in every possible way, and willed for the day, someday soon, that when she smiled, she meant it.

As she left for her break, Violet told Rosie she was meeting Eddie.

"He's your knight in shining armour, Vi," Rosie said with a wink. She saw Violet's reaction and added, "Sorry, too soon."

Eddie was waiting with two pots of tea, a cheese scone and fruit scone.

"Wasn't sure what you like," he said, pointing towards the scones.

Violet smiled. What a kind gesture. Like the little, kind gestures that had been offered by Ben as a result of a rape, a beating or mental abuse. Like the little, kind gestures that had become so perverse and twisted that Violet doubted people's integrity constantly. Something she was trying to change because little, kind gestures are the things that touch the heart most. Things in life she wanted to remember, the small moments, the thought, the intention being genuine and not manipulative. She knew in Eddie's eyes he was genuine, but something in her had to test him.

"Why are you here, Eddie?" she asked.

"Pardon?" Eddie seemed taken aback.

"Why are you here? Why did you wait for me? We don't know each other."

"Er, because I want to be here, Violet. Because in the short time we have known each other, we've developed a friendship. Because you are with a monster, and I don't want you to be hurt. Because you deserve better." Eddie shook his head and tugged his beard. There was silence for a few seconds as emotion lingered in the air.

Violet's shoulders slumped as she sighed, shaking her head. "I'm sorry, I just... I'm just not used to it, Eddie. Especially from men. Bear with me, sorry." Violet felt instantly guilty and embarrassed.

"It's ok. I get it. Tell me to back off, I won't be offended. But I'm certainly coming from a genuine place."

"I will have the fruit scone, please. I have a terrible sweet tooth," Violet said, changing the subject. She reached over the table, smiling at Eddie.

And so they sat, for twenty minutes, talking. Violet poured her heart out to this near stranger, who smiled and nodded at the right times. Who didn't judge her or look disgusted. Violet talked of her plan for freedom. And Eddie told her she could do it, that she was brave and he would help in any way he could.

In those twenty minutes, Violet knew she had made a friend for life. In those twenty minutes, Violet's faith in the male species had become a little bit restored.

# 77

# Borrowed Time

## Florence

Florence was still in bed when Jessie arrived. Not hungover like the morning before, just feeling poorly and a little weak. Florence knew what it was. Jessie knew what it was. Florence saw the upset in Jessie's face.

"Pet, it's going to happen, and it's going to get worse. I don't want treatment with nasty side effects that will only prolong the pain for my loved ones and me. We wouldn't see an animal suffer, would we, love?"

"But you're not an animal; you're our Florrie." Jessie started crying. Florence was more than a job, more than a morning call to Jessie. Florence knew Jessie loved her, just as she loved that wonderful young woman. They were friends. They were pretty much family. Florence's life was richer for having her Jessie, and she knew she held a space in Jessie's heart.

"I'm sorry, I'm sorry, Florrie. I just hate the thought of losing you. It's silly, I know. I know you will always be around me, and you'll be with your Ernie. But I love you, Florrie, and I'm not ready any time soon for you not to be here." Jessie pulled a seat close to Florence's bed and held her hand.

"I felt a pulling on my shoulder again the other night, love. It woke me, but I wasn't frightened. I knew it was my angel, my Ernie. I don't know how long I've got, but I just want to make the most of it." Florence gripped Jessie's hand.

"C'mon, love, I am going to try to get up. Put the kettle on."

Jessie stayed longer than normal as they talked about what Florence wanted.

"I have time to plan, love. Some people never get that. I can get everything in order. Our Veronica is coming over with the family for Christmas. I can see everyone. It will be lovely. You know how much I like a full house."

Jessie made sure Florence had her pot of tea and the biscuit tin before she left. Florence sat back in her recliner, notepad and pen in hand, and started making a list of things that needed doing.

Two hours later, William arrived. "Hi, Mam, it's me," he called as he unlocked the front door.

"Hi, Son," Florence called back.

Florence thought she had perked up a little, but clearly she hadn't, as William came rushing over.

"Mam, what's wrong? You look dreadful."

"Just feeling a little off, Son, don't worry." Florence looked at her middle-aged baby and smiled. He was a lovely lad. She was so proud of him.

"Mam, for Christ's sake, of course I am going to worry. You are bloody dying and don't want treatment." William started pacing the room like an irritated bull.

"Son, Son, please, this isn't helping."

"Mam, I can't watch you just bloody deteriorate." William was holding his face, his voice cracking as emotions overwhelmed him.

"Son, I will deteriorate either way. Why prolong it? Let's just make the most of my time left and not pump chemicals into my body which will keep me alive for longer but in a less able state. I don't want that, Son. I may just be having a bad day."

William looked like a little boy in the shell of a man. His vulnerability, his raw emotions. The beautiful loving side he had inherited from Ernie. The ability to express himself that he'd inherited from Florence. *He cares so much, sometimes too much*, Florence thought. But she secretly loved the attention and affection. She could never have enough hugs or get sick of hearing "I love you" every day.

"William, love, why don't you go to the shops alone this week? I will make a list. I don't need much. Then, we can have some lunch when you get back. We can watch *The Chase*, if you want? It's a celebrity one."

"Ok, Mam," William said reluctantly.

Florence wrote her list and handed it over. She always wrote in block capitals, which always made William smile.

"I'll be quick."

"Lock the door, Son," she said as he left the room.

"I will, Mam. Love you."

"Love you too. See you soon. Drive safely."

Florence heard the door close behind William and sadly sighed. It was untrue to say she wasn't frightened of dying. It is our internal programming to fight death until the very end. She was frightened. But she would be with Ernie. Her family would miss her, *they bloody better miss me*, she thought. She was loved, she knew that. She was decorated in love; it was sprinkled onto her by everyone around her. But she was tired, and since her stroke last year, she'd known she was on borrowed time. It was reality. She was frightened, yes. She was sad, yes. But somewhere inside her, she had made peace with it. And she knew her Ernie couldn't wait to see her.

# 78

# *Property Value*

## Derek

It was Saturday morning. Derek had arranged for two local estate agents to come and value the house. As he sat in his armchair, cuppa and biscuit tin by his side, he pondered about what his marriage had become. It had felt a little bit like respite from Brenda these last few months. He had enjoyed beginning the journey of finding himself and making new friends. But something was missing. That person to say goodnight to. That company in the bed, keeping the space a little warmer. That someone who opened the front door. Derek hadn't sat at the dinner table since she'd left except for the time he'd cooked for her and the first Dinner Club. Derek sighed. It was really happening, and although he knew it was for the best, he had never been a solitary character.

"At least you'll always love me, Son," he said to Des, rubbing his head. Des panted back, but Derek knew he had an ulterior motive, eyeing up the biscuit tin.

The night before, Derek had looked at his finances. There was only around fourteen thousand left on the mortgage. He could remortgage to pay Brenda out, but given his age, it would probably be a ten-year mortgage, which would hike the price up. The other option would be to sell up and both of them start again with a smaller budget.

First things first, he needed the house evaluated and then he would speak with the mortgage company to discuss. They may stretch to fifteen years.

The doorbell went. Derek rose out of his seat, making the "oof" noise he'd made every time he'd got out of a seat for the last twenty-five years.

"Mr Morgan?" enquired the man at the front door. "I'm Wayne from Property Plus."

"Derek, nice to meet you. Please come on in." Derek stood to the side as Wayne walked in.

"I understand I'm here to value the property, Derek. Is it ok to have a look around?"

"Of course."

Derek needed a pint or five. Wayne had left, letting Derek know someone would contact Derek with an evaluation on Monday. Then, a guy called Andrew had arrived from Homes For You to also assess the property. Apparently, he'd contact Derek by the end of the day with a guide price.

Derek had arranged to meet up with Bri in a few hours but would head to The Spitting Feathers earlier. First though, he would have some lunch and get his laptop out to go on the cross-dressing forum. He needed the morale boost.

Last night, Derek had experimented with Mexican food, making nachos with refried beans, jalapeños, guacamole and sour cream. And that had been just his starter. Needless to say, his eyes had indeed been bigger than his belly, and the fajitas he had made after had only been half consumed. Not a problem, as that meant lunch for today was sorted. A further bonus was that he had his menu for the next Dinner Club sorted and would add in some Tequila. He chuckled to himself—Florence would be a right hoot on Tequila. He could hardly wait.

Leftovers heated up and a beer from the fridge poured, Derek was back in his armchair, lap tray on knees and laptop on the side table. He logged on, trying to make his fajita wraps with one hand as he typed in the web address. Des came darting over and inhaled a scrap of red pepper and a small slice of mushroom that had fallen on the floor in the process of Derek's balancing act.

"Bloody hell, Son, faster than a bullet you were, you greedy bugger."

Des looked up, almost proud of himself, waiting for the next mistake that would enable him to indulge a little more.

Derek logged into the forum. He had been getting quite a few messages of support and had been enjoying reading the posts, contributing where he felt confident. There had been a few dodgy messages, which had felt uncomfortable at first and highly embarrassing. However, Derek had become more accustomed to the way of the internet forums and the "DMs", as the young 'uns called them. Some of it went over his head.

"The bloody lingo they use, Bri, it's all FFS this and WTF that. Then, there's WLTM and some terminology that is apparently about sexual things and fetishes. I mean, the mind bloody boggles," Derek had said to Bri the previous week.

"Christ, mate, sounds like a weird brothel or something." Bri had laughed.

"I mean, there are some people just after a "hook up", as they call it. But I guess you get that on social media. I have had propositions that would make a stripper blush. Most of them are genuinely nice and supportive. It's helped. Many are just like me, Bri: older men who just like to dress up now and then. Not wanting to chop their bits off or make a big scene, you know. They don't want to be the next Lily Savage or become an activist; they just want to express themselves."

"Well, good on you, mate, whatever makes you happy. I see a positive change in you," Bri had replied.

Derek smiled, recalling the conversation. It was important that his nearest and dearest had seen a change in him. A change for the better. A happier Derek. No regrets.

Derek's inbox was flashing. Clicking on the messages, there were three unread.

***What a stunning big bear you are! Would love to spend a night in the bear cave with you!***

*What the hell does that mean?* Well, he could guess, but what was with the bear analogy? No thanks, Derek thought, moving on to the next message, from Cher43.

***Hi, De1958,***
***How's you?***
***I noticed you are in the Northeast area. I am in Durham. I run a weekly support group. Well, I say support, it's more like a natter and a few beers or cuppas. We're only a small group, but a nice bunch, who talk about what they want, without judgement, and try and be supportive and fun.***
***Let me know if it's something you may wish to try, and we can talk more.***
***Alan/Cher***

Derek had never realised there were actual physical support groups. He was intrigued. Did they all go dressed as their alter ego? Was it in someone's house or public? What did they talk about? He thought it felt a bit scary, but at the same time, something he wanted to know more about. He drafted a response. He would check it later and decide whether to send it.

The last message was from wearwhatiwant54. Derek and Peter/Paula had been messaging quite a lot. They had started texting as well as messaging on the forum. It had been nice for Derek to receive reassurance, have his questions answered and views supported. It felt strange; he was lonely at times, but at the same time, Derek continued to feel emancipated, like a caged bird set free.

"I just want to be happy," he said. And with that, he shut down his laptop, put on his shoes and walked the seven minutes to The Spitting Feathers.

# 79

# *The Great Escape*

## Violet

The next fifty-six hours had been a countdown for Violet, a mode of simple survival, a covert operation. Finally, it was 8:30 a.m. on Monday morning.

"See you tonight. Love you, Vi," Ben said as she handed him his lunch.

"Love you too." *That's the last time I'll have to say that sickening lie*, she thought as she closed the front door behind him and slid down it, sobbing and grabbing her stomach.

Violet had just over nine hours to get out of the house she had shared for almost a decade with Ben, to the sanctuary of Rosie's. Ben had been sickly sweet since Thursday night, as predicted, on his best behaviour. It meant Violet had been safer and less monitored, although she'd had a lump of anxiety in her throat for days.

She immediately rang Rosie. "He's gone, Ro, he's gone," she said, relief and anguish in her voice.

"Ok, Vi, I'll be over in fifteen minutes."

Violet started gathering her belongings, putting them into the case in the spare room. Getting a few holdalls from under the stairs, she started filling them before going in the loft and getting more bags. Rosie was soon there to help. They embraced, both crying. *It's really happening*, thought Violet.

When they ran out of bags, they gathered bin liners.

Rosie's car was soon full. "I'll take these, then come back for more. Get your kitchen stuff, Violet, leave that prick with as little as you can. I hope he starves to death."

After filling her own car, Rosie was back. They filled Rosie's again and then it was time to go. Violet cried as she drove away from her home, away from her old life. She would wait for the fallout, but the fallout would be the beginning of her new chapter, of her freedom.

# 80

# *Budgeting*

## Derek

The last few evenings had been consumed by Derek trying to work out his finances. He felt like Carol bloody Vorderman, well, actually, a pound shop version, as he was getting nowhere fast, and she would have solved it all. Scribbling on another bit of paper, he swore aloud, wondering what the hell he was going to do. The house valuations had come in, and he knew what he would owe Brenda. They had an appointment with a solicitor next Friday. Surprisingly, Brenda hadn't been in touch. *The only blessing in this process*, he thought.

Reaching for another bag of crisps out of the multipack on the sofa next to him, he sat back and sighed. He would have to see a financial advisor or go to Citizens Advice about how he was going to make this work. Then, he had his eureka moment. Eddie! Eddie was a financial director at Hendersons. Surely, he would know his stuff. Would it be cheeky to ask him for some advice? Would it make Eddie feel as though he worked in a chip shop all day, then ate chips at teatime? *It has to be worth an ask*, thought Derek as he stuffed his vinegar sticks into his mouth with hungry force before opening the email app on his phone.

***Hi, Eddie,***

***How are you? Looking forward to The Dinner Club next week?***

***I was wondering, mate, you being in the finance world, do you know anyone who could help me look at my incomings and expenditure, please? I've had the house valued and need to see how I can afford to buy Brenda out. Any people you can recommend would be magical.***

***Thanks, Eddie.***

***Derek***

Sent. Hopefully, if Eddie couldn't help, he may be able to recommend someone.

Derek picked up his laptop. He had been messaging Cher43 on the forum for the last few days. Alan/Cher had told Derek more about the support group, Embrace. It sounded a small, friendly group, and Derek had plucked up the courage to agree to go to the next group in Durham on Monday night. It was a bit of a trek for him, but Derek realised that part of his new life was engaging in activities and exploring opportunities. He had wanted it for so long, he owed it to himself. It was daunting, of course it was, but he had The Dinner Club to compare it to, and that had been a phenomenal success.

Peter/Paula had also been keeping in touch. Peter was being supportive, answering all of Derek's questions. Derek found him a great source of comfort about the unknown and his innermost feelings.

For the first time in so many years, Derek was at the best place he had been in a lot of ways. This house business was just getting to him, and he had always been a worrier. Derek's phone pinged: an email.

It was Eddie.

***Evening, Derek,***

***How's you?***

***Well, I've had a weird week but in a good way. This Dinner Club lark has had a rather profound impact on me! Send your query over to me, mate, if you feel comfortable sharing, and I will try to offer some advice. I can pop over one night to discuss if needed? It's the least I owe you for helping me "see the light", ha!***

***Cheers, Eddie.***

"Wow," said Derek. He was intrigued by Eddie's new way of thinking and looked forward to finding out more. And Eddie had offered to help. "Fan-bloody-tastic, Son," Derek said to Des.

Derek sent some figures to Eddie of his income, estimates from the house valuations, a little narrative of what he currently lived on, outgoings and his ideal solution. Then, he opened the fridge, pulled out some leftover veg, cracked a few eggs and made a Spanish omelette.

Just before bed, Derek's phone pinged with an email from Eddie. *Bloody hell, that was quick,* he thought. Eddie had given a little overview but offered to visit Derek the next evening to discuss further, as long as Derek didn't mind him bringing Willow. Derek smiled to himself, thinking it would be lovely to meet her. He had always wanted to be a father, but he and Brenda sadly had been unsuccessful when it came to conceiving. There hadn't been the technology or resources to help couples get pregnant like there were these days, so they'd missed out. Of course, they could have adopted—Derek had been keen but Brenda hadn't been. *It was for the best in the end though*, Derek mused. Derek would have loved to have been a dad, though, and a grandad.

***Evening, Eddie,***

***Wow, I really appreciate it, mate, honest. Tomorrow night would be great. I will be in from about 5 p.m., and it would be lovely to meet Willow. Let me make you both dinner as a thank you, just let me know if Willow is allergic to or doesn't like anything.***

***Thanks so much, mate.***

***Derek.***

After the longest day at work ever, Derek was home and preparing veggie mince chilli, rice and nachos for Eddie, Willow and himself. Not too spicy for the little one. Derek wondered if little Willow had tasted veggie mince before. They arrived just after 5:45 p.m. Derek opened the door to a happy face smiling up at him.

"I'm Willow," Willow said, holding out her hand for Derek to shake.

Derek chuckled. "Well, hello, Willow, I'm Derek, come on in."

"Hi, Derek," said Eddie as they stepped inside, and he helped Willow take her coat off.

"I'm hungry, Derek, what's for dinner, please?" enquired Willow.

"Willow! Let's get in first, please. Out of the mouth of babes, eh, Derek." Eddie laughed.

"Maybe you can come and help me, Willow? Your daddy says you are a great help in the kitchen."

Willow beamed, following Derek until she was distracted by Des and immediately wanted to make friends, which Des would never complain about.

Over dinner, Eddie explained Derek's options around remortgaging, the likely cost and length of time versus paying Brenda each month from his salary, which would leave him short.

"That even depends on if she is happy with a monthly sum, Derek. She may be awkward and make you sell."

Derek's heart sank. He didn't want to leave his home. It had some bad memories, for sure, but it had some amazing memories too, plus it had been his father's home for the last six months of his life—a time Derek would always cherish.

"I can't move, son, it would break my heart." Derek was consumed with sadness. Of course, he had considered this, but hearing it from a financial expert just felt too real.

"You could always get a lodger, Derek. This is a big house, and it could be nice company if you got the right person. Even just short term until you paid the rest of your mortgage and freed up some cash."

Derek had never even considered a lodger. Mind you, there were some bloody weirdos about. What if he ended up with one of those gaming nerds who lock themselves in their room twenty-three hours a day and end up predisposed to becoming a serial killer? Or what if he ended up with another friggin' Brenda? He shivered at the thought.

"Ah, Eddie, I don't know. There are some right fruit loops out there," said Derek.

"You're right, but, Derek, there are also some really nice people, like you. You can interview people, get references and all that. Just something to think about that could pull in around four hundred a month if you put bills in with it."

Derek raised both eyebrows. "Really? That much? Bloody hell, I think I may just change my mind, mate. Thanks for your advice, Eddie, you're a good man.'

Willow was back playing with Des, who was fussing round her, making her giggle.

"Now, Eddie, tell me about this epiphany."

# 81

# Dinner Club Round Three

## Derek

It was the night of the third Dinner Club, and Derek was excited as he climbed into his car. He was keen for the group to connect again, and it was Violet's turn to cook. It was tainted slightly by the solicitor appointment at Marsden and Co the next night. Derek still hadn't heard from Brenda and didn't know how she would react to his proposal, but Derek had made some decisions. He couldn't sell the house; it meant too much to him. He couldn't afford to remortgage on his wages alone, so he had decided to try for a lodger. He was going to put an advert in the local paper and insist on interviewing, in a public place, as a first step. The added difficulty was Debbie. Derek had to be Debbie when he wanted, so a lodger would have to accept that. It was a big ask but he had to try and try quick. Else, it was back to square one.

Derek had been chatting to Florence the night before and had offered to pick her up, as he wasn't going to drink any alcohol tonight. Florence had been delighted, accepting his offer quickly. He had decided to be Debbie that evening, so put on a lovely new red dress. *Very Christmassy*, he thought.

This was probably the last Dinner Club before Christmas, and he wanted to make an effort. He had some black boots with a little heel and a new brown wig.

*Bloody hell*, he'd thought as he'd browsed wigs online the week before, *women have such choice; they can be anyone they want to be.*

As Derek pulled up, Florence was looking out her window and gave a little wave. Derek noticed she had her sticks as she came to the door, so got out to help.

"Evening, madam," he said in his most butleresque voice.

"Hi, my love. Nice to see you, Debbie, you look gorgeous." She smiled her cute, little, comforting smile.

"Let me help, Florence," Derek said as he approached.

"Thanks, pet, I've had a bad few days."

"Ah, I hope you feel better soon, Florence," Derek replied, helping her into the car.

"Well, this will be the tonic, I'm sure, love."

Derek climbed back into his side of the car and then they were well on their way.

Eddie was already at Violet's when they arrived. Greetings and hugs were exchanged. Derek noticed Violet's face was slightly swollen and that through her layer of make-up, bruising was visible. *What happened? Who did this to Violet? Maybe she was attacked? Mugged?* He opened his mouth to speak, but Florence got there first.

"Oooh, love, your poor face. Are you ok, love?" asked a worried Florence as she reached for Violet's hand.

"I'm ok now. I'll tell you all about it over dinner," replied Violet. Florence nodded, then looked at Derek, whose eyes remained wide with concern. Violet changed the subject to Derek, as Debbie, paying him compliments. The others chipped in, agreeing. Derek absorbed the kindness of his friends; each acceptance fuelled his confidence.

Derek's homemade soup and seeded bread had done nothing to fill him at lunchtime, so he had munched his way through his entire emergency biscuit supply by 2 p.m. and had eaten nothing since. He was still famished. Luckily, a Greek meze starter was soon served.

"Nice house you have here, Violet," said Derek, tucking in to hummus and pitta bread.

"Well, actually, Derek, that brings me on to the story of why I look a bit swollen," replied Violet nervously.

She relayed the recent events and those of the last many years with Ben, from the emotional abuse to the physical abuse. Derek was aghast and didn't do a very good job of hiding it. Florence was visibly upset, and Eddie seemed emotional also.

"Violet, love, that's horrific," commented Derek, irate and dejected that someone had put his friend through such abuse.

"Chop his balls off. His hands too, so he can't grab another woman," said Florence firmly. "And his nasty tongue as well, so he can't speak to anyone else the way he has you, pet," she added. "You are a strong, brave girl, Violet. I, for one, am very proud of you and honoured to know you." Florence held Violet's hand across the table.

Violet teared up. "Thank you, Florence, that's exactly what my grandmother would have said."

Florence weakly pushed herself from her seat and walked slowly around the table, struggling and highlighting that old age is inflicted on us all who are lucky enough to reach it. Violet rose out of her seat, and Florence embraced her as she sobbed onto her shoulder. Florence soothingly stroked Violet's head.

"It's going to be ok, my darling," Florence said gently as Violet held on, eyes closed. When she eventually opened them, Derek and Eddie were also stood next to Florence.

"You will get through this, my love," Florence said as she let go. "You are stronger than you realise, and you will heal. I promise." Then, she stood to the side, and Eddie and Derek both took turns giving Violet a cuddle.

Derek gave good cuddles. It was one of his favourite things about himself. People always commented on it. True, not everyone was a cuddler and you cannot inflict them on people who aren't that way inclined. But for those who advocated the cuddle, Derek was gold standard. He embraced her, hoping it would help.

"Cuddles when we really need them can make our hearts feel as warm as the summer sun," Derek said. It was a phrase Arthur used to say. Violet nodded.

"The only thing missing is some boobies to cuddle into," said Derek, still holding on to Violet, hoping the joke would lift the mood. Violet started laughing, followed by the rest of the group.

"Thank you, all of you," Violet said as her cuddle with Derek came to an end. "It sounds mad but I feel as though you all came into my life for a reason and at the right time."

"I think we all feel a little bit like that, pet," said Florence. Eddie and Derek nodded.

Derek firmly believed this. There was something almost telepathic about the group. Something that ran through the veins of each of them and connected them. A purpose maybe, if you wanted to be spiritual. But definitely something.

"Right, can I help with the main?" Derek asked, and a grateful Violet went into the kitchen with him. They returned ten minutes later with plates of fish pie and veg—a recipe Violet used to make with her late mother.

"This is bloody delicious, Violet," said Derek after his first mouthful. Derek had to have a word with himself to slow down—he was shovelling it in and was at risk of burning the roof of his mouth as well as looking like Augustus Gloop.

Eddie updated the group on what he had done with Willow that week, including dinner at Derek's. Derek had been touched by the love Eddie had shown Willow. *It mustn't be easy, given he's a single parent, but he seems to do a great job*. To Derek, Eddie was not only a wonderful dad, he was also a bloody nice human, of which there weren't enough of in the world.

Florence talked about Jessie, Lucy and William and mentioned that Veronica was coming for Christmas for three weeks, from next week. Her face illuminated with love.

Derek discussed his plans to explore looking for a lodger before he would reassess whether he could manage to keep his home and not have to sell it.

"If it were a bungalow or flat, I would move in with you, son, but stairs take it out of me. Mind you, I think it would be worth it, the giggles and trouble we would get up to." Florence nudged Derek as she winked at him. Derek laughed. Florence was one of a kind, and he would love to have a housemate just like her.

Violet moved the conversation on to all the things she was going to do in her future.

It was soon time to leave. The owner of the house, Violet had introduced as Rosie, had returned and greeted everyone. Derek helped a tired Florence to the car, leaving Eddie, who'd offered to help Violet wash up.

"Derek, how do you walk so well in heels? I've spent all my bloody life struggling to walk in heels, and now I struggle to walk in flats. You, you were born to wear stilettos," Florence said.

Derek burst out laughing. "Maybe I was, Florence, maybe I was."

They were soon at Florence's after chatting the whole journey home. Derek helped her into the house.

"Watch what you are doing driving home," Florence said as Derek left.

It had been a wonderful night. Emotional but something about this had allowed them to get to know each other even more. They wouldn't see each other until after Christmas now, but the new year would start with Dinner Clubs planned for the full year, which was all the Christmas present Derek needed.

# 82

# *A Friend in Need*

## Eddie

It was Sunday night, and all Eddie wanted to do was relax after his strange weekend. Somehow, the last few days, he had become some sort of counsellor. He'd also experienced some personal awakening moments.

He sat in his chair, with a coffee, thinking about the last few days. It had started on Friday night with Willow. He'd mentioned Saturday morning at Momar's and Grandpa's as always, and she had started talking about packing her bags. It was getting ridiculous. Eddie took Willow into the dining room, sat her down and poured a glass of milk each.

"Bubs, why are you packing so many bags?"

"I need the stuff, Daddy."

"You don't need all of it, Willow, not every time you leave the house."

"I do," she argued back.

"Willow, you are always coming back home. Your stuff will be here waiting for you. You can just take what you need."

Willow's voice turned small and hard to hear. "But what if it goes and never comes back, like Mammy did?"

And there it was, staring Eddie straight in the face: grief. His four-year-old and her grief. He'd been so busy thinking of his own needs and own torture that he hadn't seen how it was impacting on his baby. But what was different was his reaction. In the past, Eddie would have broken down or wanted to scream out of pain and frustration. Instead, he got up and he walked around the table to hold his daughter close, like Florence had hugged Violet the night before. Like they had all hugged Violet.

"I love you, Willow. Everything is going to be ok," Eddie said, stroking the wild red hair that his baby had inherited from her beautiful mother.

"Promise?" asked Willow.

"I promise, baby, I promise."

Eddie held his daughter as she shook and cried into him, and he told her she was loved, she would always be loved and he and her stuff would never leave her.

On Saturday morning, Willow took one big bag and a small one to Connie and Robert's. It was better than three. Eddie had researched about play therapy for grieving children. He would contact a local service on Monday. Eddie and Violet had been texting most days that week and had agreed to meet on her break at Foodways. She had thanked him for listening and being kind. It felt good to help someone in their time of need. In a bizarre way, Violet was helping Eddie see a different perspective on his relationship too. He was becoming more grateful of what he'd had with Issy: the deepness of the love, the equality. Perspective was helping him recover, and it was in turn helping him help Willow.

They sat on her break, a scone each, and chatted. She thanked Eddie for listening, and Eddie asked her if she wanted to go out for food one night next week. As soon as he said it, part of him wished he could take it back. He didn't want her to think he was trying it on or pushing her to spend time with him, not after what she had been through.

"I mean, nothing too much, even just a cuppa. But only if you are at a loose end or want to chat or need another opinion than Rosie's. Although Rosie seems great and—"

"Eddie, I would really like that. Thanks."

Eddie smiled the whole way out of Foodways and all the way to his parents'.

Sunday's plans were to take Willow swimming—she was a water baby and would stay in the pool until she was wrinkled and her tummy was rumbling away. Eddie had been thinking about going to the crem to put a Christmas wreath on Issy's gravestone. He hadn't been for a few weeks. He called Connie, asking her to pop over for an hour and inviting her to come swimming. Connie and Robert relished in any opportunity to spend time with Willow, so it was an excited acceptance.

"I'll just be an hour, Mam," Eddie said after they returned from swimming, leaving the house as Connie sat down to colour in with Willow.

He picked up a wreath from the local florist and was soon at the crem. He could walk to Issy's gravestone with his eyes closed, from all the torturous yet strangely comforting visits. Approaching her plot, he felt the familiar heavy feeling on his chest. Swallowing what felt like cement in his throat, he reached where his wife lay.

"Hi, darling," he said quietly, looking down at the cold block of granite that summarised his wife's time on earth. He stared at the words, at the hyphen between her birth and death date. That hyphen was her life, her achievements, her loves, her beauty. It was them; it was the three Musketeers. It was everyone who had been lucky enough to meet her.

Eddie put a clenched fist to his mouth. He hated this place, this cold place filled with broken dreams and destroyed hope. Yet he loved it equally, because Issy was here. He placed the wreath down and tidied up her grave, making sure the colourful, foil windmill from Willow was still firmly in the ground.

On each visit, Eddie tried to tell Issy something new Willow had discovered or achieved. There had never been much to tell her about him, as all his energy the last year had been poured into Willow, even when supplies had been low. But today, Eddie found himself talking about The Dinner Club and even laughing a little. He craved a reply so badly.

He bent down to say goodbye and did what he always did when he left: kissed the palm of his hand and placed it over her name on the gravestone.

"I love you," he said.

Eddie turned to make his way out of the crem. Walking through the grounds, he glanced at a few people, wondering what their story was.

"A widower, like me," he muttered sadly, seeing an old man sitting quietly on a bench in front of one plot. His eyes moved to the next person, and he did a double take.

"Cara?" he said, then immediately felt bad for shouting in a cemetery.

She looked up. There were no tears on her face but her eyes were red and puffy. "Oh, hi, Eddie."

Eddie walked over, hands in his pockets. He stood beside Cara, facing the gravestone.

"Your mam?"

"Yeah. I still come now and then. We had some nice Christmases when I was little. My mam loved Christmas. I hate Christmas myself, but she liked it."

She had put a small, glittery plastic Christmas tree on the base of the stone. Cara had never mentioned any other family, and Eddie didn't feel it was his place to ask about them. They were colleagues. Were they friends yet? Probably, but they were still colleagues and getting to know each other.

"Did you go to the cat and dog shelter?" Eddie didn't know what else to say and knew that was a safe subject.

"I rang them. I am going to go in next week to help them prepare for Christmas." Cara genuinely looked proud of herself, so it was unexpected when she burst into tears.

"Hey, hey, it's ok." Eddie put a hand on her shoulder, and she started crying more.

*Bollocks*, thought Eddie. *Well, I guess we're not in the workplace this time.*

Eddie stretched his arm over her shoulders, and she immediately snuggled against his torso, clearly needing some human comfort.

"Hey, come on, you're a tough little thing."

Cara slowly pulled away. "It's just hard sometimes. I don't know why she was never the mam she should have been. Maybe that's what's the hardest thing. I just wanted her to be a mam and be proud of me." She wiped her sleeve across her nose.

"Cara, I can guarantee your mam will be very proud of you, and rightly so. She always would have been. Just... sometimes parents don't always realise what's going on as they're soaking in their own issues. We're human, not perfect. I don't know your story, but I am certain your mam loved you."

Cara looked at the ground. Eddie wasn't sure if he had said the right or wrong thing.

"I just want to be happy." She sniffed as she said it, still looking at the ground.

"Hey, how about a quick cuppa? On me? There is a great little café round the corner. They may even have flapjacks." Eddie looked at Cara encouragingly.

She smiled. "Thanks, Eddie."

Eddie was conscious of time. He text Connie saying he would be a little late as he ordered some drinks. They talked about work and the animal shelter, then Eddie mentioned The Dinner Club.

"Sounds great. I'm a crap cook. Absolutely clueless in the kitchen. But I wish I was better. I will need to eat better when I move into my own place, to budget and all that."

"How's the flat hunting going?" Eddie asked.

Cara's face dropped. "It's a friggin' nightmare. It's so expensive. I can't afford bonds and admin fees. It's a right con. I worry I'll be sleeping on a sofa forever. Or that I'll be chucked out. I'm sick of it," Cara said, deflated.

Then, the lightbulb moment happened for Eddie. Derek! Derek needed a lodger. Someone who would accept him and give him privacy. Why hadn't he thought of it before? He'd had so much going on that the idea must have been waiting in the background for him to grasp it.

"Cara, I may just have you the perfect solution. A man I know needs a lodger. He's in his early sixties and has just split from his wife. He's lovely, and he has a dog."

Cara's face lit up at the mention of the dog.

"I doubt he would want a bond, and his house is lovely and spacious. I tell you what, let me give him a call later, and I will let you know at work tomorrow if the room is still available." Eddie knew it was but didn't want Cara or Derek to feel the pressure.

Cara grinned. "Thanks a ton, Eddie, that sounds amazing. And if you know him, I know he won't be a dick."

Eddie laughed. "No, no, he's not a dick. He's a quirky old thing. A little bit eccentric, I would say, but a great guy and a great friend."

# 83

# *Happy Monday*

## Derek

*Didn't Monday come round too quick*? thought Derek as he ate his overnight oats with raspberries and banana. His weekend had been quiet but pleasant. He'd caught up with Bri, spent time doing some sorting at home, conversed with Peter and had had a lovely phone call with Florence, where she'd shared one of her favourite recipes for fruitcake. It was the type of weekend Derek needed after the appointment on Friday.

Brenda had been reasonable, saying she would consider the monthly payment, but it would have to start next month, as she needed to think about her future also. She was full of crap—Linda had said she could stay there permanently, although she would want some money for housekeeping. There was something different about Brenda, and it wasn't her hair. Derek was the observant type who always noticed if someone had a new haircut or colour, new glasses or had done something different with their appearance. There was something fishy going on, and he didn't trust this reasonable side of Brenda. Perhaps she had met someone. He shivered at the thought of someone else having to put up with her. Either way, he had to start making progress on trying to find a lodger.

Bri had offered to put an advert up where he worked, and his daughter Bonnie could also advertise it within her networks. Then, on Sunday evening, Derek had received a call from Eddie.

"Hi, mate, how are you? To what do I owe the pleasure?" Derek enquired.

"Are you still looking for a lodger, Derek?" Eddie asked.

"I certainly am, son. I need to get a move on. Don't suppose you could share an advert at Hendersons, could you, please?"

"I can do more than that. I may have the perfect lodger for you," said Eddie.

"Really? Is it Florence?" asked an excited Derek.

"No, no, it's not Florence." Eddie chuckled. "It's a girl, well, woman, from work. She's a little bit of a lost soul, trying to turn her life around, Derek."

"Oh, I see, she's not in any bother, is she?" Derek asked, concerned.

"No, nothing like that. She's a really nice young lass. She's called Cara, she's twenty years old and a hard worker. She loves dogs and has a very understanding personality. I think you would really like her, and she needs somewhere to live pretty quickly."

*Eddie gives good sales pitches*, thought Derek.

"She sounds nice, Eddie. I would have to interview her though. I need to know she would be right for me and Des." Derek was still feeling nervous about a lodger. He knew he needed one, but letting a stranger into his home was a massive deal. It could be disastrous if the wrong person moved in.

"You could come to mine and interview her there? I could make you dinner, since you made mine last week. Willow has been asking after you and Des."

"That's lovely, son, and that sounds smashing, thanks. How about tomorrow night?"

"I am sure that will be fine, but I won't be able to check with Cara until I see her at work. I will confirm in the morning, mate. And thanks, Derek."

"Hopefully, I will be thanking you tomorrow. Goodnight."

"Bye, Derek."

Derek hung up, wondering if Cara could be the solution to his problem.

Derek left work and drove to Eddie's. That morning, Eddie had confirmed Cara could meet that evening. His stomach was rumbling, but Derek was unsure if it was nerves or hunger or, in fact, both. As Derek pulled up at Eddie's, Willow was waiting at the window. She started to wave, and he waved back.

Derek watched Willow disappear from the window, then the front door opened.

"Derek, Derek," she shouted, happy to see him. "Where's Des?"

"Oh, he's at home, love, but he said to say hi and he looks forward to seeing you soon."

Willow shrugged, seemingly happy with the response, and dragged Derek into the house.

Willow held his hand and led him to the lounge. There, a childlike young girl sat waiting in a chair. She was nervously tapping her foot. She smiled at Derek, getting up as he approached.

"Hi, I'm Cara. Nice to meet you." She stood there awkwardly, fiddling with the fabric of her sleeves. Derek wondered if she'd struggled to decide between shaking his hand or giving him a hug and had somehow overthought to the point she did neither.

"Nice to meet you too, Cara," Derek replied, smiling and trying to put this clearly anxious girl at ease.

"Derek, you're here and just in time for dinner." Eddie grinned, stood in the doorway, tea towel slung over one shoulder. "Come on through," he said to the two of them.

*Great*, thought Derek, pleased at the timing. *It's definitely hunger rumbles going on in my stomach*.

They sat down to BBQ chicken, corn on the cob, coleslaw and chips.

"Looks better than a bloody Nando's!" Derek was almost salivating at the food. *Bugge*r, he thought, *I shouldn't be swearing in front of Willow*. "Erm, I mean looks wonderful," he corrected, winking at Willow. She started to giggle.

Cara picked at her food.

"Do you cook, Cara?" Derek asked.

"No, but I really want to learn," she replied.

"I've been teaching myself these last few months. It's so therapeutic. I love my food, in case you can't tell." Derek laughed, patting his stomach.

They talked as they ate, Eddie adding a sentence or two every now and then. Derek noticed Eddie had a big, satisfied grin across his face. He was confident, almost cocky, although this wasn't a done deal. But Derek had a big soft spot for Eddie. He was a nice, decent guy.

Cara told Derek a little of her past. It sounded as though she hadn't had the best start in life but was doing good for herself, working at Eddie's place. She praised Eddie throughout the conversation. He had clearly made an impact on her.

"Well, anyone who thinks Eddie is a decent bloke is a good soul in my eyes. I have to be honest though, Cara." Cara looked at the table. He could almost see her heart sink, as if she was waiting for rejection. "There is something you would need to know about me if you were to move in." She looked up again. "Every now and then, I like to dress up as a woman."

Cara looked at Derek, then Eddie, then back at Derek.

"I like to dress up too, Derek. As Belle, Buzz, Ariel..." Willow chipped in, and the three adults burst out laughing.

"I quite like Belle myself, Willow. You have great taste," Derek replied.

"Well, maybe you could help me with my make-up skills, then. It would be nice to feel confident enough to find myself a nice girlfriend in the future," said Cara.

That was the end of the test; Derek knew she would be the perfect housemate.

"So, when can you move in, Cara?"

# 84

# *Family Festivities*

## Florence

Veronica was due to arrive tomorrow, and Florence was feeling in slightly better health. It may have been the prospect of seeing her firstborn. She had two full weeks of Veronica and was going to savour every moment. Florence had told Veronica about her diagnosis. Like her brother, Veronica had been in denial and became upset and angry. Florence had let her express herself and had tried to comfort and explain. There had been attempts to coerce Florence into treatment, with suggestions of new-fangled cures such as CBD oil and bizarre rare plants in the outback of Australia.

Dying makes us all selfish. People want to keep loved ones and would give anything for an extra minute, hour, day. We are never ready. Those who will be left behind become selfish, in the nicest sense of the word, wanting to cling on to and keep someone for as long as possible. It's instinct. It's love.

Florence knew this would be her last Christmas. She had made peace with that and had started her list of things to do. Jessie and Lucy were helping with it. William was too, reluctantly and with distress. It had to be done. Florence had to be practical. Time wasn't on her side, but she had the beauty of some time, and she had to make the most of it.

The Marie Curie nurses had been out that morning to explain things. William had been there, getting up and leaving the room on more than a few occasions. Florence knew how much he loved her and how difficult it was for him.

Florence had been chatting with Derek on the phone, and he had updated her of his search for a housemate. A lovely young lady was moving in. She would help around the house and with Des, and Derek was going to teach her how to cook. Florence was happy for the man that she had grown extremely fond of.

Eddie and Violet had also been in touch, emailing and texting. Florence had been checking up on Violet, making sure she was coping ok after everything she'd been through. They had all grown so close.

The first Dinner Club of the new year would be hosted by Florence. She hoped to feel in better health, even just for the day. Luckily, Jessie would be co-hosting, and Florence saw this as an opportunity to pass on some of her recipes to Jessie as well as a way to spend extra time with one of her favourite people. They had discussed the menu already: vegetable broth starter, chicken casserole and vegetables for main and homemade Victoria sponge for pudding. These had been Ernie's favourites, and Florence had always put her secret ingredient in: love. Ernie had thought she was the best cook in the world. Florence used to beam as he complimented her cooking over and over.

Yes, she would make her Dinner Club special. She would find her old black and white photos and see if her guests would like to look over them with her, sharing her tales of days gone by. She had a bottle of sherry kept to one side, and with Jessie's help, she would make it a night to remember for her new friends.

# 85

## *Rollercoaster*

### Violet

The last week had been something between a dream, a nightmare and watching a film about her life. An absolute emotional rollercoaster. It wasn't all the happiness and relief Violet had anticipated. The new lease of life. Instead, she felt sad, lonely, confused and angry. It was only after talking to Eddie about it as they'd sat in the local Italian restaurant, that she understood.

"You're grieving, Violet. You're grieving for the death of your relationship. It's a big deal. Let yourself feel what you feel and don't give yourself a hard time for feeling something. That's the best advice I ever got when I was first grieving. It's different in a way, but it's still an end."

"That makes sense, Eddie, it really does. It's just sad. I feel sad. I know it will pass."

Ben had rung her twenty-nine times on Monday evening before she'd eventually answered. She'd been greeted with a barrage of abuse and shouting down the phone. Hanging up, she'd let him ring a further four times before answering, telling him if he shouted, she would hang up. Violet had known he would be livid with her telling him what to do, but she'd also known he would be desperate to know what was going on.

"It's over, Ben. I've left you, and I'm not coming back. You aren't a nice person, and you've destroyed me, almost beyond repair. I've left so I can live a life I deserve."

"What the fuck you on about, Vi? Are you having a breakdown?" Ben seemed genuinely aghast.

"No, Ben, but staying with you was making me mentally unwell. I don't love the person you've become. You are a bully and an abuser. You've done disgusting things to me, and you've never been truly sorry. You don't love me, and I don't love you." Violet kept her voice calm and clear. Ben didn't know where she was—she had that on her side.

He laughed. "Of course we fucking love each other, Vi. Are you pissed? Listen, I will give you a day to think about this, then I expect an apology and for you to come back home, with the bloody stuff you've pinched."

Violet knew Ben was deluded and that his behaviour would change over the next few hours and days. She had to stick to the script and repeat herself.

"It's over, Ben. I'm not coming home, and I don't love you. You can keep the house, but I won't ever come back." Violet hung up, started shaking uncontrollably and ran to the toilet to vomit.

Throughout the week, Ben had demonstrated all the approaches Violet thought he would to get her to return home: grovelling apologies, promises to change, crying and pleading, telling her he couldn't cope without her, indicating he would die without her. Eventually, his tone had changed to that of threats to kill and hoping she would burn in hell. At that point, Violet had told him she would phone the police and report everything that had ever happened if he tried to threaten or contact her again. She had then blocked his number on her mobile but not his social media profiles, in case she needed evidence for the police. He would never change, and she knew that.

Rosie had been her saviour, listening, advising and supporting all week. She had brought cookies home from work for them and made her comforting soup. She had cuddled her when she'd faltered and told her how beautiful she was. She had been Violet's guardian angel. And then there was Eddie. That man she had known for just a short few months, who had become such a good friend, a confidant, the voice of reason and a real comfort.

And for all the torment, blurred reality and realisation of the last week, for the first time in a far too long time, Violet knew she would be ok. In fact, she would be better than ok, she would thrive.

# 86

# *Recipe Legacy*

## Florence

It was the first Dinner Club of the year. All normal duty had resumed after the Christmas period. Veronica had returned home but had told Florence she would be back over at the end of the month and would stay as long as needed. They both knew what that meant. Florence had thrived on having her family close and had enjoyed her Christmas immensely. The black cloud hanging over her hadn't taken the shine off their celebrations for long. Florence had talked with her children about Ernie, their childhood and the love they had as a family. The tears had fallen, there had been pleas, the why us, but the love had also flowed.

Tonight was the night Florence had been waiting for: her Dinner Club. Jessie arrived three hours before the guests to help prepare.

"Hi, Florrie," Jessie shouted, letting herself in.

"Hi, love, come on through."

"Ah, you look tired, Florrie, and pale," Jessie said, deflated.

"Well, I will just have to slap more of my new foundation on later, then, won't I?" Florence chuckled. "Come on, we've got a winning menu to create."

The four Dinner Club friends had kept in touch over Christmas. Derek had rung a few nights ago, asking if it was ok to invite his new lodger to join the Dinner Club.

"She's a lovely little thing, Florence, a bit of a lost soul. I think she would benefit from it and wants to learn to cook. Eddie can vouch for her," Derek had said.

"Of course, love, maybe we need a bairn to join us to keep us oldies feeling young, eh." Florence had laughed.

So, it was a meal for six, including Jessie. Florence and Jessie got to cooking as Florence showed Jessie what to do and watched her with delight as she embraced the challenge. Weighing and sieving, pouring and whisking.

"There's a lot more to this than you would think, mind, Florrie," commented Jessie.

"Yes, there is, my love, and you always need to put the extra ingredient in."

"What's that, Florrie?"

"It's love, my dear, always put love in."

Jessie shook her head, laughing. "You're one of a kind, Florrie, you really are." Then, she went over to Florence and hugged her, covering her in even more flour.

Once all preparation was done, they both sat back and exhaled.

"Let's share a shandy, love, to celebrate our cooking." Florence nodded towards the fridge.

"They haven't tried it yet, Florrie, it might taste of cack," Jessie joked.

"It *will* be bloody lovely, you daft bugger." Florence tutted humorously.

The guests soon arrived, to a warm welcome from Florence and Jessie.

"We've heard a lot about you, Jessie. Sounds as if you deserve a medal, and I don't mean for putting up with this one," Derek said, nudging Florence playfully.

"Hey, you cheeky sod. You won't get extra pudding for that." Florence winked.

Cara was introduced to Violet, Florence and Jessie. Shy at first, she seemed more relaxed as Jessie showed the guests to the table, where fancy name plates had been created for everyone.

"Ooh, these are lovely. Derek, we could keep ours and reuse them each night at dinner time," Cara said as she turned the name plate round in her hand.

Jessie served the starter: vegetable broth. Florence sat at the top of the table, watching her guests with adoration as their food was served.

"Yes, it is homemade bread," Florence commented as Derek reached over for a thick wedge of bread.

"You must've read my mind there, Florence," he replied as he passed the chopping board of bread around the table.

The main course was soon served, Jessie catering for everyone's needs.

"Jessie, can you come and help me at dinner times as well, please? I have a daughter who often has hungry guests in the form of Disney Princesses," Eddie joked.

"Are you not hungry, Florence?" asked Cara, noticing Florence hadn't touched much of her starter or main.

Florence bit her lip and mustered a smile, thinking that this may be one of her last meals with her precious friends.

"I'm quite full today, pet, full of love from you lot." She looked around to where her guests sat, tears welling up in her eyes.

"Aw, well, thanks for letting me tag along, Florence, and everyone really for allowing me to join the group," Cara said nervously.

"Our pleasure, pet, always room for a little one," Florence replied.

"Here, here, the more the merrier," Violet said, raising her glass. "To lifelong friendship," she toasted. They all repeated the words in unison as Florence's cheeks slowly dampened with tears.

"I'm an old softy," Florence announced, wiping her face.

Everyone tucked into the rest of their chicken casserole, and dessert was soon brought into the room by Jessie. She placed a magnificent homemade Victoria sponge cake on the centre of the table to a chorus of "oohs" and "ahhs".

"Wow, Florence, this looks amazing. Almost too good to eat, but of course I want a big slice," said Eddie.

"Get a photo of it and put it on Facebook," Cara commented.

"Actually, take a picture of us all on your phone, will you, love?" Florence asked Jessie.

Jessie rubbed Florence's shoulder fondly as she moved back from the table to get everyone in the photo. "Say Victoria sponge!"

The table started laughing, and Jessie captured the moment in time forever on her mobile phone. Passing it round the table for everyone to see, Florence sat silently, absorbing the atmosphere of happiness as each guest commented on the photo, wanting a copy. She would miss these people, each of them. Even Cara, who had only entered her world that evening. People so different, yet so perfectly matched. Pieces of a jigsaw, all connected beautifully.

Conversation turned to relationships and loved ones the group had seen and had missed over Christmas.

"It was lovely, our Veronica being here, for me and for my William. But you never get over the death of your partner, and nor should you. I always miss my Ernie at Christmas. He loved Christmas; would go all out. He made it magical. He made every day magical." Florence delicately held Ernie's St. Christopher round her neck.

Looking at Eddie, she began to speak again, "We aren't meant to be alone. It was different when my Ernie passed; I'm a different generation. People weren't expected to meet someone else. I had a life filled with love. I still do."

She smiled at Jessie. Then, she turned back to Eddie. If anything, not knowing how long she had left, she wanted her words to strike him. She wanted him to be able to feel love again. Happiness again. Because unlike her, he still had so much life left to live. "But it's never the same as having the love of your partner, that someone to snuggle up to on a cold night. The person to share your bag of chips with. The one who's there when you laugh and when you cry. The beans to your toast, and the milk to your tea. No, you never get over that loss. But you carry their heart in yours, and your mind is richer for having them, even if it wasn't for long enough. You must give love a second chance. Your loved one would always want that."

Eddie wiped a tear from his eye, his bottom lip quivering. Florence's job was done; her words had reached his heart.

"I hope I find the love you had with your Ernie, Florence," Violet said, reaching out to hold her hand.

"Me too," said Derek.

"And me," whispered a timid Cara.

"A toast," said Florence, holding up her sherry. "To love and always embracing it."

"To love," they all repeated.

There was a quiet moment of reflection before Violet asked Jessie about her job.

"I love it. Not everyone is as class as our Florrie, but it's great. I've done it for years and can't think of ever wanting to do anything else," said Jessie.

"I did care work for a bit myself, in a different life. I would love to get back into it," said Violet, a tinge of sadness in her voice.

"I'll give you the number, if you want? The managers are good, and they offer a training package if you want to become a supervisor. I'm starting mine next month."

"Oh, wow, erm, yes, yes please. That would be great," replied Violet excitedly.

Violet turned to Florence. "This Victoria sponge is the nicest cake I have ever had."

"I will share the recipe, pet. The men love it," she said, winking, then looking at Eddie.

Violet laughed, a girly laugh, and Florence saw a little twinkle in her eyes and a blush in her cheeks. Florence had no doubt Violet would meet a man who would adore her the way her Ernie had adored her. That's if she hadn't met him already.

# 87

# *Evolution*

## Derek

Almost a fortnight had passed. It was Thursday, and it was Derek's turn to cook. Well, technically, it was Cara's turn, but she felt nowhere near ready, so Derek was continuing to help her cook and to eat better. They had developed a nice little friendship and cohabiting arrangement, each giving each other space and respect, whilst still being supportive.

Derek noticed how much Cara loved to talk about her day at work. Her job meant the world to her, and she would talk about Eddie and Danielle with admiration. She mentioned the courses and extra responsibilities she was receiving. Derek always praised her and asked questions. He would see her face brighten, like a child on stage at their dance show. He had warmed greatly to Cara, who he felt was trapped somewhere between a child and an adult.

She, in turn, asked about his working day, if he'd had a nice catch up with Bri and how his cross-dressing support group was going. She encouraged him to express himself and listened to his views from his forum. She eagerly walked Des, fed and brushed him. They were an odd coupling but they worked, and it meant Derek could stay in the house and pay a monthly sum to Brenda, who had begun an "internet dating journey", as she called it.

*Good luck to her*, Derek had thought, remembering what Florence had said about love. His time would come.

Florence had emailed the night before, saying she wouldn't make The Dinner Club but was sending her love. She had been feeling off and would hopefully make the next one. He had sent well wishes back and told her she would be missed.

Cara came out of her shell at The Dinner Club that week. She helped Derek prepare for the evening and picked up some tips and ideas. She even helped Derek choose his outfit for the night. Violet and Eddie both asked Florence's whereabouts when they arrived. Derek updated them of the email.

"I'll give her a ring in a day or two, check she's ok," Violet said.

"I'm sure she'll appreciate that," Derek replied warmly.

The food was enjoyed that night, with positive feedback from both Eddie and Violet. Cara continued to get to know Violet, and after a few reminders from Eddie, in jest, that they were "not at work now", she relaxed and talked a bit more, rather than just listening.

As the last mouthfuls of dessert, a ginger and lemon cheesecake, were consumed, Derek let out a sigh of contentment.

"Well, that was rather good, even if I do say so myself." He looked at Cara, giving her a wink as he announced his satisfaction.

"It was delicious, Derek and Cara. A lovely night. The only thing missing is our Florence," Eddie said as he drank the rest of his beer.

"Hopefully, she'll be better soon and can make the next one. That will be you cooking, is that right, Eddie?" Cara asked.

"Yeah, and there won't be any flapjacks on the menu." He grinned.

As the group moved into the lounge for one last drink, Violet shared her plans for her future.

"I've rung the agency Jessie works at. I'd love to go back to care work. It was Ben who stopped me progressing my career in health and social care, and although I do enjoy working at Foodways, it's not really my calling."

"Good on you, pet. You should definitely go for it. Sometimes, the most awful of things give us that chance to start again, in more ways than one," Derek said reflectively as he looked at his beer. There was a brief silence before Derek returned his gaze to Violet. "You have a beautiful nature and would make a lovely carer." He was pleased she seemed to be doing well, given her recent trauma, and even better that she had a new focus.

"I think you would make a great foster mam, Violet," Cara chipped in.

"Th-thank you, both, those are such lovely things to say," she stammered.

"You are an amazing woman, Violet, you truly are," said Eddie, looking fondly at Violet.

"Wow, this room is full of love. Imagine if our Florence was here—she would have us all in tears." Derek chuckled.

After Violet and Eddie left, Cara and Derek cleared up and said their goodnights.

Derek got into bed and contemplated the last six months. In the last month alone, Derek had attended three cross-dressing support meetings and had found them all really helpful. The group was a small, non-intimidating, welcoming group, and he had been keeping in touch with them. Derek's whole social circle had expanded, and it felt good to not feel suppressed and directionless.

His world had evolved so much in under six months. He was living his best life. He was proud of himself for breaking free from the shackles that had been drowning him, for being true to himself.

# 88

# A Hard Goodbye

## Florence

Florence spent the evening in a restless state, flicking between TV channels and picking at the sandwich she had made herself. She felt trapped in her bungalow and trapped in her head.

It had taken her over two hours to send the damn email to Derek, and as soon as she'd sent it, she'd regretted it. Florence was a strong woman, perhaps not physically these days, but emotionally, she was bold. Life hadn't always been kind, and Florence had experienced much loss, in many ways.

Florence sighed as she held the St. Christopher around her neck. "Not long, my love," she said as she closed her eyes, then kissed her beloved's necklace.

She had wanted one last adventure, medication of fun, rather than the tablets and treatment that would delay the inevitable. She'd wanted to feel alive, even if for a short time, not just to lie back and die. But as her ultimate demise crept in, she didn't feel as bold, even with the thought of being reunited with Ernie. Because now it wasn't just William, Veronica and the kids she would miss. It wasn't just Jessie and the other carers. Now, it was her wonderful friends, who in such a short time, had brought a brighter light to her world. Brave Derek and his courage, his kindness and humour. Sweet Eddie, who she felt such a connection to and really hoped she'd shown he could find love again without it meaning a betrayal to Issy. Beautiful Violet, who was one of those people who simply didn't realise what potential they had. Even young Cara, who seemed to have landed into the group at perhaps the right time; as another member was due to leave, whether she wanted to or not.

Florence let out a sob, a small wail, like a wounded animal. She pulled the blanket that sat on her lap up to her chin, holding the edge as she cried, desperate for some comfort. It was pointless; she knew her fate. Although The Dinner Club had been an experience of a lifetime, it had quickly become another thing she would lose.

A text message alert broke her tears. Her shaky hand reached for her mobile from her side table. It was William. Florence managed a sad smile as she opened the text from her son.

***Hi, Mam, just to remind you I'll be over in the morning, then we can maybe go for a slice of cake and cuppa somewhere. Sleep well, Mam, I love you.***

Florence raised her hand to her mouth, stifling her sobs as tears cascaded down her face. She looked at the wall, where a family photo hung. Over forty years old. The colour had faded but the smiles hadn't. Her beautiful family: William, Veronica, Ernie and herself, on holiday in Blackpool, not a care in the world.

"I love you," she said, blowing them a kiss. She took a deep breath, a sip of her tea that was now cold and said, "Now, where's that notepad?"

# 89

# *Healing*

## Eddie

Willow was on a waiting list to see the child counsellor at Blossom's, the local child and adolescent counselling service. They would meet Willow with Eddie and discuss options around play therapy for grieving.

The darkness was getting lighter for Eddie; his thoughts weren't consumed with his own emotional struggles so much anymore. He knew it meant he was closer to healing. The wound that had ripped open his heart was starting to mesh together. Undoubtedly, it would never fully heal, but it would start to repair, and he could live with the scars. He had to.

Focusing on helping Cara move into Derek's had helped. There was something about that kid that he championed. She was the one in the egg and spoon race who kept dropping the egg, the last one picked for the football team, the one who never came first. He was rooting for her, and she didn't even know it. But when he said something that she interpreted as kind and selfless, when he did a gesture like share his flapjack or show interest in her, when he offered the simplest act of human kindness and recognition, the flame in her damaged soul shone so bright that Eddie could see it radiate out of her. He wanted to make her life easier, better.

Then, there was Violet. Innocent, fragile, resilient, inspiring, beautiful Violet. Whose presence filled a room in a way she would never realise. Whose eyes told a story of pain and of strength. He just wanted to be around her. *She gives me hope that people can have their happily ever after, that death isn't the end.*

She had become someone who made him sing again in the shower and made him want to get up early every morning for something other than the need to piss. The good morning text just before 8:30 a.m. each day brightened his day before it even properly began. Violet, who Cara asked after almost each lunchtime as they ate together, and as much as he tried not to, Violet who he was well and truly falling for.

He felt guilty about having feelings for another woman and had been internally battling with himself for a few days. He had told no one. There is a judgement held by people when someone starts dating after their partner dies. Maybe people feel they will forget. *Christ, I bet some people wish they could forget, then they wouldn't live in an emotional prison*, thought Eddie. There was something about loyalty over happiness that people focused on. *We aren't solitary creatures*—Florence had said it herself.

Then, Eddie had dreamt of Issy, just as he'd done before the start of The Dinner Club experience. There she was in his dream, her striking red hair blowing in the wind. Her porcelain, flawless skin. Standing there in a long dress. She was smiling, walking backwards ever so slowly as he was walking towards her, saying her name over and over. She kept walking backwards, gracefully, never taking her eyes off him, never stopping smiling. Then, she waved and was gone.

Eddie woke up knowing it was ok. Issy was ok, and he would be ok.

It was soon his turn to host the next Dinner Club. As usual, the group email was sent the night before. Eddie was making home-battered cod, double-fried chips and mushy peas, served with wedges of tiger bread smothered in butter. He couldn't wait. Willow was going to be staying at home. She had become almost obsessed with Derek and now Cara after meeting her, constantly asking when they were coming round to play. Eddie had to keep reminding his little madam that they were his friends and not hers but that he would share. Violet hadn't met Willow yet. This made Eddie really nervous, but it was something he wanted to happen. He knew Willow would adore Florence and would see her as another grandmother. *She'll run rings around them all*, he thought, laughing to himself.

Violet arrived at Eddie's first. He opened the door, Willow standing by his side. Violet looked so beautiful in a teal green dress, her hair shiny and natural.

"Evening, madam," Eddie said. "This is Willow. Willow, this is Violet."

"Hello, do you like horses?" Willow asked excitedly.

"Well, as a matter of fact, I do like horses, very much," Violet replied, smiling at Willow.

"Yeeessss! Let me show you mine. Through here," Willow announced, dragging Violet into the lounge.

"I wouldn't protest; she's an insistent little thing," Eddie said, following them.

Derek and Cara soon arrived.

"I rang Florence and got no answer. Then, we went round to pick her up, and she wasn't in. Very unlike her, Eddie. I'm a bit worried," Derek said, flustered.

"Maybe she's at her son's and forgot? Or maybe she's asleep. I bet she will ring when she wakes up. Don't worry, come on in," Eddie replied.

"Mmmm, can't wait to eat what you're cooking," said Derek, soon distracted by the smell of the fish.

The friends enjoyed their food and company as usual, with some added entertainment from Willow, who asked if they were eating Dory or Nemo or Flounder. Eddie put her to bed before serving caramel cheesecake for pudding.

"Think I will pop back round to Florence's in the morning before work," said Derek. "I just want to check all is ok. She might still be poorly. Sounded like a virus, but I haven't heard from her for a few days."

"Sounds like a plan. Let us all know when you get hold of her, please?" said Violet.

It was soon the end of the night, and everyone had a full belly. Derek and Cara left first, a slice of cheesecake each packed up for the next day.

Eddie walked Violet to the front door.

"Thank you, Eddie, I had a great night. It was lovely to meet Willow. She is a wonderful child, so well-behaved, a real credit to you."

"Thanks, I'm very lucky," Eddie replied. "I'm pleased you've met her, Violet. I would like for you to get to know each other more." He said it almost without thinking. *Shit, was that too much?* Then, he saw the smile on Violet's face and was instantaneously reassured.

"Let me know when you get home safely, Violet," Eddie said, his hand on the door handle.

Eddie paused, turned back round and looked into Violet's eyes. Both of them were frozen; a moment in time where just he and she existed. He wanted to say something else, ask if he could kiss her, but he couldn't talk. His heart was racing—with excitement or nerves? He wasn't sure. Feeling his legs wobble, he leant forward and kissed her on the lips, the sensation that he may just collapse with nerves coursing through him. A tender, sensual kiss returned by Violet as she gently put her arms around his neck, and he wrapped his around her waist.

Eddie slowly pulled away and touched Violet's cheek comfortingly. She placed her hand on top of his momentarily before they stood facing each other again, in silence. *What now?* Eddie thought as a million emotions surged through him. Did he want a relationship with Violet? Christ, would she want a relationship with him? His palms were sweating as he stood staring like an awkward teenager at Violet. And then reality hit him with the biggest question of all, a question that made him sick to his stomach: had he betrayed Issy?

"I-I'm s-sorry, Violet. I'm erm, I'm not really sure what happened there. Well, I know what happened of course but—" Eddie stammered, interrupted by Violet, who grabbed his hand, stepped in close and gently kissed him on the lips.

# 90

# *Greener Grass*

## Violet

Violet sat in the lounge with Rosie, who was hanging on her every word, animated, looking as though she may explode with excitement at any time.

"Vi, I *knew* it. I bloody knew he fancied you. Eeeh, God, he's gorgeous."

"Bloody hell, calm down." Violet laughed. "It was just a kiss."

"No, it bloody wasn't, Vi. It meant something to him, I'm telling you. He wouldn't put himself out there like that, not after what you've been through and what he's been through, the poor bastard."

"Rosie, less of the swearing, please." Violet sniggered.

Rosie rolled her eyes. "I'm so excited for you, Vi. You need to get him into bed, snare him, keep that one. Eeeh, imagine Ben's face. The ugly, nasty lowlife will turn green." Rosie was now clapping her hands in delight.

Violet grinned. "Ro, I can't rush anything. It's all so overwhelming. I'm not used to all this, you know, niceness. Plus, it's complicated. Eddie's grieving and has a child."

"Bugger it, Violet, life's too short. I won't let you let this pass you by." Rosie put her arm around Violet. "You deserve happiness, you deserve to be adored and to be loved how you love others. You are beautiful, Vi, inside and out."

"What would I do without you?" Violet said as she hugged her friend, her rescuer and the person who always made her feel better.

Violet realised she was crying. She didn't know if they were tears of relief, tears of the past or tears of happiness. What she did know was that after years of feeling love was cruel, hurtful, spiteful and cold, that something inside her felt warm and accepted by Eddie.

Violet went upstairs and climbed into bed, a sigh of contentment as she pulled the quilt over her and felt the softness of the pillow below her head. All the tiny things she had felt since she'd left Ben. Sure, it wasn't over completely; he was still sending nasty messages on social media. But they had reduced, she had stuck to the broken record technique, telling him it was over which had turned to ignoring him completely. She didn't know when he would give up or the extremes he may go to, but she felt mentally prepared, alongside the safety planning she had put in place. She was learning to once again enjoy all the things that most people took for granted: being able to have a slice of toast in peace, knowing she could go to bed without being assaulted, her heart not racing with anxiety every time the key went in the front door. Not being called names daily and feeling worthless. Not having to get dinner done just the right way but it never being right or it being wrong compared to the week before. The mind games, the obsessive routines, the mental torture, the violence, the degradation, the torment, the utter exhaustion. Much of which became her routine. She was realising just how insane and dangerous some of the behaviours of Ben and, subsequently, herself had been.

But the grass was greener, she was starting to heal. She could see a future—a happy, safe future—and secretly, in her own head, a future with the man who had just tenderly kissed her goodnight.

Violet went to sleep comfortable and safe that night, with a smile on her face.

# 91

# *Finding Florence*

## Derek

Derek had been trying to get in touch with Florence all day yesterday, with no success. He had driven past her bungalow and rang the bell—no answer. He was sure there was an explanation, but he was beginning to get worried.

"She might be staying with her son and maybe forgot her phone," suggested Cara.

"Perhaps, love. I might pop over later."

Derek had messaged Violet and Eddie that morning to ask if they had heard from Florence. They hadn't, but everyone had agreed to update each other if she got in touch.

To distract himself, Derek and Cara went to Foodways for shopping. The weekly shopping trip had now become an event for the odd couple, and they both enjoyed the outing. They were like a comedy duo, bouncing off each other, giggling and thoroughly utilising the opportunity as an adventure for new experiences and food.

Derek felt as if Cara were the granddaughter he had never had, and he knew, although she may not admit it so quickly, Cara was fond of him. Last week, when Cara had been paid, she'd returned from work with a present for Derek and herself. Matching lap trays. Derek had been delighted and touched by the gesture.

She was a good kid, and there was more than a financial benefit to having Cara in the house. She had become a friend and part of his and Des's family.

After returning from Foodways, Cara took Des out for a walk, and Derek decided to go over to Florence's to check if she was around. As he arrived, there was a car outside her house. He exhaled, thinking Cara was probably right and she had been away with family. Walking up the drive and knocking on the door, he prepared the little lecture he would give her in his head.

Someone who wasn't Florence answered the door. He recognised him from the very first Dinner Club meeting. "Oh, hello, William, I don't know if you remember me, but I'm your mam's friend Derek," said Derek, holding his hand out.

"Yes, yes, I do. Hi, Derek." William's clothes were ruffled, and he looked as though he hadn't slept. He took Derek's hand weakly.

"Is your mam home?" Derek asked. "I've been a bit worried about her. She didn't come to The Dinner Club on Thursday night."

William took a deep breath and stepped aside. "You should come in, Derek."

As Derek walked in, he noticed a pile of boxes in the hallway and knew something wasn't right. Where was Florence? He looked back at William, William's pale, expressionless face looking back. Dread engulfed Derek as his mouth became dry. He could almost hear his heart pulsating in his ears. He swallowed, hoping the siren of thoughts screaming in his head would dissolve. "Erm, what's up, William? Is everything ok?"

"No, everything isn't okay." William shook his head, tears welling in his eyes. "I haven't had a chance to tell people, apart from family, but Mam passed away yesterday afternoon."

Derek put his hand on the hallway wall, steadying himself as reality span around him. He closed his eyes, hoping he would wake up to find this was all just a dream, but instead all he could see was Florence's kind face. She couldn't have gone; she'd only just come into his life. Precious Florence. Florence who had accepted him, who had shown kindness, love, support. She just couldn't have gone. Gradually opening his eyes, he was back to looking at William, although this time it was a blurry image as William stood there, frozen to the spot, tired eyes wide. It was almost as if William were stood behind a cascading waterfall of tears. Derek moved towards William and comforted the man who was almost a stranger, but because of Florence, felt like family.

"No, she can't be," Derek blubbered. "I mean, what... what happened? I don't understand." He pressed his hand to his chest, almost as if holding his heart in place would stop it breaking.

"Come through, Derek," William said, walking into the lounge. Derek followed slowly, unsteady on his feet. William sat on his mam's cherished recliner, holding his face in his hands, sobbing.

"She had cancer and refused all treatments." William shook his head. "The last fortnight, she deteriorated massively. We knew it was coming. But nothing prepared me for this. She was my mam... my mam," he said, his voice breaking.

Derek's mouth dropped. He'd had no idea. Florence had seemed so well, healthy for someone her age and so spritely. Derek took a deep breath. It was too much to absorb. Why hadn't she said? Why hadn't she told him? He never got the chance to say goodbye.

Derek looked at the wall, needing a second to compose himself. He was greeted by a family photo that hung happily on the wall, showing an unmistakable younger Florence with her family. Derek wiped his eyes with the sleeve of his jumper and returned his gaze to William. "I had no idea, William. I am so very sorry. Your mam, she said she had a virus. I... I wish I'd known. Maybe I could have helped," he said, deflated.

"She didn't want people to know, Derek. My mam was a proud woman—you'll have already known that from meeting her. She wanted to have some fun, to meet new people and, I guess, in some way, leave memories for them."

"Your mam, in the short time I knew her, had a monumental impact on me, William. I mean it. She, well, your mam was one of a kind, and she came into my life at a time I needed a friend just like her." Derek let the tears fall down his cheeks as he looked at William, who was nodding. Here he was in Florence's lounge, crying in front of her son... a stranger.

"My mam, gone. I don't know what I'm going to do without her," William whispered, staring at the family photo on the wall.

"I'm so sorry, I really am. She was an amazing woman. Like no other eighty-two-year-old I've met. I'm so grateful I got a chance to know her, I truly am," Derek said gently. "Can I do anything? Anything at all to help?"

"Not at the minute, but thanks. I'll be in touch. Will let you know funeral plans and all that."

"Ok, well, my number is in your mam's phone, but here it is again in case I can do anything to help," Derek said, jotting his number down on a notepad next to Florence's recliner. When he pulled back, he grimaced. Florence's writing was on the page next to it. Her last Foodways shopping list. "And I'm so sorry again for your loss," he said, filling up again as he said goodbye to William.

Derek left and sat in his car for a few minutes, shocked and upset. It was hard to imagine never seeing Florence again.

"Why didn't you bloody tell me?" he said, hitting the steering wheel. "I never got to tell you. I never got to bloody tell you how much you meant to me." Derek put his head on the steering wheel and sobbed for Florence, for William, for himself and for The Dinner Club.

Cara's face dropped the second Derek stepped through the door. Was it his bloodshot eyes? "What's up, Derek?"

"She's dead, Cara. Florence has died." Derek collapsed backwards against the wall, fresh tears streaming down his cheeks.

"Oh shit, no." Cara ran over to Derek, trying to cuddle him as best she could.

"I just can't believe it," Derek said, shuffling away from the wall to sit on the bottom step of the stairs. "We never even knew she was unwell. She never said. I never got to say goodbye." Derek wiped his nose with the back of his hand as Cara sat next to him and stroked his back.

They sat on the stairs for a few minutes in silence as Derek sobbed.

"I need to tell the others; they'll be devastated," Derek said sadly, taking his phone out of his pocket.

For the rest of the weekend, Derek walked around in a daze. The Dinner Club members kept in touch, checking in on each other, as friends do, but Derek just felt numb. Florence, despite only knowing her a short time, had made a significant impact on his life. She'd had that ability, that essence to imprint. Her character of gratitude, simplicity, humour and love. Her cheeky side, her maternal heart. Derek sobbed, missing his friend already.

# 92

# Missing Dinner Guest

## Derek

The next Dinner Club had been cancelled. Florence's funeral was the day after, and all members agreed it was too soon and wouldn't feel right. Florence had a humanist funeral, a lovely service, and Derek was honoured to witness how much she was adored by everyone in her life. *She'll be back with her Ernie now*, he thought, holding Violet's hand as they sat on a pew. Florence had been a massive part of their club, their lives, and they knew it was going to be hard without her. Derek knew she would want them to continue, but he felt torn. It wouldn't be the same again.

That weekend, Cara tried her best to keep Derek occupied: they walked Des together, cooked together and watched films together. Derek appreciated it so much. He knew life would go on, it just felt very sad and colourless at the moment.

At lunchtime on Wednesday, Derek noticed a missed call from William on his mobile. He rang William back.

"Hi, William, how are you holding up? Stupid question, I know."

"Ah, we are getting there. It's up and down, you know. I just miss her so much."

"I bet, mate, I bet. I miss her too," Derek replied.

"I'm ringing, as I found some envelopes when me and Veronica were sorting the bungalow. They're addressed to you, Violet and Eddie. Can I drop them off at some point?" William asked.

"Of course, William. And if there is anything I can do, you know where I am. That offer still stands. Florence meant so much to me. She still does," Derek said, smiling sadly as memories of her laughing and dancing played in his mind.

William had dropped the letters off on Monday. It was Thursday now, and The Dinner Club members were meeting at Violet's. He'd told them all about the letters, and they had decided it would be a good idea for them to meet that week and open them together. It felt important to support each other, and in his heart, Derek knew that Florence would want it that way. All had invited Cara, but she had declined, saying she would attend the next one but felt this one had to be the three of them.

Derek had pulled up at Violet's, pleased to see his friends but with a bittersweet twinge that Florence wouldn't be there. Eddie was already there. Derek laughed when Violet told him the menu: vegetable soup, gammon with chips and apple crumble and custard. These were foods that Florence had loved, although she'd told stories of gammon being too salty in pubs but still always going back for more.

"Florence will be watching over us and laughing, love. Not too much salt on the gammon though, eh?" He giggled. Violet chuckled and then held her hand to her heart sadly.

"Come here, love," Derek said, embracing her as she let out a little sob. "C'mon, it's ok. It will be ok."

The three sat at the table, their envelopes on their placemats, an all-consuming void where the fourth person, Florence, would have been sitting. They all looked at the empty chair and then their envelope.

"Who's going first?" asked Eddie nervously, looking around the table. No one volunteered.

"We know you had a special connection, Derek, so would you like to go first?" Violet said.

Derek nodded tensely. He opened his envelope and cleared his throat.

*My dearest Derek (or should that be Debbie),*

*I owe you the biggest thank you I can muster for creating something that's made my last few months so memorable. I only wish you had come up with your idea years ago! You've made a lonely old woman very happy, and you are a good cook to boot.*

*I think you're wonderful as Derek or Debbie, and you should always continue to be yourself and express yourself in the way you want, son, not in the way you think you should. Be who you want to be, dress how you want, talk how you want (not too much swearing), make new friends, and when you are ready, find love again, son.*

*Don't end up lonely and missing that special person to cuddle up to at night. Whoever loves you just the way you love them will be very lucky indeed.*

*You are a great man, a kind man, and in the short time I've known you, you've felt like a son to me.*

*All my love, pet,*

*Florence x*

Derek wiped his eyes with his free hand and looked into the envelope. His hand shaking, he pulled out and glanced at two recipes titled "Florence's family dishes". There was a third folded piece of paper that read:

*READ TOGETHER ONCE ALL ENVELOPES ARE OPEN.*

He held the letter to his chest. He would cherish his letter and his memories of Florence forever.

An already emotional Violet decided to go next. Eddie stroked her shoulder as she opened her envelope. Like Derek, she had two recipes and a folded piece of paper with the same message to read together once all envelopes had been opened. She also had a personal letter. She kissed the paper and began reading.

*Beautiful Violet,*

*You have beauty and strength flowing through you despite the hurt that has been inflicted on you. You have never let cruelty harden your kindness or turn it to anger at the world. Your resilience is truly admirable, and I see a love in your heart that needs to be shared.*

*You will be the most wonderful carer, just like my Jessie, and you must promise me you will pursue this. I believe you can do anything your heart desires, pet.*

*Your swine of an ex did not deserve you, and you must never go back to him (I know us women don't like being told what to do, but you have to take this one as gospel). Love is right under your nose, Violet. Hopefully, sitting next to you now.*

Violet stumbled on the last few words and paused, her face turning crimson. She purposely avoided making eye contact with anyone else in the room. "Ummm..." she muttered before turning back to the letter.

*Love. Let yourself be loved and love back without pain and hurt. Find your you again, and find the person who loves you for exactly who you are, pet.*

*Look after Derek. He's a strong man, but they all need a little bit of nurturing once in a while from us women!*

*Start a new adventure with our Eddie. Let him love you in the most beautiful way. He is one of the good ones, I promise.*

*Smile that stunning smile as much as you can, pet, and on hard days, hold your loved ones close.*

*I hope to meet your mam over there to tell her just how fond of you I am.*

*All my love, pet,*

*Florence x*

Violet broke down, sobbing onto Eddie's shoulder. Derek watched him tenderly stroke her hair and reassure her. Florence was right with everything she'd said.

"I'm sorry, between losing Florence and the mention of my mam..." Violet said.

"Violet, love, stop apologising. Florence would have told you off for saying sorry," Derek said. The three of them managed a laugh despite their grieving.

"She put a lot of thought into this, the lovely old bugger," said Derek, smiling. "Last but not least." Derek looked across at Eddie, who looked back, fragile.

Eddie took a deep breath and opened his envelope, finding four pieces of paper, like his friends. He read out his letter.

*Our Eddie,*

*I don't know where to start with you, as I truly don't think you realise how special you are. You go to work every day, doing a hard job. You run your house, and most importantly, son, you're the best dad to your Willow.*

*I won't ever forget how I felt when I lost my Ernie: the pain disabled me, and it never goes away, son. You have a baby who is your reason to continue, to never give up.*

*I never met anyone after Ernie. I was lonely, and the loneliness never went. My Ernie will be telling me off right now for never giving love another chance. We never forget the ones we lose, and we never replace them. We carry their hearts in our heart. But to never let love in again is to die with part of our soul lost, lonely and sad.*

*Let love in. I saw in your eyes that you wanted to, and I saw the way Violet lit up your soul. Don't fight it, don't feel guilty, and don't have regrets, pet. Let love in.*

*You're a bloody marvellous dad, never forget that. Your daughter will be so proud of you, as you are her. She is the luckiest girl in the world to have you. You must make yourself happy for you, for her and because Issy would want that.*

*All my love, pet,*

*Florence x*

Eddie looked up, silent tears streaming down his face.

"Come here, you two." Derek pushed himself out of his seat, his chair squeaking against the floor. He stood back from the table with his arms open. Derek needed a hug right now as much as he needed to give his friends that comfort. Violet rose quickly and stepped into Derek's embrace.

"I miss her," came Violet's muffled voice. She opened up the hug to Eddie, who stepped into the cuddle. Three people brought together over friendship and loss. Three friends supporting each other through a shared void.

"You're a good hugger, mind, Derek," Eddie said as he let go of the group embrace.

"It's these big guns," Derek said jokingly as he flexed his muscles. Derek's quick wit helped the atmosphere as they took their seats again.

They all got their extra note out of their envelope. Derek started reading his out, it becoming immediately apparent that they all had the same recipe: an extra special recipe made by Florence.

*<u>Florence's Recipe for Relationships</u>*

*Unlimited LOVE,*

*A generous portion of FRIENDSHIP,*

*Equal measures of SUPPORT and GRATITUDE,*

*HUMOUR to taste,*

*A sprinkling of SARCASM, INDEPENDENCE, LUST and BICKERING.*

*Never let your relationship get too hot or too cold. Never let love burn, don't take it for granted, and always keep an eye on it. Tell one another when it leaves a bad taste in your mouth, and add spice when needed, as a team. Never be greedy with your portion, instead, savour the taste of your love and happiness.*

*Cook together and eat together. Enjoy your food and take your time. Make mealtimes your time. No phones. No TV. Always sit opposite each other so you can see into each other's eyes.*

*There is always room for pudding—make your life sweet!*

Derek finished reading. He looked up at his friends, who were holding hands and smiling at him. Eddie and Violet leant over the table and grabbed one of Derek's hands each. The three members of The Dinner Club sat silently, with red eyes and snotty noses, remembering their friend Florence, remembering the impact she'd had on them and knowing they would never forget her.

# Ten Months Later

# 93

# *Happy Ending*

## Cara

Cara had been helping Derek prepare for the Christmas Dinner Club. The last few months, she had become a bit of a whizz in the kitchen, to the point where she was trying to get Derek to apply for *Couples Dine in With Me* with her.

"Bugger off, Cara," Derek would say, laughing. "Imagine them rooting through our drawers, Christ!"

"But we can show off our culinary skills, Derek," Cara would plead.

"No chance. I'm happy feeding Eddie and Violet and Bri now and then, but that's enough for me."

*I will work on him*, Cara decided.

A lot more than cooking had changed for Cara. She was eating better than she ever had and didn't have negative associations with food like she used to. Living with Derek wasn't the healthiest, as he piled food on her plate, but she had started jogging, sometimes taking Des out with her, if he could be bothered. Other times, she listened to audio books as she jogged around the estate—her own time for relaxation.

Cara had decorated her room and felt fully at home. Derek gave her space to come and go but was always there when she needed him. She was content. More than that, she was happy and not filled with fear of her happiness potentially being cut short, snatched away and ruined. She was enjoying life. She saw happiness around her in Eddie and Violet, with colleagues at work, with Derek. He had made new friends from his cross-dressing group and forums. She was proud of him for being himself.

She had started internet dating and had been on dates with a few women. Nothing serious right now, but it was nice to meet other young women, and it was a boost to her confidence. She could date without the fear of having to do anything she didn't want to for a bed for the night. She could be herself in personality and sexuality.

She was loving her job at Hendersons. She had ongoing training, job satisfaction and a purpose. Cara felt in control for once. She had achieved things and knew people around her would always catch her if she fell. Not that she intended on ever falling again.

# 94

# *Home*

## Violet and Eddie

"Quick, we're going to be late," Eddie shouted up the stairs.

"Ok, ok, I'm coming," called Violet.

It was the last Dinner Club before Christmas, and Derek had promised an early Christmas dinner with all the trimmings.

Violet had been living with him and Willow for just over three months. Eddie had taken on board everything in Florence's letter, and it had been the catalyst in ensuring he'd seized the moment and been honest with himself without feeling disloyal to Issy. It had been a big deal for him, but he'd had Willow to consider as well. The worrying had been pointless; Willow had warmed to Violet from the start and their bond continued to grow.

Violet had always wanted to be a mother—she had told Eddie this. She had also made it explicitly clear she did not want to replace Issy and that she would never be Willow's mother but would try her hardest to be the next best thing.

Eddie and Violet's love had grown naturally and with ease. Violet now knew how equal, respectful, tender and supportive love could be. They were a perfect fit, like chips and tomato sauce, the sand and the sea, the comfiest slippers. It was true love.

They arrived at Derek's, greeted with the usual cuddles and slobber from Des. Cara had a Christmas jumper on, and Derek was dressed as Debbie, looking glamourous, with tinsel as an accessory on a headband. The friends had a wonderful day eating, chatting, laughing and, of course, toasting to absent friends.

"We've booked a holiday. I haven't been on holiday in years," said an excited Violet.

"Where you going, pet?" asked Derek.

"Italy. We're going to Italy. A lovely little place you will know, called Florence."

# 95

# Follow Your Heart

The Christmas Dinner Club had been a success. It had been a feast and a half, with vulturelike Des hovering around at all times. Of course, there was always something missing: his little Florence. Although Cara was now a regular at The Dinner Club and Willow made the odd appearance, it would never be the same without Florence. Derek was ok with that. He would never want her replaced. Different was ok.

Clearing up the last of the dishes as Cara showered, Derek looked above the dining table and smiled. There, in a frame, was the photo of The Dinner Club at Florence's that Jessie had taken on her mobile. Looking back, he wondered if Florence had wanted that picture taken for a reason: for the others to remember her by.

"You look so happy, love," he said, eyes focused on Florence. "But I wish I could have said a proper goodbye."

Derek remembered what Arthur used to say about people coming into your life for a reason, a season or a lifetime. He thought of The Dinner Club members and how they would be friends for life. But he also thought about Florence and that perhaps the members had come into her life for a reason: a final adventure, people to share her much-loved recipes with, her ingredients for living. He would never forget her or their wonderful memories.

"To you, Florence." He held the last of his prosecco up.

Florence would remain in the group, even if it couldn't be physically at the dining table. Although Derek had started The Dinner Club, he felt as though Florence had made the most profound impact on it. Her observations had instigated change while she was alive and embedded happiness and confidence in her passing. He hoped she was watching over them.

"Well, Des, got to clear the rest of this up, my old son," he said, looking down at his loyal companion.

There was a lot of preparation to be done for his visit from Peter/Paula, wearwhatiwant54, at the weekend. Derek thought back to his personal goals he had made all that time ago when Brenda had left:

1) Be true to himself.

2) Meet people who will accept him as he is.

They had felt so daunting at the time, so unachievable. Derek began washing the dishes and let out a big sigh. He knew he had done it; he had achieved what he'd once thought was impossible. Thirteen little words. Helped along by a touch of magic and some incredible friends.

"Derek Morgan, you bloody did it!"

# Acknowledgements

Firstly, thank you to you, for choosing and reading my debut novel. I hope it left a delightful taste in your mouth and your soul feels full.

I began writing The Dinner Club in November 2019. The character Florence is based on my beloved Grandmother who died suddenly as I was writing my manuscript. I wrote through my grief and my heart broke and healed many times during the process. When Cassandra at Cahill Davis Publishing offered me a publishing contract, it felt a magical gift that my Grandma would live on in print and that readers could meet the characters I loved creating. Thank you, Cassandra and all at Cahill Davis for believing in my book and for believing in me.

Thank you to my number one fan, best friend and partner, Paul. For your unconditional support and encouragement, for always being the first to read my work, and for your love that makes me feel nothing is impossible. You make my world a better place.

Massive thanks to all my family, who have always asked, encouraged and championed me, as a human and as a writer. In particular to my Mam and Auntie Carole, who read all my work, tell me how proud they are, and never tell me off for swearing too much!

A great big thank you to my friends who surround me with positivity and support. A special thanks to those who asked to read my work and made me feel like all the hours spent at my writing bureau were indeed for a purpose. Huge gratitude to Debbie and Caroline for reading my work, asking constantly and being wonderful cheerleaders! For Elizabeth and Pat who read my manuscript and who's feedback was crucial. Thank you also to Lisa, Mim, Angela, Marnie and Sarah.

Thank you to all my colleagues, who see me as more than a manager and inspire and nurture my creativity in and outside of work. Special thanks to Neil B, who asked about and encouraged my writing from the very beginning.

A final and sincere thank you to my social media writing community. People who were once a profile of a fellow writer and reader became a community and friends. I'm supported and inspired every day by the hundreds of people who take time from their daily demands to communicate with me, it makes my heart happy.

As The Dinner Club is my debut novel, I would be super grateful if you can submit a review wherever you can! If you post it on social media please use the hashtag #tdcha so I can find it. And feel free to follow me on my social media and say hello!

<u>Instagram:</u>
@helen.aitchison_writes
<u>Twitter:</u>
@aitchisonwrites
<u>Website:</u>
www.helenaitchisonwrites.com

With thanks and love, Helen

# About The Author

## Helen Aitchison

Helen Aitchison is a writer from North East England. She is the director of a Community Interest Company, Write on the Tyne, which provides creative writing courses and mentoring with a focus on engaging marginalised people. Helen also teaches for her local council, is a freelance writer for StoryTerrace and an on-line journalist for Radio Gateshead.

Helen has 20 years' experience in the health and social care sector, from frontline support work with victims of domestic abuse to senior management for a national charity supporting homeless and vulnerable adults and young people.

This experience, along with life events we all can face, inspired her to begin her writing journey in 2019. To date, she has had a number of poems and short stories published in anthologies and online media, as well as being shortlisted for Story Tyne Award 2019 and longlisted for The Alpine Fellowship 2020.

She writes in any spare time she can capture, alongside a healthy obsession with reading, travel and exercise.